A Gexalatian Tale Series
BOOK TWO

Return
to
Gexalatia

E. PAIGE BURKS

For information about this title or to order other books and/or
electronic media, contact the publisher:
InfinityFlowerPublishing,LLC
www.infinityflowerpublishing.com
info@infinityflowerpublishing.com

ISBN: 978-0-9984620-8-0

Interior Design:

Dedicated to James.
Your support makes these books possible.

PROLOGUE

The mouth of the Eluvios as it meets the Bay of Antiquus,
Siccita.
The eighty-eighth day of fall, the 904th year of
the reign of King Paraximus Lamia.

WATER LAPPED AT THE BOW of the Madelief as she drifted through the canyon of the Eluvios River, open water and their traveling companion, the Marianya, in the distance. Her crew was settling in for the night, the boatswain doing his final rounds. He glanced aimlessly over the masts, unconcerned about the shape of the rigging. They had only been sailing for a day, and the trip down the Eluvios was one that most of the crew had taken many times.

The man paused to test a knot when a sudden rumble below deck made the Madelief shudder and shift. The boatswain scowled as he crossed toward the hatch, where thick bars of chalargentum were latched shut.

"There's naught to fear, Mister Gannon."

The boatswain jumped at the sound of the old man's voice, turning to look at him.

"Water dragons can feel the rain," the old man said, his

gnarled fingers curled around the rounded end of a cane. "This one's no different."

Gannon looked over the man, disgusted by the sight of him. He must have been at least a hundred years old, which was ancient for an Inerse. He was hunched, his skin wrinkled and sagging over his haggard face. He moved slowly, as if it pained him to walk, but his eyes sparkled when he spoke of the beast below. He had a crooked grin, flashing missing teeth, and a sparkle in his old eyes that was disturbing.

"I'm not fond of these creatures," Gannon said.

The old man's grin widened. "Scared are ya?"

Gannon scowled, crossing his arms.

"Ain't nothing to be fearin', boy," the man continued, looking back into the hatch. "Tis a youngling." He looked up to the boatswain. "Too small to harm this vessel."

Gannon could feel his scowl deepening as he watched the old man hobble away. He hated the dragon master. Their encounters always left him feeling unsettled and icky somehow. He leaned over to look into the hatch, seeing a shape curling in the darkness below deck. Faint blue shimmered in the pale moonlight, and a yellow eye blinked up at him as the dragon hissed, acrid sulfur-breath wafting up to his nose.

Pity streaked through the sailor for the beast. The journey would be long, and it would be caged below until they reached the northern-most coasts of Ymber, where it would then be sent to the mines in Perfide. The mines were carved from the backs of dragons and the hands of slaves. That was no way for a living being to be treated, even if it was a dragon.

Gannon sighed shortly, turning away. It did no good to dwell on it. The dragon master was responsible for its well-being. It was his job to man the ship and make sure their journey was smooth. He made his way toward the aft of the ship, pausing to knock on the captain's door.

"Enter."

Gannon pushed open the door, seeing the captain sitting at his desk, a quill in his hand and his log book open. "Everything is secure, Captain."

The captain nodded, strands of blond hair falling from the ponytail over his shoulder. "Get some rest, Mister Gannon." A wry smile creeped across his face. "We hit the bay tomorrow."

Gannon nodded. "Aye, Captain." He stepped back, closing the door behind him. Despite feeling weary, Gannon found himself lingering on the deck, looking up at the clear night sky. His mind was wandering as stars dashed across the darkness of the night. He always enjoyed the silence of the stars, with the faint creaking of the boat below. It was settling, helping him to clear his mind and prepare to sleep.

A sudden trumpeting call from below deck shattered Gannon's thoughts, making him jump. He frowned, ready to berate the dragon master for not sedating their cargo, when a light flashed before his eyes, the smack of wood to wood filling the air. For a moment, all Gannon could do was stare stupidly, seeing a flaming arrow stuck into the deck.

"We're under attack!"

A shadow suddenly appeared overhead, more arrows raining down onto the deck. Gannon barely had time to duck behind cover, feeling the wind of an arrow as it whizzed past him.

"Man the cannons!" the captain barked, ringing the warning bell. He pointed to two men as they stumbled from the crew quarters. "Put out the fire! We can't lose the sails!"

Gannon jumped to his feet immediately, helping a crewmate push a cannon into firing position. He tried to focus on his job, but chaos was erupting around him. The vessel suddenly became alive with the disordered murmur of terrified and confused sailors, some of whom were greenhorns they had picked up at port, lads barely of age and having never seen battle. Men were scrambling to arm themselves with water pails and load cannons, but they were no match as another shadow fell to the deck with a crash. The wood groaned, the sound of monstrous claws digging into it permeating the bedlam.

Gannon was frozen to his spot as he looked up to see a massive red dragon. It roared, sending flames skittering across the deck. An easy flick of its tail sent a handful of men slinging across the railing and into the waters below. A rider aimed a bow toward Gannon's shipmates, felling them with each draw of the bowstring.

Gannon struggled to turn the cannon as the man beside him was struck in the chest. Gannon knew the shot had pierced his heart as he collapsed to the deck, his eyes unseeing. Panic and fury was filling the boatswain, but it wasn't enough as sharp pain exploded across his back, shoving him to his knees. He looked up, feeling dismayed as he realized there were more of the flying beasts, and more riders raining blazing arrows down on them.

Gannon dragged himself behind the cannon, the pain keeping him still. He could only watch as the red dragon murdered his shipmates, using massive teeth to crunch their bodies and fling them overboard. Any shots or attempts to harm the dragon were deflected by its thick wings. Gannon knew the ship and her crew was lost.

The ship was soon alight with fire, the blue dragon below trumpeting and twisting, trying to free itself from its prison. It crashed heavily against the bars, its cries desperate. It was answered by the shadows of dragons overhead, a small green-scaled one suddenly swooping down to allow a man to leap from its back. The man raced toward the bars sealing the hold, using a blast of magic from his hand to break the lock before throwing the door open. He whooped and whistled, the green dragon sweeping back down to catch him.

Gannon gasped as a flash of blue streaked from the darkness, twisting from the flames that were consuming the ship. It twirled as it flapped its wings, causing the fire to twist around its bright blue body as it rose into the sky. It was beautiful, and its call of freedom was deafening as it joined the others of its kind in the sky.

"Fly Raimi!"

Gannon was caught off guard at the sound of the Loquelan words. Were these riders Fornaxian?

The red dragon arched its neck, sending a final blast of fire across the deck. Gannon could hear the cries of his mates as the flames licked at powder kegs and he scrambled to his feet, a sudden blast sending him hard into the dark waters below.

Sorona, Ymber.
The second day of winter, the 851st year of
the reign of Queen Liana Estrella.
Thursday, December 22, 2011.

T HIS WAY," RAPHAEL COMMANDED quietly, waving his sisters on. "Quickly."

Bailey and Ellie jogged past him, deeper into the trees. In the distance, smoke was curling from the burning remains of Sorona, filling the surrounding groves with its pungent stench. Raphael followed the twins, kneeling beside them behind some thick brush. Between the branches, they could see the manor.

"Are you sure we should be doing this?" Bailey asked softly.

Raphael looked at her before shifting his eyes to Ellie. "We need to see if Father is alive," he said. He knew they were doing this more so for Ellie; she refused to leave without their father.

Bailey followed his gaze, seeing her sister's eyes searching the grounds frantically. "I have a bad feeling about this," she whispered.

Raphael moved to his feet. "Stay here," he said shortly. "I'll take a look around." He looked to Ellie, seeing the desperation in her eyes. "If they come back, you two run to the dragons." He looked back to Bailey. "Don't wait for me."

Bailey's heart twisted in her chest, but she nodded. She grabbed Ellie's arm as Raphael began to move from the trees toward the manor.

"Do you think he's still alive?" Ellie whispered, fear in her voice.

"I hope so," Bailey returned. She held her sister tighter. "I hope so."

※

Raphael jogged across the open courtyard, his eyes scanning around. His stomach turned at the sight of charred bodies lying in the grass, but he pressed on. He didn't want to see the people he'd once known this way. He paused as he reached the side door that opened into the kitchen. It was quiet inside, the crackling of flames still filling the air.

He moved slowly inside the kitchen, seeing that the place had been ransacked. Tables and utensils were strewn about, and blood streaked the floor. A tin of flour had been upturned, and monstrous foot prints were tracked around the room.

Raphael felt his heart seize as he paused to look at them. They were massive, with four-clawed toes, much like a wolf's paw print, but Raphael knew they didn't belong to any such beast. He tried to shake the fear that was creeping over him, his hand slipping to the sword at his hip. He did not want to come face-to-face with an atrox.

Despite his fear, he pressed on, his heart racing as he turned the corners of the manor house slowly. All around him was carnage; dead bodies, rugs smeared with blood, and charred remains of tapestries and the wonders that had once decorated their home. It seemed like it took forever, but finally he reached the second-story platform.

The stone stairs were blackened by the fire, but still strong and able to support his weight. The carpet had burned away, but Raphael would know the way to his father's library with his eyes closed. He crossed to the door quickly, pulling at the iron handle. The door was shaking on its hinges, part of the wood crushed as if the door had been kicked in.

The stench of death immediately made Raphael's breath catch, and he pressed his hand over his face. He didn't want to proceed any further, but he knew he had to. He needed to know. Carefully, he let go of the door, wincing as it slammed against the stone wall, leaving the library open to him. Inside, light was filtering through torn curtains, illuminating a bloody streak across the floor. Raphael knew what he would find as he took a shaking step inside.

In the middle of the floor, Lord Willem Atturon was dead. His eyes were unseeing as he lay on his back, his blood staining the floor around him. Raphael felt sick as he turned away quickly. His father's throat had been slashed by monstrous claws which left his flesh gaping open.

Tears filled Raphael's eyes as he fought to control himself. He turned around once again, seeing that a large hairy body was lying next to his father's, its head cleaved from its shoulders. A sword was lying on the ground, the blade bloodied. Raphael crossed slowly toward the carnage, bending beside his father.

"I'm sorry," he breathed, his tears falling faster. They made a soft splat as they landed on Willem's face. "I should have been here." He pressed his hand against his father's cold forehead, his head bowed. "I could have saved you."

He drew a slow breath, looking out the window to compose himself. He knew he couldn't stay much longer. He reached quickly for his father's sword before jumping to his feet. He paused in the doorway to look over his shoulder, remembering his father's words to him.

"I'll take care of them," he said quietly. "I'll get them to Regius Carmen."

With that he turned, running to the stairs and back toward where he had come from. Just as he hit the bottom step, he froze, seeing shadows moving at the end of the hallway. Soft sounds filled the hall, growls and dog-like laughter echoing toward him. His heart caught in his throat as he dashed toward a nearby doorway.

"Smeeelll something," one of the beasts growled. Their claws ticked on the floor as they moved closer.

"Yesss," a second rumbled. "Fresssh meat."

Raphael held tightly to his father's sword as they growled and yipped in excitement. His heart was pounding loudly in his ears, and he wondered if they could hear it. Every muscle in his body was tense, his ears straining to hear as they came closer. He knew what he had to do, but he didn't know if he could kill both of them.

Another rumble filled the hall, this time nearly on him. Raphael was frozen as the end of a snout appeared around the doorway, sniffing the air deeply. The atrox bared its fangs, saliva dripping from its jowls. "Don't be ssscared," it snarled, pushing the door to the room open slowly.

Raphael jumped forward, just as the beast's head came into the room, swinging the blade. The monster howled as the sword sliced into its face, sending it reeling from the room. Its partner snarled angrily, charging forward. Raphael dodged under its monstrous claws, rolling to his feet in between them.

The leader laughed, the sound throaty and sending a

chill over Raphael. "Nowhere to ruuun," it growled, stalking slowly around Raphael.

Raphael gritted his teeth, holding his sword up. Behind him, the injured atrox was whimpering between snarls. He glanced over his shoulder, seeing that his sword had slashed out one of the monster's eyes.

"Kill!" the injured one snapped. "Kill Inersse!"

Raphael turned to face the injured one just as it leapt at him. He barely managed to block its bloody claws with the sword, pulling a knife from his belt with his free hand. With a battle cry, he dove toward the atrox, digging the knife into its chest where its heart was. The monster squealed in pain and collapsed to the floor as Raphael yanked the knife from its chest.

"No!" the leader howled. "Brother!"

Raphael spun to face it as it bared down on him. He grunted in pain when the beast slammed him to the floor, his sword the only think keeping the monster's teeth at bay. He pressed his free hand against the blade of the sword, feeling it cut into his hand as he tried to hold the beast off. Its breath was acrid as it snapped massive teeth in his face, saliva dripping onto his face. Desperation was seeping through him, his arms trembling with the effort. He knew he couldn't keep it back much longer.

A sickening crack suddenly filled the air, and the atrox reeled backwards, whining and growling in pain. Raphael was surprised to see a hatchet protruding from the monster's head. It staggered backwards and collapsed to the floor, dead.

Raphael rolled over quickly, surprised to see Bailey standing over him. She held out her hand, her eyes worried. "What are you doing?" he demanded as he caught her hand and let her pull him to his feet.

"You were taking too long," Bailey said, turning to look

into the hallway. "I was worried."

"Where is Ellie?" Raphael asked, jogging after her as she ran toward the kitchen.

"I sent her to the dragons," Bailey said, closing the heavy kitchen door behind them. "She's okay."

Raphael nodded as he looked around. "Grab whatever you can find," he said, seeing a basket of fruit. "Whatever you can carry, and then let's get the hell out of here."

Bailey nodded as she dug some dried meats and bread from where she knew the cook kept things hidden. She crammed as much as she could into a flour sack before they ran out into the fading daylight. She didn't feel safe until the dragons were in view, Ellie sitting tall on Bartuk's back.

Coracinus Mountains, Ymber.
The second day of winter, the 851st year of
the reign of Queen Liana Estrella.
Thursday, December 22, 2011.

NYX FROWNED, FOLLOWING JET. SHE didn't know how she was supposed to feel as they wound their way through a trail. They'd been walking since before sundown. Jet made her rest while the sun was at its highest, but he said they needed to move at night. It was safer and he said it would be less taxing on her body. She wasn't so sure about that.

The moons had lent enough light to the burial grounds, but here the mountain faces cast long shadows, leaving them in a thick, murky darkness. Every nerve ending in her body felt like it was tingling, anticipating a fall into some abyss she couldn't see or a bite from some monster she couldn't fathom. Her heightened senses and eyesight were a help, but she knew it wasn't good enough. She wasn't suited to this super-darkness, and she tripped, crashing heavily to the ground.

She gasped as sharp stones dug into her hands. Despair caught at her for a moment. She was in a strange land with someone who, she assumed, didn't care what happened to her, and now she was in pain, scrapes stinging on her hands and her knees.

Nyx was surprised when she looked up, seeing Jet's dark eyes sparkling as he stood by her, a hand reaching down to her. Her heart caught in her chest as she realized a soft light was hovering just over his shoulder. She recognized the augarlux.

"Are you sure that's safe?" she breathed as she caught his hand, allowing him to help her.

"Doesn't seem like we have a choice," Jet said.

Nyx frowned at him. "Why?" She watched as the light swirled in a small mass beside him, shifting as he turned away from her.

Jet sighed. "Don't you ever stop asking questions?" he asked, the irritation heavy in his voice. "You couldn't see, so I summoned it for you."

Nyx realized she was trembling. "Thanks," she whispered. "I could have done it myself."

Jet suddenly stopped, rounding on her. "Let's just get this out of the way," he said sharply. "You're to do nothing unless I tell you to." There was an anger in his voice that Nyx couldn't place. "I'm know this place and everything in it." His voice echoed quietly off the walls around them, making the darkness feel pressing and sucking. "If you wish to survive, you'll do as I say."

Nyx wrapped her arms tightly around her middle, the feeling to flee heavy in her mind. She wasn't sure what she'd done to anger him so much, but he'd been like this since they crossed. She was beginning to wonder if it was her, or if there was something he wasn't telling her.

"You'll have to trust me."

Nyx's heart was racing as Jet stood in front of her, his dark eyes watching her. "What is it you're not telling me?" she breathed.

Jet's eyes narrowed at her, as if he was irritated that she could read him. "Nothing I haven't already said," he snapped. "Every moment we spend here in the open brings us closer to being found."

Nyx was pretty certain she didn't want to know who was waiting for them somewhere in the darkness. She felt small and alone as he turned away from her, pressing forward. She followed closely behind him, clinging to the light of the augarlux.

✦

Nyx wasn't sure how long she'd been following Jet through the darkness of the mountains. She could feel weariness pulling at her eyelids, and she could feel her feet dragging against the stone beneath her. She wiped at her face, wishing she could draw on reserve energy, but she didn't have any left. The thin air and the stress of getting to this point were finally dragging her down.

She felt the toe of her boot catch an uneven spot, and she stumbled forward, barely catching herself. Her palms and knees were still stinging from her earlier encounter with the ground. "I need to rest," she whispered meekly. She looked up at Jet, seeing that he paused a few feet away from her. He was clearly unhappy.

"We can't stop here," he said slowly, as if trying to force his voice to be calm.

Nyx bowed her head. "I'm exhausted," she breathed. She didn't even have the strength to fight with him. She hadn't slept in too long, afraid to close her eyes for fear of what she would see.

Jet scowled darkly, walking toward her. "There are caves ahead," he said shortly. He caught her hand, pulling her up.

Nyx gasped in surprise when he swept her feet from under her, holding her close to his chest. She was tense as he carried her effortlessly. "Is all your energy an Acerbi thing, too?" she asked.

Jet shook his head, his eyes turned ahead. "It's training."

"Oh, right," Nyx breathed. "Military." She let her head rest against his shoulder, the fatigue heavy in her bones. "I wish I could be more helpful." Her voice was small.

Jet frowned. "Me, too."

Just as he promised, they reached a series of caves. He carried her inside, setting her down carefully. He waved the augarlux to the floor, dimming it as he dropped his bag beside it. "Rest," he commanded, watching as Nyx eased to the floor. "I'll keep watch."

Nyx drew a ragged breath as she watched him stand in the entrance, the augarlux throwing light on his back. She felt tired and sick, and she reached into her pocket, feeling the toaster tarts Seth had given her. She pulled the package from her pocket, feeling her stomach turn.

Her heart hurt. She missed Seth and Anna and Dorothea. She wished she could go back and stop all this from happening, but knowing it was done sent a sharp pang of hurt through her. Pitifully, she opened the toaster tarts, breaking off a chunk and putting it in her mouth. Silent tears slid down her face as she savored the taste.

They were strawberry. Her favorite.

Despite feeling consuming sadness, she was desperately hungry, and she finished off the pastries, tucking the plastic wrapper back into her pocket. She wiped at her face as she let her head rest against the wall, trying to sleep. She was worthless without any energy.

She didn't know how much time passed as she dozed lightly. She could feel the bad memories fading as her mind succumbed to a much-needed sleep. She didn't dream of anything, and the darkness was welcome. She could have stayed like that forever, but Jet didn't let her enjoy it long.

"Wake up," he said quietly.

Nyx lifted her head, seeing that he was kneeling before her, his hand on her shoulder. "Five more minutes," she said groggily.

"We have to go," Jet said, glancing over his shoulder in a distracted way. "We're being followed."

Nyx felt his words hit her like a bolt of lightning, and she was on her feet in an instant. "By who?" she breathed.

Jet shook his head, waving his hand to call the augarlux to him. "We need complete darkness," he said softly. He wrapped his hand around the augarlux, effectively extinguishing it.

"But I can't see," Nyx breathed. She was terrified as she stood in the dark.

"I can," Jet said, catching her wrist gently. He swept her into his arms, carrying her from the cave.

Nyx gasped when a blast of air suddenly hit her face, and she realized they were moving. And very fast at that. She buried her head into Jet's shoulder, trying not to think about what was happening. She drew a sharp breath when Jet suddenly stopped. He lowered her to her feet gently.

"Summon a soft light," he said.

Nyx did as he said, mustering a pathetic augarlux. Jet caught it in his hand, infusing it with his energy to brighten it some and then pressing it back into hers. It was cold to the touch, blackness pressing against the gold inside. "If you need me, use this to call me." He pointed, his dark eyes glinting in the faint light. "Follow the trail to the forest."

Nyx felt her heart lurch as she realized he was leaving her. "But, I don't know how," she breathed, feeling panic assailing her. "I don't know where I'm going."

Jet's eyes narrowed in the faint light. "You'll be fine," he said sharply. He reached into his bag, pulling three long knives from it. They were tucked safely in leather sheathes. "Take this." He handed her one.

Nyx shook her head as she took it, her hands shaking. "I thought you couldn't bring—"

"It's chalargentum." At her blank look, he sighed. "Silver-steel," Jet said bitterly. "Try to remember your training." He pulled the bag over his head, dropping it unceremoniously around her shoulders. "Now shut up and go."

"But where are you—"

Jet turned to look at her, his dark eyes dangerous. "I'm going to do what I do best," he said, his voice clipped. "I don't need an audience."

Nyx drew a sharp breath. Her heart skipped a beat as she realized he was going to kill the ones following them. She was mute as she nodded her head. She didn't want to see anyone else die.

"Wait for me at the forest," Jet said. He turned away from her. "If I haven't come by sunrise, then follow the trail to the nearest town. There is a map and some supplies in the bag." He drew a slow breath, unable to look at her. "Someone will find you and make sure you get to Liana."

Nyx felt tears in her eyes as he suddenly vanished, leaving her alone. Her heart was racing with fear as she stared around the canyon. She was desperately afraid as she turned, pushing on down the trail. Her hands were shaking as she lifted the augarlux over her head, lighting the way.

⚜

Jet drew a slow breath, forcing himself to be calm. Being free of Nyx suddenly made him feel like a weight had been lifted from his shoulders. He wasn't good at separating things, and all he'd been able to think about was how miserable he felt every time he looked at her. He couldn't tell if it was from the weeks before, or if it was because of everything he'd just put her through. He tried not to think about it as he took a moment to clear his head. It wouldn't do to be distracted.

He lifted one of the two weapons he'd taken, pulling the scabbard back to reveal a long-bladed dagger. He lifted it, running his finger across the blade. He felt satisfied when a red line appeared on his skin, blood beading from it as the wound sealed itself, the magic pulsing through him healing the cut quickly. Liana had had these blades specially commissioned, for times like these.

He shifted his attention from the blade, sliding it into the scabbard at his side. He could feel the others in the distance, their life force distinct against the blackness of the canyon. He knew they could probably feel him, too, but only because he was allowing it. He knew he was much stronger than they were, and this would be an easy fight.

Slowly, he crept through the darkness, coming to a bend in the trail. He stilled, holding his breath as voices could be heard.

"She hasn't returned," one whispered in Sarotian.

"That doesn't matter," another snapped. "The message has been sent."

Jet frowned, feeling his heart skip a beat. What message were they talking about?

"Enough chatter," a third said, clearly the leader. "Our primary mission is complete. They will die in the canyon. We need to make our way back."

Jet narrowed his eyes, feeling bitterness well inside him suddenly. What was their mission? And who had their message gone to? He could hear footsteps coming closer, and he waited until the first man rounded the bend. It was easy enough for him to catch the man off-guard, swinging his head painfully into the rock wall.

The man slumped to the ground as a second drew a sword, swinging it at Jet. Jet dodged it easily, blocking the second man's arm as he dealt a swift blow to his chest. The second man fell back, gasping for air, his sternum crushed under the force. Jet didn't toy with the third man, slinging a blade at him. It struck home, sinking into the man's eye, rendering him useless as he collapsed to the ground.

Jet walked toward him, yanking the dagger from the dead man's flesh. This had been too easy. He turned his onyx eyes on the second man, seeing him gasping as he pressed his back against the stone walls around them. Jet had spared him because of the badge on his sleeve. He'd noticed it immediately.

Fear was in the man's eyes as he watched Jet toward him. Despite the darkness, he could see the silver of the dagger gleaming with his comrade's blood. He couldn't find words as Jet walked toward him, kneeling slowly.

"Who is your captain?" Jet asked softly. His eyes shifted to the badge. "Second Lieutenant."

The soldier shook his head. "I won't tell you," he said angrily. Pain was etched across his face as he drew a hard breath.

Jet smirked lightly. "That's interesting," he said slowly. "I believe I'm still your superior."

The soldier scowled at him. "You are a traitor," he snapped bitterly. "A deserter. I don't have to answer to the likes of you."

Jet scowled at him. He couldn't stop the anger that welled in him suddenly. In an easy motion, he dug the dagger into the soldier's leg. He watched, unfazed, as the man cried out softly, his breaths ragged. "Shall we try that again?"

The soldier turned his face away. Pain furrowed his brow, but he shook his head. "I'll never talk," he gasped.

Jet nodded slowly. "I suppose it doesn't matter," he said slowly. He yanked the dagger from the man's flesh, listening to him whimper. His body wasn't healing. Jet knew all three were Inerse. It seemed like a strange choice, to send mortals to find him and Nyx. A bad feeling seeped through Jet.

"Who else is with you?" he demanded.

The soldier shook his head, weak laughter leaving his lips. "It's too late," he breathed. He was dying, his body growing weaker with each passing moment. "Your princess will be dead soon."

Jet gritted his teeth, fury gripping him at having been duped. "She's not my princess." He slammed the soldier roughly into the stone wall, driving his dagger into the man's heart. He stepped back from the dead man, wiping the blade on the man's clothes.

He was stupid for having thought this would be easy.

Nyx lifted the augarlux, watching as light cascaded around her. The canyon was eerily silent, just like the burial grounds had been. It didn't make her nervousness ease as she pressed forward. She didn't have any idea of what time it was, or what the forest would look like when she reached it. She thought to take out the map, but she knew she had to keep moving. She didn't think it would be much farther.

The sudden shifting of rocks made her jump, and she spun around, using the light to illuminate the path behind her. Fear filled her as she realized she was alone, and she turned away, letting her hand rest on the sheath at her side. Her hands were shaking as she struggled through the canyon, a hill suddenly cresting in front of her. The path going up was rocky, and she felt the ground shifting beneath her boots as she scrambled to the top. She felt her breath catch as she reached the top of the hill.

Before her, an expanse of forest reached for miles. Just as Seth had told her, it was beautiful, covered in glistening white snow. She pulled at her jacket, a cold breeze pushing into the canyon. Her heart was racing suddenly as she stared at the landscape. Gexalatia didn't look anything like she had imagined. Large, winding tree boughs arched around, making the forest look like a gnarled mass of monster limbs. Tree-tops reached for the sky around the limbs, a fine sheet of white powder coating everything.

Once again, she saw the moons glittering brightly in the night sky, the light of countless diamond stars filling the void of the night. This put anything in the Texas sky to shame.

Nyx looked down, seeing that the pathway down to the forest was steep. She held tightly to the strap of her bag, trying to make her way down. She gasped when she lost her footing, skidding and sliding down the rocky trail. She landed in the snow-covered grass hard, feeling the wind knocked from her for a moment. She rolled onto her back, coughing as she tried to catch her breath. Once she felt less like she'd been hit in the gut, she rolled onto her stomach.

A gasp left her lips as she looked down, seeing stems of grass poking through the snow. She sat up quickly, feeling startled. The grass was a deep cerulean in the white light of the augarlux, which had slipped from her fingers and rolled across the snow. Nyx stood quickly, taking a step back. She'd never seen grass so blue and beautiful.

She turned her attention away from it, pulling the bag

Jet had given her from around her shoulders. It was heavy as she let it fall to the ground, kneeling beside it. She pulled it open, digging through it. Just as he said, it was filled with a blanket and a leather flask and some other things. Under the blanket, she found a paper folded neatly, and she pulled it out. She frowned when she saw more knives glistening in the bottom of the bag. She sighed as she realized that's why the bag was so heavy.

Carefully, she unfolded the paper, seeing that it was indeed a map. She smoothed it across the snow, so that the light from the augarlux was casting over it. She frowned, seeing that words were written on it in a language she couldn't make out. She guessed it was the language Jet and the others spoke, and she felt a scowl pull at her face.

She couldn't read maps. And she definitely couldn't read a map that she'd never even seen before. She fell back in the snow-covered grass, sighing deeply, trying to push the fear that was rising inside her away. Jet had told her to follow the path into the forest. He had told her to wait for him until sunrise, and it wasn't sunrise yet.

Her stomach twisted painfully with anticipation as she turned her eyes back toward the canyon. She hadn't heard any noises, and she didn't know what Jet was up against. What if he didn't come for her?

Nyx shook her head, forcing the thought away. She would handle those things when she got to them. She drew a ragged breath as she folded the map back together, laying it carefully inside the bag. She slung it over her shoulders, bending to scoop the augarlux into her hands. She figured the safest place was away from the main trail, and she turned, seeing the darkness of the trees had become illuminated by a soft light. Flowers were opening inside the tree line, where the snow couldn't touch them, emitting a gentle light as they unfurled their petals.

Slowly, Nyx walked closer, bending to look at the flowers. She drew a sharp breath, seeing how large and beautiful they were. As she came within arms' reach, the glow suddenly brightened, as if the flowers knew she was there. Amazed, she reached out her hand, wanting to pluck one. She drew a sharp breath when the flower suddenly zipped closed, turning dark. Nyx frowned at it, turning her head when all the flowers around her suddenly dimmed, curling around themselves. She thought maybe she'd been the cause, but then the sound of footsteps came softly behind her.

She straightened and turned, thinking it was Jet. Relief was filling her, but it was too soon as she saw bright blue eyes glowing down at her. A woman formed against the light of the augarlux, a vicious grin on her face. Her eyes were smug as she spoke coldly to Nyx in an unfamiliar language.

Nyx clutched the augarlux painfully in her hands, her heart racing. "I—I'm sorry," she managed. "I don't understand—"

Faster than Nyx could react, the woman was on her, cold hands wrapped tightly around her neck. Nyx gasped a strangled cry, fighting desperately to draw a breath. The augarlux fell from her fingers as she dug her nails into the woman's wrists, trying to break her iron grip. Terror streaked through her as she realized that one of the woman's arms was rough, scales twisting up to her elbow. Claws pressed into Nyx's flesh from the tip of her fingers.

Nyx couldn't tear her eyes away from the woman's face as she coughed and gagged. She was desperate as she tried to think, feeling her knees buckle, a fog pressing against her mind. The woman's weight was heavy as she held Nyx down, a malicious grin sliding across her face.

The blade.

The thought hit Nyx suddenly, and she reached for it, her fingers fumbling for it against the blackness that was threatening to consume her. Nyx heard her attacker gasp when she swung the knife, releasing her suddenly. Nyx coughed and choked as she twisted on the ground, turning to see the woman standing over her. She was dressed in a black leather uniform, a coat of arms emblazoned into the leather over her left shoulder. Thin sheets of armor covered her chest and other strategic places.

Nyx realized she'd gotten lucky with the dagger, managing to drive it between pieces of armor.

The woman began to speak, her words sounding angry as her eyes blazed. She yanked the dagger from her side, twirling it in her clawed and scaly fingers. Her uniform began to turn darker as her blood stained it. It didn't seem like the wound fazed her at all, no trace of pain on her face.

Nyx couldn't understand her, and she gasped hard, shuddering breaths shaking her as she pulled herself back from the woman. There was one thing that was clear. This woman intended to kill her. She raised her arms to defend herself when the woman descended on her again, murder in her eyes.

Coracinus Mountains, Ymber.
The second day of winter, the 851st year of
the reign of Queen Liana Estrella.
Thursday, December 22, 2011.

J ET COULD FEEL THE COLD wind blowing into the canyon from the forest. He was close. He'd felt the momentary spike of fear that traveled through the augarlux and he knew Nyx was in danger. His heart caught when a sudden scream filled the night. He broke into a sprint, his eyes catching the scene before him.

A blue-haired woman was kneeling over Nyx, trying to drive a knife into her as Nyx barely held her back. Fear and pain was etched across Nyx's face as she screamed again, begging for the woman to stop. Her cries went unheeded.

The ferocity that filled him was white-hot, fueling the rage already burning inside him. In a swift motion, he leapt from the canyon. He twisted through the air, sending a blade humming in the direction of the woman. He felt his breath catch in his throat when the woman suddenly disappeared, the blade driving into the ground just shy of Nyx's head. He landed easily, his back to Nyx, seeing the woman standing before him.

She surprised him as she stared at him, her eyes growing wide with unimpeded emotion. "Jet," she breathed in Sarotian. She pressed her closed fist over her heart, bowing slightly. "General."

Jet stood motionlessly, feeling the same emotion that was on her face. "Savra?" he breathed. He hadn't expected this.

His heart twisted hard in his chest. He didn't think after so long he'd still have such strong feelings for her. She hadn't changed much in all the years he'd been absent. She was still small, with a slight build and a ferocity that took most by surprise. Memories assaulted him as he stared at her, conflicting feelings filling him. His eyes narrowed as he looked at her arm, which had been replaced with a dragon claw.

"I didn't want to believe it when I heard..." she whispered. Her eyes shifted back to the blonde-haired girl on the ground. "Is it true?" She looked up at him. "Are you really taking this girl to Liana?"

Jet clenched his jaw, surprised by the uncertainty in her voice. It reminded him of different days, when he was a different person. He almost felt a yearning to be that person again, until the wind shifted, the smell of Nyx's blood hitting him. "Yes," he said stonily.

He watched her brow lift in surprise. Obviously, she expected another answer.

"Why?" she breathed, her eyes confused. "Our King will have you back. You could come home." She looked at Nyx. "Liana's heir would be more than enough to win his favor." Pain crossed her face. "We could be together again. Like we used to."

Jet didn't look at Nyx as she gasped painfully, unwilling to take his eyes off her attacker. He gritted his teeth as the smell of her blood made his stomach turn, reminding him of his duty and his promise to her. He didn't trust himself to move just yet as he watched the blue-haired woman, rage seeping through his veins.

"What makes you think that I would still want to be with you after all this time?" he asked through gritted teeth. "No one came for me while I was in Liana's clutches, not even you." He struggled to tap his rage, knowing now was not the time to be impulsive. "Now stand down or die."

Savra seemed taken aback as she watched his face. "You know I would have done anything for you."

Jet smirked darkly. "But you didn't," he said darkly. "You're dead to me."

The surprise that had been on her face melted away to anger. "You would betray us all for the one who took your life away?" she demanded. She motioned to Nyx with the dagger she'd taken from her. "For this girl?" She tilted her head, thick strands of hair falling away from her eyes. She flexed her taloned hand, the claws sparkling in the moonlight. "You've changed."

Jet was glad that Nyx couldn't speak Sarotian. "A century in a dungeon will do that to you," he said slowly. "Let's not make this any uglier than it has to be."

Savra's eyes suddenly blazed. "Do you really think that will scare me?" She held the dagger in front of her, prepared for a strike. "My orders are clear: bring you back to King Paraximus. Dead or alive." Her eyes shifted to Nyx, hatred curling her lips. "I'll kill her first, so you can wallow in your failure." A sadistic smirk slid across her face. "Then I'll cut your throat."

Jet felt the distinct urge to roll his eyes at her. "Come

now," he said shortly. "Do you really think you could kill me?"

Savra twirled the blade, grinning sardonically. "We'll see, love." With a single step, she flashed into nothing. Her movements were fast, but Jet's eyes followed her easily.

He lifted his arms to stop her as she twisted, her leg swinging at him. He caught her foot, the force of her blow causing a shockwave where they met. He intended to stop her there, but she maneuvered away from him, her fist arching through the air. The blade in her hand whistled as she swung it at him. Jet didn't toy with her as he caught her wrist, stopping her dagger and dealing a hard blow to her side. He felt her bones give under the force. Savra staggered back, pain on her face as she caught herself.

Jet knew he should have taken her moment of discomfort to kill her, but his thoughts stilled him. He remembered seeing her beside him, slaying their enemies on the battlefield. It felt almost unfair to kill her so easily. She used to be so beautiful, covered in the blood of her victims, making murder an art form as only she could. He realized what he was feeling was disappointment.

Savra lifted her clawed hand, sensing his hesitation, a burst of magic suddenly erupting from her palm. It was hot and blue, like dragon fire, but Jet wasn't bothered as he lifted his hand in a swirling motion. Silver light formed a shield in front of him, rippling as it absorbed her blast. Her eyes were angry as she stared at him.

"Where is the Savra I used to know?" Jet taunted. "Has lovesickness dulled your skills?" He could feel the sizzle of her discharge in his fingers, but he knew that she was no match for him. Had she always been this weak and he'd just never noticed? Or had his years of captivity made her soft, too?

Once again, the disappointment weighed heavily in his chest, especially when he remembered the way Nyx's golden magic had literally dripped from her fingers. In his mind, there would never be anything that would compare to that moment. That was true power.

Savra glared at him for a long moment, hatred creasing her face. "Our lord will be coming for you," she said, her voice biting. "Even if you escape me, others will be coming for your blood." Despite the ferocity she was forcing, Jet knew she was terrified. She knew he was going to kill her. "I'll give you one last chance. Come back to Celo Cavus with me."

"I'll never go back there," Jet said easily.

He leapt toward her to deal the killing blow, but he tensed when Savra suddenly lifted her hand, a blinding light filling the night. The force of her magic caused him to stagger back, and he stepped closer to Nyx as her clawed arm began to morph, growing from the end of her elbow. It began to drip to the ground, the way Sophia's golem had. A strangled roar filled the night as the claw grew into an iron-scaled dragon. Jet felt his jaw clench.

The dragon curled around Savra, her eyes blazing with the fire of a thousand suns, and Jet recognized her instantly. "Isn't she beautiful?" Savra asked, holding out her remaining hand, her other arm ending at the elbow. Jet knew that it was dangerous, powerful magic she'd used to bind the dragon to her body like that.

The black dragon turned her head, a low growl echoing inside her chest. She let her chin rest in Savra's hand. Recognition sparked in her eyes as she gazed at Jet, but she bared razor fangs defensively when Savra moved toward her.

"I'm sure you thought she'd been slain by Liana's soldiers," Savra said, watching as the dragon flipped her tail between them. Her scales glittered in the moonlight, heat rolling off her body from the furnace that blazed inside her, melting the snow where she stood. "But I saved her." She turned her blue eyes to Jet. "For you."

Jet didn't move as Savra climbed onto her back. "You should have let her die," he said darkly. "She's no one's slave."

Savra laughed. "I brought her back from the edge of death," she snapped angrily. "Hessa knows who owns her life."

Hessa arched her body then, lifting leathery wings.

"Now you and your princess will die," Savra said, pursing her lips. "I won't stop the others who will come for you." She shook her head, looking disappointed. "You could have lived."

Jet lifted a hand to shield his eyes as a scorching blast of wind from Hessa's wings sent a flurry of snow and grass around them. Just as easily as she had come, she disappeared like a shadow into the sky. Jet cursed silently to himself, staring for a long time into the expanse of the night. He shouldn't have let her live.

It was Nyx's soft sobbing that finally brought him back to himself. He turned, seeing her footprints in the snow. She must have fled when he and Savra were fighting, which was probably the smartest thing she'd done since they'd arrived. He followed her footsteps, finding her leaning against the thick trunk of a tree, holding her arm tightly to her body. Blood was dripping across her fingers and staining the snow beside her.

When Jet stepped toward her, she twisted away, gasping in pain. "Let me help you," he said, trying to force his voice to be gentle.

"No," she snapped. Tears were falling quickly down her face. "I just want to go home." She sniffled and drew a ragged breath. "I just want to go back home."

Jet caught the sigh that tried to squeeze past his lips. "You can't go back there," he said quietly. He watched her cry for a minute longer. "You need to get up."

Nyx shook her head, lifting her hand. Her eyes were wide as she stared at her own blood on her fingers. "Why is this happening?" she whispered.

Jet caught her bloodied hand in his, seeing her eyes shift to his face. "This will keep happening if we don't get away from here." He held her gaze for a moment when she didn't move. "Savra will come back."

"Why did you let her get away?" Nyx suddenly demanded, her voice choked. "You just stood there and let her go." Accusation was thick in her voice.

Jet could feel his teeth grinding together as he gazed at her. "I can't win a fight against a dragon," he said, trying to keep the fierce edge from his words. His eyes shifted down, the stark and coppery scent of her blood making his chest feel tight. It was different, and he swallowed thickly, feeling something stirring inside him.

"You didn't even try!" Nyx yelled, pulling him from his thoughts. She seemed to gather herself, as she leaned forward to sit. "Holy shit, she had a dragon." She gasped in pain as her thoughts raced in her head. "And her arm..." How was any of this even possible?

Jet arched a brow at her. "You're being ridiculous," he said quietly. He knew Nyx was in shock, but he also knew she was right. He had let Savra get away, and he'd let her do more than he should have. He should have killed her as soon as he saw her. Nostalgia had gotten the better of him as he wondered how different she might be, and he couldn't let that happen with the others he intended to kill.

Nyx frowned at him, feeling the adrenaline in her system beginning to subside. It made the wound on her arm worse. "*I'm* being ridiculous?" she demanded. "She tried to kill me." Her gaze was guarded as she cradled her arm. "I thought your job was to keep me alive."

Jet scowled at her then. "You know nothing about what's going on here," he snapped. "I don't owe you any explanations."

"Yes you do!" Nyx countered, anger creasing her face. More tears flooded her eyes. "She *tried to kill me*!" She held his gaze as he glared at her. "Why did you let her get away?"

Jet sighed in disgust. "She has information that we need."

Nyx narrowed her eyes at him then. "Which is what?"

"Well, Paraximus' plans for us, for starters."

Nyx tried to absorb his words. She couldn't make her mind accept what she'd just experienced, and she knew that was stupid. "She grew a dragon from her arm," she mumbled.

Jet nodded, pressing his lips together tightly. "*Drac'duni*," he said softly.

Nyx looked at him. "What?" she asked.

Jet sighed for the millionth time. "It's powerful magic," he said shortly. "That dragon is technically dead." The thought made him fight down a grimace. "She's used a necromancer's magic to bind the dragon's spirit to her body, but it comes at a price."

"Her arm?" Nyx asked, pain creasing her face again. At Jet's nod, she tried to sit forward. "Who is she?" Her gaze was guarded as she looked at him. "You guys sure had a lot to say to each other."

"Her name is Savra," Jet said, kneeling in front of her. "She was a captain in Paraximus' lower ranks. I'll take care of her next time."

"How do you know that?" Nyx asked softly, drawing a

hitching breath. She watched his face, remembering what he'd said about being in the military.

Jet frowned darkly then. "I was her commander."

Nyx shifted her eyes to him, surprise in them. "You were part of Paraximus' military?" Her voice was breathless.

Jet smirked darkly. "Once upon a time. But not anymore." He held out his hand. "Let me see."

Nyx gasped, feeling dizzy when Jet pulled at her jacket, sending white-hot pain through her. More tears filled her eyes and she breathed a soft curse. Her heart was racing from the pain. She looked at the ground, feeling her stomach turn at the sight of her blood staining the snow.

"You can heal this," Jet said finally, drawing her from her thoughts. He pressed the torn sleeve of her jacket against the wound to try to stem the bleeding. The last thing they needed was a crimson trail leading straight to them.

Nyx looked at him, feeling a bit ill as she did so. "How?" she breathed. Her brow furrowed. "Can't you just magic it or whatever like Seth did?"

Jet arched a brow at her. "No," he said shortly. "Seth draws from the same source you do. That's how he could do it before."

Nyx clenched her jaw. She didn't know anything about her magic. She didn't even know how to do something like healing. "So, do I say the magic words or what?" she asked, looking up at him.

Jet smirked lightly, fighting down irritation. "Come," he said. He helped her to stand before guiding her toward his bag. He lifted it over his shoulder, leading her away into the trees. "We need to find some sort of cover." He doubted Savra would let them lick their wounds for very long. Once they had put some distance between them and the tree line, he stopped Nyx. "Sit."

Nyx followed his order, gasping in pain as she sank down onto a thick tree limb. The cut was still bleeding, and it hurt more just to look at it. It was deep, and she remembered still the sting of Savra's blade when it pierced her skin. She tried not to think about it as she turned her eyes on Jet, seeing him drop his bag on the ground and kneel before her.

He was grateful that Savra hadn't used a poisoned blade. That would make things more complicated.

Nyx turned her face away when he caught her arm in his hand. "I can't look," she breathed. She turned her eyes away, seeing the glowing flowers had once again opened around them, lending Jet enough light to see despite the reaching monster-trees around them.

"You need to gather your magic," Jet said, letting his eyes inspect her wound for any sign of poison. Her skin was pink and raw, the blood having stopped. She was healing quicker than an Inerse would have, but her wound should have sealed itself by now.

Nyx gasped when he wiped at the searing cut with his fingers, fighting the urge to yank her arm away. She missed the way his eyes lingered for too long. "That hurts, dammit!" Despite the pain, she closed her eyes, remembering how he'd told her to channel her magic.

"Just focus," he said softly, looking up at her. "Push it toward your arm."

Nyx drew a ragged breath as she let her mind go blank, feeling the warmth of her magic as it began to pool in her chest. She thought about what she wanted, just like she'd done with the augarlux, feeling the heat traveling down her arm and into her wrist. She opened her eyes slowly, gasping when she saw bright sparks jumping across her skin. They moved like a needle and thread, pulling her skin together painlessly.

"How...?" She felt sick suddenly as she watched. She hated needles and the motion of the sparks was making her stomach turn.

Jet looked up at her. "Talk about something. It'll distract you."

Nyx bit her lip as she looked away, staring at the flowers. "What are those flowers?"

Jet followed her gaze. "Infinity flowers."

Nyx gasped when he tilted her arm, making the cut twinge painfully. "Infinity flowers?" she whispered, feeling tears welling in her eyes again.

"They go through cycles," he said. He let his fingers drift across the sealing wound, feeling the heat of her magic pressing back. She was learning. "They close in the light and open in the darkness. But when they have a source of power to draw from, they bloom constantly." He glanced up at her face. "People who keep them allow them to bloom infinitely."

"Oh." Nyx felt her heart lurch when she glanced at him, and she turned her face away quickly. Her head spun dangerously, making her feel faint, as she realized how close he was to her. She remembered very vividly the urge she'd felt to kiss him, and she hated that she was feeling it again.

"Relax," Jet said. "You're done." It was odd to think that she was so fragile after what he'd seen her do.

Nyx looked down, realizing her good hand was clenched, her nails digging into her palm. Her hands were caked with dried blood and it made her stomach turn, even though it was her own. She nodded shortly, drawing a quick breath as she turned her eyes away. "Good," she said softly. She could see that the newly healed flesh was pink. She pulled her sleeve down quickly, even though it was torn from Savra's blade. She couldn't look at her arm without remembering the way Savra's eyes had flashed as she stood over her.

Jet felt satisfaction seep through him as he moved to stand. "Better?" Now they could get moving again.

Nyx swallowed thickly as she nodded, residual magic pulsing through her body. "Thanks." She frowned at the torn fabric.

Jet nodded. He surprised her when he reached down, scooping the snow he could find into his hands. He caught her hands in his, using the snow to wash away the blood. He said nothing as he finished, standing and swinging his bag over his shoulders. "Let's go," he said. "We need to be on the other side of the forest by sunrise."

Nyx grimaced. She looked down when he held her dagger out to her. She didn't want it, but she was ready to be far away from here.

The forest was silent as they wound their way through, the trail becoming less of a trail and more of something that Nyx was sure Jet was taking liberties with. She couldn't see a path anymore, and she was pushing through thick foliage, trying to stay on Jet's heals. Tall, ancient trees rose around them, their boughs bending in arcs across each other. The infinity flowers bloomed all around them, becoming bright and fading as she walked past them. Insects jumped out of their way, flashing in the darkness. The bright moonlight was touching the forest floor in some places and Nyx could see easily without the help of Jet's augarlux.

The weariness in her body became worse as the night wore on, even though she tried to fight through it. She tried to take in all the new and amazing things around her, but it made her feel like her brain was being overloaded. She also tried to ignore the way her blood-soaked clothes were becoming dry and crusty.

She jumped suddenly when a cry pierced through the trees. "What was that?" she whispered, shifting her eyes around. Fear filled her as she tried not to think about Savra.

Jet paused, looking at her over his shoulder, his lips twisting slightly with humor. "The Sarotian word is *anthis*," he said slowly. His onyx gaze searched the trees. "It's a small, winged creature."

Nyx grimaced, relief filling her. "Like a bird?" she asked meekly.

Jet shook his head. "It has hands, like a monkey," he said. "And teeth."

"Oh, great," Nyx said, pushing her way closer to him. "I'm ready to go now."

Jet smirked then. "They don't eat flesh," he said, turning and continuing. "Only fruit."

"That's fine," Nyx said hurriedly. "But I'm not interested in meeting one today. So let's go."

Jet watched as she pushed through the vines and foliage past him. He was enjoying this too much.

"Is Sarotian the language you speak?" Nyx asked suddenly, looking over at him. They'd been walking in silence for a while, and her thoughts had been rampant. She didn't know how he could be so calm.

Jet nodded. "It is the common tongue," he said. "There are others, but Sarotian is the diplomatic language."

Nyx frowned. She paused to catch herself as she climbed over a fallen tree. She was surprised to see that the bark of the tree was a deep green, and the leaves that covered the ground were bright blue like the grass had been. The snow was barely visible here, having been caught by the limbs of the trees around them.

"Is that what you were speaking with Savra?" she asked suddenly. When she didn't receive a reply, Nyx paused, looking over her shoulder at him. There was a soft scowl on his face as his eyes shifted around the trees. "What?"

Jet shot her a glance. "It's nothing," he said dismissively. He didn't offer more. He thought he could hear something in the distance, but he wasn't certain. Nyx attributed the distracted look in his eyes to their run-in with Savra, missing the things he thought he was sensing.

Silence fell over them for a long moment, allowing Nyx's thoughts time to coalesce into a myriad of questions she wanted to voice. "What was she saying to you?" she asked finally, suddenly curious, despite the way her heart fluttered at the thought of Savra. She paused, looking up at him. Something in his face had changed when he and Savra were speaking, his eyes betraying hidden emotions. Nyx hadn't been able to fully discern them, especially since she'd been rolling on the ground in pain.

Jet stopped beside her, crossing his arms. He wasn't sure he wanted to tell her about it. He was trying not to think about it. But he could tell from the sparkle in her emerald gaze that she wasn't likely to let this go. He sighed shortly, aggravated.

"We used to sorta have a … *thing*," he said, feeling his face twist into a bitter scowl with the admission. "She knows things about me, just like I know things about her."

Nyx felt a flare of jealousy streak through her. She didn't like the idea that there were people who actually *knew* Jet. He didn't share his past with her. "You mean she was like a girlfriend?" she asked carefully. Silence stretched between them for a long moment as she pushed on through the forest. She knew she was prying at a Pandora's box.

Jet sighed after a while. "If that's what you want to call it," he said finally.

"And you were in the military together," Nyx said,

frowning. She shook her head, confusion filling her. "And you were her commanding officer." She felt her frown deepen as a thought hit her. "You had to have known what she was capable of. Why were you going easy on her?" She sighed, feeling bitter suddenly. "You never go easy on me."

Jet had a sixth sense when it came to hand-to-hand combat. He would never let her get away with the same thing twice, always forcing her to improvise. It didn't make sense that he wouldn't know Savra's moves already. The jealousy nagged at her again. She stopped suddenly, feeling her heart skip a beat and her stomach turn. "Do you still have feelings for her?"

Jet sighed in aggravation as he shook his head, conflicting feelings jumbling inside him. He didn't dare tell her the truth. "Just shut up about it," he snapped. "It's none of your business." He turned his head then, another unusual sound catching his attention. He tried to tell himself that it was nothing; he just wasn't used to Gexalatia's sounds anymore.

Nyx felt her heart sink. "Whatever." Her insides were twisting and coiling, making her feel sick. She didn't like that Jet was keeping secrets from her. It just wasn't fair, because all his secrets seemed to put her in danger. She felt her stomach flip as it occurred to her that she wasn't certain if Jet was really on her side or not. "So, you're going to take care of her the next time we see her?" Her voice was cautious.

Jet's eyes shifted to her. He didn't like the way she said that, and it made him feel dirty somehow. "I told you I'd handle it," he snapped. He sighed in disgust. "You need to learn to trust me."

He knew his father had probably filled Savra's head with all sorts of nonsense about revenge, playing on her emotions to convince her to come after him and Nyx. That was the only reason, because Savra had to know that she couldn't win, even with her *drac'duni*. Just like Nyx said, he did know her moves before she made them. Nothing had changed much in the years that he'd been in prison, except that it seemed Savra had forgotten him. If she remembered what he'd done at all, she never would have agreed to come after him.

Nyx scowled at him suddenly. "You're always talking about trust," she snapped. "But how can I do that with you keeping so many secrets?" Suspicion suddenly seeped through her. What was Jet really hiding?

Jet's face pulled into scowl. "I don't have secrets," he hissed suddenly. "I told you what you wanted to know." The accusation in his voice was heavy. "It will be a miracle if you make it to Regius Carmen alive."

Nyx tried to keep the angry look on her face, but she was failing as her heart twisted painfully. Tears began to fill her eyes. "I didn't ask for this," she said quietly. "I didn't ask for someone to murder my aunt, and for you to bring me here." Her tears were suddenly falling faster. "You should have just left me alone." Bitterness was welling inside her, and she turned away from him. "I wish I'd never met you."

Jet rolled his eyes suddenly. "Oh, here we go," he said angrily. He trailed after her as she pushed through the trees away from him. "It's always about you, isn't it?"

Nyx shook her head, brushing at the tears on her face. She didn't care what Jet was supposed to do, she didn't want to be near him anymore. She rounded on him. "Why don't you just leave me, then?" she yelled. "Like you said, someone will get me where I need to go."

Jet gritted his teeth, angry words on his lips, when suddenly he froze. He turned his head slightly, listening. Just like before, the slightest silence around them, followed by soft knocking. It suddenly occurred to him that it was code.

"Don't ignore me!" Nyx suddenly barked at him.

Jet turned to her, narrowing his eyes, her outburst having interrupted his concentration on the soft pattern. "Shut up, Nyx," he said quietly, his voice dark.

Nyx shook her head, bristling. "Don't tell me to shut up!"

Jet reached out quickly, backing her into a tree and clamping a hand over her mouth. He ignored her when she gasped in surprise, her emerald eyes wide as she struggled against him. "We're not alone," he said quietly, looking around the trees. He couldn't hear the knocking anymore, and it made a scowl cross his face. He released Nyx when she pulled at his hand.

Her eyes were wide with fear. "What's happening?" she breathed.

Jet shook his head. "Keep moving," he said, catching her arm and pushing her ahead of him. His strides were long and quick, and Nyx felt like she was sprinting suddenly to keep up with him.

The Abjure Forest, Ymber.
The second day of winter, the 851st year of
the reign of Queen Liana Estrella.
Thursday, December 22, 2011.

NYX TURNED HER EYES AHEAD, pushing her way through the trees. The sudden rush of adrenaline made her forget her weariness and their fight. They ran for a moment before Jet stopped her. His dark eyes scanned the trees around them, as if he was sensing something Nyx knew she couldn't.

"Are we alone?" she whispered.

Jet didn't say anything, listening. "For the moment," he said softly. He turned back to her.

Sudden, fierce pain shot through him as a force shoved him forward. The pain started in the back of his shoulder and traveled down to his fingers, and he turned his head. He gritted his teeth, seeing an arrow had struck him, sinking deep into his flesh.

"Oh my god," Nyx breathed, stepping away from him. "You've been hit!"

Rage filled him as he lifted his hand, yanking the arrow from his shoulder. If she'd kept her damn mouth shut, he would have expected this. The ache was annoying as he caught Nyx, listening to her gasp in small, terrified breaths, pushing her forward.

"Move."

Nyx felt panic fill her as she broke into a dash through the trees. She ducked under a large branch, a scream escaping her when an arrow hit a tree next to her with a resounding smack. Suddenly, all around them arrows were filling the trees. Nyx was gasping for air as they fled, feeling the forest working against her suddenly. Her legs tangled in brambles, bringing her crashing to the ground. She cried out softly, tears filling her eyes as Jet caught her, pulling her easily to her feet.

"Don't stop," Jet said, ducking his head as another arrow whizzed by.

"I can't," Nyx breathed, fear rendering her useless suddenly. She struggled forward, feeling her body giving out. She didn't have the energy or the strength for this. She didn't know how Jet could go forward, even after he'd been injured.

Jet sighed suddenly, the sound irritated. Nyx watched in surprise as he threw up his arm, a burst of magic filling the air. When the arrows struck, it flickered, a silver shield protecting them. Without missing a beat, Jet swept her into his arms.

Nyx gasped when he suddenly leapt forward, shooting into the reaching boughs of the big trees around them. Her eyes were wide as her brain tried to understand how this was happening. Jet was nimble as he leapt through the trees. It suddenly seemed as if this was easier than being on the ground, and she held tightly to the front of his shirt, fear coursing through her. Jet landed in a tall, thick-branched tree, turning his eyes over his shoulder.

"How are you doing this?" Nyx breathed suddenly.

Jet looked down at her. He eased her to stand beside him. "Practice," he said. His dark eyes were arrogant.

Nyx held tightly to his arm as she looked down. The tree was massive, rising well into the sky, giving her a good view of the forest. It looked like a white-covered ocean as it stretched out on either side of them. It was frightening, knowing there were people out there that could see them, but Nyx didn't know where they were hiding.

"Did we lose them?" she whispered.

Jet looped an arm around her middle to steady her. "I doubt it," he said darkly. "We've just bought some time." He schooled his face into calm as pain suddenly began to course through his shoulder, where the arrow had struck him. He tried to stop the sigh that he felt on his lips. He shouldn't have been in pain like this.

Nyx looked up at him. She realized that he was too calm. Her eyes shifted to the blood that was staining his t-shirt. "Are you hurt?" she asked softly.

Jet's eyes shifted to her. He didn't like that she seemed to know what he was thinking. "I'm fine." He turned to her, lifting her into his arms. "We can't stay here."

Nyx gasped, feeling her stomach flip as Jet suddenly dropped from the bough. She hated the feeling of falling as Jet landed lightly on another branch. He paused, and Nyx felt her breath catch in her throat, straining to hear what he was listening to.

Nyx held tightly to him when another arrow suddenly flew toward them. She gasped, holding down a scream as Jet turned quickly, dropping from the tree. His jaw was clenched against the pain as he landed on the ground, collapsing momentarily to a knee. He cursed softly in Sarotian as he pulled another arrow from his side.

"Are you okay?" Nyx asked quickly, fear filling her. Her breaths were quick. She did see pain on his face this time as he tossed the arrow away.

"I'm fine," he snapped. His onyx eyes were narrowed angrily. "Keep moving." He gasped softly as he pushed her forward.

Nyx couldn't stop the fear that was coursing over her. She knew Jet was trying to hide his injuries, and it made her feel more afraid. How much pain was he really in?

Soon, the trees opened into a clearing, a field stretching before them, surrounded on either side by more trees. The grass was tall, and it was like trying to run through water as Nyx fought her way through, feeling the shoots tangling around her feet. She glanced over her shoulder, seeing Jet was behind her, a hand pressed to his side.

He paused as he turned to look behind as well, and Nyx stopped, trying to catch her breath. She wished she would have known that this was going to happen. She definitely wouldn't have come here.

Jet could feel his heart racing as he stood there. Shallow breaths were ghosting over his lips, and he pressed his hand harder over the wound to his side. His blood felt like it was on fire, and the pain was making fury fill him. He didn't deal well with pain. He could hear more knocking and the rustling of someone approaching. It made him uncomfortable. He couldn't pinpoint exactly who was hunting them.

"What's happening?" Nyx asked, gasping softly for a breath as she straightened.

Jet narrowed his eyes. "Savra said more would come," he said bitterly. He lifted his hand, seeing his blood staining it. It suddenly made sense, what those men had said about the message. They'd been left behind to somehow cue the others that he and Nyx were coming. They'd been herded right into a trap.

"We can't stay here," Nyx said, seeing the blood on his hand. "You're hurt."

Jet turned his eyes on her. "I'm fine," he said coldly. He'd been injured much worse. This pain was just enough to irritate him. It was enough that if he saw Savra, he'd kill her before she stepped foot from her dragon's back.

Nyx frowned at him. "I saw you," she said, disbelief filling her voice. She remembered the look on his face when he'd been struck. "You might be a badass when you're not hurt, but you can't fight like this."

Jet winced, drawing a ragged breath as the burning surged. His eyes shifted back to the trees. He needed to be ready for whoever was coming for them.

Nyx stepped toward him, afraid. "What should I do?" she whispered, watching his face carefully.

Jet shook his head. "Just stay alive," he said. The soft rustling was becoming louder, and he turned his eyes back to the trees. "They're here."

Nyx drew a ragged breath, stepping back, behind Jet. "Who?" A dark shadow suddenly emerged from the trees, standing on the edge of the field. Nyx reached for Jet, catching the back of his t-shirt. "Who is that?" Her voice was shaking.

Jet drew a short breath, shaking his head. A smirk was pulling at his lips. He watched as the shadow uncurled into the shape of a man. "I should have known," Jet said, a hint of cruel humor in his voice. He turned to look at Nyx, catching her hand and uncurling her fingers from the fabric. "Let me take care of this."

Nyx felt her heart skip a beat as Jet walked away from her. She realized she was trembling as she watched him. She sank down into the tall grass, hoping to avoid drawing attention to herself. She drew her dagger just in case, watching between the blades of grass as Jet walked toward their pursuer.

"So, it is true," the man said, taking several steps toward them. His Sarotian was very distinct to Jet, from a province on the edge of Siccita.

Nyx felt her heart sink at the cruel tone to his voice, despite not understanding their language. She gasped as he came into the moonlight.

He was a big man, with large, broad shoulders. His arms were huge and muscular. Dark brown hair was teased into thick, spiky chunks on his head. Even from her distance, Nyx could see his brown eyes glowing softly in the light of the moons. He wore a uniform like the one Savra wore, the same coat of arms pressed into the leather. It was barely visible though, as a plate of armor emblazoned with some sort of beast covered his chest. Pieces of armor covered his forearms and the tops of his legs, shimmering as the moonlight bounced off the metal. Nyx noticed that a large weapon was strapped to his back, something that looked way too heavy for anyone to be able to wield successfully.

Jet lifted his chin, dropping his hand from his side. "What is that?" he asked, regarding the man with narrowed eyes. He knew this man. He was an Acerbi, and he once served under Jet as his Lieutenant. It vaguely occurred to Jet that his father was testing him, sending ones he knew to battle him. Paraximus wanted to know how strong he was and how in control of the monster he was. Jet didn't like that.

Lue lifted his chin, his eyes shifting to Nyx over Jet's shoulder. "You *are* doing Liana's bidding." He laughed shortly. "How did that wretch charm you into taking up her cause?" His eyes shifted back to Jet. "Did she promise you that pretty little girl?"

Jet clenched his jaw, but he forced a light smirk, looking down at his bloodied hands. The only thing he desired in this moment was to see Lue dead. "What's it to you?" he asked scornfully. His eyes were following Lue's lumbering form, his mind searching for any disadvantage he could exploit.

Lue was still grinning as he walked slowly toward Jet. "She must have offered you something big, General," he said. He laughed again. "You used to take whatever you wanted. It just doesn't make sense."

Jet shifted his eyes to Lue's face, feeling defensive. Lue was trying to close the gap between them. He'd always been one for close combat. That was how Jet knew that there was someone else with him. Lue carried a war hammer, not a bow. Purposefully, Jet angled his shoulders. Lue would be more than happy to have his subordinates strike Nyx down while they were engaged in hand to hand battle.

"I wouldn't do that," Lue said suddenly, drawing Jet's gaze. He was grinning darkly. "My men will kill her if you try to get to her."

Jet gritted his teeth. He didn't like this at all. "So why haven't you done it yet?" Jet asked, watching Lue carefully. "If you're sent to kill her, why are you stalling?"

Lue shook his head. "You misunderstand," he said. He lifted a beefy hand, pulling the large hammer from his back. The hammer sparked with magic as Lue charged it. "It's your head Our King requires. Taking the princess will be a happy coincidence."

Jet leapt back quickly as Lue lurched forward, swinging his hammer. He felt the air stir and crackle, realizing how close Lue had come as he landed a few feet away. He grimaced, knowing he was too slow. The poison that was burning him from the inside out was slowing his reactions. Lue was large and lumbering, but he was swift with the swings of his hammer. Jet knew the only chance he had was to take Lue's weapons away.

Lue advanced on him again, swinging his hammer in a downward motion. Jet barely managed to avoid it as it smashed into the ground, the magic it emitted leaving a deep crater. "It looks like my poison is working," Lue said boastfully, leaping at Jet again. "You're slow."

Jet gritted his teeth, knowing this had to end here. "It seems cowardly of you to have to cheat to kill me." He summoned all his strength, feeling the magic that pulsed through him combating the burning inside him. He felt a pain shoot through his chest as the *fax* suddenly twisted. He knew that wasn't a good sign.

Lue suddenly appeared beside him, faster than Jet had expected. He swung his arm with unexpected force, and Jet braced, stepping into the blow, summoning a shield. Pain suddenly ricocheted through every bone in Jet's body, but he let his shield dissolve, catching the hammer. He felt like he'd been struck by lightning as he held onto it, feeling Lue's magic pulsing through the handle, sending jolts of pain through every fiber inside him. He ignored it though, baring his fangs in a dangerous smile. He'd caught the hammer as it swung, effectively stopping Lue's blow.

Lue snarled suddenly. "Impossible," he growled.

Jet shook his head, using his grip on Lue's hammer to swing Lue around, sending him flying. He gasped, feeling the beast whispering softly in his head. He knew he was tottering dangerously on the edge of losing control, but he also knew there was no other way. Only the *fax* could give him the strength to kill Lue right now.

"You've forgotten, Lue," Jet said darkly. His onyx eyes

flashed dangerously as he stepped toward Lue. "The beast can't allow me to die by the hands of a pathetic weakling like you."

Lue's eyes were suddenly wide. He didn't have any words as Jet suddenly sprang at him, forming his Geminaci blades. He barely managed to stop Jet, attempting to swing his hammer. Jet ducked it easily, moving much faster than Lue could track him. Jet swung his blades in an expert move, slicing cleanly into Lue's flesh, bringing him crashing to the ground.

"We're done," he said darkly. He kneeled over Lue, who was gasping in pain. With an easy swing, he used his blades to slice Lue's head from his body.

Jet drew a ragged breath, wincing suddenly. The beast's whispering was suddenly more intense as Lue's blood began to stain the ground. The beast twisted painfully, reaching for it through Jet's body. Jet gasped, falling to a knee. He had to stop it and get it back under control. He couldn't let it take over. Not right now. Nyx was still in danger.

He forced himself to his feet, turning away from Lue. The beast inside roared with displeasure, but Jet shook his head, trying to clear it. He needed to focus. He took several painful steps away from Lue's body, feeling the *fax* suddenly attempt to take control. It felt like clawed fingers were digging into his heart, and he fell to his knees.

"Stop," he breathed. "I can't do this right now."

The *fax* raged. *I will have this body.*

Jet shook his head against the monster's throaty words. "Not today," he growled, forcing himself to stand. He ignored the pain as his eyes found Nyx immediately.

Fear was on her face as she ran toward him through the tall grass. "Are you okay?" she asked breathlessly as she reached him.

Jet nodded, his hand pressed against his chest. He saw that tears were in her eyes.

"I can't believe you did that," she whispered. Her eyes took him in, searching for wounds. "There's no way you should have been able to stop him like that."

Jet forced a smirk. "I thought I told you— " Surprise stilled the rest of the words on his lips as whistling caught his ears. He stepped to the side thoughtlessly, narrowly avoiding another poison-tipped arrow. The smack that it made when it hit flesh was deafening, as was the pained cry that left Nyx's lips.

She reeled backwards, falling to her hands and knees. She dug her fingers into the blades of grass around her, gasping another strangled cry. Jet looked over his shoulder for the archer, reaching for her to shield her from any more shots and pulling her quickly into the trees. He knew it was dangerous to turn his back; if his body took any more damage, the *fax* could take control, but they couldn't stay out in the open anymore. He thought the faint glint of armor caught the moonlight in the distance, but he was distracted when Nyx whimpered as he helped her slide to the ground.

"Shit," Jet breathed, eying the arrow protruding from her shoulder. The scent of her blood was filling the air as it ran across her shoulder and her fingers as she pressed her hand against her shoulder. She was drawing shuddering breaths, her brow furrowed with pain. The *fax* was still twitching in his mind, begging for just a drop, daring him to reach out and let it run across his fingers. Jet tried to ignore it as he assessed the situation, clenching his fists.

Nyx clenched her jaw tightly, the pain of her muscles straining unmatched by the pain that was suddenly coursing through her. She lifted a hand to reach for the arrow, but she gritted her teeth when her fingers brushed it, trying to stop the cry that escaped her lips. Tears were rolling down her cheeks.

Guilt was flooding Jet as he kneeled in front of her. That arrow was meant for him. "I need to pull it out," he said, watching her tear-filled gaze rise to meet his.

Nyx shook her head, sobbing softly as she looked at him. "No," she managed. She leaned away when he reached for her, fear in her eyes. "Don't touch me."

Jet held her gaze, knowing this was going to hurt her. "I have to," he said sternly. "You can't heal with it still in there." He managed to catch her, her struggling weak as she cried harder. "I'll make it quick."

Anger creased her face suddenly, barely reaching her eyes. "Don't you dare," she half-growled. She surprised him when she used her feet to push him away, more force in her pushing than he expected. "Get away from me!"

Jet caught her ankle as she tried to kick him, pulling her toward him. It caught her off guard, causing her to fall on her back. He sighed in annoyance as he climbed over the top of her to keep her still, pinning her good arm with his knee and grabbing hold of the arrow shaft. "Stop it," he said, annoyance in his voice. "You're acting like a baby."

Nyx let her head fall back in the grass, the pain shooting through her whole body. She felt nauseous and her head was swimming. The burning in her veins was worse as Jet's weight pressed against her skin. She turned her face away from the arrow, Jet's hand causing a pins-and-needles feeling as he braced it against her shoulder. Her mind felt foggy suddenly, everything around her swaying and making her feel like she could just fall into darkness at any moment.

"On three," he said, watching her face. She was pale and her eyes were unfocused. The *fax's* voice was suddenly too quiet, as if waiting in anticipation. Jet knew something was wrong as he watched her face relax suddenly, and her eyes close. "Nyx?"

His heart dropped and he gave a quick yank, feeling the barbed tip dislodge from her flesh, hoping it would be enough to snap her back to reality. She didn't react and he pressed his hand against the bleeding wound, feeling his chest constrict. The *fax* twisted hard against him suddenly, relishing the feel of her warm blood flowing over his fingers. Jet clenched his jaw hard against the monster's whispering. Now was not the time for this.

Taste it.

"Stop it," he breathed, lifting his hand to his face. The sickly-sweet stench of poison made his stomach turn, but the smell of her blood made him freeze. He stared hard at it as it beaded and rolled slowly across his fingers.

Just one drop, the *fax* begged.

Jet felt his thoughts slow to a halt. The voice was so tempting, making his body ache for the power that he knew was contained in her veins.

You can take her strength, the *fax* reasoned.

Images began to flood his mind. He could see the battle fields stretched before him and could feel the carnage that had been caused by his hands. He could feel a strength pulsing through him that he hadn't felt in more than a century. The *fax* promised that all of this could be his again, and all it would take was one taste. One taste, and he could have her power; the strength that made magic run like water.

We could be whole again.

Jet's eyes focused on his hand, a sick feeling overwhelming him. Whole again? He clenched his fist, suddenly slamming it into the ground. Rage was filling him, silencing the beast that he harbored and shattering the images in his mind.

Pain slowly crawled through his wrist and into his arm,

helping his mind to focus on something other than the voice.

He was whole now. He didn't need the empty, bullshit promises the *fax* thought it was offering.

He realized he was trembling from the effort it had taken to keep the monster at bay. He shook his head slowly, drawing a ragged breath, the silence in his mind making him wary. He knew it could come back at any moment, and maybe with urges stronger than these.

Jet looked down to Nyx, gathering her quickly into his arms. He needed to move now, while he could still think rationally. She was hot to the touch, and he knew that the poison was spreading through her body quickly. She needed help.

5

The Abjure Forest, Ymber.
The third day of winter, the 851st year of the
reign of Queen Liana Estrella.
Friday, December 23, 2011.

JET KNELT SLOWLY, SEEING FAINT rays of sun peaking over the trees. He knew he didn't have much daylight. He let Nyx slide slowly from his arms, watching as her brow furrowed. Sweat was rolling down her temples, and her face was red. She hadn't moved in the last hour, since he'd picked her up and carried her to the edge of the river.

The water was cold as Jet dipped his hands into it, watching a cloud of red form around his fingers. The scent of her blood was still pungent to his senses, but at least the beast had gone silent. He scrubbed at his skin, trying to clean all her blood from his hands. He felt sick thinking about the monster's whispered words.

Once he was satisfied and his hands were sufficiently raw, Jet opened his bag and pulled the blanket from it, tearing a strip from the end. He plunged it into the frigid water before pressing it against Nyx's face. She didn't stir like a conscious person would have, or even respond to the icy water against her face.

Jet knew that her time was short. He sighed around the heavy feeling in his chest, knowing that his options were limited.

Somewhere, in the boughs of the trees, hidden from sight, was a plant that could stop the poison that was flowing through her. The only problem was he didn't know where to find it, and he didn't know if he could make it in time. He knew there was a village somewhere, as well, but that seemed like a bigger gamble than looking for an antidote. The villagers were likely tribesmen and probably wouldn't take kindly to their intrusion.

He sat slowly beside her, his heart heavy. If she knew how to channel her magic properly, she could have healed from this easily.

Jet pressed the back of his hand against her face, feeling how hot she was still. The compress seemed to be doing nothing. He drew a slow breath, deciding there was one last thing he could try. Maybe he could force her magic to generate and heal her. He moved to his knees, prepared to try, when a sound suddenly caught his ears.

He was on his feet in an instant, his Geminaci blades in his hands. If one of Lue's men, or even Savra, had come to finish them off, he wouldn't make it easy. Surprise filled him when the call of a rapere suddenly filled the morning air, along with the sound of laughter.

A tall orange beast broke through the brush, starting at the sight of him. It flapped stubby wings, clacking a monstrous beak. "Easy," a man cooed in Sarotian from its back, patting its neck. "Easy girl."

Despite the confusion filling him, Jet didn't lower his weapons. He watched as the man's eyes found his, his grey eyebrows lifting in surprise.

"What is it Papa—oh!" Another rapere appeared behind the first, clearly a large male with a bright crest and glistening blue feathers. A girl, no older than Nyx, sat atop it, her face pulled in surprise.

"Stay on your mount, Melinda," the man commanded, sliding from his own bird-beast. He handed the reins to her, a silent warning passing between them.

Jet eased his stance slightly as the older man took a step toward him, his grey eyes shifting to Nyx.

"Do you need help?" he asked. Concern was on his face as he stared at Nyx. "Is she ill?" The man motioned toward a saddlebag that was bulging at the bird-beast's back. "I'm a doctor. I can help you."

Jet frowned then. "A doctor?" he asked warily. "What is a doctor doing in the middle of the forest?"

The man looked to Jet, his eyes still concerned. "I live with the Abjureans, in the village of Festra," he said evenly. "We're returning from a supply trip." He seemed to be wondering the same thing about Nyx and Jet as his grey eyes shifted over them.

Jet let his weapons slowly dissolve. The man took that as a sign to proceed, and he moved rapidly toward Nyx, kneeling beside her. Jet knew he was useless as he watched the old man's practiced hands touch her face.

"Fever," he said absently. His eyes shifted over the blood that stained her shirt, a frown pulling at his face. He pressed his fingers against her wound, lifting them to his nose. The scent of the poison made his face wrinkle. His eyes drifted down to her unusual clothing, trying to hide the surprise that was pulling at his face as he looked up to Jet. "What happened to her?"

"Poisoned arrow," Jet said shortly. He didn't particularly

care for the way the old man was looking at them, as if he knew something he shouldn't have.

The old man stood, motioning to the girl to bring the mounts forward. "Can you get her onto Palla?" He motioned to the orange bird.

Jet hesitated. He wasn't sure if he should trust them, but what other choice did he have?

"I must take her back to Festra," the old man continued, urgency in his voice. "She will die without an antidote."

Jet grimaced lightly, nodding his head. He was silent as he lifted her, watching the doctor climb onto his mount. Jet handed Nyx's limp form to the man, watching as he turned his mount quickly, letting it speed into the trees.

The girl was still sitting on her rapere before him, and she held out her hand. "Let's go."

Jet caught her wrist, allowing her to pull him on behind her, her mount speeding after the first.

"We're not far from the village," the girl said, glancing over her shoulder at him. "My father will heal her."

Jet frowned at the back of her head, holding onto the back of her saddle. He hoped what she said was true. He didn't want to think about the other possibility.

Before too long, the massive trees and thick brush began to give way, a path forming among the boughs. The sun was at its highest, barely over the tops of the trees, throwing morning light across the ground. It was disorienting to Jet. He had become used to Earth days, which were three times longer than Gexalatian days. He couldn't dwell on his thoughts long, however, when the brush suddenly dropped away, revealing a giant wooden ramp.

The doctor's rapere raced up the ramp, which curled around the gigantic trunk of an older-than-ancient tree. The ramp led high into the air, and Jet felt his breath catch in his throat. All above him was a village, built into the boughs of the trees.

The buildings were nearly to the middle of the trees, perched on the wide branches, which acted like roads between the structures. Stairs and wooden ramps twisted between the branches, connecting the village. It was much larger than Jet thought it would have been, with homes and what appeared to be a smith and a carpenter. Toward the center, a tall structure stood, carved into the trunk of another massive tree. It was decorated with symbols and creatures, painted brightly in yellows and oranges. Behind it, a long set of stairs wound up the massive tree, to a mansion perched high into the canopy.

Jet was still trying to take it all in as Melinda's rapere came to a halt in front of a small house. "What is this place?" Jet asked softly.

Melinda smiled slightly, brushing her tousled brown hair from her face. "This is Festra." She caught the reins of her father's bird as Jet slid from behind her to take Nyx into his arms.

"This way," the doctor said, walking up wooden steps and into the house. "Bring her in here."

Jet did as he said, looking around. It was clearly their home, filled with their personal belongings. A stove stood in the far corner, a small fire inside the grate. It was the only light in the house until the doctor waved his hand, summoning an augarlux. Jet frowned at the man, having felt the pull of the magic he'd used. It was the same source that Jet drew from.

"Lay her down," the doctor said as he placed the augarlux on a shelf above a bed.

Jet did as he was told, stepping back toward the doorway as the doctor began to flit around the room. He'd grabbed a case, which Jet hadn't noticed as they'd come through the door, and now he was digging through it.

"Melinda!"

Melinda's round face appeared in the doorway. "Yes, Papa?" she asked.

"Bring water," the doctor ordered.

"Yes, Papa," Melinda said, all business as she disappeared into the other room.

Jet glanced over his shoulder, seeing her pouring water from a bucket into a wide-rimmed bowl. "Can you help her?" he asked, feeling useless as the girl rushed past him to hand her father the bowl.

"She will be fine," the doctor said distractedly, pouring different vials of liquid into the water. He didn't look up from what he was doing. "Melinda, take our guest into the front room."

Melinda nodded, turning her eyes on Jet. "This way," she said, motioning toward the other room. Jet made to protest, but Melinda shook her head. "My father needs to do what he does best." She offered a small smile. "She will be all right."

Jet frowned at her before looking back to Nyx. He didn't want to leave her, but he watched the doctor scoop the concoction with a cup, holding it to her lips. He cooed soft words to her to encourage her to drink.

"Sir?" Melinda prompted.

Jet turned his attention back to her.

"At least take a rest," she said earnestly. Her eyes shifted over his torn and bloody clothing. "You look like you need it."

Jet sighed shortly, knowing there was nothing more he could do. He didn't like feeling helpless. He relented finally, following Melinda into what was essentially a kitchen, dining room, and family room, all rolled into one. She motioned to a thickly padded chair, which he slowly sank into.

Melinda eased onto a short stool across from him, her blue eyes studying his face. "What in the world happened to you two?"

Jet frowned at her, looking away. "It's none of your concern," he said, his words a bit more clipped than he intended.

Melinda seemed surprised as she sat back on her stool. "Sorry for the intrusion," she said meekly. She rose slowly to her feet. "Papa has some old clothes that you can have." She appraised him for a moment. "You look to be about his size."

Jet didn't say anything as she disappeared into the back room. He could hear soft whispers as they spoke to one another. He let his head drop into his hands, feeling like shit. He should have been able to protect Nyx.

Heavy footsteps across the wooden floor caught his ear, and his head snapped up. He turned in his chair, watching as the doctor walked toward him. Behind him was Melinda, a bundle in her hands.

"How is she?" Jet asked quickly, moving to his feet.

The doctor motioned for him to sit, easing onto the stool Melinda had once occupied. "She will be fine," he said, clasping his hands in front of him. He leaned forward, and Jet felt himself bristle at his posture. "What the hell happened to you two?"

"Just like I told your daughter, it's no one's business but mine," Jet said defensively.

The old man didn't seem fazed. "She was poisoned with infinity flower poison," he said shortly. "Not the most common or easiest to make." His greying eyes narrowed. "Seems like the person after you knew what he was doing."

Jet clenched his jaw. He should have seen that coming. There were provinces in the northern parts of Siccita, near the mountains, that were renowned for their use of infinity flower poison. Only someone from those provinces could have recognized it so quickly. He lifted his chin slightly. "I suppose a defector would be familiar with infinity flower poison, wouldn't he?"

The doctor's eyebrows lifted then, the tiniest hint of a smile pulling at his face. "Well played," he said evenly. He leaned back on the stool. "The people here call me Branimir." He watched Jet expectantly.

"You shouldn't know about us," Jet said slowly. "It will only put you and those you care about in danger."

Branimir did smirk then. "I've lived too long and seen too much to be afraid," he said, looking to his daughter. "And my girl can fend for herself." He looked back to Jet. "But *your* girl…she needs training."

Jet felt a scowl pulling at his face. "Training?" he asked, an edge to his voice. "What are you talking about?"

"Don't be daft, boy," Branimir said. "I saw her clothing." His eyes shifted toward the back room. "I may be old, but I'm not stupid." He pinned Jet with something akin to a glare, but heavy with disappointment. "What business does an Earth girl have here?"

Jet felt his heart leap in surprise. He was at a loss for words for a moment, watching Branimir look to Melinda. "How do you know that?" he asked finally.

"You aren't the only one with secrets," Branimir said, moving achily to his feet. Disapproval was on his face. "You should have left her there. Gexalatia is no place for her."

Jet frowned at the man's back as he crossed to the stove.

"She will need a few days, and then you can take her," Branimir continued. "But you should visit the smithy and at least buy her some protection." He shook his head. "Gods above know she'll need it with whatever wretches are hunting you still out there."

6

The Temple of Daya, Celo Cavus, Siccita.
The fourth day of winter, the 906th year of
the reign of King Paraximus Lamia.
Saturday, December 24, 2011.

PARAXIMUS LIFTED THE MIRROR SLOWLY, watching the glass ripple, an image forming before his eyes. A scowl pulled at his face as he watched a boy slay one of his monsters before boosting one of the Atturon girls onto a dragon.

"How can this be?" he said softly, looking up to Daya's statue. His eyes found Mara, who was clinging to the shadows.

Mara took a step forward, a hood hiding her face. "You will send more of Daya's spawn." Her voice was gravelly and unsteady as she spoke, a side effect of her need to take the blood of children. She was hungry, and Paraximus had intentionally kept her underfed. She seemed to be more pliable when the promise of sustenance was at stake.

"That was not our deal," Paraximus ground out.

Mara turned her head slightly, looking up at the statue.

"Daya does not play your mortal games," she said quietly.

"What have I done to offend her this time?" Paraximus demanded. He was tired of her game. Everything she promised came at a price, and nothing was as cut and dry as she claimed it would be.

Mara turned to look at Paraximus. Underneath her hood, he could see that her skin was cracking like clay on a hot Siccitan day. Her eyes were hollow, hunger pervading her aura. She took a step toward him, baring rows of teeth. "Tis not you, my king," she said evenly. Her tongue flitted across her lips then, as if she was sizing him up as prey.

Paraximus' hand slipped to the sword at his hip. He knew better than to underestimate a hungry Erosi. "Do not think I will be easy prey," he said slowly, narrowing pitch-colored eyes at her. "It takes more than the blood of children to piece a body together."

Mara scowled, seeming to come back to herself. "Apologies," she whispered, bowing low. "You must understand one thing, King Paraximus."

"And what is that?" he asked, easing his stance slightly.

"Daya is but one side of the wheel," Mara said, lifting her head.

Paraximus frowned at her in confusion. "The wheel?" he asked.

Mara nodded. "The light and the darkness," she continued. "Where there is light, darkness is certain to linger, but the darkness has no purpose without light." She tucked her arms under the cloak she wore to hide her crumbling body. "Daya manipulates the darkness, but she has no control over the light."

Paraximus' eyes shifted to the statue beside them, clenching his fists. "What good is her power if it can be turned back?" he growled.

Mara's face lifted in a grotesque half-smirk. "You must crush the light," she said. She lifted her chin. "Send waves of Our Lady's children. You will have what you desire."

Paraximus shifted his eyes back to Mara before lifting the mirror in his hands. He knew that every day that he wasted only brought his prey closer to Liana, and closer to a place where even Daya's magic could not touch them. He turned away from Mara, hearing her draw a sharp breath.

"I have given you what you need," she said, an urgency in her voice. "You will keep your end of the deal."

Paraximus rolled his eyes as he walked toward the temple doors. "You will have your blood," he tossed over his shoulder. He motioned to a guard who stood outside the door, a young boy by his side.

At his command, the guard pushed the boy into the temple, pulling the door shut quickly. The sounds of screaming were lost on Paraximus as he walked down the cobbled pathway toward the foyer of the castle that stood stark against a tall waterfall. Once inside, he lifted the mirror, pressing his fingers against the glass. He watched as the glass rippled, beginning to form into a bright, midday sky.

The sound of running water filled his ears, and a shape began to form out of the ripples. Darwren's dark curls framed his face as he leaned over the water Paraximus was using to channel himself. He bowed his head, pressing his closed fist over his chest.

"My king," he said respectfully.

"Darwren, it is time," Paraximus said, feeling put-out. "You must breach the wall and find the girls."

Darwren's brow furrowed in confusion. "My king?" he asked.

"I will open a gate for you," Paraximus said, ignoring the uncertainty on his servant's face. "You will lead the Sagiers and take both of the Atturon girls. Is that clear?"

Darwren nodded quickly. "Of course, My Lord," he said quickly. He knew better than to ask more questions, even though they were written across his face.

"Your time is limited," Paraximus continued. "Do not disappoint me."

Darwren bowed his head. "I will not return without them," he said.

Paraximus nodded. "Good." He didn't feel confident about this. He was certain Daya had some plan in her mind to foil his attempts to take control of the Visus.

"Is there word from Savra, My King?" Darwren asked, breaking through Paraximus' thoughts.

Paraximus blinked, feeling his chest tighten with rage suddenly. "Savra will report to me when she has completed her task," he said, his words clipped. It had been too long. He was certain she was trying to buy time or that she was dead. But once he had the Visus, Jet wouldn't matter anymore. Once he had control of the Visus, all of Gexalatia would bow to him. "Do as I have instructed."

Darwren nodded mutely.

Paraximus pressed his fingers against the glass once more, pushing the magic Daya had bestowed on him into the liquid surface. He could feel the icy energy pulsing through his veins, feeling like claws dragging under his skin. In his mind, he could see a portal beginning to open, beasts digging their way from the earth to stand beside Darwren and his handful of soldiers.

"Go now," Paraximus commanded.

Darwren hesitated only for a moment to glance at the hellish beasts beside him before stepping into the swirling water.

The Plains of Pacier, Ymber.
The fourth day of winter, the 851st year of
the reign of Queen Liana Estrella.
Saturday, December 24, 2011.

HE SUN WAS SETTING ON the eastern horizon, throwing long shadows across the ground. In the distance, Ellie could see Paries' Wall, standing tall against the darkening sky. They had been traveling close to the wall, making their way toward the bay. Raphael said it was the surest way to stay hidden and out of danger, but the coiling in Ellie's gut said otherwise. They had found a small grove of trees to build their tent in for the night, but the open, snowy grasslands left Ellie feeling exposed.

"Do you feel it?"

Ellie glanced at her sister, nodding slowly. "The darkness?" she whispered.

Bailey nodded, reaching for her twin's hand. "We're not safe here."

"We won't be safe until we're in Regius Carmen," Ellie said quietly, feeling her heart twist.

Both girls turned their heads, watching Raphael cut meat from an agrestis carcass, tossing chunks of it to the dragons. He had done his best to keep them safe since the attack on Sorona, but the girls knew that it wouldn't last.

"I had a dream last night," Bailey whispered, her deep blue eyes following Raphael, making sure he didn't hear their conversation.

Ellie felt her breath catch in her throat. "Did you see it, too?" she breathed.

Bailey's brow furrowed. "I saw the Sagiers," she whispered, her voice pained. "I saw myself being dragged away as Raphael…" She shook her head, looking down at the ground. Ellie could feel her twin's fear.

"We aren't going anywhere," she said quickly, holding Bailey's hand tightly. "We will make it to Regius Carmen." Her own hands were trembling. She'd seen what her sister had, and more. She'd seen blood and death, and it was more than she could stand to think about. Fortunately, she didn't have to think about it anymore as Raphael called them over, smiling in a way that set Ellie's heart at ease.

She followed her sister as Bailey moved to stand and walked toward the fire. Raphael and Bailey's words were lost on her as she watched her siblings laugh and joke with one another, as if they were simply on a camping trip. Ellie knew, as long as they were together, everything would be okay.

The night was too dark to see when Bailey woke. She drew a sharp breath, feeling on edge. She glanced over her shoulder to where Raphael was asleep beside her before looking to her sister on her other side. Neither had stirred at all, and she wondered if she'd been dreaming and it had jolted her awake. Carefully, she eased from the opening of the tent they were sharing, looking around slowly. The plains were quiet, long tendrils of grass that had broken free of the snow fluttering lightly in the soft wind. Bailey drew a slow breath, trying to ease the uncomfortable feeling from her chest.

The fire was smoldering, lending little light to their camping area. Bailey walked to the fire, placing a thick piece of wood on top of it. She stood there, waiting for it to catch, wrapping her arms tightly around her middle. She kept shifting her eyes around, the hair on the back of her neck prickling. She tried to tell herself that it was just the dark; she and Ellie had never been outdoorsy, so it was creepy to be out here, where it felt like a thousand eyes were watching them.

"Bailey?"

Bailey jumped at the sound of her sister's voice, turning to look at her over her shoulder. She watched as Ellie walked toward her. "What is it?" she asked quietly.

"I can't sleep either," Ellie whispered, pressing her shoulder against Bailey's. Her eyes scanned the darkness just beyond the fire. "It's like a thousand eyes are watching us."

Bailey nodded. They stood there in silence for a long time, until the light from the small fire began to fade. "We should try to get some sleep," Bailey said finally. Her throat felt dry, and her eyes were tired, but she didn't want to fall asleep.

Ellie nodded, turning back toward the tent. She reached for the flap, pulling it aside, when a soft sound made her freeze. Her head snapped toward the sound, her blood running ice-cold in her veins.

"Bailey?" she breathed, her voice trembling. "Did you…"

Bailey was frozen behind her, looking into the darkness as well. "Yes," she breathed.

Ellie gasped when Bailey roughly grabbed her arm, pulling her behind her. Glittering eyes were suddenly appearing just beyond the edge of their camp. A stench like the smell of rotting meat was in the air, and Ellie's heart dropped to her feet.

"They found us."

"My, you girls are hard to find."

Ellie clenched her sister's arm as a man stepped from the darkness, the tall grass parting around him. His eyes were glowing softly in the moonlight, his dark hair falling across his forehead. He wore Siccita's crest across his chest, a red cloak across his shoulders.

Bailey took a step back into Ellie as the man walked closer, the atrox around him stepping into the dying firelight. "Please," she said, her voice quivering slightly. "Don't hurt us."

The man paused, tilting his head. "Who said anything about hurting you?" he asked, baring a fanged smile. "We would never do that." He nodded over his shoulder to one of the hairy beasts. "We need you alive."

Bailey lifted her fists, prepared to fight the atrox that was advancing on them, when it suddenly let out a piercing scream. The bloodied tip of a sword cleaved clean through its neck, it's head falling with a thud to the ground.

"I don't think so," Raphael said, standing between the girls and the man. His sword was lifted, blood dripping from the blade.

The man smirked then, crossing his arms. "Are you supposed to scare me, boy?" he asked patronizingly.

Raphael returned his smirk. "No, but she will."

The man turned quickly, feeling a burst of wind against his back. He rolled quickly out of the way as a dragon crashed to where he'd been standing, catching one of the monsters in her teeth.

"Hurry," Raphael barked. "Get to Bartuk."

Bailey grabbed Ellie's arm, yanking her sister after her as they ran toward the monstrous dragon that landed behind them.

"Stop them!" the man commanded furiously.

Ellie gasped, flinching as the sound of howls filled the night. She slid into the safety of Bartuk's wing, clambering onto his back, looking around for her sister.

"Bailey?" she breathed, her heart dropping to her feet. Bailey was nowhere to be found. "Bailey!"

Raphael's head snapped up at the sound of panic in Ellie's voice, causing him to take his eyes from the beast he was squaring off with. He gasped as it swung a massive paw, raking claws down his chest and sending him sprawling to the ground. Pain made stars shoot across his vision, and his hands were hot with his blood, which was oozing from his wounds and soaking into his clothing. He tried to draw a breath to call for Ellena, but blood was bubbling past his lips, muting his voice.

⚜

Bailey rolled to her feet, having narrowly avoided a beast's claws. She watched Ellie duck behind Bartuk's wing before turning her eyes toward the man leading the assault. She made a quick decision, sprinting toward the tent.

It was ripped open, where Raphael had cut through it to get to them quickly, and she ducked inside, seeing her father's sheathed sword lying on the ground next to where she'd been sleeping. She grabbed it quickly, throwing the sheath away.

She watched as an atrox knocked Raphael to the ground, fury overtaking her. She ran toward the beast, swinging her sword in a clumsy and brutish way. Fortunately, it struck home, driving into the monster's chest.

The beast whirled to face her, causing the sword to slip from her grasp. It bared grotesque fangs at her and took a staggering step toward her before collapsing to the ground. Bailey was stunned for a long moment, but then she heard Raphael choking. She ran to him, sliding to the ground beside him.

"Raphael," she breathed, pressing her hands against his wounds. It was useless, they were too large and bleeding too profusely, but she had to try. Tears were flooding her eyes as pain furrowed his brow, blood spilling over his lips.

Bailey turned to look at the man leading the assault, seeing his arms crossed smugly. Despite them having killed three of his beasts, there were still more behind him.

"Stop this!" Bailey screamed hoarsely. Tears were streaming down her face. "I'll go with you!"

The man lifted a hand to still his minions. "*Both* of you will surrender to me," he said. "My king will have you both."

Bailey shook her head, looking down at Raphael. His eyes were pleading with her not to go, but she knew that there was only one option. She looked up when Ellie suddenly appeared beside her.

"You have to heal him," she said, her voice trembling.

The man sighed, as if he was being put out. "Magic cannot heal an Inerse," he said shortly. "If he lives, he lives. Otherwise—" He shrugged. A sinister smirk came to his face. "But I won't kill him."

Bailey moved to her feet. "Give your word," she said. She knew she wasn't in any place to be giving commands, but she needed to know Raphael would live.

The man lifted his hand in a mock salute. "You have my word," he said, annoyed. "Not that it should be worth much to you."

Bailey looked at Ellie, catching her hand. "We'll go with you."

The village of Festra, Abjure Forest, Ymber.
The sixth day of winter, the 851st year of the
reign of Queen Liana Estrella.
Monday, December 26, 2011.

THE CEILING OF BRANIMIR'S HOUSE had become monotonous. Jet had memorized all the twists in the thatching, able to count the number of reeds to a bundle. He drew a slow breath as he sat up in the chair, looking down at the sleeping girl in the bed he sat beside. She looked better, and Branimir said her illness had passed, but she hadn't woken yet. Branimir assured Jet that it was just because her body needed to heal.

"How is she?"

Jet turned to see Melinda walking toward him, a tray in her hands. He wanted to snap at her, frustrated with her question, but he ducked his chin and bit his tongue. "Same," he muttered.

Melinda sat the tray on the bedside table, easing to sit on the edge of the bed. She pressed a hand against Nyx's face. "Nyx?" she said softly. "It's time to wake up."

Jet titled his head as he watched her, feeling the gentle pull of warm magic filling the air. He frowned lightly. "You're Auresi?" he asked.

Melinda looked at him, offering an abashed smile. "I'm neither," she said. "My mother was human, and my father is Acerbi." She shrugged lightly. "I can draw from whatever source I choose, but I can only use it to help heal others. Unfortunately, my body heals and ages like an Inerse's."

Jet's frown deepened. "How is that possible?"

Melinda shrugged again. "I don't ask questions anymore," she said. "I just accept the gift that the gods have given me and use it the best I can."

Jet wanted to roll his eyes. That sounded like a cop-out answer, but the way she said it was innocent and as if she truly believed it. He turned away from her as Branimir's footsteps echoed through the house, the front door closing behind him.

"Were you able to see Wyn?" Melinda asked, standing in the doorway.

Jet watched as Branimir nodded, shedding his cloak.

"He asks for you to come after mid-sun," Branimir said, meeting Jet's gaze. "He doesn't have anything built, but he can craft something for her."

Jet nodded, feeling uncertain. He didn't say anything as Branimir came into the room to observe Nyx.

"It is time for her to wake," he said absently, to no one in particular.

Melinda stood near the foot of the bed. "I did what I could," she said.

Branimir nodded his head. "Then we will wait." He turned, looking at Jet. His greying eyes shifted over the old clothes Jet was wearing and the scruff that was forming across his face. "You should get outside. Sitting in here is doing you no good." He grinned through his grey-streaked beard. "Not to mention, you look like hell warmed over."

Jet narrowed his eyes at the man.

"Melinda, show him the bath house."

Melinda nodded, looking at Jet. "I'll prepare some things for you, and then we'll go."

Jet sighed. "Fine," he clipped. He didn't like her perpetual cheerfulness and he was growing tired of her father's ability to make him feel inferior. He moved to his feet, though, the thought of a bath too tempting to ignore. If they were to be stuck here, he might as well make the most of it.

The water was hot, filling the bath house with steam. It made the air feel thick as Jet stepped into the room. Beneath the floor, he could hear pipes rumbling and shuddering, bubbles making the water murky. He was alone as he walked toward the edge of the pool, looking down into it.

He took a moment to kick off his boots, Branimir's old pants too short as he looked down at his feet. They hung a few inches above his ankles, and he scowled. He yanked the old shirt that Melinda had given him off and tossed it aside, as well as the too-short pants. He was glad to be rid of them as he stepped into the water.

He wasn't happy with the situation at all. He didn't want to be in Festra, he didn't want to be waiting on Nyx to wake up, and he didn't want to be wearing second-hand clothing. He stared mindlessly at the bubbling water as he sat there, wishing that they could just be in Regius Carmen already.

Facing Savra and Lue made his brain feel jumbled, and he didn't like it. Things were cut and dry in the beginning, but they felt less so now. Especially with Savra. He didn't give a crap about Lue, but seeing Savra again made old, uncomfortable feelings stir in his chest.

Jet turned to lay his arms on the side of the pool, resting

his chin against them.

Since their encounter, his thoughts hadn't stopped turning to what used to be his home. Thinking about it now made him scowl, but it was hard not to want to go back to Celo Cavus. It was all he'd known. His whole life had revolved around that place, and he'd been trained to return there and protect it with his life. Even now, something deep down told him that continuing to Regius Carmen was the wrong thing to do; that he could still win back his father's favor by taking Nyx to him.

He closed his eyes quickly, pressing his forehead against his arms. Did he even want that?

Jet clenched his jaw tightly.

No. He didn't want that. Everything he'd said to Savra had been true. Maybe she still had feelings for him, but it didn't change the fact that *no one* had come for him. It didn't wash away a hundred years of sitting in a dark cell, left to rot for Liana's amusement. As much as he loathed Liana for what she took from him, he loathed the rest of them for not trying to free him.

No amount of wealth or acceptance could make him go back to Celo Cavus. The only reason he'd ever set foot there again would be to slaughter Paraximus and anyone else who got in his way.

Jet lifted his head, staring at the wall.

It didn't matter if seeing Savra still made his heart race. He would kill her for betraying him. He would kill her, if nothing else, because she had been the reason Liana had captured him in the first place. Logically, he knew it wasn't Savra's fault he'd been imprisoned, but if he hadn't cared so deeply for her, Liana wouldn't have been able to complete her ruse. If he hadn't loved her, it never would have worked. He'd kill her to free himself.

The thought made his chest clench.

He would never love anyone ever again. So far, it had only brought him misery. He wouldn't be bound by that same misery ever again. He was in control of what happened in his life from now on, and no one else would ever take that away from him again.

⚶

The first thing Nyx noticed was that she was warm. A blanket was pulled up to her chin, and soft light was pressing against her eyelids. She drew a slow breath and pulled the blanket closer. She almost thought she could smell the faint scent of her aunt's cooking, and it made her stomach rumble. She sighed shortly, knowing she should get up. There were chores to be done…

"Nyx?"

She frowned, not recognizing the voice calling her name. She opened her eyes slowly, seeing a wooden wall that didn't look familiar. Her heart dropped into her stomach, and she turned to look over her shoulder, feeling her stomach clench with fear. A girl, not much older than herself, was sitting on the edge of the bed, smiling gently.

"How are you feeling?" she asked. Her blue eyes were kind, but it did nothing to assuage the feelings that made Nyx's stomach turn.

"Where am I?" Nyx managed around the lump in her throat. "Who are you?"

"My name is Melinda. You are in the village of Festra."

Tears suddenly filled Nyx's eyes. "I'm not dreaming?" she whispered.

Melinda's face softened and she shook her head, auburn curls bouncing around her face. "No," she said, mistaking Nyx's tears. "You're safe." She pressed her hand against Nyx's cheek in a comforting gesture. "You're in a safe place now."

Nyx felt her tears coming faster, and she turned away

from Melinda. She curled her fingers tightly into the pillow beneath her head, crushing reality coming over her. Her aunt was gone. Earth was far behind her. Any semblance of her former life was gone.

"Shh," Melinda soothed, rubbing her back gently. "Everything is all right now." Sadness was heavy in her own heart as she listened to Nyx's quiet crying. She couldn't even imagine what the blonde-haired girl had been through.

Nyx sobbed softly into the pillow until there were no tears left. The pain was still there, but her mind was empty. She turned to look at Melinda, seeing that a chair had been pulled toward the bed. "Where is Jet?" she asked, her voice hoarse from the crying.

Melinda offered another gentle smile. "He's gone to the bath house," she said. "You both were in quite a state when we found you."

Nyx felt her brow furrow. "We?"

Melinda nodded. "My father and I."

"Melinda?"

Nyx looked up, seeing another room beyond the doorway. She heard the floorboards shift, and an older man came into view. His eyes were light and turning opaque with his age, and grey strands were streaking his dark navy hair and beard. His appearance surprised Nyx, but she could see the resemblance in his face to Melinda. He smiled gently.

"Welcome back," he said, tucking his hands into his pockets. "You gave us all quite a scare."

Nyx's frown deepened. "What do you mean?" she asked, sitting up in the bed. She winced as an ache shot through her body.

"I'm not surprised you don't remember," the old man said, leaning on the doorframe. "You were severely injured and the poison had done a number on you."

Nyx pressed her hand against her shoulder, vague memories of trying to kick Jet in the face surfacing in her mind. "Who are you people?" she asked, looking between them.

"My name is Branimir," the man said kindly, "and this is my daughter, Melinda. I am a doctor." He took a step into the room. "I know this all must be very confusing for you, coming from Earth to Ymber."

Nyx felt her heart drop into her stomach again. "How do you know where I've come from?" she asked defensively, easing away from Melinda slightly.

Branimir offered a smile. "Don't be alarmed, child," he said. "You aren't the first, nor the last, to pass through the Limen." He lifted his chin, as if there was more he wanted to say, but didn't.

Nyx pressed her back against the wall the bed butted up to, pulling her knees toward her chest. "I don't want to stay here," she said. "Please, just take me to Jet."

Melinda turned to look at her father, whose face was furrowed with disapproval. "I can take her to the bath house," she offered. She looked back to Nyx. "The warm water would do well to ease your stiffness."

Branimir seemed like he would protest, but he simply nodded. "Your old clothes should fit Nyx," he said. He offered her another kind smile. "Melinda will take care of you."

Nyx looked back to the girl, who rose from the edge of the bed.

"Give me just a moment," she said before stepping into the other room.

Nyx didn't know how to feel as she slowly pulled the blanket from her legs. She looked down at her clothing, feeling sick again. Her jeans and her t-shirt were covered in blood. She wasn't sure if it was hers or Jet's. Her torn jacket had been laid across the foot of the bed, and it was bloodied as well. She swallowed thickly as she moved to her feet, feeling the aching spread through her whole body. She swayed slightly, feeling lightheaded as she braced her hand against the bedside table.

Melinda reappeared, moving quickly to her side. She held a basket in one hand and threaded her free arm through Nyx's. "Careful," she said quickly. "Your body is still recuperating."

Nyx let Melinda assist her, feeling steadier with each step. She glanced at Melinda, suddenly feeling silly. "Thank you," she said.

Melinda looked to her, her smile returning. "You're welcome," she said kindly. She helped Nyx into the front room, pausing before she opened the door. She reached for a cloak to pull around Nyx's shoulders. "You can't go out in those clothes. This cloak will keep you covered up for now."

Nyx drew a slow breath, nodding as she pulled the cloak tightly around her arms. The air was cold as she watched Melinda pull the thick door open, reminding her that it was snowy and wintery in Gexalatia. The heavy scent of foreign sap hit Nyx's nose as she shuffled to the door. Her eyes widened and her footsteps halted as she took in the view.

Massive trees rose all around them, houses built seamlessly into the boughs. Lights were on in the windows and lanterns lit the pathways that wound from one bough to the next, connecting the little village and keeping out the darkness of tree-cover. A few people were milling just outside of their homes, readying their raperes and agrestis to prepare for a day of hunting and gathering.

Nyx turned her eyes toward the center of the village, seeing the elaborate designs etched into the trunk of a tree as thick as a large building. Soft orbs of light were dancing around the top of the structure, illuminating what appeared to be a picture story carved into the wood. At the top was another massive building, complete with windows and floating orb-lanterns.

"What is that?" she asked breathlessly.

"That's the Sacred Tree," Melinda said. "And at the top is the home of our chief."

Nyx shook her head, amazed. "How is all of this here?" she whispered, letting her eyes rove over the floating village again.

Melinda grinned. "Festra has stood for many hundreds of years," she said simply. "It's been this way as long as I can re-member." She walked down the steps from their house, turn-ing to assist Nyx.

Nyx looked at the path that led from the front of their house toward the rest of the village. It was smooth, carved into the tree and worn from use. Along the edges, bright blue and orange flowers glowed softly, leading the way. The flow-ers were different from the infinity flowers, almost like Earth flowers, but glowing softly.

Insects flitted from one bloom to the next, also emitting their own soft glow. Nyx had to stop and stare as what looked like a butterfly flitted lazily in front of her. It was all so beau-tiful and amazing, and her legs felt stronger as she followed Melinda toward a rope bridge.

"This way," Melinda said, stepping onto it.

Nyx grabbed the rope-railing tightly, feeling the bridge sway a bit. It was wide, to her surprise, with lantern posts ev-ery few feet to light it. Below, the shadows seemed to stretch into a bottomless void, and Nyx swallowed thickly, knowing it could be a very long way to the forest floor. She looked up at the sound of footsteps, seeing a man walked toward them, leading a tall bird-like creature. He smiled and said something to Melinda in greeting, which she returned, his eyes surprised as they landed on Nyx. He halted, his bird-mount at his side, looking at Melinda and speaking in what Nyx assumed was

Sarotian.

Melinda offered him a bright smile and caught Nyx's arm, laughing softly. It seemed that whatever she said appeased the man, and he smiled brightly at Nyx, bowing his head.

"He says his name is Breddyn, and that he's delighted to meet you," Melinda said, leaning in to whisper to Nyx.

Nyx nodded and offered a smile in return. It seemed to be enough for Breddyn, as he turned and continued on his way, his bird following at his heels, flapping small wings and ruffling bright blue feathers. "What is that?" Nyx asked, staring after the creature.

"They're called raperes," Melinda said. "We use them as transportation."

Nyx nodded mutely, staring after the beautiful creature. Everything was so amazing, she didn't have words for it all. She couldn't stop staring at everything they passed as they finally made it to a two-story-tall wooden building.

Melinda led the way up the steps to the second floor and pushed the door open. A short hallway went in both directions to the left and right, a wall in front of them. Melinda inclined her head to the left. "Ladies are this way."

Nyx turned to follow her, hearing the light shuffle of feet behind her. She glanced over her shoulder, feeling her heart leap into her throat.

"Nyx?"

She turned quickly, ignoring the aches that filled her body, throwing her arms around Jet's middle. Tears flooded her eyes again as she gripped the back of his shirt, pressing her face against the scratchy material.

Melinda watched as he bent his head, drawing a slow breath as he held her. Something like relief was on his face as he looked down at her. Nyx pressed harder into him when his arms came around her tentatively.

"Why are you crying?" he asked, his voice reverberating inside his ribcage.

"I woke up and you weren't there," Nyx said, still clinging to him tightly. She seemed to pull herself together some, and she stepped back, a scowl on her face. "Don't ever do that to me again."

Jet arched a brow as his arms fell to his sides. He didn't know what to say as he looked over her shoulder to Melinda. "What are you doing out of the house?" he asked. "You should be resting."

"I thought she could use a warm bath," Melinda said in explanation. She lifted her basket. "And a change of clothes."

Jet looked back down to Nyx, seeing her brow furrowed lightly. "Go with Melinda," he said. "She'll take care of you."

Worry was etched in Nyx's face. "But, I—"

Jet shook his head, cutting her off. "We're safe here," he said slowly.

Nyx felt her heart twist, thinking about the terror she'd faced in such a short time. "Are you sure?" she whispered.

Jet nodded. "Get cleaned up," he said. "We'll talk when you get back."

Nyx took a step back from him, realizing she was wringing her hands. "Okay," she said, turning away from him and walking toward Melinda.

"We'll see you in a bit," Melinda said to Jet.

He nodded, watching them turn the corner.

Nyx was still threading her fingers together tightly as she walked beside Melinda. Her mind was racing, relief and sadness mingling inside her. She tried to shake it off as they reached a wooden door, which Melinda pushed open, revealing a large pool. A tall ceiling arched over the pool, reminding Nyx of the inside of a church.

Steam was rising from the water, filling the room with

moisture and the heavy scent of the tree the bath house was built into. The water was bubbling softly, pipes from the floor below lending a constant flow to the water to keep it from becoming stale. A wall was built to the right, and Nyx assumed it separated the girl side from the boy side. Melinda closed the door behind them and set her basket down, beginning to untie her wrap-dress.

Nyx felt her face flush. "What are you doing?" she asked, embarrassed.

Melinda paused, looking up at her. "What do you mean?" she asked, clearly confused. She offered a small smile. "You don't bathe with your clothes on, do you?"

Nyx turned away as Melinda shed her clothing. She was too self-conscious to even shower after gym class, let alone be expected to get in a gigantic bathtub with another person. She heard the splashing of water and glanced over her shoulder, seeing Melinda sitting in the hot water. She ducked her head under, her auburn curls flattened against her head as she surfaced.

"Come on," she said. "You'll feel a lot better."

Nyx's face was on fire with embarrassment, but the water did look nice. "Just, don't look over here while…you know, okay?" Nyx stammered.

Melinda laughed then. "We're both women," she said. "It's nothing to be ashamed of." She turned her back to Nyx. "But if it makes you more comfortable."

Nyx pulled her gross, blood-stained clothing off quickly, practically running into the water. It was initially almost too hot for her to bear, but, just as Melinda said, her sore muscles needed it. Relief was washing over her as she sunk deeper into the water, until she was up to her chin.

"Better?" Melinda asked, glancing over her shoulder.

Nyx nodded. "Yes," she said, staying mostly submerged.

She offered a small, genuine smile for the first time since she'd woken. "You were right."

Melinda seemed satisfied as they sat at opposite sides of the pool, enjoying the water. Silence was heavy between them, broken intermittently by Nyx scrubbing her arms.

"I brought the good soap," Melinda offered, drifting across the pool toward where she'd set her basket near the side. She pulled a wrapped bar from the basket and handed it to Nyx. "Here."

Nyx took it, lifting it toward her face. "This smells great," she said, surprise in her voice. "What is it?"

"It has Pipoue in it," Melinda said. "I made it myself."

Nyx rubbed it in her hands, lathering them. "I know this is dumb, but what's Pip-ooey?" she asked, the word feeling funny in her mouth.

Melinda laughed softly. "It's a type of berry," she said. "They grow in the Abjure forest near waterfalls."

Nyx set the soap on the clothe it had been wrapped in on the side of the pool, watching as the soap washed away the flecks of blood still on her hands. "Is that where we are?" she asked. "The ab-jurr forest?"

Melinda nodded, still seeming humored. "Your accent is atrocious," she said.

Nyx looked down at the water, focusing on rinsing. "Sorry," she managed.

"I didn't mean to embarrass you," Melinda said quickly, worry on her face. "I guess I just thought you would at least know Sarotian."

Nyx shook her head. "I know very little about this place," she whispered.

"Oh," Melinda breathed softly. She watched Nyx's eyes shift around uncertainly. "Why did you come here, if you don't mind me asking?"

Nyx looked up at Melinda, feeling unsure. Should she tell Melinda the truth? Could she trust Melinda? Would Jet be mad if she did?

"I, uh, was taken to my home, um, Earth," the word felt foreign to her, "from here when I was a baby." It was weird to talk about her whole life as if it was some faraway place now. "Jet came to bring me back here." She shook her head. "I didn't know that this place even existed until a few months ago."

Surprise pulled at Melinda's face. "Really?" she asked. "So why did you have to come back?" She leaned in slightly. "Is it dangerous there?"

Nyx shook her head. "Oh, no," she said quickly. "I love it there. I didn't want to leave."

Melinda's face softened. "Then why did you have to?"

Nyx turned her face away, feeling her heart twist. "I'm not sure," she whispered, feeling those words echo in the pit of her chest.

Silence fell over them again as Nyx stared absently into the pool, her thoughts roiling.

"Nyx?" Melinda's voice was soft and timid.

Nyx looked up at her. "Yeah?" she asked.

"I want to help you," Melinda said softly. "I can teach you about Ymber, and about Gexalatia." She drifted closer to Nyx in the water. "Jet said you would be here for some time, and I can help prepare you for whatever your journey is."

Nyx felt surprise fill her, and she nodded her head. "I would like that," she said finally.

Melinda smiled again, swimming toward the steps that led out of the water. "Great," she said, climbing out. "First things first, you need proper clothing."

Nyx felt her cheeks flare again with embarrassment. She hoped she'd get used to this life quickly.

The village of Festra, Abjure Forest, Ymber.
The sixth day of winter, the 851st year of the
reign of Queen Liana Estrella.
Monday, December 26, 2011.

NYX FELT BETTER AS SHE followed Melinda down the path and toward her house. The clothing Melinda had given her was uncomfortable and itchy, like the shirt Jet had worn, but Nyx had noticed that the dress Melinda gave her was patched and re-stitched, clearly well-worn. She'd pulled her work boots on underneath the dress, carrying her dirty clothing in a bundle. The cloak was heavy around her shoulders, keeping the cold out for the most part.

Melinda seemed to think that her clothing was salvageable, but Nyx wasn't so sure. How would they possibly wash all the blood out?

The walk from the bath house to Melinda's home was short, and Nyx realized that the rope bridge wasn't as intimidating as it had seemed at first. It was strong and didn't sway underfoot like she expected. Foot traffic was heavy as they walked back, and Nyx began to wonder what time it was.

She tried not to stare at the men and women and children milling about.

Most had dark navy hair, like Melinda's father, and dark, tan skin, which Nyx ordinarily would have attributed to the sun. Only, in Gexalatia, there wasn't much sun. Even now, it hadn't made over the top of the trees, swinging in an arc toward the east, where Nyx knew it would set. Things here were so disorienting.

Nyx continued to watch the people walk from the bridge and toward a ramp that wound toward the ground. Some were leading raperes, and others were leading tall, deer-like creatures with thick, almost elephant-like legs. They had faces that reminded Nyx of a camel and their hair was the same soft blue as the natives. Nyx began to wonder if blue was common like brown was on Earth.

She pried her eyes away from the sights around her as the steps of Melinda's house came into view. She was surprised to see Jet sitting on the bottom step, leaning against the second step, idly twirling a long blue stem of grass. He looked up when they approached, his brow lifting slightly. Nyx knew she wouldn't have caught it if she hadn't been watching his face.

He looked like he would say something snarky as his eyes shifted over her, but Nyx beat him to it. "Shut it," she said shortly.

Melinda glanced between them, obviously confused by the interaction, but she said nothing.

"I was just going to tell you that we need to get to the smithy," Jet said, a smirk still pulling at his face. He stood, stretching his arms over his head. The shirt he'd been given was a bit too small, lifting with the motion to reveal a glimpse of his torso.

Nyx was still frowning at him, trying to keep her eyes

from drifting, when Melinda reached for her bundle.

"I'll see what I can do with these," she said pleasantly.

Nyx felt guilty. "Are you sure?" she asked quickly. "I don't want to put you out."

Melinda shook her head. "Nonsense," she said, turning to go up the steps. "You have more important things to do."

Nyx looked to Jet, seeing his arms were crossed as he waited. "Let's go then," she said, waving her hand at him to lead the way. She trailed after him, taking a moment to really take in the shirt and trousers he'd been given. They were threadbare and re-worked like the dress Melinda had given her, clearly some type of wool dyed a soft brown color. The shirt looked like it was at least a size too small, and he had the legs of the trousers tucked into his boots. "You look ridiculous."

Jet looked over his shoulder. "You think you look any better in that?" he asked, motioning to her dress and the cloak Melinda had lent her. "You look like a child."

Nyx scowled at him. It wasn't her fault the cloak was a bright blue with flowers embroidered on it. "So why are we going to the smithy?" she asked. She frowned to herself. "And what's a smithy?"

Jet sighed in aggravation. "You don't know what a smithy is?"

Nyx shook her head, keeping her own snarky comment to herself.

"It's where the blacksmith does his thing," Jet said. "He's going to build you armor."

Nyx looked up at him, feeling like she should have known that, as often as they'd had their horses shod. Of course, the farrier had always come to them, but still. "Armor?" she asked. "What for?"

Jet looked down at her, his customary scowl coming to

his face. "So I don't have to worry about you getting shot again," he said shortly.

Nyx swallowed thickly, unconsciously reaching for her shoulder. "Oh."

"Yeah, oh," Jet said as they crossed the rope bridge. He glanced down at Nyx after a moment, reading into her silence. "They make armor pieces for archers here."

Nyx looked up at him, wondering what that meant.

At the confusion on her face, he continued, "it's light and meant to allow the wearer to move freely."

"Oh," Nyx said, feeling better. She was picturing a suit of armor like a medieval knight would wear. She looked up the path, seeing a building with smoke curling from a chimney. "Is that it?"

Jet nodded as he led the way, walking up a short set of steps, and pushing a door open.

Nyx blinked against the darkness inside the smithy, feeling immediately how hot it was inside. She winced as the ringing of a hammer on metal filled the air. Sparks lit the room, the glow of a fire throwing bright orange light across the rest of the room. Orbs were strategically placed to lend light as well.

Jet stepped toward a man as the door shut behind them, who had paused in hammering what looked like a blade for a plow. Nyx crossed her arms in front of her and hugged them tightly to her middle as Jet and the man conversed for a moment. She took a step back as the man set down his heavy hammer, brushing his hands across a leather apron and approaching her.

His tone was rough as he spoke to her, wiping sweat away from his forehead with the back of his hand.

Nyx looked to Jet, seeing humor on his face. She fought down a scowl, knowing he liked to watch her squirm. She was further irritated when he stepped toward her, saying something in Sarotian to her that she didn't understand. When she didn't comply with his order, he reached for her wrists, lifting her arms. She didn't like the way he tossed words over his shoulder, making the blacksmith laugh.

"He needs to measure," Jet said to her finally, leaning in to whisper to her when the blacksmith turned away for a moment.

Nyx scowled at him but said nothing as the blacksmith wrapped some sort of tape measure around her in various places that she wasn't entirely comfortable with. Once he was finished, he said something to Jet, to which Jet nodded before ushering her out of the workshop.

"What the hell was all that?" Nyx asked as they stepped out of the heat, the door swinging shut behind them.

"We need to work on your Sarotian," Jet said. He was unhappy, a sudden change from the way he'd been apparently joking with the blacksmith. "No one can know where you've come from, or that you speak English."

Nyx frowned at him as they walked back toward the bridge. "Why?"

Jet didn't look at her, his brow furrowed. "It's dangerous."

"But Melinda and her father speak English," Nyx said slowly.

"That's different," Jet snapped. "They're the only ones we can trust, and even then, we still need to be careful." He glanced over at her. "Anyone could say something about us to the wrong person, and we could be in a lot of shit."

"Oh." Nyx felt her breath catch in her chest, but she didn't say anything else as they made their way back to their hosts' home. She tried to push Jet's uncomfortable words from her mind, turning her eyes to the flowers. She noticed that the flowers along the path were glowing brighter, as were the insects, and the sun was slipping away quickly.

"What's up with the sun here?" she asked, pausing to look over the tree tops. "It doesn't last."

Jet paused as well, following her gaze. "It's called perpetual twilight," he said slowly. He looked at her. "It's why our senses are so sharp."

Nyx frowned unhappily. "Will I ever get used to this place?" she asked through a sigh.

Jet smirked. "Let's hope so."

Melinda was elbow-deep in a buckle of sudsy water when Nyx and Jet walked through the front door. She looked up as they came in, a smile coming to her face. She pulled Nyx's shirt from the water and wrung it out, holding it up.

"What do you think?" she asked.

Nyx walked closer, surprised to see that it was actually much whiter than it had been when she'd put it on a few days ago. "It looks great," she said, returning Melinda's grin. "I hope you haven't been working too hard to get it clean."

Melinda shook her head. "Just a little amuun," she said easily. "Took the stains right out."

Nyx frowned. "A-moon?" she asked.

Jet sighed. "Bleach, basically," he quipped. He ignored the way Melinda frowned at his clipped words.

"Oh," Nyx said, ignoring his tone. She walked toward Melinda's wash tub. "Do you need any help?"

Melinda's smile returned. "Sure," she said.

Nyx had never washed her clothes by hand before, and it was a neat experience as Melinda showed her how to use a washboard and how to twist the water out of the clothing. She was so absorbed in what she was doing, she missed the way Jet frowned at them as he sank down onto a chair.

IO

The Plains of Pacier, Ymber.
The sixth day of winter, the 851st year of the
reign of Queen Liana Estrella.
Monday, December 26, 2011.

PAIN WAS SHOOTING THROUGH RAPHAEL'S en-
tire body, making his mind feel like it was on fire. His
limbs felt numb and cold as he stared at the darkening sky.
He'd been lying there, alone, for too long.

Bartuk and Ellena had settled beside him, the warmth
from their bodies lending him some comfort. But that wasn't
enough.

All he could think about was how he had failed; he'd
failed his sisters, and he'd failed his father. He couldn't stomach the thought of disappointment in his father's face. His
disappointment had always been worse than his anger.

Raphael drew a ragged breath as he closed his eyes. His
chest hurt with each breath he drew, and a fog was setting
in across his mind. He wondered if this was what it felt like
to die. Weakness was seeping through his body, making his
breathing feel difficult and labored. He felt Bartuk shift next

to him, a soft rumble shaking his chest.

"It's okay," he managed.

Bartuk bent his neck, pressing his scaly nose against Raphael's cheek. The heat from the dragon's breath should have been unbearable, but Raphael barely felt it now. He could only hope that Bartuk could somehow know his thoughts.

He wanted the dragons to find Ellie and Bailey. He wanted them to be rescued, and he knew it wouldn't be because of him. A tear slipped slowly from his eye as a rough, gasping cough forced its way past his lips, the taste of coppery blood in his mouth.

The pain surged a final time, and Raphael knew it was useless to try to hold on any longer. He let darkness consume his mind, feeling nothing but the call of a deep, comforting void.

A hunting party was moving slowly through the tall grass. A young, dark-skinned woman knelt slowly, sliding a twisted rope of woven grass from the neck of a small *damer*. It flopped a long tongue from its mouth which was lined with sharp teeth, lowering a flat, pig-nose toward the ground, a thick-haired tail braided against its hind quarters. It broke into a jog, a whine twisting from its throat as it hit on the scent of prey. The woman motioned to her companions, flipping a thick blue braid of hair over her shoulder and jogging after the *damer*.

They wound their way across the plains and into a thick grove of trees. The woman, Kadira, pushed her way through the tall grass, feeling her feet still as the trees opened to reveal a camp. She held up her hand quickly to still her hunting party, seeing the last tendrils of smoke curling away from a dead fire. The *damer* was still scenting, small grunts coming from its lips as it walked around the encampment, digging lightly at the dirt with clawed paws.

"What is this?" a man to her side whispered.

Kadira shook her head. The foul stench of a corpse hit her nose, making her scowl. "Search the camp," she ordered.

Her party moved about the camp slowly, looking for anything that could be of use to them. Kadira was surprised when she walked around the torn and crumbling tent to see a massive hairy body lying on the ground, the beast's head missing. She covered her nose and mouth, realizing the stench was coming from the beast.

"Should we scavenge it?" her companion asked again.

Kadira shook her head. "No, Tarke," she said quickly. "Its flesh is no good to us."

"Kadira, over here!"

The leader turned her head, jogging to the side of another of her companions. "What is it, Sami?" she asked. She drew up short when she saw the woman kneeling beside the body of a young man.

Sami looked up, her light blue eyes hopeful. "He's still alive," she said.

Kadira walked closer, kneeling to look at him. His clothing was bloodied and torn, thick gouges in his chest. She glanced back at the headless monster, realizing that it must have been the thing that had injured him so badly. "Find some limbs," Kadira said finally, looking up to Sami.

"We can't take him back with us," Tarke said quickly, scowling at her. "He's dead weight." He motioned to the blood on the ground. "He'll be dead before we reach the village."

Kadira turned her scorching gaze on him, rising slowly to her feet. "Would you want to be left to die a dishonorable death, Tarke?" she asked bitingly. She watched shame cross the younger man's face.

Tarke ducked his chin and adjusted the bow at his back. "No."

Kadira looked around, motioning to the tent. "Cut some strips for the limbs," she ordered. "And be sure to bring the rest with us."

Tarke moved away from her like a scolded child, silently obeying her command. The rest of the party were gathering any other useful materials they could find, and Sami returned shortly with two thick limbs.

Kadira helped her and Tarke to fashion a stretcher and lift the man's lifeless body onto it. She knew that the Khanh would be unhappy with her, but she couldn't leave this man to die alone. If nothing else, they would give him an honorable burial to allow his soul safe passage to the afterlife. If he lived, she knew she'd have to do a lot of bargaining with the Khanh.

Just as they were ready to take him, a trumpeting call suddenly filled the air around them. Kadira jumped at the sound, watching as her party members lifted their weapons. She spun quickly toward the sound, alarmed to see two large dragons circling overhead.

"What do we do?" Sami whispered.

The *damer* was tucked tightly against Kadira's leg, growling softly and trembling. She kept her eyes on the dragons overhead for a long moment before looking to Sami. "I don't think they mean to hurt us," she said softly. "They would have done so already if that was their intention."

Sami and Tarke were tense beside her still, and Kadira motioned to them to lower their weapons. They did so gingerly. They were surprised when the dragons called once more, swooping lower to the ground.

"This man must be their master," Kadira said slowly. She slung her weapon across her back slowly, turning back to the make-shift stretcher. "They will let us take him."

Sami was unsure and Tarke looked like he was upset, but they both put their weapons away. Sami reached to lift the other end of the stretcher. As they began to carry the man from the campsite, the dragons stayed overhead, as if supervising their trip home.

Kadira knew the Khanh would be pissed, but what choice did she have? She called after the *damer* as they began to make their way home.

Forn, the Royal City of Fornax.
The twelfth day of winter, the 851st year of
the reign of Queen Liana Estrella.
Sunday, January 1, 2012.

T HE HALLS OF THE CASTLE were silent as Rian walked them. His boots clicked on the dolomite floor, the coolness of the mountain seeping into the castle. Rian knew it was too early in the morning for the servants to be eavesdropping. He tried to bolster his confidence as he pushed open the heavy throne room door.

"You asked for me, Father?"

The sound of claws digging into the dolomite echoed around the room, a massive white dragon unfurling from behind a throne. If Rian hadn't expected it to be there, he wouldn't have seen it against the white stone. It flashed a bright green eye at him, a low rumble vibrating the stone walls. It moved slowly, flipping its tail from in front of the king's throne.

The man sitting in the chair was just as ancient as the dragon, with a long, curling beard that matched the dragon's scales in whiteness. It was in stark contrast to his sun-darkened skin. He didn't move to stand from his chair, his ancient face wrinkled into a permanent frown. His eyes were nearly opaque, his eyesight nearly gone with his age. He held out his hand, motioning for his son to come closer.

"Rian," he said, his crackling voice filling the room. "You have not done as I instructed."

Rian came closer, kneeling on the steps of the dais. "I'm sorry, Father," he said gently. "But you know where my heart lies." He clenched his fists. "I cannot sit by and let more of our kin be slaughtered."

The king's frown melted deeper into his face. "That is not for you to decide, Rian," he said slowly. He leaned forward slightly, causing the beast curled behind him to lift its head. "Now stop this foolishness. Disband your Pangere."

Rian gritted his teeth, unable to look up at his father. He couldn't do that. "I cannot do that, Father," he said, his voice clipped. "The Sky Dragon came to me. You know I have been charged with this task by the gods."

His father sighed, leaning back in his chair. The white dragon rested its head across its master's lap, closing its eyes as the old man ran his hand across the dragon's face. "I know what this means to you, my son," he said. "But this must stop. You must find a way to fight this through peaceful means."

Rian's head snapped up. "King Paraximus will not listen to peace," he said desperately. "He is murdering our dragonkin, and you just sit by and let it happen!" This was not the first time he and his father had had this conversation. His father didn't believe in dreams, but Rian knew what he'd seen and what he'd been told to do.

The king sighed once more. "Listen to me, Rian," he said, his voice firm. "I am not much longer for this world." He did move to stand then, the dragon rumbling its unhappiness. It pushed its head against the king's side to brace him. "It is time you take your place and stop this foolishness."

Rian moved to stand as well, feeling rage shifting in his chest. "I would never let this happen if I were king."

His father's face twisted with anger. "You will treat me with respect," he barked. "I am still your king."

Rian winced at his father's tone, slinking back. "Yes, Father," he said, bowing his head. "Forgive me."

The king held out his hand then. Rian rose quickly, catching his father's hand and looping it around his arm. Despite his frailty, his grip was still firm as Rian walked with him. "Please do not make me issue orders to you, my son," he said softly, a lament in his voice. "I understand your mission more than you know, but you must understand my position." He paused, his eyes unseeing as he caught Rian's hand. "I cannot bring our people against Siccita. We would not survive. Gods or no gods."

Rian turned his eyes away, knowing his father was right. Fornax was too small; even though the dragons that Siccita and Ymber used for battle were bred in the fires of the mountains, there was no way an army of dragon riders could stand against Paraximus' armies. "I understand, Father," Rian said finally, defeat in his voice.

The king patted his hand then, a small smile coming to his face. "Your heart is in the right place," he said. "Don't let that change."

Rian ducked his head as he led his father toward the dining hall for breakfast. He knew that his father was right and he knew that he was playing with fire, but he also knew the atrocities that their dragons were facing was too much. Someone had to do something, and that someone was him.

The training fields were quiet early in the mornings,

just the way Rian liked them. He preferred to practice alone so that he could mull over his thoughts in peace. He had just gone through the first two practice stances when a shadow fell across him.

"I take it your meeting didn't go well this morning."

Rian looked up, sighing shortly. "Unless you're here to spar with me, I'd appreciate some alone time," he snapped. He knew he was being unkind to his friend, but she had a knack for showing up at the worst times.

Zaida crossed her arms, frowning at him. "You know I'm on your side," she said evenly.

Rian eased his stance and lowered his practice sword. "I know, Zaida," he said. "I'm sorry."

Zaida offered a half-smile. That was one thing Rian could always count on; Zaida never took anything personally and was always logical and even-keeled. He couldn't remember a time he'd seen her truly upset, but he also couldn't remember a time when she'd really been happy, either.

"I will take you up on your offer," she said, flipping a long, black ponytail away from her deep brown eyes. She pulled two short swords from her back, tossing the scabbards away.

Rian shook his head. Zaida was a fierce swordswoman, preferring two-handed weapons. And she never used a practice sword. He turned and tucked the wooden sword into the rack, picking up his own sword.

It wasn't as heavy as the wooden sword, and felt warm in his hand. The grip seemed to have been molded to fit his fingers, and the blade curved slightly, a dragon etched into the silver-steel. It felt like an extension of his arm. But it didn't make him feel safe from Zaida as she twirled her twin blades.

She didn't say anything, watching as he nodded that he was ready. Her face was smooth and unreadable as she lunged for him, swinging her blades in a cutting motion. Rian dodged her attack, twisting under her as she lunged a second time. They traded even blows back and forth for a while, both of them beginning to pant. Finally, they reached a stand-off.

"You should just give up, Zaida," Rian said, smirking at her. "You know you're not going to beat me."

Zaida sighed as if she was annoyed. "Once more," she commanded. "Bring all you have."

Rian drew a breath and grinned. He leapt at her, swinging his saber as hard as he could. He knew her next move would be a block, and he tried to maneuver around it, but Zaida knew his moves, too. She surprised him by dodging his blow, whacking him across the shoulder with the flat of her blade before rounding out her finishing move by pressing her opposite blade against his neck. She offered her narrow half-smile again as Rian eyed her bitterly.

"I hate you," he said, pushing her sword away from his face.

Zaida shrugged triumphantly. "Don't be so predictable." She trailed after him as he walked from the field to pick up a water flask. He took a swig before offering her some, which she accepted.

"I think it's time for us to go north," Rian said suddenly.

Zaida lowered the flask slowly, frowning at him. "North?"

Rian nodded. He looked down at the sword in his hands. "I know what I saw, Zaida," he said softly. He gripped the hilt of his sword tightly. "Eomryr Lani spoke to me."

Zaida was watching him passively. "I believe you," she said simply. She closed the flask and tossed it on the ground.

Rian's gaze was distant as he remembered how real the dream of the Sky Dragon had felt. It was almost as if he could smell Eomryr Lani's fragrant breath and feel the burn of the god's scales. His eyes had flashed in a myriad of colors, so beautiful that Rian had awoken in tears. The god's voice had echoed down to his soul, not so much a sound as it was a feeling. Rian knew he'd been blessed with Eomryr Lani's presence, and he knew he was tasked with a mission.

"But my father doesn't," Rian said bitterly, running a hand through his auburn hair.

"Your father believes in what he can see," Zaida said. "And he's never seen the gods." She watched him. "You're not like him, Rian. You aren't grounded in reason."

Rian looked up at her, frowning. "Thanks, Zaida," he said, annoyance in his voice.

Zaida blinked, her brow quirking as she realized what she'd said. "You know what I mean," she said quickly. "You follow your heart. Your father follows what he can touch with his hands."

Rian nodded, flashing her a small grin. "I knew what you meant." He tucked his sword away and pulled the scabbard belt around his hips. "We still have to go north. Eomryr Lani told me to save our kind, and I fear that Liana may be our only hope."

Zaida blew a slow breath through her lips. She clearly didn't like his words, but she'd never question her leader. "Shall I prepare the others?"

Rian nodded. "The sooner we can get to Regius Carmen, the better."

12

The village of Festra, Abjure Forest, Ymber.
The thirteenth day of winter, the 851st year
of the reign of Queen Liana Estrella.
Monday, January 2, 2012.

JET EMPTIED THE CONTENTS OF a small, dirty bag into his hands. Nyx had thought he was crazy, digging in the mountain's soil for some gold, but he'd intentionally left them some money hidden away for their return. He'd known this trip wouldn't be cheap, but he didn't realize it would be quite so expensive.

"That's fifty *pecuns* for the pants, Sir."

Jet handed the woman her fee, watching as she folded the pants and handed them to him.

"Are you sure you don't want the coat to go along with these?" she asked.

Jet's gaze shifted to the clothing that was lain out in the make-shift store. Apparently, the woman was the wife of Garibold, Festra's merchant. He was rarely in town, usually on a supply trip to the mountains or to the sea to bring back goods, and his wife and their son ran the shop in his absence.

This time, though, he'd brought back some premium items, including the *stuba*-skin clothing. Jet knew he couldn't pass on that.

"Can I see it?" Jet asked, nodding his chin.

The woman smiled and nodded, turning and handing it to him across a counter. Her hair was tethered back in braided plaits, the length swinging with her motion. Across the room, her son was talking quietly to another customer. Jet noted that the boy seemed well-versed in the weaponry his father had acquired.

The *stuba*-skin coat was thick and heavy in his hands as he took it from the merchant's wife. Jet rubbed his fingers across the material, noting the fine quality. *Stuba* was notorious for being difficult to work with, not to mention that the creatures were hell to try to trap. But there was nothing better than cut-resistant and fire-proof clothing.

"I'll take it," Jet said, handing the woman more money.

"Thank you, Sir," she said, smiling broadly.

Jet nodded to her and turned to leave the shop. He glanced once more at the boy, seeing that he was putting a sword away, having sent his customer to his mother with a different blade. He caught Jet's eye and smiled.

"Need a weapon to go with those?" he asked, indicating the *stuba* leather.

Jet paused, studying the weapons on the wall. He couldn't imagine Nyx trying to wield any of the swords; they were too big and she was too clumsy. His eyes landed on a recurved bow, and an idea sparked in his mind. "What can you tell me about that bow?"

"Ah, this one," the boy said, pulling it down from where it was displayed on the wall. He handed it to Jet. "Made from agrestis bone. Lightweight, but very resilient."

Jet was impressed with the craftsmanship as he looked it

over. The bone was indeed light and it felt thin in his hands. He knew it would be a good weapon for Nyx, if she could ever learn to master a weapon. He sighed as he pulled more money from his pouch. This trip was bleeding him dry.

Nyx looked to Melinda as she stirred a pot of stew for tonight's dinner. She was talking about the boy who lived up the way, Ean Gallson. Nyx appreciated her friendship, but she was tired of hearing about Ean and how much Melinda liked him. She stirred the stew absently, wondering when Jet would finally be back from the merchant.

"You're not hearing a word I'm saying, are you, *Soramicus*?" Melinda asked suddenly, a smile on her face.

Nyx snapped back to reality, drawing a sharp breath. "Sorry," she said quickly. She felt her cheeks tinge pink a bit. She wasn't completely comfortable with Melinda's nickname for her yet, but she appreciated the sentiment. Melinda said it meant friend, but Jet told her it was closer to sister.

Melinda was still humored as she crossed the room, taking the spoon from Nyx's hands. "I'm sorry if I talk too much," she said, kneeling beside the hearth and the stool that Nyx was perched on. She looked mildly embarrassed. "I never have anyone to talk to."

Nyx felt a small frown pull at her face. "You don't have friends in Festra?" she asked softly.

Melinda offered a half-shrug, focusing on stirring the food. "My father and I aren't natives, or Inerse," she said in explanation. "Even when my mother was alive, we were still only kept around because Papa is a doctor."

Nyx felt her heart ache for her new friend. "Sorry," she said gently.

Melinda looked up at her, her smile returning. "Nothing to be sorry for," she said easily. "I'm content with my place."

Nyx didn't like the way that sounded, but she couldn't argue as footsteps echoed on the stairs outside. "That must be Jet," she said, moving to stand.

The door opened, and, just like she thought, Jet entered the small house. Nyx noticed the myriad of things he was carrying, including several changes of clothes, her eyes catching the bow that was slung across his back.

"What's all that?" she asked, walking toward him.

Jet set the clothes down, swinging the bow from his back. "Stuff," he said dismissively.

Nyx caught the bow in her hands when he set it down. "Why did you buy a bow?" she asked, holding it up. She noticed that big, cat-like creatures were carved into the handle, similar to the ones that had been protecting the Limen.

"You're going to learn to use it," Jet said, handing her a pile of clothes.

Nyx looked up at him, frowning as she absently took the bundle. "A bow?" she asked. "Why?"

Jet sighed in annoyance. "Change your clothes," he said shortly. "We're going to train."

Nyx looked down at the fabric in her hands, realizing it was thick, dyed a bright blue. It was a bit scaly-looking, as if it had been made from a lizard.

"Oh wow," Melinda said, crossing the room to run her hands over Nyx's new clothes. "*Stuba* leather." She looked up at Jet, surprise on her face. "This must have cost you quite a bit."

Jet seemed rather pleased suddenly. "I can afford it," he said dismissively, reaching for the bow. He looked to Nyx. "Hurry up."

Nyx scowled lightly at him, turning and trudging into the bed room. Melinda was behind her, sitting on the bed as Nyx began to change her clothes. "What's stooba?" she asked, shrugging out of Melinda's old dress and pulling on a soft satin shirt.

Melinda's lips quirked. "We need to work on your pronunciation," she said, giggling softly.

Nyx rolled her eyes. "Why is Sarotian so hard?"

"You'll get it," Melinda said encouragingly. "Don't worry." She looked down at the coat as Nyx pulled on the pants. They were a perfect, albeit snug, fit. "*Stuba* is great. It's hard to make because the creatures it comes from are extremely acidic, but once it's cured it can't be cut and it can't be burned." She looked up at Nyx. "Jet must really want to keep you safe."

Nyx arched a brow as she pulled on the coat. It was light, despite the thickness, falling perfectly to just above her hips, fitting her snugly. "Well, it is his job," she said absently, fiddling with the buttons. The satin shirt he'd given her was comfortable, but it was thin and Nyx knew the cold wind would blow right through it.

Melinda shook her head. "You two could stand to be nicer to each other," she said.

Nyx looked at her friend as she sat in a chair and pulled on her boots. "You mean Jet could be nicer to me," she said.

Melinda shrugged. "It's just because he likes you."

Nyx paused in lacing her boots, feeling her face turn hot. "What?" she blurted. "I don't know what Jet you see, but that's not what I see."

Melinda grinned conspiratorially. "Oh, come on, Nyx," she said. "I see the way he watches you."

Nyx yanked the laces on her boots tighter than she meant to, shaking her head. "You're wrong," she said shortly. She looked up at Melinda. Melinda was a romantic at heart and she always saw the good in people, even Jet. "He looks at me like I'm a problem."

Melinda giggled again, moving to stand. "A problem because he likes you. And we all know men are stupid when it comes to feelings."

Nyx bit her lip to stop her own giggle as she followed Melinda into the living area. Jet had already retreated outside, and Nyx walked to the door, pulling it open. "We'll be back for dinner."

Melinda nodded, checking the stew. "Have fun," she said teasingly.

Nyx shot her a look before closing the door behind her and trotting down the steps. She was surprised how comfortable her new clothes were as she saw Jet waiting for her at the end of the bridge. She noticed that he'd put on new clothes too, a pair of gray trousers and a black shirt underneath a black leather jacket. She wondered what kind of creature the leather was made from as she reached him.

"Here," he said, holding out the bow to her.

Nyx took it slowly in her hands, looking it over. "I've literally never used a bow before."

Jet rolled his eyes, turning to walk across the bridge. "I figured," he tossed over his shoulder.

Nyx quickened her pace to fall into step beside him. "How much longer do we have to be here?" she asked.

Jet shrugged. "A few more weeks," he said. He looked down at her. "Why?"

Nyx looked down at the bow in her hands. "I dunno," she said softly. She was finding that she sorta liked it in Festra. She looked up at Jet quickly when he stopped.

"We can't stay here," he said shortly. "You know that."

Nyx nodded quickly. "No, I know," she said. "I was just wondering."

She was silent as she followed Jet across the bridge and toward a set of stairs that wound up toward the smithy. Melinda had made her feel welcomed, and it had helped over the last week as Nyx reconciled the fact that she could never go back to her old life. In fact, being with Melinda almost made her look forward to living in Gexalatia. Melinda reminded her of Anna.

"How are your studies going?" Jet asked suddenly.

Nyx's head snapped up, her eyes narrowing in concentration at the Sarotian words. Since she'd started working with Melinda, he would randomly talk to her in Sarotian to test her. "Fine," she returned, the word feeling funny in her mouth. She watched as Jet glanced at her as he reached the top of the steps, a smirk on his face.

"Your accent sucks."

Nyx sighed, understanding those words perfectly. Melinda only said them all the time. "I'm doing the best I can," she said bitterly in English. "You try learning a new language in such a short period of time."

Jet shook his head, turning away. "It took me less time to learn your language," he said arrogantly.

Nyx scowled at the back of his head as she followed him down the path. Woop-dee-effin-doo, she thought to herself. She kept her mouth closed as they passed the smithy, a platform coming into view. Jet walked up the steps onto it, opening a wooden gate. Nyx was surprised to see a training field, complete with practice swords and shields, hay-bale targets set up at the far end for archery practice. She looked up at Jet as he shrugged out of his jacket, picking up a quiver of unsharpened arrows.

"All right," he said, holding one out to her. "Let's see it."

Nyx grimaced as she held up the bow. She'd only ever seen them used on TV, and she knew nothing about them. She lined up the notch on the end of the arrow on the string like she thought she was supposed to, surprised by the tension when she tried to draw the string back. She sighted one of the targets, feeling her arms straining at the unnatural feel of the weapon. She let the arrow fly, watching as it flew a few feet and slid pitifully to the ground, less than half the distance to the target.

"Oops," she breathed, looking up at Jet. She wasn't surprised by the look on his face, one that made her think he wanted to facepalm.

He drew a slow breath as he turned his eyes back to her. "You suck."

Nyx shrugged. "I told you I've never done this before," she said pathetically. She watched as he picked up another arrow, holding it out to her.

"Try again," he commanded. "This time aim higher."

Nyx wasn't sure how that would help, but she notched the arrow and aimed a bit higher than she thought she should. She released the string, surprised when the arrow stayed in the air a bit longer. Unfortunately, it slid pathetically short of the target like the first. Nyx glanced up at Jet, seeing him reaching for another arrow.

"Are you sure that this is something I can learn?" she asked as she took the next arrow.

Jet shrugged. "Can't be sure you'll learn anything," he murmured.

Nyx narrowed her eyes at him, scowling lightly. "Thanks for the vote of confidence," she said. She drew the bowstring back, determined to make him eat crow. There was a little bit more strength in her draw, and she let the arrow fly. She gasped in surprise when it struck the hay bale, even though it was barely on the corner.

Jet seemed surprised as he crossed his arms. "Maybe you can be taught."

Nyx sighed in disgust at him. "Just give me another," she

said, gesturing to the pile.

"Ask in Sarotian," Jet said, turning his dark eyes on her.

Nyx could tell he was toying with her, amusement barely concealed behind his eyes. "Da'mihi," Nyx ordered.

Jet arched a brow as he reached for one, twirling it in front of her. "What?" he asked teasingly, "No please?"

Nyx snatched the arrow from his fingers, sticking her tongue out at him. She notched it and yanked the string back, feeling Jet settle just over her right shoulder. She was surprised when she felt his hand on her elbow.

"Here," he said, lifting it slightly. "Your hand should be almost to your cheek."

Nyx drew a slow breath, realizing her heart was racing suddenly. She could feel the warmth from his body as he mirrored her stance. He used the toe of his boot to push her left foot out some.

"A wider stance allows you to get a better pull," he continued.

Nyx felt her face flush as his left hand covered hers, his fingers twining with hers to adjust her hold on the arrow. She could feel his chest against her back as he drew a breath, lifting her hand slightly to help her aim.

"Take a slow breath," he said. "Keep both eyes open." He caught her right hand, making sure it was pulled back to the right place. When Nyx had drawn a full breath, he let go of her hand. "Exhale slowly to keep your hand steady. When you get to the end of your exhale, release."

Nyx could feel her arms straining at holding the string taut for so long, but she focused on her breathing. As she blew a shaking breath between her lips, she reminded herself to keep both eyes open as she sighted the target. Finally, she reached the end of her exhale, knowing it was now or never. She released the string in her right hand, feeling Jet step back from her. Her eyes widened as the arrow sailed across the course, striking the target with a hard smack.

"I did it," she breathed, staring at the arrow protruding from the bale. It was nowhere near a bulls-eye, but it was center-mass and deep. She turned to look at Jet, seeing that his arms were crossed tightly.

He didn't let his face betray anything as he looked from her to the arrow. "Practice your form," he said dismissively. "That's only one."

Nyx frowned at him. Just a second ago he'd been so supportive, and now he was cold as the evening wind that was pulling at her. Not that that should have surprised her. "Where are you going?" she asked as he picked up his jacket.

"To talk to Wyn," he said as he turned toward the entrance to the field. "You can handle this for a few minutes, can't you?" He was back-pedaling, that smug smirk pulling at his face. "It's pretty hard to hurt yourself on practice tips."

Nyx sighed in disgust as she turned back to the quiver. "Whatever," she mumbled, listening to the sound of his boots on the platform fade. She notched the arrow, feeling her cheeks turn red again as she tried to mimic what she'd just done. It was weird and different without Jet guiding her.

Jet's footsteps were heavy as he crossed into the smithy. He stepped into the dim light, looking around for the blacksmith. He caught sight of the burly man at the forge, embers lighting up his face as he fanned the flames. Jet could see a shimmering piece of metal lying in the embers.

"Ah, Brani," Wyn said suddenly, looking up from his work. He smiled. "Come to check on your commission?"

Jet nodded, the fake name he'd given Wyn sounding weird. "Just wanted to see your progress," he said, intending to flatter the blacksmith. He had a feeling that praising the man's work would help get it done faster.

Wyn left his project in the fire and crossed toward a table. "Tis the finest chalargentum I could get," he said, holding out a thick piece of metal peppered with dings from a hammer. The burly man was entirely too proud of himself. "Hadda pay Garibold's lady a pretty penny for it."

Jet took it in his hands, turning it over to examine it. "This is indeed fine metal, Wyn," he said, offering a smile.

Wyn returned his grin as he took the piece back. "'Twill protect your *adamate puella* from damn near anything."

"Oh, she's not—" Jet bit his tongue quickly. It was best to let Wyn think whatever he wanted to think. They wouldn't be here long enough for it to matter.

Wyn frowned at him lightly. "Oh, betrothed then?" he asked, offering a smile. "'Pologies if'n I made an assumption." He leaned in as if he would elbow Jet conspiratorially. "Hope she ain't pledged to another. Pretty thing like that won't be free long."

Jet forced a smile. "I assure you, that's not the case," he said. He was trying to keep as much of their identities under-wraps as he could, but Wyn was a nosey bastard. It was worse with the way Wyn's words made him feel sick at the thought of delivering her as a bride to someone, which was interesting. Jet had never cared about what happened to other people, but he *did* care about what happened to Nyx.

Wyn clapped him on the shoulder then, stepping back toward his forge. "Good man," he tossed over his shoulder. "Best to keep 'er to yerself."

Jet tried to keep a friendly look on his face, but he was failing as he turned and left Wyn to his work. He forced himself to draw a calming breath as he stepped into the cold air. It was a drastic change from Wyn's sweltering forge, but it didn't help to ease the knots in his gut. Jet pushed the man's words from his mind as he walked back toward the practice field.

Around the pathways, the lanterns were lighting themselves, floating orbs glowing softly inside glass cases. The insects were flitting about, glittering in the evening shadows. If it weren't for the cold, they would be singing softly in the waning light, calling for mates and whatever else bugs did. Jet used to enjoy the night sounds, but lately he'd been too distracted to care.

He walked up the steps to the practice field, not surprised to see Nyx not training. He frowned lightly as he walked through the gate. "What are you doing?" he demanded.

Nyx lifted her head from where she was lying on the wooden floor, her hands above her. Softly illuminated butterflies were dancing around her hands, landing gently on her fingers. She was grinning as she sat up. "Look at this," she said excitedly. She waved her hand, a colorful array of butterflies flittering away from her, circling around her. "They won't leave me alone."

Jet sighed shortly, shooing them away as he stood beside her. "They're attracted to your magic," he said. She behaved like a child. Part of him wanted to be annoyed, but part of him was twisting in knots again. How could she be so innocent and so infuriating at the same time?

Nyx's eyes widened. "Oh," she said, watching them flit away. The child-like happiness didn't fade from her face as she looked up at him. "That's cool."

Jet sighed again, offering his hand to her. "Did you even do anything while I was gone?" he asked bitterly.

Nyx nodded as he pulled her to her feet. She motioned to the bale across the way.

Jet stopped short when he turned to look at it. A handful

of arrows were jutting randomly from the target, but three had found the bulls-eye.

"I guess I'm better with a bow than we thought," she said, turning to look at him.

Jet nodded mutely. Surprise was still filling him. He'd never seen anyone take to a weapon so quickly. He shook his head as he turned his eyes to her. "Go get your arrows," he said. "We need to get back."

Nyx's eyes brightened then. "Yes, dinner!" she said quickly before jogging to the target to collect the arrows. "I'm starving!"

Jet drew an annoyed breath as he waited for her at the edge of the practice field. Darkness was creeping up on them quickly. Jet turned his head as orbs of light began to flit to life in the distance, filling the night air with light. They floated up into the air, illuminating the temple carved into the middle of the huge tree that Festra was built around. Jet could see that the massive tree appeared to be a conglomeration of many thick branches as the augarluxes floated in and out of them.

"Whoa," Nyx suddenly breathed next to him. "I've never seen it like that before." Her eyes were wide as she stared up at the temple. The lights were like fireflies as they floated around the carved beasts on the front of the temple.

Jet didn't say anything as he stepped in front of her, breaking her reverie. "Come on," he said shortly. "Melinda is expecting us."

Nyx frowned at his back, but remained silent as she followed him. Since when did he care what Melinda thought or wanted? She jogged to keep up with him, realizing he was walking quickly. "Why are you in such a hurry?" she called.

"Just come on," Jet snapped.

Soon they were at Melinda's door. Nyx was surprised to

see that she was waiting for them on the porch. She moved to her feet, smiling warmly as they neared. "You're a bit later than I expected," she said.

"Sorry," Nyx said as she reached her friend. She held up the bow and quiver of arrows in her hands. "Training ran long."

Melinda's smile didn't waiver. "It's fine," she said briskly. Nyx noticed that she was dressed in a nice, embroidered pinafore with a puffy-sleeved blouse underneath. She was also wearing her good cloak and her hair had been teased into more kempt curls.

"What's the occasion?" Nyx asked.

Melinda looked mildly surprised for a moment, but then her smile widened. "Tonight is the first night of *Cael Hiems*," she said.

"Kale he-ums?" Nyx asked, frowning. "What's that?"

"It's the celestial winter celebration," Melinda said. "I was waiting for you two." She became bashful suddenly. "I thought you might want to come with me."

Nyx's brow rose in surprise and she looked up at Jet. "Can we?" she asked cautiously.

Jet sighed in annoyance. "Do what you want," he said, waving his hand.

"Do I need to change?" Nyx asked, motioning to the *stuba* clothing she was wearing.

Melinda shook her head. "No," she said quickly. She reached for Nyx's ponytail, pulling the band that held it in place. "This will be fine."

Nyx let her fluff her golden curls, missing the way Jet's eyes lingered for a moment before he turned away to head up the steps.

"Dinner is on the hearth if you're hungry," Melinda offered, glancing at him.

Jet nodded silently as he disappeared into the house.

"What was that about?" Melinda asked quietly as she turned to Nyx, holding out a wrapped biscuit. "I grabbed this for you."

Nyx shrugged as she took it, taking a bite. "Seemed normal to me. Like I said earlier, he could stand to be nicer."

Melinda seemed confused for a moment, but then she caught Nyx's arm, leading her toward the chapel. "Let's hurry," she said excitedly. "I don't want to be late."

Nyx fell in step with her as she ate her biscuit, watching as the rest of the village emerged from their homes and flooded the walkways toward the chapel. "So, tell me again what this is," Nyx said quietly. She watched as other villagers began to surround them, talking excitedly.

They were all dressed in what Nyx would consider their Sunday best, the men in clean shirts without elbow patches and nice trousers, carrying hats in their hands, while the women wore nice, deep blue dresses and thick, wool cloaks. Some wore bonnets on their heads and some not, while clean-faced children dodged between the adults, obviously playing. Nyx caught snippets of conversations, understanding words here and there.

"*Cael Hiems* is the yearly winter celebration," Melinda whispered, so as not to draw attention. "The villagers worship the goddess Caeles. She is said to be the bringer of the snow and the protector of the harvest." She glanced down as a boy and girl pushed past them, shrieking happily. "We celebrate her for the next ten days."

"Oh," Nyx breathed, looking up at the amazing chapel as they neared. It was massive, towering over them with sharply pointed cathedral windows carved into the face, where the augarluxes floated lazily in and out. "What are the creatures that are carved into it?"

"Those are Caeles' children," Melinda said. "They are the creatures of the forest and are said to live among us to help us and protect us."

"Ah," Nyx said, looking at the massive beasts. Her eyes landed on what resembled a tiger, with massive claws and teeth, two tails spiraling from its hind-end. "What's that one?"

"Those are *leonis*," Melinda said. "They're very rare now, but said to be Caeles' sacred animal." She pulled Nyx toward the door to the chapel. "It is said that if you see one, you are blessed with Caeles' favor." She offered a teasing grin. "Assuming you don't get eaten."

Nyx nodded mutely as they filed into the church, Melinda's attempt at humor evading her. Her eyes were taking in everything, her senses feeling as if they were on overload.

Wooden pews were all around them, looking as if they had grown up from the tree just for the people to sit on. The floor was well-worn and smooth, as were the benches. At the front of the chapel was a raised dais, and a statue of whom Nyx assumed was Caeles stood on it. Her hands were outstretched, her eyes closed, butterflies resting in her palms and along her arms. Animals were curled around her feet, and deer antlers protruded from the top of her head. Her hair had been stylized as if a wind had caught it, wrapping it around her narrow torso. Nyx saw that a flute was lashed across her chest and hanging around her hips.

Behind the dais, a set of stairs spiraled toward a balcony, where Nyx could see what looked like a choir. A doorway was behind Caeles' statue, shadowed heavily against the flickering lights of the augarluxes. Nyx thought she could make out more stairs, but they were too far away for her to be sure as Melinda guided her into the back row of pews. All around them, people continued to mill in and find seats, visiting with people they knew. It reminded Nyx of church on Sunday mornings, and made a stab of loneliness flit through her.

"I hope you enjoy this," Melinda said, pulling her from her thoughts. She was smiling brightly. "This is one of my favorite celebrations."

Nyx tried to mirror her excitement, but was having trouble as the church began to hush. She turned her eyes toward the dais, not surprised to see a woman in white robes walk in front of the statue. She began to speak in a pleasant, yet booming, voice. Nyx furrowed her brow hard, trying to concentrate on what she was saying. The echo of the room made it difficult for her to pick out any words.

"Do you recognize anything?" Melinda asked after a long moment.

Nyx shook her head. "The echo is distorting her words too much," she whispered.

"She's basically welcoming everyone and talking about Caeles," Melinda interpreted. "The story of Caeles is that she was a slave-girl, the daughter of a poor farming family. She was sold as a child to help her family and to keep her safe, but she saw the suffering of her people. As she grew, she fought to help them, using her connection with the animals of the forest to help her people survive. She brought much good to her people, eventually catching the eye of one of the gods. For her deeds, she was granted immortality, even though she was Inerse."

"Hn," Nyx said, letting her eyes drift around the church. It was beautiful in the flickering lamp-light, images of the forest surrounding them.

"There is of course more to her adventures," Melinda continued.

"I'd love to hear more another time," Nyx whispered,

still trying to take in the whole temple around her.

The sudden sound of a flute made Nyx jump, and she looked toward the front, seeing a small girl standing at the front of the dais. She played a slow, somewhat haunting tune on her flute, and Nyx found herself entranced. She drew a sharp breath when a voice suddenly began to echo in the temple, vibrating deep into her chest. The flute girl was joined then by a stringed instrument that Nyx couldn't see, the three sounds melding and twining around the walls of the temple. More voices began to join the chorus, and Nyx felt a chill run down her spine.

The way the music caressed her senses was the way her magic felt as it pressed against her chest, filling her with wonder and hope. She was mesmerized and she closed her eyes, letting the heavenly sounds engulf her and carry her away. The whole cathedral seemed to vibrate with the weight of the song, and it made tears spring into Nyx's eyes. She'd never experienced anything as powerful and moving as the dulcet tones that were pulsing against her. She was lost to the music for a long time, disappointed when it finally ended.

Nyx's eyes flashed open when Melinda caught her arm. She looked around, seeing that the villagers had all risen to their feet, and she followed Melinda's lead. She noticed that they were watching the dais expectantly.

"The Ka is back," Melinda whispered excitedly.

Nyx glanced at her. "The what?" she asked.

"The Ka," Melinda repeated. "The chief of the village. Ka is a very ancient word for warrior or battlefield and the title given to our chief." She suddenly drew a sharp breath, happiness and surprise on her face. "He doesn't spend much time in Festra since he's usually away in Regius Carmen."

Nyx watched as a tall, broad-shouldered man stepped

through the doorway behind the statue of Caeles. He had long, dark hair that was tethered away from his face, save for two long strands that fell across either cheek. Even from her distance, Nyx could see that beads were threaded into his hair. His neck and arms were tattooed with what she assumed were ceremonial designs. Heavily embellished white and gold robes were wrapped around his body, and he carried a staff in his hand, the head of what appeared to be a hawk carved into the top. He jingled with the weight of the gold pieces on his robes and the rings that hung from the top of his staff. His voice was booming when he addressed the gathered crowd, a gentle smile coming to his face.

Nyx wasn't sure what he was saying, but the words felt kind and loving. She glanced at Melinda, seeing that her friend was totally captivated by the words of the Ka. "What is he saying, Melinda?" she whispered.

Melinda blinked from her reverie, looking at Nyx. "He's welcoming his people," she said. "He's explaining that he is sorry he's been away for so long. The Queen Mother has called her advisors to her side, and he must answer her call, but he hasn't forgotten the one he serves, the goddess Caeles. He has come for her celebration and will remain until the end of *Cael Hiems*."

Nyx turned to look back at the man, listening to his unfamiliar words echo around the chapel. Melinda continued to translate his message as he began to tell the tale of Caeles and how he became a priest in her order. His story wasn't particularly spectacular, except for the part where he was a priest for a strange goddess that Nyx had never heard of, but the whole ceremony was delightful and different. Even though she knew she would miss the wonderful music, Nyx was glad when the service ended.

She and Melinda eased into the crowd with the rest of

the villagers, walking back to Melinda's house in silence. They were crossing the rope bridge, most of the crowd that had been with them having dispersed at this point. It made Nyx realize how far on the outskirts of town Melinda and her father really were.

"So, what did you think?" Melinda asked, breaking the silence.

Nyx looked at her friend and offered a smile. "I really liked it," she said. "The singers were amazing."

Melinda returned her grin. "Just wait until *Agita Nocturna*," she said excitedly.

Nyx sighed shortly. "I'm pretty sure you're just making words up now."

Melinda laughed softly. "It's the fifth day of Caeles' celebration," she said in explanation. "We have a huge party and dance and sing and it's wonderful." Her eyes were wistful. "Everyone brings a homemade dish of sweets or bread. I even made my own dress for this year."

Nyx felt out of place as she listened to Melinda describe the party. It made her think, not for the first time, about the life she'd left behind and all the things she was missing out on. Sadness tried to creep in, but she pushed it away, determined to adjust to Gexalatia.

13

The village of Grassmire, Siccita.
The fifteenth day of winter, the 906th year of
the reign of King Paraximus Lamia.
Wednesday, January 4, 2012.

BAILEY STOOD AT A WINDOW which overlooked a courtyard. Below, villagers were carrying on about their business, trading goods and visiting with people they knew. Their smiles seemed foreign and faraway.

"Are you sure we have to do this?" Ellie whispered, drawing her sister's attention.

Bailey's arms were crossed tightly as she turned. "There's no other choice," she said sternly. "I'm the only one who can distract them while you escape."

Ellie's shoulders sagged and she looked around the room cautiously. "Don't speak so loud," she said fearfully. "They'll hear us."

Bailey crossed the room and sat on the bed beside her younger twin. She caught Ellie's hands. "They aren't listening right now," she said gently. She pressed her hand against Ellie's cheek. "I'm sorry that this has happened." She sighed deeply, her strong façade cracking. "I should have taken better care of you."

Ellie shook her head. "No, it's no one's fault," she said quickly. Tears began to well in her eyes. "I just wish Raphael—" A soft choking sound escaped her lips.

Bailey hugged her sister tightly. "I know," she said, keeping her own tears in check.

It had been nine days. Nine painful, long, arduous days since they had been taken captive. Nine days that Raphael would not have survived.

"We can't think about that now," Bailey said then, holding her sister's shoulders. "You need to focus on what you have to do."

Ellie wiped at her face and nodded. She knew that there was more than just their own safety riding on their plan; she and Bailey had shared a vision after they had witnessed the power King Paraximus possessed to summon portals. They knew that his power would continue to grow and, in time, he would be unstoppable.

"When he sends his guard in to bring dinner, that's when you run," Bailey said. "And you don't stop until you get back to Ymber." Her voice was forceful. "Understand?"

Ellie nodded. "What will you do?" she asked, her voice trembling.

Bailey offered her a playful smile. "I've got some tricks up my sleeve," she said bravely. "Don't you worry."

The truth was that she didn't know. After they surrendered to Paraximus' lackey, Darwren, a portal had opened, allowing him to bring them to Siccita without crossing Paries' Wall. Fortunately, to help avoid any unwanted attention, the atrox had been returned to the depths from whence they had crawled, leaving only Darwren and his men to bring them to Paraximus. Bailey knew this was an advantage and that they had to move fast. The village of Grassmire was merely the first stop on the long road to Celo Cavus. If Ellie could escape now, it would be easy for her to make it back to Ymber.

The confidence in her sister's voice didn't uncoil the knots in Ellie's stomach. She didn't know what she would do when she escaped. If she escaped. She wasn't a survivalist like her brother and sister. Her first instinct in the face of danger was to crumble. She knew she needed to be brave, but she wondered if she could.

"Are you sure I can do this?" she asked Bailey.

Bailey's eyes widened for a moment. "Of course you can," she said. Her brow furrowed. "You are stronger than you think, Ellie." Her blue eyes were pleading. "You must believe this."

Ellie looked down at her hands in her lap, which she was wringing slightly. "I'm not like you and Raphael," she whispered. "I'm not brave."

Bailey shook her head. "You are." She rubbed Ellie's shoulder. "You must be brave now."

Ellie felt her heart skip a beat in fear when footsteps could be heard down the hallway.

Bailey turned her head as well, her face set in grim determination. "Darwren made a mistake bringing us to this inn," she said, summoning her courage. "We will make him pay."

Ellie watched as Bailey rose to her feet, crossing the room quickly and picking up the metal tea pot that had been brought to them with this morning's breakfast. She stepped behind the door, prepared for it to open. She nodded to Ellie as the footsteps stopped, a rapping on the door.

"Dinner," a gruff voice called.

Ellie stood slowly, walking to the door and opening it.

She stepped back quickly, seeing a soldier standing there with a tray of food. "Just…over there," she motioned, feeling her voice quivering.

The soldier didn't seem to notice or care as he stepped into the room. His back was to the door, and just as he leaned forward to put the tray on a table, Bailey pushed the door shut, swinging the tea pot hard at his head. The soldier didn't know what hit him as he slouched to the floor.

Ellie's heart was racing as she looked at her sister, seeing her pull the soldier's sword from his belt. "I can't believe you did that," she said, her hands trembling.

Bailey caught her sister's arm, looking into her eyes. "It's time for you to be brave," she ordered. "I will distract them." She pulled the sheath from the sword, dropping it on the ground. "You run and you don't stop. You find a horse or rapere or anything that moves and you get the hell out of here."

Ellie nodded, trying to force down the fear that she felt for her sister's safety. She didn't have words as Bailey pulled open the door, looking cautiously into the hallway. A lump was forming in her throat. This might be the last time she saw her sister.

Bailey was focused as she motioned for Ellie to follow her. They tip-toed down the hallway, Bailey pausing at an open door. She lifted her sword, prepared to fend off any attackers as she peered into the room. She gasped in surprise after a moment, suddenly disappearing into the room.

Ellie ran to the doorway, seeing Bailey snatch another blade off a table.

"Father's sword," Bailey said, holding it up with a triumphant grin. She unbuckled the belt quickly, pulling it around Ellie's hips. "This will protect you."

Ellie caught her sister's arms then, looking into her face.

She didn't have to say anything, her twin reading her emotions. She drew a shuddering breath when Bailey pulled her into a tight hug.

"Everything will be fine," Bailey whispered. "I will find you."

Ellie caught the slight hitch in her sister's voice, and her heart sank. She didn't have time to say anything as Bailey suddenly let go of her.

"Good luck, Ellie," Bailey said, stepping away from her. "I love you."

Ellie was frozen for a moment as Bailey disappeared down the steps. She held her breath as she counted to ten, knowing she needed to give Bailey time to lure the guards away. It didn't take long before a ruckus could be heard down the stairs, and Ellie pushed her fear away. She didn't think as she darted down to the first floor and into the main area of the inn.

Just as they expected, it was full of dinner-time regulars, a loud din filling the room. Ellie found it easy enough to slip into the crowd, elbowing her way toward the door. Her heart leapt when it opened, fading light falling into the tavern. She was almost to freedom.

"Hurry!" a voice suddenly shouted.

Ellie's feet stilled, and she ducked behind a group of men, watching as two soldiers burst through the door. They ran quickly toward the stairs, no doubt looking for her. Once they went by, Ellie ran to the door, feeling out of sorts as she burst into the cooling night air.

It was strange to see normal people, doing normal things, while she was a fugitive. It seemed like at any moment someone would point her out, but no one batted an eye as she faded into the marketplace crowd. Her heart was still racing as she stole glances over her shoulder, watching for the tell-tale flash of red cloaks.

Once she'd moved up the street with the crowd, she ducked down an alley, pressing her hand to her chest. She leaned against the wall, forcing herself to draw slow and even breaths. She knew she needed to calm down. She needed to think clearly. She needed to find transportation.

After a long moment, she poked her head back into the street. People had begun to leave, disappearing into their homes and eateries for the evening. Ellie knew that left her in the open, but she straightened her shoulders and trudged forward anyway. She tried to pretend she was a shopper, looking at the goods that the merchants were beginning to pack away. She kept her eyes peeled for any sign of a stable. She didn't have any money, but with any luck she could wait until dark and steal a mount.

Ellie was so focused on what she needed to do, she didn't see where she was walking. She nearly jumped out of her skin when she collided with a tall young man.

"Oh, sorry!" he said, catching her arms. "I'm so clumsy." He had a satchel swung over his shoulders, no doubt full of goods from the market. Ellie noticed his darkly tanned skin and unusual clothing, including thick riding breeches and thick cloak with a dragon emblem embroidered into it. She knew immediately that he was foreign, but she couldn't place his accent.

Ellie stepped away from him quickly, ducking her head. "It's fine," she murmured, continuing quickly down the street. The last thing she needed was any commotion to bring unwanted attention. She missed the way the man watched her, a frown on his face.

14

The village of Grassmire, Siccita.
The fifteenth day of winter, the 906th year of
the reign of King Paraximus Lamia.
Wednesday, January 4, 2012.

IAM ADJUSTED HIS PACK, WATCHING the girl who
had run into him scurry away. Her pale blonde hair was
unkempt, and her bright blue eyes had been distracted. He
didn't like it. She looked afraid as she walked down the dirt
road, her eyes skirting everywhere.

Liam sighed.

Rian was expecting him back soon with the food he'd
bought, but Liam knew that something was amiss. He turned
slowly, tailing the girl at a distance. She didn't seem to notice
his presence, which he thought was odd, considering her hy-
per-vigilance. She seemed to become more distressed as the
evening darkness dragged on and street-lamps began to flair
to life.

Finally, she stopped at what Liam could see was an inn.
She walked toward the barn where the patrons' mounts were
sheltered for the night. Liam could tell she was trying to

stay in the cover of darkness, but she was bad at it. She was terribly noisy as she pulled the barn door open, trying to sneak inside.

"Hey," Liam called as he walked closer.

She jumped in surprise, fear on her face as she whirled to face him. She reached for the sword at her hip, but her hand was trembling as she struggled to pull it from the scabbard.

"Whoa, easy," Liam said, holding up his hands. "I don't want to hurt you." He offered a reassuring smile. "You look like you need help."

The girl managed to free her sword, but Liam could tell from the way she held it that she didn't know what she was doing. "I don't need help," she said breathlessly, panic in her voice. "Now leave me alone. I can't attract any attention."

"Whose attention?" Liam pressed. He watched her eyes dart around.

"Just go away," she begged.

Liam took a step toward her, wondering what had her so frightened. "Just let me help," he said. "Whatever it is, we can sort it out."

She shook her head, holding her sword in front of her. "I don't want to hurt you, but if you don't go away I'll have no choice."

Liam kept his hands where she could see them, but he didn't back down. "This really isn't necessary—"

"Over there!"

The girl jumped as a yell filled the street. Her eyes were impossibly huge as she looked over Liam's shoulder.

Liam turned quickly, pursing his lips.

Three soldiers were approaching them, their red cloaks catching the lantern light. Their swords were drawn, and Liam knew instantly that they were after this girl.

"I can't go back," she breathed, panic in her voice.

Liam stepped to her quickly, grabbing the sword from her fingers. He was surprised at how light it was, the edge of the blade sparkling as he held it in front of him.

"Surrender the girl to us," one of the soldiers commanded.

Liam maintained a defensive stance. If there was one thing he hated more than Siccitan garbage, it was being bossed around by them. "For what reason?" he demanded. "Has she broken the law?"

The soldiers moved in. "It's no concern of yours," the leader barked. "Hand her over."

Liam smiled grimly. "I'm gonna have to go with no on this one." He surprised the leader when he leapt toward him, swinging the girl's blade.

It was easy to maneuver as he blocked the first's blow, kicking the second away, and using the momentum of the first to throw him into the last soldier. They each tried to regain their footing, but a few solid punches left them on the ground.

Liam turned back to the girl, seeing surprise on her face. He moved toward her quickly and caught her hand. "Come on," he said shortly. "I can get you out of here."

Her hand was still shaking as she held to his tightly, running after him. The night was dark enough to hide them as they clung to the shadows until they reached the edge of the village. Liam didn't let her stop running until they were well away, pulling her into the tall brush and away from the road.

They both were panting hard when they finally stopped. Liam doubled over, his hands on his knees as he tried to catch his breath. He glanced up at the girl when she sank to the ground, sobbing softly.

"It's okay," he said, misinterpreting her tears. "You're safe now."

The girl nodded her head quickly, brushing at her eyes. She looked up at him. "Thank you," she managed. She looked down at the ground as if she wished to say more, but her thoughts were too jumbled.

Liam straightened as he managed to control his breathing. "You're welcome," he said. "Now, time for some answers."

She looked up at him, her eyes afraid again.

"Who the hell are you and why the hell were those thugs after you?"

Her brow furrowed. She seemed like she wasn't sure if she could trust him, but she shifted her eyes over him, drawing a slow breath. "My name is Ellie," she said slowly. "Ellie Atturon. King Paraximus' soldiers kidnapped me and my sister."

Liam frowned at her. "Atturon?" he asked. "Is that supposed to mean something? Why would Paraximus want you?"

Ellie looked down at the ground and shook her head quickly. "No, I shouldn't involve you anymore," she said, gaining some courage as she got to her feet. Heartache furrowed her brow. "People close to me get killed. Just forget I was here." She held her hand out for her sword. "You didn't see me."

Liam huffed sardonically as he handed her the blade. "It's too late for that, sister," he said. "We're both on their list now."

"Just go," Ellie said as she sheathed the sword. "I have to get to Regius Carmen."

Liam arched a brow at her. She must be of importance if Paraximus wanted her and she was trying to get to Liana. "You said they took you and your sister. What about her?"

Pain crossed Ellie's face then. "I made her a promise,"

she whispered, tears crowding her eyes. "I have to get to the Queen Mother. It's the only way I can help her." Ellie knew that Darwren would be on alert. He would have Bailey under lock and key, and maybe even have summoned more of his atrox. If that was the case, there would be no way to get to Bailey without powerful magic ... magic she didn't have.

Liam crossed his arms as he gazed at her, weighing his options. He knew that she would be a burden to take with them on their journey, but did they have a choice? He had just rescued her from certain death and he didn't want to just abandon her in the middle of nowhere. It was clear that she had no idea what she was doing and she'd probably get herself killed or captured before she even reached Ymber. Also, there was whatever this girl was hiding. Something that made her valuable to Paraximus, and maybe even a threat.

He drew a put-out breath, rolling his neck. He knew what had to be done. "You can come with us," he said shortly. "My group and I, we're going to Regius Carmen to see the Queen Mother too."

Ellie's eyes filled with hope. "Are you sure?"

Liam ran his hand through his dark hair, aggravated. "Listen, you have to get Rian's approval, so no promises, but I'll take you to see him."

Ellie nodded quickly. "Yes, okay," she said, relief in her voice.

Liam was sure that Rian would have his hide, but there was nothing he could do now. They were stuck with this girl, for better or worse.

Celo Cavus, the capitol city of Siccita.
The fifteenth day of winter, the 906th year of
the reign of King Paraximus Lamia.
Wednesday, January 4, 2012.

HE Siccitan air was hot as it blew over the walls surrounding the outer courtyard. Mist from the massive waterfall that Celo Cavus sat below was thick in the air, making it moist and humid. Hessa's wings stirred the mist, making rainbows swirl around them in the light of the moons. The beauty of the night belied the dangerousness of Savra's arrival.

To the south of the wall, the sprawling city slept, lantern lights fading out for the night, unaware of the monstrosities that hid just beyond the castle walls. The Siccitan wildflowers and trees that grew in the outer courtyard were enough to convey the utopia that Celo Cavus had once been, but Savra knew better. She knew the cruelties that were committed daily, in the bowels of the castle where they could be hidden.

Savra eased from Hessa's back, phantom pain causing

her to look down at her missing arm. It had been many years since she'd had Hessa bound to her, but the magic still took a toll on her body. It was worse now as Savra thought about the bitterness that was filling her.

Hessa had been mortally wounded the day that Jet was captured by Liana. Unable to help her lover, she'd done the next best thing and tried to save Hessa. Savra knew that Hessa was the only thing he loved unconditionally, and she knew that she needed to keep the black dragon alive. She didn't think it would be possible, and she did the best she could for several days, trying to nurse Hessa back from the brink of death.

But nothing worked. Even the Royal Dragon Master said that she couldn't be saved. Hessa's heart was broken, he claimed. She didn't want to live anymore. It was then that Savra learned the strength of the bond between rider and beast.

Savra turned her navy-blue eyes on Hessa then, watching as she lowered her head in submission. "I'm sorry, Hessa," she said softly. "I wish I didn't have to do this to you."

Hessa's body began to dissolve, melting into a thick tar-like liquid that swirled toward the end of Savra's elbow. Pain coursed through her as the dragon's magic latched onto her bones, digging into her much like she imagined ivy dug into stone. The dragon magic burned in her veins, but it was only temporary. Savra flexed her clawed and scaled fingers, trying to ease away the ache of the binding magic. She used to feel guilty for doing this to Hessa, forcing her to continue to live this way, but now she only felt rage.

She would use Hessa's magic to kill Jet and his princess. After that, there would be no need to keep Hessa bound to the living world, and Savra would let her soul finally rest.

The night was silent, save for the gentle roar of the waterfall, and it put Savra on edge. She walked slowly toward the steps that led to the entry way of the castle. It swept up into massive, tiered arches as she stepped inside, guards posted silently at the doors. They were like decorations, seen and never heard.

Massive tapestries and banners decorated the main entry, as well as paintings and artifacts that looked priceless. Most of these things had been looted from castles and temples that had fallen to King Paraximus' hand. He displayed them more as a statement than because of their beauty; he took what belonged to more powerful civilizations, and he'd take whatever anyone else had, too. Many ambassadors left Celo Cavus knowing there was no hope for their kingdoms.

The entry way opened to her left into a grand ballroom, which was dark and empty. Balls and celebrations were not often, and they were lavish and scandalous when they did take place. Again, they were a show of power, a way for the king to display the cultures that he'd taken. These displays would last for days, with Paraximus' courtiers and other nobles enjoying their spoils. Everyone wanted to be part of the celebration, and no one wanted to be on the receiving end of his wrath.

Savra realized her nails were digging into her skin, and she unclenched her fists as she reached the royal throne room. A huge door stood between her and her king, but it didn't offer her any comfort. She knew he was expecting her. She knew she wouldn't escape his fury. Slowly, she placed her scaled hand against the door, pushing it inward.

The throne room was empty, void of any of the usual faces that hung around the castle. Savra knew it was because of the time. It was late, and most were asleep at this hour. The sconces around the room were still lit, however, lending light from one end of the room to the other. Savra dreaded the long walk from the door to the dais. She clenched her jaw tightly as she looked up, seeing Paraximus sitting on his throne.

His face was smooth, a hard set to his jaw that was characteristic. He didn't betray any emotion or thought as she came closer. His dark eyes followed her, his dark hair tied back from his face. A ring sparkled on his right hand in the light, a crest worn and faded on it. Savra was always intrigued by the fact that it was the only jewelry he wore; he had so much wealth and gold and things he'd stolen, certainly there would be something he'd choose. But he'd always been a simple man, tall and strong and powerful.

Savra moved to her knees as she came to the bottom of the dais. She pressed her fist over her heart. "My king," she said, bowing her head.

"Savra." His voice resonated in the empty room, a dangerous edge to it.

She didn't dare look up, knowing that he would kill her just as soon as he would hear her out.

"Have I wasted the power of the *drac'duni* on you?"

Savra's eyes shifted down to her clawed hand, and she shook her head. "No, my king," she said quickly.

"Then *why* have you not done as I asked?"

Savra glanced up then, flinching at the anger in his voice. Her first instinct was to prepare to save her own life, but she knew if he so desired her blood, he would take it. She forced herself to keep her eyes downcast. "It is my fault," she said. "I was not prepared to face Jet." She hadn't expected to still feel so strongly about him, but he'd made his choice, and it wasn't her. She looked up then, feeling anger pulsing through her. "But you will have what you desire."

Paraximus was standing over her. He titled his head, strands of his long hair falling over his shoulder. A thick, red mantle hung across his shoulders, covering black *stuba* clothing. The leather was pressed with the Siccitan crest. He was a striking and terrifying figure as he looked down at her, his face creasing slightly with his impatience.

"How can I believe that, Savra?" he demanded. "Jet should have been easy for you, with the power of the dragon. Have I chosen poorly?"

Savra shook her head. "No, my king," she said, hearing the anxiety in her voice. "I will kill Jet, and I will bring you the princess." She clenched her hands. "Or I will die trying to serve you."

Paraximus didn't seem placated by her answer. His frown was becoming more prominent. "I have heard these words from you once already," he snapped. "I will not hear them another time."

Savra bowed her head. "Of course, my king." She glanced up fearfully when she heard him step toward her.

His face softened, something akin to compassion sweeping his features. "My dear Savra," he said, catching her chin in his hand. "You must not let your heartache drive your actions. Jet will never return here by his own will. He will never come back to you."

Savra held his gaze, fear coursing through her. Her heart was beating double-time. His touch made her blood run cold. He could snap her neck at any moment, and she would be helpless.

Paraximus brushed her navy hair away from her eyes, enjoying the fear he saw in them. "Channel your rage and your hatred," he said. "Remember, Jet abandoned us all." His face hardened, his next words pointed and dangerous. "He is a traitor, and you are his executioner."

Savra tried to hide the shaking breath she drew when he released her. "Nothing would make me happier than to bathe in his blood," she said.

Paraximus nodded, turning to walk back to his throne. He settled in the chair, motioning with his fingers. "Now go," he said, his voice deceptively gentle. His eyes were boring into her. "If you fail me again, the only blood spilled will be yours."

Savra nodded, moving to her feet and bowing. She couldn't get out of the throne room fast enough, feeling the weight of his threat sitting on her heavily. He didn't make those comments idly, and he would be delighted to slaughter her in whatever manner he saw fit.

Once she reached the entry way, she quickened her pace to the galley. She needed to refuel and get herself together again. This time she wouldn't fail.

16

*Meeting House of the Anemoi, The Plains of
Pacier, Ymber.
The fifteenth day of winter, the 851st year of
the reign of Queen Liana Estrella.
Wednesday, January 4, 2012.*

KADIRA KEPT HER EYES DOWNCAST. She stood in the presence of the elders, who were bickering back and forth between themselves. A tall man stood beside her, his thick, muscular arms crossed. Bright tattoos wound across his ebony skin, and a deep blue cloak was slung across his shoulders. When he shifted, beads rattled against his broad chest, brushing against the agrestis-skin clothing he wore. His normally gentle and handsome face was set in a scowl.

The man she had brought back had finally awoken. The healer wasn't sure he would survive, but he had, against the odds. The Khanh had let him stay because he was on the edge of death, but now there was much bickering about what his fate would be. And about the dragons.

Kadira felt terrible, and she stole a glance at the village leader beside her. She didn't want to put anyone in this position, but she didn't want the man to die, either. She knew she'd done the right thing, even if her clan couldn't see it.

"Kadira, what say you?"

Kadira's eyes widened at the Khanh's harshly-spoken words. He turned to look at her, his squared jaw still stuck in a scowl. "Forgive me, Khanh," she said, bowing her head, "but the goddess did not put us on this earth to turn away from anyone in need."

The Khanh's scowl deepened. His bright blue eyes were not angry, but deeply unhappy. "We do not deal with outsiders, Kadira," he said shortly. "We have become responsible for this man's life."

Kadira felt desperation seep through her. "I've sat at his bedside every day since he came here," she said quickly. "I sense no evil in this man." She turned to face the accusing eyes of the elders. "We must allow him to gain his strength." She looked back to the Khanh. "Then I will personally see him from our village."

The elders murmured more, the Khanh turning to listen to them. Kadira could tell her words were softening him. Finally, he held up his hands, defeat on his face.

"Enough," he said. He looked at Kadira. "I will grant you this, Kadira." He placed a hand on her shoulder. "But you are responsible for this man's actions and whatever consequences this may have."

Kadira nodded her head, relief making her heart skip a beat. "Thank you," she said, bowing her head. Once the meeting was dismissed, she turned to leave the meeting room as well, but the Khanh stopped her.

"Kadira?" he called.

She paused, looking over her shoulder at him.

He sighed as he held her gaze. "You know how the elders will talk. They will say I am too soft with you because you are my bride."

Kadira nodded quickly. She forced a small grin. "Is that not why you are lenient with me, Rais?"

Rais pressed his lips together. It was rare for anyone to call him by his name instead of his title, but he found it endearing when it came from her. "I try not to be," he said seriously. "I can't let them think that I make biased decisions."

Kadira nodded seriously. "I know, Raisy," she said, using his pet name from when they were children. She watched his eyes soften. "I appreciate you taking this chance for me."

Rais nodded and looked away as if to hide the effect she had on him. "How is he, anyway?" he asked.

"He doesn't know where he is," Kadira said, crossing her arms. "But he should be strong enough to go on in a few days. His dragons have kept a loyal post since we found him."

Rais's brow furrowed. "Do you think he poses a threat to us?"

Kadira shook her head, seeming appalled. "Of course not," she said quickly. She wanted to say more, but caught herself. She knew what he was thinking from the look on his face.

"We can't be too careful, Kadira," he said solemnly. He walked toward her, catching her hand. "You know this."

Kadira nodded, leaning into his touch as he smoothed a rogue hair from her face. "Once he is well enough, I will send him on his way." Despite the stranger's arrival, her mind had still been on the upcoming wedding celebration. Gazing into his eyes made her heart flutter.

Rais nodded, placing a chaste kiss on the end of her nose. "Good."

Pain was crawling across Raphael's body like insects to a feast. It was the worst in his chest, which was wrapped with thick strips of cloth. Whatever the healer had applied to his wounds made them numb, but it didn't stop the rest of him from feeling run over by an agrestis. He could feel the grimace that seemed permanently etched into his face as he stared at the thatched ceiling of the hut.

Beyond the woven-reed door, he could hear muffled voices. He couldn't make out the words, knowing they were in the language of the tribe anyway. He looked toward the door when the voices drifted away, feeling the cold air gust in as it was pulled to the side. He watched as a tall, dark-skinned woman walked toward him, her deep blue eyes swirling with concern and reserve. Her hand-made clothing smelled of livestock and wood-fire smoke as she knelt near his bed.

"I'm glad to see you are awake," she said, her Sarotian thickly accented.

Raphael nodded, feeling uncertain. "Yes, thank you for your care," he said, his voice hoarse. He had vague memories of this woman and another with thick, curly brown hair and the same dark complexion, but it felt like something that happened in another lifetime. "Where am I?"

"I am Kadira," she said, tendrils of bright blue hair falling around her face. "You are with the Anemoi."

Raphael frowned. The Anemoi tended to stay closer to the coast and Paries' Wall. "Why are you so far in-land?"

Kadira drew a slow breath, smiling thinly. "We follow the herd during the winter," she said, as if it was obvious. "They bring us here."

"Hn." Raphael leaned his head back against the soft blanket underneath him. "I need to leave soon." He looked over at Kadira, feeling his stomach twist. "Your chief will let me leave, yes?" The Caelin tribes were notorious for hating outsiders, some going so far as to kill trespassers. And he needed to get to his sisters.

Kadira arched a brow, her brown eyes amused. "Do you tire of our hospitality?"

Raphael shook his head absently, worry flooding him. "No, of course not," he said quickly. "But I need to go." He winced as he tried to sit forward. "I need to find my sisters."

Kadira rose to her feet then, pressing her hand against his shoulder. "You are in no condition to leave," she said sternly. She watched his eyes turn away, distress on his face. "Tell me your name."

Raphael glanced at her. "Raphael," he said quietly. "Raphael Atturon."

Kadira frowned at him. "Well Raphael At-tur-on, you need more time to heal," she said. "The Khanh will be happy to see you go once you are strong enough."

"The Khanh?" Raphael asked.

Kadira nodded. "Our leader, Khanh Rais," she clarified.

Raphael nodded. He could feel a pit forming in his stomach. At least they planned to let him leave. But, he feared, by then it would be too late.

"You should rest," Kadira said, seeing the way his face twisted with pain. She reached for a wooden cup on the table near the bed, pouring liquid from a clay pot. "Drink. It will help you sleep."

Raphael took a sip of the steaming liquid as she held the cup to his lips. It was bitter but warm as it went down his throat. He closed his eyes as Kadira put the cup down, trying not to think about his sisters. If Paraximus wanted them so badly, then they had to still be alive. And once he was well enough to go, he would find them and bring them home.

17

The outskirts of Grassmire, Siccita.
The fifteenth day of winter, the 906th year of
the reign of King Paraximus Lamia.
Thursday, January 5, 2012.

BAILEY'S BREATHS WERE SHORT AND ragged as she leaned forward, blood dripping from her mouth. She could hear Darwren's hard, angry footsteps as he crossed the wooden floor of the empty barn.

"Don't let her out of your sight!" he barked to a nearby soldier. He turned his attention to his men outside. "You! Find the other one!"

Bailey groaned softly as she let her head loll to the side. The side of her face was throbbing from the force of his blow. She pressed her tongue against the inside of her lip, feeling where it had split against her teeth. She tried to use the back of her hand to wipe her mouth, but both hands were bound together tightly, with ugly red bruises forming against her pale skin.

Bailey knew that Darwren and his toadies would be for-midable, but they'd taken a bit more of a beating from her than she expected. She guessed it had something to do with the order that she and her sister weren't to be harmed, but she knew that Darwren was resenting that now. She stole a glance up at the guard standing over her, a smirk coming to her lips.

"That's quite a shiner there," she said quietly, watching the guard's eyes shift to her, one of them nearly swollen shut. He scowled darkly but otherwise didn't react. It made her happy, despite her situation.

Morning light was beginning to shine through the broken slats of the abandoned barn. Darwren had moved her here, away from town and away from any watchers once he'd had her under control. Thankfully, Ellie had gotten away. Darwren's soldiers hadn't turned up any information on her, other than she'd managed to evade some of his men. From what Bailey could discern, a couple of his lackeys had been found with nasty bumps on their heads.

She drew a slow breath, tasting dust on her tongue. She could see it swirling in the air, caught in the beams of light. She knew Ellie had found help. There's no way she could have escaped otherwise, but that was okay with Bailey. Knowing her sister was safe and alive, that was all that mattered. It would help her endure Darwren's cruelties and whatever else was in store for her.

18

The outskirts of Grassmire, Siccita.
The fifteenth day of winter, the 906th year of
the reign of King Paraximus Lamia.
Thursday, January 5, 2012.

To SAY RIAN HAD BEEN unhappy to see Liam with a guest would be an understatement. He'd wanted to kick Liam's ass, but one look into the girl's frightened blue eyes and Rian knew that Liam had done the right thing, despite his better judgement.

It was now dawn, and Rian stood beside his red dragon, Raimi, at the crest of a hill that overlooked the township of Grassmire. Behind him, dark against the morning sky, rose Paries' Wall, two stark watch towers called the *Custos Obduros* jutting from it. It was the main entry into Ymber from Siccita, and heavily guarded, with men stationed at the gate and in the towers, prepared to shoot down any invaders. They planned to skirt the towers to the east and fly straight toward the mountains where Regius Carmen was hidden.

"You look troubled."

Rian turned to look over his shoulder at Zaida. Her ra-

ven hair was catching the morning rays, her pale skin seeming paler than normal. Her eyes were steady and unwavering as she gazed at him.

Raimi shifted beside Rian, turning her head to Zaida for a nose rub. She purred lightly as Zaida used the heel of her palm across Raimi's face. Rian could feel the heat of her body as she pressed her shoulder against him, trying to move closer to Zaida. It had taken Raimi a long time to warm up to the other Pangere members, but not Zaida. Raimi loved Zaida in a way that was unusual for a dragon.

"I don't know about this girl," Rian said, pressing his hand against Raimi's side. Her scales were smooth and warm, like river stones that had sat in the sun all day.

"I don't sense anything foul about her," Zaida said, absently rubbing Raimi's face still.

"That doesn't mean she won't be a burden," Rian said tersely. He sighed as he glanced once more toward Paries' Wall. "There is much distance to cover before we reach Regius Carmen."

Zaida dropped her hand and turned to follow his gaze. "There's more to her story than she's told us," she said. "Why would Paraximus want two little girls?"

Rian looked to her and arched his brow. "That's the question, isn't it?"

Ellie was exhausted. She hadn't slept a wink, despite being nestled between a fire and a large green dragon. She had lain awake all night, staring at the sky, trying to keep her fear at bay. What was happening to her sister? Was she okay?

Movement near her caught her eye, and she lifted her head from the woven mat that she was lying on. Liam sat up from the green dragon's embrace, his dark hair tousled. The dragon stretched her front paws, yawning deeply before turning to blow hot, acrid breath across her charge's face. Ellie watched as he grinned at his mount, petting her nose gently, whispering soft words to her. She was close enough that she could hear the dragon purring deep in her chest.

Liam shifted his eyes to Ellie then, seeing her watching him. He pushed himself to his feet, his dragon uncurling her tail from around him. "Good morning," he said lightly.

Ellie nodded mutely, sitting up as he came to kneel by the embers of the fire.

"How did you sleep?" he asked.

Ellie shook her head as she watched the beams of morning light glint on his hair. His suntanned skin looked darker than it had the day before in the waning light. "I couldn't sleep," she said hoarsely.

Liam frowned lightly as he looked at the fire. "You thinkin' of your sister?"

Ellie nodded. She could feel her stomach twisting into a knot, but she knew there was nothing she could do. Somehow, that didn't help. It just made the knot worse. Ellie looked up sharply when Liam suddenly stood, turning to look over his shoulder.

A tall woman with pale skin and dark hair walked into the clearing, the sandy-haired leader trailing behind her. Her dark brown eyes landed on Ellie, pinning her with a gaze that she knew wasn't good. She crossed her arms in front of her thick leather chest-piece, which had a dragon etched across it in a manner similar to the others.

"What's with the sour face, Zaida?" Liam asked, a grin pulling at his lips. "The sun hasn't been up long enough for you to be so irate."

Zaida narrowed her dark eyes at him, her lips pressing even thinner. "I have some questions for your new friend," she said, walking toward Ellie.

Ellie felt her heart drop into her feet. Despite her nervousness, she held Zaida's gaze as she approached. "What do you want to know?" she asked, her voice stronger than she expected it to be.

"Where did you come from again?" Zaida asked, eying her carefully.

"I'm from Sorona," Ellie said. She motioned toward the north. "A province in Ymber."

"And how did you get on this side of the wall?" the leader suddenly asked, his brow furrowed. "Ymberians wouldn't come here to Siccita."

"I was taken," Ellie said, repeating what she'd told them last night. "Paraximus sent his soldiers to take me and my sister."

Rian was still frowning. "How did they even get across the wall?" he asked, shaking his head. "Your story makes no sense."

Ellie felt desperate suddenly. "I know it's hard to believe, but it's true," she said, afraid they would leave without her. "Somehow, Paraximus can summon portals. That's how he was able to take us and get us across without anyone noticing."

Rian crossed his arms then, lifting his chin. "And why would he want you?" he asked, an edge to his voice. His eyes skirted over her. "You're just a little girl."

Ellie scowled at him. "I'm an Atturon," she snapped. "My family has been the keeper of powerful magic for eons."

Rian was still doubtful. "What power is that?"

Ellie crossed her arms, digging her nails into her skin. "The Visus."

Rian shook his head, glancing at Zaida. "Visus?" he asked.

"Sight," a voice suddenly called behind them.

Ellie turned her eyes quickly over Zaida's shoulder, surprised to see another woman stepping into the clearing. Her hair was in a thick plait down her back, a surprising shade of pink. Her eyes were a deep brown like Zaida's, though. Under her arm was a silver helmet with a blue plume, her cloak the same color. Ellie hadn't seen her before.

"Where have you been, Amaya?" Zaida suddenly demanded.

Amaya shrugged, her blue dragon lingering on the edge of the tree line. "I wanted to scout ahead," she said easily.

Rian scowled darkly at her then. "You could have been spotted," he barked at her, anger on his face.

Amaya raised her hands in an apologetic gesture. She pulled a bag from around her shoulders. "I brought breakfast," she said, as if that made her rogue actions better.

Ellie watched as Rian pressed his hand to his face, sighing shortly. She was surprised to see that Amaya had found giant *pom-moms*. They were ripe and bright orange, making a satisfying crunch when Liam bit into his. When Amaya's eyes landed on Ellie, she froze.

"Who's this?"

Zaida sighed, put out. "Ellie Atturon," she said shortly. "She was just telling us why Paraximus kidnapped her and her sister."

Amaya's eyes grew large suddenly. "You're an Atturon, huh?" she said, excitement in her voice. She suddenly skipped toward Ellie, grabbing her hand. "You can see futures, right?" She grinned broadly. "Do me! I want to know if I'll marry a rich lord."

Ellie stared at Amaya stupidly, wondering how she even knew about her family. "I—I'm sorry," she said slowly, feeling her cheeks flush. "I can't control it."

"So you're a Seer?" Rian said, drawing her gaze.

"Duh," Amaya said, rolling her eyes at Rian. "You're never heard of the Atturon family and the Visus?"

Rian shook his head. He didn't realize that Zaida's brainless and gossipy cousin was so well-read.

"I can't control it," Ellie said again, looking at Rian. "Paraximus took me and my sister because he wants to use the Visus." She shrugged helplessly. "But we were never trained to use it. We can't control what we see or when."

Rian's face grew solemn as he looked at Zaida. Some silent communication passed between them, because Zaida turned away, walking toward her black dragon. "I guess that settles it, then," Rian said, looking between Liam and Amaya. "Prepare to ride out."

Ellie turned to look at Liam as he kicked dirt over the fire to extinguish it. He caught her eye as he walked toward the green dragon. "Guess you're with us," he said, swinging a saddle across her shimmering scales.

Ellie walked toward the dragon, seeing her turn her head, blowing hot air across Ellie's hands, scenting her. "What's her name?" she asked, looking at Liam.

"Emma," he said with a small smile. "She's my girl."

Ellie looked at the green dragon again, realizing she was pressing her nose into Ellie's hands. "Hi Emma," she whispered, petting her softly. "I hope you don't mind me being along for the ride."

Emma surprised her when she stepped toward her, her sticky tongue peeking out to lick Ellie's hands. Again, the rumbling purr filled Emma's chest.

"She likes you," Liam said as he strapped his bedroll and other bags to her back.

Ellie nodded, feeling a genuine flicker of happiness in her chest. She waited for him to strap on his heavy armor, much like the others. He plunked his silver helmet, complete with a nice green plume, on his head before swinging onto Emma's back. He offered Ellie a hand once he was astride.

"Hold on!" he said as Emma lurched into the sky.

Ellie glanced over his shoulder, seeing Rian's bright red dragon spiraling higher into the clouds, Zaida's black dragon and Amaya's blue dragon joining them. The morning air was moist as the group banked away from the sun and toward the bay, the only noise the sound of rushing wind and beating dragon wings.

19

The village of Festra, Abjure Forest, Ymber.
The seventeenth day of winter, the 851st year
of the reign of Queen Liana Estrella.
Friday, January 6, 2012.

THE HOUSE WAS SILENT. MELINDA had gone out with her father to tend to a neighbor's wife and child, and Jet had disappeared off to somewhere without any indication of when he would return. Before she left, Melinda had handed Nyx a children's book. She could feel frustration welling inside her as she looked at the words and the hand-drawn pictures.

Melinda had been an absolute angel, helping Nyx learn Sarotian. Unfortunately, it was not as intuitive as Nyx had hoped it would be, and it made looking at the words on paper more difficult that just saying them out loud. Despite it being for children, Nyx couldn't figure out what the book was even about. She'd been staring at it and the pictures for a long time, practically since Melinda and her father left. She sighed shortly, blinking her tired eyes and setting the book down on the table.

Nyx needed a break. She got to her feet and crossed to the hearth, letting the fire inside warm her hands. Despite how small it was, the cabin was still a bit drafty, and Nyx was unused to the Gexalatian winter. The trees caught most of the snow, but they didn't do much to keep the biting wind away.

Nyx could feel her mind drifting as she stared absently into the soft glow of the hearth. She hadn't had much alone time since coming to Gexalatia. Stabbing loneliness caught up with her as she stood there. Her mind turned to her home in Lucky; what was going on there? How were Anna and Seth? How was the farm? And her aunt...

Tears filled her eyes. She hadn't had time to mourn her aunt. So much had happened in such a short period of time. But it didn't keep the pain away. Her tears came harder and more violently as she stood there, thinking about Dorothea.

It was so hard to imagine that she was gone, just like that. Nyx remembered the harsh words she'd spoken to her, and regret filled her along with the grief. She wished she'd never been mad at her aunt, but she was glad that their last interactions hadn't been on bad terms. She was glad that she'd told Dorothea that she loved her.

She shook her head after a while, trying to keep her mind from questions that she didn't want the answers to. She'd seen enough violence, and her mind sometimes supplied her with the bloody kitchen. It was something she wished she could erase, but it seemed to dig in harder when she tried to forget. She didn't want to think about the pain her aunt must have experienced, or whether she was tortured before she died, or if her death was slow. But her mind liked to mess with her, making bile rise in her throat.

Nyx stepped away from the hearth, grabbing her coat and pulling around her shoulders. She knew she was going to be sick, and she yanked the front door open, staggering out into the cold winter air. Her stomach turned, and she didn't try to stop it. Tears and vomit mixed on the ground, making her feel pathetic. She was glad no one was there to see her like this. After a few more moments of dry heaves, she straightened, pulling her hair away from her face.

She sank slowly onto the steps to the house, feeling empty inside. She leaned back, letting her head rest on the top step, so that she was staring at the canopy of trees overhead. It was quite beautiful, she realized, with rays of sunlight piercing through the bright blue of the leaves. Every so often, birds and small creatures would flit from one branch to the next, their soft calls echoing gently.

The time slipped away from her as she laid there, staring at the sky between the leaves. The sun was different here, shifting in an opposite and lower pattern than she was used to. She couldn't tell what time it really was as the sun moved from west to east. She could have been sitting there for hours or for minutes. Thankfully, her mind was empty and silent.

"Nyx?"

She blinked then, lifting her head to see Melinda and her father standing on the path. She sat up quickly, wiping at her face. She didn't realize how cold her fingers were as she did so. "Hey," she said quickly, hoping she didn't look as haggard as she felt. "How was everything?"

"Mika's wife and baby will be fine," Branimir said as he took a step closer. His eyes creased as he looked her over. "You look ill."

Nyx shook her head. "Just tired," she said, offering a small smile. She looked to Melinda, hoping to change the subject. "I couldn't read the book you gave me."

Melinda smiled, her curls bouncing around her face as she shook her head. "That's okay," she said quickly. "I just wanted you to try." She walked closer, holding her hand out to Nyx. "Come on, I'll help you."

Nyx caught her hand and let Melinda pull her up. The girls followed Melinda's father into the house. Nyx realized that it was indeed much warmer than the outside air, the heat almost stifling on her cold skin. She watched Branimir begin to put his things away into a small closet, while Melinda began to flit about to prepare dinner.

"Bring the book," Melinda said over her shoulder. "I can cook and teach at the same time."

Nyx returned Melinda's little grin, picking up the book and easing to sit on a stool next to the hearth. She cracked the cover open, admiring the pictures once again. They were quite beautiful, clearly hand-drawn and colored. "Where did this come from?" she asked, glancing at her friend.

Melinda looked over at her. "My mother," she said, reserve in her voice. "She made it for me."

Nyx felt her brow rise in surprise. "Oh," she said, feeling a newfound appreciation for the book. She let her fingers drift over the artwork. "She drew this?"

Melinda nodded as she stirred her pot. "She was a very talented artist," she said softly. "But we were very poor and couldn't really afford paints and canvas." She frowned lightly, something that Nyx rarely saw her do. "Whatever she was able to get, she used to make this for me."

Nyx stared down at the book, noting the care of the brush strokes. Despite the color being faded, the pictures were still filled with bright blues and oranges and yellows. All happy colors for a child to delight over. A stab of grief filled Nyx. She would never have anything like this from her time as a child. They'd had to flee so quickly, she'd only had the necessities Jet had grabbed for her.

"But anyway," Melinda said, breaking the silence, "try

reading the first page to me."

Nyx pressed her lips together tightly. She drew a short breath as she looked over the words, feeling cajoled by them. She stumbled through the first page, grateful for Melinda's gentle coaching with words she was unfamiliar with. She was surprised to realize that the book was about a butterfly princess who had been taken by an evil caterpillar before being rescued by a beautiful butterfly prince.

As Nyx reached the final page, a beautiful castle on hill with a sunrise behind it, two butterflies dancing in the breeze, she realized that she felt more like herself again. The tension that had sat in her shoulders had eased, and the aching blackness of her grief had released her, allowing her to breathe more easily. It felt like opening the window to let sunlight in again.

"Well?" Melinda asked, sitting on another stool across from Nyx. The pot was sitting over the hearth, warming. "What did you think?"

Nyx nodded, offering a genuine smile. "I liked it," she said. "It helps to have you instructing me though."

Melinda's grin widened, and she scooted her stool a bit closer. "Listen," she said, sudden nervousness coming over her. "Remember after the first night of *Cael Hiems* when I told you about the *Agita Nocturna*?"

Nyx nodded, realization dawning on her. "That's tonight, isn't it?" Nyx suddenly remembered Melinda baking sweet rolls the day before, stashing them in a large jar so that they wouldn't get eaten.

Melinda nodded. "I thought you might want to go," she said excitedly.

Nyx felt surprise fill her. "Do you think it's safe?" she asked quietly. "I'm still not sure I can talk to anyone."

Melinda waved her hand quickly. "Nonsense," she said.

"You're doing great."

Nyx looked down at her hands, realizing she had nothing to wear. "I don't even have a dress," she said.

Melinda caught her hand and pulled her after her. "I have just the thing."

Nyx followed her into the bedroom, watching as she pulled open a chest, lifting a dress from it. She smiled up at Nyx, holding up the thick fabric. "What do you think of my new dress?"

Nyx reached slowly for the dress, seeing that it was made of several different patterns. The body of the dress was a rich blue, while the skirt was a yellow, happy paisley. Thick, white fur circled the collar. Nyx knew it must have been a gift Branimir had been given in exchange for medical care.

"It's great," Nyx said, seeing Melinda's face light up. "You made it yourself, right?" She ran her hands across the fur, feeling how soft it was.

Melinda nodded. "I've been working on it all week," she said happily.

Nyx offered her a smile. "It's beautiful." She and Jet had been training all week, so she'd barely noticed whatever Melinda had been doing, between being gone and being too tired to function.

Melinda was positively beaming as she talked about where the fur had come from and that she had saved her money for many months to be able to afford the fabric. She paused after a moment though, seeing the distracted look on Nyx's face.

"Are you worried about what Jet said?" she asked.

Nyx blinked, surprised. "I didn't think you heard that," she said, feeling embarrassed suddenly.

Part of the reason Jet had stormed out this morning was because Nyx had made the mistake of telling him she liked it here in Festra. Of course, he totally blew up, telling her that they couldn't stay and she couldn't get attached. He'd made sure to throw in some mean things about her aunt, and that had set off her mood for the day. He definitely knew how to hurt her in the worst ways; ways that weren't physical and left lasting scars.

Melinda gave her a knowing look. "This house is too small for secrets," she said, smiling sympathetically.

Nyx looked down at the ground, more embarrassed. "I guess so," she said. She sank down onto the bed beside Melinda, feeling defeated. "I just wanted to experience part of this place." She let her eyes drift out the window, somber. "With all the things we've been through, I just want happy memories to take with me."

Melinda's face softened. She couldn't imagine what Nyx must be feeling. She reached out to take her new friend's hand, squeezing it tightly. "Well, I have something for tonight that you'll like."

Nyx perked up, watching as Melinda began to dig through the trunk again.

"What else is in there?" Nyx asked, leaning forward as Melinda knelt on the floor.

Melinda looked up at her, grinning slightly. "This is where I keep my treasures."

Nyx watched as she lifted a partition inside the trunk, revealing a cache of things. She leaned over the top, seeing a variety of knick-knacks and a thick leather book. Curiosity got the better of her as Melinda pulled a white garment from the bottom. Once it was free, Melinda stood, letting it uncurl down her front. Nyx realized it was a dress.

It was thick, white fabric, sewn into gentle puffs. It had sleeves that came down to the elbows and a thick, puffy collar. Despite the thickness of the fabric, it still fell in gentle, flowing waves. Gold-brown stripes ran around the middle and the bottom of the dress. It had a lace-up corset sewn into it. It was obviously sewn with much care and well-loved.

"What do you think?" Melinda asked, her eyes excited.

"It's beautiful," Nyx said, confusion furrowing her brow. It was clearly too small for Melinda and Nyx wondered where it came from. Melinda was a bit too tall and a little bigger in the bust.

Melinda's grin widened. "Why don't you wear it for the festival?"

Nyx felt her confusion fade slightly, her spirits lifting. "Are you sure?" she asked.

Melinda nodded. She looked down, running her hands across it. "It's time it was worn again."

Nyx reached for the soft puffs, admiring the work. After watching her aunt sew for so many years, she could appreciate the effort. "Is it one of your old ones?" she asked. She took it when Melinda offered it to her, gesturing for her to look in the mirror.

She watched as Nyx held it to her front, a surge of emotion overtaking her. "This was the dress my mother made for her first festival."

Nyx caught the slight hitch in her voice and she looked up at her friend in the mirror. The immense value suddenly hit her, and she turned quickly to Melinda. "Oh no," she said, holding it out to her. "I couldn't wear your mother's dress."

Despite the way her eyes were welling with tears, Melinda smiled. "Of course you can," she said. "You're just about her size. It's a perfect fit."

Nyx wasn't sure what to say as she looked down at the dress in her hands. With the loss of her aunt still so fresh in her mind, she couldn't even begin to imagine wanting to allow anyone to touch her things. Tears began to crowd her eyes as well, and she laughed as she wiped them away. "Look at us," she said, more small laughs escaping her with her tears. "Crying like this."

Melinda laughed too. "We shouldn't be sad that they're gone," she said. "We should be happy they were here."

Nyx nodded, Melinda's words a comfort to her broken heart. "Thank you," she said, blinking the tears away. She didn't want to cry. "This means the world to me."

Melinda smiled broadly, suddenly hugging her. Silent thoughts passed between them as they embraced, and Nyx felt comfort like she hadn't since she left her old life behind. When Melinda released her, she was still smiling, her excitement mounting as she crossed to pick up her blue dress.

"We're going to be the best dressed ladies at the festival," she said, holding up her dress next to Nyx in the mirror.

Nyx looked to her friend, sharing in her excitement. "I can't wait," she said. "Tell me what it will be like."

Melinda giggled, catching her hands and leading her to sit on the side of her bed. Nyx knew that she would always be grateful for Melinda and her father as she listened to Melinda talk about the ceremony and the dancing and the food. She wished she didn't have to leave this small village, but she knew that wasn't her destiny. She had to return to Regius Carmen, but a fun night wouldn't hurt.

The sun had set some time ago, but an air of excitement filled the Laxman residence. The girls were flitting about, getting ready for the festivities. Branimir was sitting at the table, a thin pair of glasses perched precariously on his nose. He shifted grey eyes to look toward the bedroom at the sound of giggling. He sighed deeply, a small smile pulling at his lips. It was nice to hear the girls' laughter. He turned the page of the book he was reading absently.

"Alright, Daddy, we're going."

Branimir looked up over the top of his glasses, standing slowly. "You two look amazing," he said, smiling under his beard. He crossed toward them, catching their hands and spinning them around. "Let me take a look."

Both Nyx and Melinda giggled again. Melinda was wearing her new dress, her hair done in looping curls around her face. A silver barrette held a swoop of hair away from her face, while a light splash of makeup made her cheeks rosy. Nyx was wearing Carmin's white dress, her golden hair plaited away from her face, delicate tendrils falling around her ears. A silver butterfly pin had been tucked into her braid.

"What's the matter, Daddy?" Melinda asked suddenly.

Branimir blinked, realizing there were tears in his eyes. He caught their chins gently in his hands, looking between them. "You both look very beautiful," he said. He looked to Melinda. "Very fine young women that I'm proud to know."

Melinda hugged him tightly and Nyx felt a lump form in her throat. She was surprised when Branimir held out his arm for her to join them, and she did, feeling love all around her. The feeling of belonging made tears prick at her eyes as well.

"Now then, you need to get going," Branimir said, clearing his throat and stepping back. "Don't want to be late."

Melinda nodded, crossing to pick up her jar of desserts. She and Nyx pulled cloaks on at the door, talking quietly to each other in excited voices as they skipped out into the night. Branimir stood in the doorway, trying to catch his breath and calm his pounding heart. It was wonderful to see Melinda spending time with someone other than him, and he'd come to care for Nyx like another daughter. She was so kind and sweet, and the brightness of her soul shone in whatever she did. His and Melinda's lives were richer now because of her. Branimir knew he would be sad to see her leave, but Melinda would be devastated.

Nyx walked in step with Melinda, listening to her talk about who all would be there. She hadn't had the chance to meet very many of the villagers, save for the ones that would come to the house for medicine. Most of them seemed nice, but Nyx knew that Melinda had one particular person on her mind.

"What about Ean?" she asked, looking over at Melinda.

Melinda's cheeks flushed. "Well, of course I want to see him," she said, caught off-guard.

Nyx shot her a teasing grin. "You should introduce me to him," she said. She'd never met him before, only seen Melinda exchanging pleasantries with him on occasion.

Melinda's eyes widened at the thought, but she nodded. "Of course," she said.

Nyx laughed to herself as the temple came into view. Much like the first night, it was alight with glowing augar-luxes. Nyx was surprised as they joined a group of girls as they entered the temple. Instead of like before, with pews growing up from the ground, the room was empty. The dais was still at the front, but a chorus of musicians occupied it, already tuning their instruments and playing jovial music. People milled around, greeting one another and sharing the things they'd brought. Nyx could see that a banquet table had been set up on the left side of the room, and she followed Melinda toward it. Her eyes widened at the assortment of foods that was sitting on it.

"Wow," she whispered, looking down the long table. "This is a ton of food."

Melinda grinned at her. "Remember, only Sarotian," she said.

Nyx nodded, feeling her heart skip a beat. "Right," she said in the foreign tongue. "You'll have to help me."

Melinda caught her arm, walking her down the table. "Is there anything you'd like to try?" she asked.

Nyx looked over all the desserts. "They all look so good," she said, grinning. "Which would you recommend?"

Melinda began to point out the things she enjoyed, talking about who made them and such. She occasionally introduced Nyx as her cousin to people as they walked along, and Nyx felt her nervousness easing away. She was surprised at how easily she understood their words and how easy it was to talk to them. Most people seemed to love Melinda, but as they walked toward the main dance area, Nyx noticed a group of girls who were scowling at them.

"Who are they?" she asked.

Melinda followed her gaze, her ever-present smile fading. "Valerie and her crones," Melinda said quietly.

Nyx frowned. "That doesn't sound good," she commented.

Melinda steered her away from them. "They act like their one goal in life is to make other people miserable," she said. She led them toward a series of benches on the opposite side of the room.

Nyx sighed. Of course there were mean girls in Gexalatia. There were mean girls everywhere. She just hated the idea that Melinda was the one they picked on. She was lost in thought for a moment, surprised when a shadow appeared before them. She looked up, seeing a sandy-haired young man before them.

"Good evening, ladies," he said, a smile on his face.

Melinda surprised her further when she jumped to her feet. "Good evening, Ean," she said, her smile so large that it barely fit on her face. "I'm so glad to see you could make it."

Ean returned her smile, and Nyx bit her lip hard to stop her own grin. It was painfully obvious that Ean had been bitten by the same love-bug that Melinda had. "As am I," he said politely. He looked to Nyx, who stood slowly. "Are you going to introduce me to your friend?" His voice was playful.

"Gods, I'm so rude," Melinda said, her face paling slightly. "This is my cousin, Nyx."

Nyx nodded to him politely, watching as he did so in return. Apparently, handshakes weren't a thing here. "It's nice to meet you," she said, the Sarotian words rolling easily across her lips. "Melinda has told me much about you." Her smile grew slightly as Ean looked at Melinda.

"I didn't know you talked about me to your family," he said.

Melinda's face flushed, matching his. "All good things," she said quickly. "I just told her about how you're a miller."

"Oh," he said, relaxing some.

Nyx nodded. Watching them be embarrassed around each other was almost painful, and she excused herself to get a drink. They didn't really seem to notice that she slipped away, their eyes too busy trying to catch the other's movements or expression.

Nyx sighed once she was far enough away. She wondered if that's how she looked when she used to try to talk to Randy. Anna used to give her a hard time about her puppy eyes, but thinking about it now made her chest ache. She missed Anna so much. She tried to shake the sadness away as she reached the banquet table, picking up a cup filled with pink liquid.

She slowly brought it to her nose, smelling it. It was sweet, whatever it was, with a hint of citrus. Slowly, she tilted the cup to her lips, tasting it. She was pleasantly surprised to find that it tasted the way it smelled, save for a slightly alcoholic aftertaste. She took another sip of it as she let her eyes shift over the food on the table again. She took a long moment to select a dessert, what appeared to be a roll, drizzled with perhaps chocolate. She picked it up and turned to go back to join Melinda and Ean's awkwardness when she suddenly realized there was someone behind her.

She gasped in surprise, fumbling her drink and barely avoiding a broad chest. "I—I'm so sorry," she fumbled in Sarotian. Her face flushed as she realized who she'd almost run into. She remembered what Melinda had told her about etiquette, and she bowed quickly.

"Please, child," the Ka said, catching her shoulders. "There is no need for formalities on this night."

Nyx looked up at the big man, seeing him smiling. He was even more intimidating up-close, tall and large, but he had gentle brown eyes and a kind smile. He wore the same ceremonial robes, littered with gold and beads, and he jingled as he moved.

The Ka seemed to sense her hesitation. He looked down at the dessert in her hand and made a pleased sound. "I see you've found Mrs. Alairya's sweet rolls," he said conversationally. "They're quite good."

Nyx looked down at it, nodding. "I've never tried them before," she said, not feeling so confident in her Sarotian anymore.

The Ka titled his head, and Nyx felt her heart sink. No doubt he was picking up on her shitty accent. "I don't believe we've met before," he said then.

Nyx shook her head quickly. "No, forgive my rudeness," she said quickly. "I'm Melinda's cousin, just visiting for a while. My name is Nyx."

The Ka's eyes widened then in understanding and he

offered a kind smile. "Well I do hope you enjoy your stay, Nyx," he said. His smile grew. "And I hope you enjoy tonight's festivities."

Nyx returned his smile, feeling that it was infectious. "Thank you, Ka," she said, bowing her head.

He patted her on the shoulder before walking away, greeting others of his congregation as he went.

Nyx realized her knees were trembling as she sighed raggedly. That was the last interaction she'd wanted to have, but she felt a surge of adrenaline at the realization that she'd done it on her own. She'd remembered her manners, and, most importantly, the right things to say. She took a bite of her dessert as she walked back to where she'd left Ean and Melinda, feeling damn proud of herself.

Jet walked silently up the path, his hands shoved deep into his pockets. After a day of hunting, he felt much better. His mind felt relaxed and still, the stirring of the beast quiet for the time being. As the house came into view, he felt a frown pull at his lips. He knew he'd been rude to Nyx, and a lot of it was just because he didn't feel like himself, but he knew, too, that he shouldn't have taken it out on her.

He wasn't sure what he would say to Nyx when he saw her, but he knew that she wouldn't want to speak to him. It was stupid really; he knew the things he'd said to her were mean, but he just couldn't stop them once they started flowing. He just wanted her to see that Festra was temporary, and he felt like she was getting too attached.

He was quiet as he walked up the steps to the Laxman's house and went inside. He was surprised at how quiet it was; it was pretty early in the evening. He looked around, seeing Branimir look up at him from a book he was reading. His grey eyes narrowed slightly in disappointment.

"You've returned finally," he said, looking back down at his book.

Jet frowned. "Where are the girls?"

"Out," Branimir said dismissively. "The festival is tonight."

Jet's frown melted into a scowl. "And you let Nyx go?" he demanded. "What if something happens?"

Branimir shrugged, looking at Jet over the top of his glasses. "She's an adult," he said simply. "She knows enough Sarotian to blend in. I saw no harm."

"Of course not," Jet snapped, turning back to the door. He yanked it open, feeling anger filling him. How could she be so stupid?

He stormed up the path, thinking of all the things he wanted to say to her. He was tired of being here, tired of babysitting her, and tired of feeling like she ignored everything he said. He looked up as the temple came into view, his pace slowing.

The augarluxes floated lazily around the carved walls, lending a magical light to the ceremony. Inside, music floated into the night, carrying on it the sound of laughter. Jet felt his feet still, the anger fading slightly.

He knew what Nyx had been through. She'd been ripped from everything she knew and everyone she loved. And now she was stuck with him, for better or worse, but probably for worse. Melinda and Branimir had offered her some normalcy. The way she interacted with them hadn't slipped by him. She cared about them, and that was dangerous. If their secret was discovered, Branimir and Melinda would be the first with targets on them, and Jet knew Nyx couldn't live with that.

Jet sighed shortly as he pressed on, feeling the warmth from the fires inside the temple. It was brightly lit, and dancers were twirling on the floor in traditional village dances. He looked around, feeling his breath catch when he caught sight of her and Melinda.

They were practicing the dances off to the side, Melinda teaching her the steps. They were both smiling and laughing, Nyx's white dress twirling around her as she and Melinda moved. Her thick golden braid swung down her back, and Jet clenched his jaw to bring himself back to reality.

He stalked toward them, Melinda catching sight of him first. The happiness faded from her eyes, and Nyx turned to follow her gaze. Jet wasn't surprised when she crossed her arms as he reached her.

"What are *you* doing here?" Nyx asked darkly, her green eyes accusing.

Jet mirrored her stance. "Making sure *you* don't do something stupid," he snapped.

"Well, as you can see, I'm fine," Nyx said, gesturing around. "Nothing dangerous here." She turned away from him. "Feel free to go home."

Jet was hot on her heels as she walked toward a bench and plopped onto it. "No, you're coming with me," he said heatedly. "You know this is a bad idea."

Nyx looked up at him. Normally, she'd want to yell and scream and bitch him out, but she'd thought about what she would say to him all day. She crossed her arms and leaned back in her seat, knowing the one thing that would aggravate him the most. "No."

Jet arched a brow at her. "Excuse me?" he asked.

Nyx tilted her head. "I said no," she said pointedly. "I'm not leaving."

Jet was mute for a moment, and Nyx thought she broke his brain. "Don't make me drag you out of here," he said finally, clearly scrambling.

Nyx shook her head, laughing humorlessly. "You won't," she challenged. "I'll make a huge scene." She looked around triumphantly. "All these people will see us."

Jet scowled darkly. He looked like he wanted to throttle her, but instead, he sank down beside her. "I hate you so much," he whispered.

Nyx noticed that Melinda has vanished, probably to dance with Ean. She didn't blame her. She wished she could escape, too. "The feeling is mutual," Nyx quipped. She drew a calming breath as she watched the dancers.

It was delightful watching them laugh and twirl and be happy. The music was wonderful, resonating in the temple in a way that made her heart feel light. It reminded her of the church functions she used to go to with her aunt when she was younger. Except, something about this felt more genuine. These people really knew each other, and had all their lives. They were happy and content and looking forward to spending time with their neighbors in celebration.

Nyx felt sadness settle in her stomach and she sighed slowly. "It's weird," she whispered absently.

Jet turned to look at her, his arms still crossed tightly. "What?" he asked, the unhappy edge still in his voice.

"Watching them be happy," Nyx whispered, her brow furrowing slightly. "It's right there, so close and so far away." She looked over at him. "Wouldn't you like to be happy again?"

Jet rolled his eyes. "I'll be happy when you're someone else's problem."

Nyx sighed again, this time in exasperation. "I should have seen that coming," she said.

"Yeah, I guess you should have," he snarked.

Nyx shook her head, disappointment filling her. "Let's just stop talking."

They sat in silence for a long time. Jet was letting his bitter thoughts roll through his mind, sneaking glances over at her. He was surprised when she sighed silently, her brow furrowing sadly. Her eyes shifted over the dancers and the temple, her expression defeated. Guilt suddenly flooded him. He looked down at his hands for a brief moment, the musicians changing the song from a group dance to a gentle waltz.

Jet knew what he had to do to make it up to her.

Nyx looked up at him when he stood, confusion on her face as he held out his hand.

"Dance with me."

Nyx shook her head. "I'm not falling for that," she said. "You'll just—"

"Just shut up. It's not a trick." Jet reached down and grabbed her wrist, pulling her to her feet.

Nyx was stunned into silence as he pulled her toward the edge of the dancers. She let him lead her into the crowd, feeling surprised but comfortable. "Is this your way of apologizing?" she asked.

Jet rolled his eyes again. "There's nothing for me to apologize for," he said shortly.

Nyx wished she had a witty retort, but she kept her mouth shut as he held up his hand. She glanced around, realizing this was a dance she didn't know. She mirrored the others around them, holding her hand up to his. The dance reminded her of something she'd seen in movies, but she kept up with Jet. She tilted her head when he smirked slightly.

"What?" she asked.

"You're doing better than I expected," he said.

Nyx narrowed her eyes at him, surprised when he suddenly caught her hand and pulled her into his arms. Once again, she was amazed at the grace with which he pushed her around the floor, no steps out of place, the waltz rolling and smooth like waves on the ocean. She looked around the room at the others, trying to find Melinda and Ean, more surprised when he lifted his hand from her back to catch her chin gently.

"Eyes on me," he said.

Nyx felt her face flush and her heart skip a beat, remembering the first time he'd said that to her. Her stomach twisted in knots as she remembered how dumb she'd felt that night. It almost made her want to stop dancing right there and just walk away, but something in the way Jet was holding her made her feel like she never wanted this moment to end. She wondered what he was thinking as he pressed his lips together tightly.

"What now?" she asked, trying to force a small laugh. "You look like you sucked a lemon."

Jet rolled his eyes, letting go of her quickly when the song ended. "This is just tiresome," he said.

Nyx followed him off the dance floor and back toward where they had been seated. "I don't need you here," she said as she trailed after him. "Just go home. Melinda and I will be fine."

Jet scoffed as he sat on the bench. "Things never go well when I leave you alone," he said shortly. He didn't look at her as she sat slowly next to him.

Nyx was beginning to feel like she wanted to leave, just to get him off her back. She let her elbow rest against her knee and let her chin rest against her hand as the music became jovial and up-beat. She perked up when Melinda spun through the crowd of dancers, suddenly jogging across the floor toward her.

"Come on!" she said excitedly, holding out her hands.

"This is the dance of Caeles! It's the best one!"

Nyx was nervous and surprised as Melinda caught her and dragged her into the throng. She fell in step with the others, the dance sort of like a line dance. She caught arms with the person next to her, letting them lead her in a circle. She glanced at her friend, seeing her laughing and happy, feeling her heart soar. She didn't feel alone or like a stranger as she caught hands with the villagers, joining them in their celebratory dance.

⚜

Jet couldn't keep his eyes off of Nyx as she twirled around the floor with the others. He had never been one for celebration, but she laughed and danced, the dress that Melinda had given her flaring around her, making her look like a flower. The music was filling the air with a happiness that was almost tangible. It seemed weird to be sitting here, watching her enjoy this time, when he knew what was at stake. If they were found out…

Nyx's laughter suddenly drew him from his reverie as she spun out of the circle of dancers, reaching out her hand. "Dance with me," she gasped, out of breath. Her emerald eyes were sparkling happily.

Jet shook his head. "I'm good."

Nyx gave him a knowing look, catching his hand anyway. She pulled him toward the floor. Once they stepped inside the ring, he was forced to go with the flow. He knew this dance from his schooling, but he knew it to be a commoner's dance.

Part of him thought to be offended, but then he realized that he was following along, and suddenly it didn't matter. It wasn't necessarily joy that he felt, but he felt a sense of belonging as he caught the hands of a towns girl, hearing her laugh as he spun her away, back into the chaotic turning of the group. As his eyes shifted around, ease suddenly spread through him. This night, at least, they wouldn't be fugitives. He had just resolved to enjoy himself, when he suddenly caught Nyx's hands.

She laughed as he led her around for a turn. "Isn't this great?" she asked.

Jet didn't have a chance to answer as the beat forced her to turn, catching the hands of the man he recognized as the town butcher. He couldn't explain it, but sudden bitterness welled inside him as he watched her dance with the man, seeing them laughing together.

"You don't need to be jealous."

Jet's eyes suddenly shifted to the girl before him. He hadn't realized that he had caught Melinda. "I'm not jealous," he answered her in Sarotian.

She smiled gently. "Brand is married," she said.

Jet frowned at her, wishing he could spin her away. He wasn't particularly interested in talking to her, especially not about what she thought she perceived.

The music ended abruptly, with a final flare of twirling one's partner away. The villagers bowed to one another, their laughter and clapping filling the night air. The band was taking a break between songs, and Nyx made her way toward Jet.

Jet felt frozen as she held his gaze, her smile softening as she came toward him. He felt his heart leap in anticipation at what she might say, and he frowned. What was happening to him?

"That was so much fun!" she said happily. Strands of her hair had escaped her braid, falling in unruly waves around her face.

"Hn," Jet agreed absently. He crossed his arms as he watched her look around the room.

"Do you want a drink?" she asked.

Jet frowned at her sudden change in demeanor. "I'm still not okay with this," he said shortly.

Nyx rolled her eyes then. "Just pretend to be normal for a little bit, okay?" she said, leading the way toward the refreshments table. She turned to look over her shoulder at him. "I mean, if I didn't know you better, I'd think you were having a good time for a minute."

Jet felt his frown melt into a scowl. He didn't say anything as they arrived at the crowded table. It seemed everyone had the same idea about needing drinks and desserts. He watched over Nyx's shoulder as she picked up different things to try off the table, finally handing him a cup with some sort of wine in it.

"Wow," she said suddenly, some sort of sugary confection halfway to her lips. "This is great."

"Ean's mother made those," Melinda said, appearing suddenly. "She makes them every year." She was smiling broadly.

Nyx looked up at Jet then, holding her dessert out to him. "Try this," she said, smiling as she chewed. "It's great."

Jet sighed in annoyance. He didn't want to try the food and he especially didn't want to be standing here like gossiping hens, but something compelled him to take it from her. It was sticky in his hand as she passed it to him, but it was sweet and surprisingly delightful when he took a bite.

"Well?" Nyx asked as he handed it back to her.

Jet shrugged, trying to maintain the scowl on his face. "It's okay."

Nyx turned to Melinda then, giggling. "That means he likes it," she said, dissolving into laughter with her friend.

Jet rolled his eyes and took a sip of the wine to rinse the taste from his mouth.

Nyx could feel the effects of the wine as she held onto Melinda's arm. It didn't seem like she'd had that many cups, but then again, she couldn't remember after about the third one. If it wasn't for Melinda's grip on her, she knew she'd be staggering all over the place.

Melinda looked up to Jet. "Will you take her home?" she asked softly. Her face was flushed a bit as well, but she wasn't nearly as drunk as Nyx. "I'd like to stay a bit longer."

Jet nodded, sighing deeply. "Fine," he said.

Melinda grinned broadly as she passed Nyx's arm to Jet. "Thanks," she said, turning to go back to the celebration.

Jet looked down at Nyx when she suddenly started giggling. "What's so funny?" he asked, annoyed.

Nyx pressed her finger to her lips, shushing him loudly. "She wants to kiss a boy," she said conspiratorially.

Jet sighed in disgust. "Come on," he said, leading her down the path toward the bridge. It was late and anyone not at the celebration was either drunkenly staggering home or safely tucked into bed asleep.

"I think it's nice," Nyx continued. Part of the reason they'd had to usher her out, aside from the drunkenness, was that she'd started blabbering in English. Jet was pretty sure that she couldn't remember any Sarotian words at this point.

She sighed then, leaning against him. "I wish I had someone to kiss."

Jet looked down at her, wondering why he was doing this. He wasn't a babysitter. He didn't say anything as they walked down the pathway. He should have just left her with Melinda. He didn't want to hear about any of her silly daydreams.

Nyx surprised him when she stopped, taking a shaking step backwards to look up at him. "Wouldn't you like to have a girlfriend?" she asked in English, a little louder than he would have liked.

"Keep your voice down," he reprimanded.

Nyx gazed at him, unfazed. "Well?" she prodded. A big, teasing grin started to spread across her face and she leaned forward to whisper not-so-quietly. "I won't tell anyone if you're secretly still in love with Savra."

"Seriously?" he demanded. He wasn't sure what was worse, having this conversation or knowing that she had thought about this conversation. "Why in hell would I still be in love with her? I'd like to…" He caught himself, feeling the dark scowl on his face. "You know how I feel."

Nyx frowned at him. "I don't believe you," she said, waving her hand. The motion made her rock on her heels. "I think all of this is just for show."

Jet stared at her for a long moment, feeling his insides twisting and making him feel sick. There was a small part of him that kept questioning how he really felt about Savra, but he would never, ever admit that out loud. He sighed finally, glancing away, knowing she wouldn't remember this tomorrow. "There might be a small chance," he said shortly, his voice quiet. He felt shitty with the admission.

Nyx's brow rose as she leaned forward, surprise on her face. "Really?" she drawled in disbelief. Some emotion Jet couldn't place flitted across her face.

"Really what?" Jet asked, crossing his arms tightly.

"How could you still care about her?" Nyx demanded. "She's a monster."

Jet caught her arm then, practically dragging her across the bridge. "We're not having this conversation," he said over his shoulder.

Nyx staggered after him, mumbling unhappily, suddenly stopping as they reached the path that led to the Laxman's house. She pulled her arm out of his grasp, ignoring his protests as she doubled over and vomited. She felt Jet's arms around her as her knees buckled, the alcohol finally getting the better of her.

20

The village of Festra, Abjure Forest, Ymber.
The seventeenth day of winter, the 851st year
of the reign of Queen Liana Estrella.
Saturday, January 7, 2012.

JET CROSSED HIS ARMS AS he watched Nyx jogging down a narrow trail. She turned her head to look around, as if searching for him, but she didn't look up. Jet sighed, shaking his head to himself. From where he stood on the thick bough, he could see where she was going.

He kneeled slowly on the bough, letting a hand rest on the thick bark as he leaned forward. A small smirk pulled at his lips as he watched her coming closer. When she was just about beneath him, he dropped from the bough. He was surprised when he landed, his claws digging into dirt.

In front of him, Nyx had rolled to her feet, an arrow notched in her bow string. She was unusually winded as she stared at him. "I can't believe you fell for that," she said between breaths.

Jet was still as he watched her, his smirk never wavering. He dug his fingers into the cold soil, knowing how he was going to exploit her weaknesses. "You look out of breath," he said teasingly.

Nyx's eyes narrowed. She knew that he was trying to taunt her and force her to make a mistake. She also knew that the headache pulsing behind her eyes was seriously putting her at a disadvantage. Her hands were sweating as she held the bow tightly. She knew he wouldn't let her stew for too long, she just wasn't sure how she was going to defend against him.

Jet lunged toward her, dodging her arrow easily. He reached for her leading arm, catching her wrist. He watched as she clenched her jaw, letting go of the bow and trying to grab his arm to break free. He was too strong, though, as he twisted her arm behind her back.

Nyx yielded to the pressure, falling to a knee to try to keep him from hurting her. "I give up," she gasped breathlessly. When he let go of her, she hissed in pain, her muscles aching from the force of his hold. She looked up when he kneeled beside her, still smirking.

"How's the hangover?" he asked.

Nyx wanted to punch him. "Shut up," she growled. She moved to her feet, watching as he stood beside her. "So now that you've sufficiently tortured me for the day, what are you going to teach me?"

Jet gave a short laugh. "First, tell me what you did wrong."

Nyx sighed in aggravation as she picked up her bow. "I didn't have anything to hit you with when you grabbed me," she snapped.

"Close," Jet said. He motioned for her to give him her bow and arrows. "You could have summoned a weapon."

Nyx was frowning at him as she gave him her things. "Like what?" she asked bitterly. "I wouldn't know what to do with one if I did."

Jet pursed his lips, thinking for a moment. "Most people have a weapon of choice," he said slowly, looking at her as if to size up what hers might be. "What do you think yours would be?"

Nyx shrugged, put-out. "How would I know that?" she demanded. "I've never even wielded a weapon until now."

Jet sighed in aggravation. "What sort of weapon feels right in your mind?" he pressed. "There has to be something."

Nyx closed her eyes briefly, echoing his sigh. "I don't know," she snapped. "A sword." When she opened her eyes again, she saw Jet looking at her. "What?"

"Nothing," Jet said. "We'll go with a sword." He held up his hands, forming his double-ended blade. "This is my weapon of choice." He twirled it easily. "A Geminaci blade." He waved his free hand, summoning its partner. "Two ends and two weapons."

Nyx's brow was furrowed as she watched him. She wasn't sure if she could do that. They were so solid and sharp, just like real weapons. "So how do I make something like that?" she asked.

Jet let the magic dissipate. "Hold out your hand," he said.

Nyx turned her palms up, rolling her eyes.

"Not like that," he said shortly. "Like how you would hold a sword."

Nyx felt silly as she made a hollow fist. "This feels stupid," she said quietly.

Jet shushed her. "Focus," he said. "Imagine what you want to make."

Nyx closed her eyes and drew a steadying breath, thinking about what she thought a sword would look like.

"Can you see it?" Jet asked.

Nyx nodded.

"Good," Jet continued. "Now push the magic into your hand, focusing on what you want it to look like."

Nyx grimaced as she tried to feel the magic that pulsed through her. She'd only felt it when she'd used it to heal wounds or in limited spurts, but never like the flow it was supposed to be. She knew it should feel hot, like water running through her limbs, but she felt nothing.

After a moment, she drew a frustrated breath, opening her eyes. "I can't feel the magic," she said, looking up at Jet. She felt like a failure when he frowned, as if he didn't understand.

"You can't feel it?" he asked.

Nyx shook her head. "It normally feels like hot water, running down my arms," she said, looking at her hands. "But I can't find it."

Jet's frown deepened. This was a new one. He didn't know what that felt like, to not feel the magic. It was something innate in him; something he never lost touch with. He pressed the back of his hand to his forehead, thinking for a moment.

Nyx felt her heart sink at the look on his face. "Sorry," she said quietly. "I feel like a total failure."

"We just need to find a way to center your mind," Jet said.

"I'm not doing any stupid yoga poses," Nyx snapped at him.

Jet shook his head. "That's not what I meant. There are certain things that can help you engage the magic."

Nyx watched as he stepped toward her, his hands catching her waist. Her face flushed red at the feel of his hands around her. She was glad he couldn't see her face as he spun her around.

"Loosen your stance," he said, turning her so that her back was to him. "What I'm going to teach you is called Praesen's Paces."

"Great," Nyx mumbled. She didn't want to look like a jackass waving her hands around to try to form magic, but she knew that's what was about to happen.

She blinked, feeling Jet's hand move from her waist to her hip to guide her.

"Take a half-step back."

Nyx did as he said, feeling as if she was in a battle stance. Without thought, she lifted her hands, much like she had done a million times before during their hand-to-hand combat exercises.

"Praesen was a very strong *Ignotsi* warrior," Jet said, his hands on her elbows. "Legend says that he went to battle with an Acerbi mage." His hands moved to her wrists, lifting her hands into a formation she knew from their practice. "He was struck with magic more powerful than his own, and it threatened to consume him."

Nyx drew a slow breath, feeling silly as he pulled her right arm, pushing her body to follow the flow.

"He learned to control the invading magic," Jet continued, "becoming the first *Ignotsi* to wield a magic that wasn't his own. He created this technique to call on the dark magic at-will. The trick is to envision the magic like something you can control with your hands."

Nyx watched as he guided her hands in a half-circle, wondering what the point of this exercise was. She fought down annoyance when he pulled her hands to her side, feeling like some kind of stupid anime character.

"You're not focusing," Jet said after a moment.

Nyx pulled out of his grip, turning to look at him.

"That's because I feel stupid," she said bitterly. She looked like her feelings were hurt. "I should be able to do this." She looked down at her hands. "You can do it, so why can't I?"

"It's all in your head," Jet said. "You're the one stopping you from doing what you want." He shrugged. "Not to mention, I've done this my whole life and the hand—" he caught himself, fighting the urge to grimace, "your aunt didn't teach you anything."

Nyx clenched her fists as she looked up at him. Anger and hurt flooded her at the mention of Dorothea. "This is all so stupid," she said. "I hate this."

Jet crossed his arms. "This is what's going to keep you alive," he said shortly. "You have to learn to use the magic."

Nyx scowled up at him. "What if I don't want to?" she demanded. She looked around the forest, with its blue leaves and blue-barked trees, feeling her heart sink. "I didn't even want to come here!" Nothing in this place was familiar or made any kind of sense.

Jet stepped toward her, catching her shoulders. "You're here now," he snapped. "So you might as well get on board with all of this."

Nyx pushed his hands away. "Stop touching me," she snapped, feeling her headache from earlier pushing against her forehead. She pressed her hand against her face as she stepped away from him. "I hate it here." She looked up at him, feeling angry as she thought about all the things she'd been forced to do since she met him. The anger was worse as she recalled his words from the night before. She knew he thought she'd forget, but she hadn't. "I hate you."

Jet scowled back at her. "That doesn't change anything," he said angrily. "You're still here, and you can learn to survive, or you can die."

Nyx surprised him when she lunged at him, shoving him

hard. "Why did you bring me here?!" she screamed. "This isn't my home!" Tears were suddenly in her eyes. "My aunt died because of you!"

Jet caught her hands when she tried to punch him. He didn't have any words as she began to sob softly.

"You've ruined my life," she managed around her tears.

Jet's jaw was clenched tightly as he held onto her wrists. He supposed a normal person would apologize, but what did he have to be sorry for? It wasn't his idea to do this to her. He let go of her when she pulled away, sinking to the ground.

"I hate everything about this place," she whispered, wiping at her face.

"Seemed like you were having a good time last night with Melinda," Jet said slowly, his voice guarded. He watched as she looked up at him, her eyes sad.

"It would have been better if you weren't there," she snapped.

"You know it's dangerous," he quipped.

"So I'm just supposed to hide under a rock and learn how to kill people until we get to wherever the hell we're going?" Nyx demanded.

Jet shook his head. "Of course not."

"Then why can't I just try to fit in?" she asked. "I was fine last night." She used the sleeves of her coat to dry her eyes. "I think you just can't stand to see me happy."

Jet rolled his eyes then. "Don't be ridiculous," he snapped. "You were only fine until you got so drunk you could barely walk. And then you couldn't stop blabbering in English." Nyx looked up at him, seeing that he was mad. "What would you have done if someone had heard you?"

"So I'm not allowed to have a good time now?" Nyx demanded. Inside, her heart was twisting. There were a lot of other words that she wanted to throw at him, but she managed to keep her tongue in check.

"That's not the point, Nyx," Jet growled. "And you know it."

Nyx looked down at her hands, knowing he was right. "Whatever," she managed. "I still hate you and I still hate this place."

Jet sighed then, looking away. He was silent for a long moment, wondering what the hell he was going to do with her. Every time he thought she was making progress, she took one giant step back. He turned back to her when she got to her feet.

Nyx brushed her clothes off and tucked a stray strand of hair behind her ear. She steeled herself as she looked at him, forcing her feelings down. "Teach me how to summon a weapon."

Jet regarded her for a moment before nodding his head.

The outskirts of Grassmire, Ymber.
The twentieth day of winter, the 851st year of
the reign of Queen Liana Estrella.
Monday, January 9, 2012.

ELLIE COULD FEEL AMAYA STARING at her over the flames. It was unnerving; all of the dragon riders had been looking at her funny since they discovered about the Visus.

"Here you go, darlin'."

Ellie's head snapped up, seeing Liam standing over her. In his hand was an *aurant*, another orange piece of fruit. Ellie took it slowly from him, offering a small smile. "Thanks."

Liam nodded, sinking down beside her. "You're gonna be sick of *aurants* and *pom-moms*," he joked. He looked over at Amaya, seeing her smile softly at him.

Ellie watched the interaction silently, feeling like she was intruding suddenly. Despite the way Liam doted on her and called her all sorts of pet names, it was clear that his affections were for Amaya. Ellie couldn't blame him. Amaya was beautiful with deeply tanned skin and her pink hair, and her smile was stunning. She and her blue dragon were magnificent together.

"At least we won't drop dead of scurvy," Zaida said suddenly, making Ellie jump. Her eyes were emotionless as she looked down at the blonde-haired girl. "Rian wants to see you."

Ellie held her gaze, pointing to herself. "Me?" she squeaked.

Zaida arched a brow silently.

"You'll be alright," Liam said, squeezing her hand gently. "Probably just wants to talk some more about your Sight."

Ellie nodded as she got to her feet. She followed Zaida silently into the trees, away from the main camp. Rian always seemed to be off on his own, away from the others unless it was necessary. Zaida was like a phantom, lingering on the edge of the camp, awaiting Rian's call. Ellie wondered if there was anything Zaida wouldn't do for Rian.

Finally, they came to a clearing. Rian's red dragon was curled across the middle of it, her head lifting from the ground when they came closer. Ellie felt her skin crawl when the dragon's pupils narrowed, knowing that it was the universal sign for, *'I'm going to set you on fire if you come any closer.'*

"Easy Raimi," Rian said, standing from where he was kneeling, poking at a small fire. He looked to Zaida and nodded, effectively dismissing her.

Ellie could feel the winter chill setting in as she stood there, watching him. The smell of salt water was on the air; Ellie had seen the bay in the distance from Emma's back.

"I wanted to apologize to you," Rian said, drawing Ellie's gaze.

Ellie tilted her head, surprised. "For what?" she asked, rubbing the cold from her arms.

Rian beckoned her closer to the fire. "Sit," he said, offering a friendly smile. "Let's talk."

Ellie moved closer, looking over at Raimi. She was uncomfortable, but Raimi had let her head rest on her massive front paws, her large green eyes closed. She saw a blanket laid out beside Rian, and he motioned for her to join him. She sat slowly, the warmth of the fire a relief. She wasn't used to the cold at all.

"Hungry?" he asked, holding out a piece of whatever he'd been cooking to her.

The smell of it made her stomach rumble, and she took it gratefully. "Thank you," she breathed, taking a timid bite.

Rian watched her eat, realizing that he hadn't seen the scared look on her face ease since she'd joined them. "I hope Liam and Amaya are treating you well," he said conversationally.

Ellie nodded as she devoured the food in her hands. "Yes," she said. "They're very kind."

Rian nodded, offering her more to eat. "You can have the rest," he said.

Ellie thought to decline politely, but the rumble in her stomach was more insistent. It was hard only eating fruit after not having a decent meal. "So, what was it you wanted to talk about?" she asked, picking a piece from the chunk of meat.

Rian leaned back, placing his weight on his hands. "I just want to know more about you, Ellie Atturon," he said, glancing at her. "And I'm sure you have questions for me."

Ellie paused, looking down at her hands. She realized that Rian was waiting for her to respond, and she drew a slow breath. "Why are you going to Regius Carmen?" she asked softly.

Rian grinned then. "Straight to the point, huh?" he

teased. When Ellie looked down again, he sat forward. "We want to force Paraximus out of Fornax."

Ellie looked at him. "We?" she asked.

Rian nodded. "Me and the rest of the Pangere," he said, motioning to the others just beyond the trees.

"Pan-jaire?" Ellie asked.

Rian smiled again. "In Loquelan, our native tongue, it means dragon fang," he explained. "Paraximus takes our dragons and turns them into war beasts, using them for purposes they aren't meant for. I've seen them bound with unnatural magic and slaughtered like simple-minded creatures." He scowled. "Dragons are meant to be respected. But we are under Paraximus' thumb, and we cannot escape him without Liana's help."

"Oh," Ellie said. "I've read a bit about Fornax. You worship the dragons, yes?"

Rian looked over at her. "Not the dragons, but Eomryr Lani, the Sky Dragon."

"Ah," Ellie said, nodding her head. It sounded silly to worship a dragon to her, but she kept her opinion to herself. "And what makes you think Liana will help you?"

"Well, I sorta saw something," Rian said, suddenly abashed.

Ellie was intrigued. "Saw something?" she prodded.

Rian nodded, using a stick to poke the fire. "Eomryr Lani spoke to me in a dream."

"Oh," Ellie said, realization dawning on her. "You had a vision."

Rian nodded again. "That's partly why I wanted to talk to you," he said. He ran his hand through his hair. "I don't understand what he wants me to do."

Ellie shook her head quickly. "But I can't control my Visus," she said quickly. "I would help you if I could."

Rian nodded, offering a small smile. "I know," he said, reaching to grasp her hand reassuringly. "I just thought—"

Ellie gasped as his hand wrapped around hers. She felt like her breath had been stolen, and her fingers clenched tightly around his. Her eyes widened suddenly, turning a bright blue. She was frozen for a moment, images flashing before her eyes. She tried desperately to break her body free of the grip of the magic, but it was like electricity shooting through her painfully, wrenching a scream from her lips. Once it finally released her, she yanked her hand away from his, practically throwing herself away from him. It seemed like it lasted a long time, but it was merely a brief moment.

"Ellie?" Rian asked, his voice alarmed. He was on his knees, clearly concerned. "Are you okay? What happened?"

Ellie pulled herself away from him, pressing her hands against her face, feeling pained and breathless. She could feel sweat running down her temple, and her body was trembling. "S—stay there," she managed, holding out her hand to stop him.

"Are you okay?" he asked again. Behind him, Raimi had lifted her head, a growl leaving her lips. He held up his hand to silence her.

"Rian!" Zaida's voice rang out from the trees.

"It's alright, Zaida!" Rian called, moving to his feet. "Stay where you are!"

Ellie was trembling fiercely as she tried to catch her breath, the electrifying pain finally leaving her limbs. Her eyes were still glowing brightly as she looked up at Rian, fear on her face.

"What did you see?" he asked softly.

"I saw…" She pressed her hand against her face again, her breaths shuddering. "I saw him." She looked up at Rian. "Eomryr Lani."

Rian's eyes widened with surprise. "What did he say to you?" he asked, feeling goosebumps rising on his arms and neck. He'd just thought it was a dream, but for a Seer to hear him...that was something else.

"He said you have to go to Festra," Ellie whispered.

Rian frowned. "Festra?" he asked.

Ellie nodded.

"Where is Festra?" he asked. "And what's in Festra?"

Ellie leaned forward, feeling exhausted all at once. "It's a village," she said. Her eyes suddenly felt heavy, a weariness she'd never felt before coming over her. "To the west."

Rian jumped toward her when she suddenly lost consciousness, falling into his arms. "Ellie?" he asked. He looked up, over his shoulder. "Zaida!"

Zaida was quick as she ran toward them. Surprise flashed across her face as she saw him holding Ellie in his arms. "What the hell happened?" she demanded, the closest thing to anger Rian had ever seen on her face.

"We were just talking," Rian said as she came closer. "I think she had a vision."

Zaida frowned as she kneeled beside them. "A vision?" she asked. "Of what?"

Rian looked at her, holding her gaze. "She said she saw Eomryr Lani."

Zaida shook her head, scowling. "Not this again," she said, irritated. She moved to her feet. "We're already on our way to Regius Carmen."

Rian caught her wrist, keeping her from leaving. "Please, Zaida," he said, pleading on his face. "She said we have to go to Festra."

Zaida sighed shortly as she looked at him and Ellie. "And what is in Festra?" she demanded.

Ellie stirred then, groaning softly.

Zaida watched as Rian let go of her hand, helping Ellie sit up. She crossed her arms tightly.

"Ellie, are you okay?" he asked quickly.

Ellie nodded her head, using the back of her hand to wipe at her eyes. "What…" She looked up at Zaida. "What happened?"

"You fainted," Rian said, watching her carefully as if she would break at any moment.

Ellie had her hand pressed against her head as she nodded. "The vision," she whispered.

Rian nodded. "Can you tell Zaida what you saw?"

Ellie looked up into Zaida's hard face, feeling intimidated by her steely gaze. "I saw the Sky Dragon," she said slowly. "He said that we must go to Festra."

Zaida still didn't look convinced. "No one has told me what's in Festra," she snapped shortly.

Ellie frowned, confusion on her face as she looked down at her hands. "I saw…" She shook her head. "I know this will sound weird, but I saw a girl."

Rian looked up to Zaida. "A girl?" she asked stonily. "What is special about this girl?"

Ellie felt her cheeks tinge pink. "I—I'm not sure," she lied. "We're meant to help her." Ellie felt bad about lying, but she knew that they wouldn't believe her if she told them who this girl was supposed to be. She looked to Rian. "Eomryr Lani told me to save her."

Zaida's eyes shifted to Rian then, a scowl on her face. "This is ridiculous," she snapped, turning away.

"Zaida, wait," Rian said, moving to his feet. He glanced at Ellie to make sure she was okay before jogging after her. He jumped in front of her, stopping her just outside the clearing. "Wait, let's talk about this."

Zaida was still scowling darkly at him, her arms crossed

tightly. "This is ridiculous, Rian," she whispered heatedly. "You know I'll follow you to the ends of the earth, but we don't owe this girl anything."

Rian shook his head in confusion. "She said she saw Eomryr Lani," he said.

"She could say anything!" Zaida snapped angrily. "We don't know her! This could be a trap!"

Rian took a step back, caught off guard by her outburst. "Why are you so angry?" he asked.

Zaida pressed her hand against her face. "Because," she said quietly. "You don't think about the rest of us." She shook her head. "You only think about what you have to do."

"That's not true," Rian said quickly.

"It is true, Rian," she said then, something like anguish crossing her face. "You're our leader, and we'll follow you, but don't lead us blindly into something that could get us all killed."

"I thought you trusted me," Rian said, hurt on his face. "I thought you believed me."

Zaida nodded, her stoic mask slipping back in place. "I do," she said, composing herself. "But I don't trust *her*."

Rian glanced over her shoulder, seeing the little blonde Atturon girl still huddled next to the fire. "Please," he said, catching Zaida's hand. "Trust me on this one. We'll know why we're being sent to help her once we've done our jobs."

Zaida looked down at his hand on hers, her heart twisting in her chest. "Fine," she said shortly. "But if it looks like a trap, we're gone."

Rian nodded. "Of course," he said, offering a smile. He suddenly hugged her. "Thank you."

Ellie closed her eyes, hearing Rian and Zaida's muffled voices in the distance. She shuddered as she thought about what she'd seen. When Rian had touched her hand, bright light like an explosion had filled her mind. She'd had no thoughts and no sense of time or self. She wondered if that was what it was like to be dead; to just exist with nothing else to ground her spirit to anything else.

Then she'd seen him; Eomryr Lani, the Sky Dragon.

He was massive, wrapping around the stars. The green of his mane had been the oceans and the white of his scales the mountains. His eyes had sparkled with the wisdom of the ages, and Ellie felt herself falling into whatever he was, becoming lost in time.

He had spoken to her, but his words had been more like her own thoughts, filling her mind with pictures instead of words. That was when she'd seen the girl. She had hair that was blonde like sunlight, with bright green eyes. Ellie had immediately felt the purity of her spirit, something so powerful it rivaled the pull of the Sky Dragon himself. Ellie couldn't explain it, but she felt like she *knew* this girl. And somewhere in there, beyond Eomryr Lani and the girl, she'd felt her sister.

She blinked suddenly from her reverie at the sound of footsteps.

"How are you feeling?" Rian asked as he neared.

Ellie nodded. "I'm fine," she lied. Deep down, she was scared and awe-struck and so many other emotions she couldn't place. She'd never felt something so powerful. She was also afraid for Bailey. If she had shared the vision, Darwren would know what they knew.

Rian sat beside her, looking her over. "It's a strange feeling, isn't it?" he asked suddenly.

Ellie looked up into his eyes. "Yes," she said, knowing he understood exactly what she was feeling. "I feel torn apart and put back together."

Rian nodded his head, looking into the fire pensively. "That's a pretty accurate description," he said slowly. He looked back to her. "Get some sleep. Tomorrow we're going to Festra."

Bailey gasped for a ragged breath, feeling drugged. She slumped against the wall, struggling to try to stay awake. Her mind felt overwhelmed, her weakened state causing the vision to have sapped her strength.

"What's wrong with her?" a muffled voice demanded.

More muffled voices filled her head, but she couldn't focus on them. She drew a ragged breath as a cold hand gripped her chin, lifting her head.

"Her eyes," a woman's voice said softly. "Look at her eyes."

Bailey closed her eyes quickly, knowing that they knew her secret now.

"She's seen something," Darwren said, his voice gruff. He caught her chin roughly, forcing her to look at him. "Tell me what you saw."

Bailey looked at him, a breathless grin pulling at her face. Her arms and legs felt heavy, Darwren's face blurring in and out of focus. She wasn't sure she had enough words to throw at him, her head swimming.

The woman turned to look at Darwren, an ugly scowl on her face. "Idiot," she snapped. "You've been starving her and now she's too weak."

Darwren scowled back at her. He motioned for a guard to bring him some water.

The woman took the flask he offered, holding it to Bailey's lips. "Now then," she said gently as she pulled the flask away. "Tell me what you saw."

Bailey let her head lull to the side. What had she seen?

"Dragon," she breathed finally.

The woman looked to Darwren. "What does that mean?"

Darwren shook his head. "They had dragons when we caught up to them."

The woman turned back to Bailey. "What else?" she asked kindly. She offered a deceptive smile. "You can tell me, I won't let them hurt you."

Bailey could feel darkness edging into her mind, sleep closing in on her. A sudden memory flashed before her eyes. "Girl," she whispered. "With hair made of sunlight."

"Where?" the woman pressed, urgency suddenly in her voice. "Where did you see this girl?"

"Festra."

The village of Festra, Abjure Forest, Ymber.
The twenty-second day of winter, the 851st
year of the reign of Queen Liana Estrella.
Wednesday, January 11, 2012.

THE EARLY MORNING AIR WAS cold, burning Nyx's lungs as she ran through the undergrowth. She and Jet had woken, well before the sun, to come down to the forest floor to train. Melinda had told them that there were plenty of animal trails to be found, and Jet was attempting to teach her to hunt.

Nyx had her quiver slung across her back and her white bow clenched in her hand. She jogged down what looked like some sort of deer trail, hearing the sound of water in the distance. She reached a fallen log and paused, listening for the sound of her game. It was slight, a few yards in front of her, attempting to disappear into thick brush. With grace she didn't think she possessed, Nyx vaulted over the log and ran quicker, trying to remember to mask the sound of her footsteps.

Soon, she came into a clearing, where a creature sat

on its haunches, sniffing the air. It resembled a rabbit with bright blue fur and floppy ears. Nyx notched her arrow, pulling the bow back slowly. She drew a slow breath to steady her hand and released. The creature flopped to the ground, kicking in death throws before finally laying still in the thick leaf-litter.

Nyx drew a slow breath as she walked toward it, pulling her arrow from its thick hide and tucking it back into her quiver. She picked the rabbit-creature up by its back legs, noticing fangs that protruded from its lips like tusks.

"Sorry, little guy," she whispered. She hated the thought of killing things, but she knew this was a skill she needed to learn.

Slowly, she made her way back toward the entrance to the game trail where she'd left Jet. She let her senses take in all of the forest around her, hearing the chirping of birds and humming of insects. It was neat; the forest was very much alive. Finally, she game to the end of the trail, seeing a small fire smoldering nearby.

"Jet?" she called. She looked around, the rays of morning sun finally piercing the top of the trees. She didn't see him anywhere as she walked toward the fire and dropped her kill near it.

Unease started to fill her as she stood there, looking around. She noticed that the trees around her had gone silent. Her hand drifted to the dagger at her hip.

"Jet?" she called again.

Her heart leapt in her throat when she suddenly sensed a presence behind her. In a quick motion, she drew her dagger and spun, her eyes catching the movement of another blade. She dodged the attack quickly, swinging her own dagger at her assailant. She lifted her hands quickly, prepared for another strike, the sound of laughter suddenly filling the air.

"Asshole!" she yelled, watching Jet tuck away his own dagger, still smirking smugly. "You nearly gave me a heart attack!"

"Oh, come on," he said teasingly. "It's good practice."

Nyx huffed as she walked toward him and the fire. "Don't do that to me."

"Is this all you got?" he asked, motioning to the rabbit-thing.

Nyx nodded. "Is that not good enough for you?" she asked shortly, still mad about him sneaking up on her.

Jet shrugged. "It's fine," he said. He tilted his head. "Bring it over here."

Nyx grimaced as she picked up the carcass, holding it gingerly in her fingers. "Where are we going?" she asked as she followed him a short distance away.

"You need to learn to skin it," Jet said easily. "And you don't do it where you camp."

"Oh, disgusting," Nyx said. She felt queasy as she thought about cutting the creature apart. "I don't think I can do that."

Jet shrugged. "You'll learn," he said dismissively. He motioned for her to bring the animal toward a tree with a forked branch poking from the side. "You can hang it here."

Nyx did as he instructed, noticing that blood was dripping from its lips. She looked up at Jet as he stood beside her. She had been a bit surprised at him this morning. He'd actually been in a good mood and willing to teach her things today. She wondered if her armor was almost ready. That was the only thing that explained it.

"Get to it," he said, suddenly drawing her from her thoughts.

"What?" Nyx asked, feeling grossed out. "I have to cut into it?"

Jet crossed his arms. "Well I'm not doing it," he said shortly.

"Oh god," Nyx said, stepping toward the carcass and lifting her knife. She felt her stomach turn as she timidly cut into it. "I think I'm gonna be sick."

Jet sighed over her shoulder. "It's not that bad," he said. "It's already dead. It's not like you're hurting it."

The sound of the knife tearing at its skin made her shiver, her stomach flipping hard. She pressed the back of her hand against her mouth, feeling bile in her throat. She shook her head quickly and walked away, vomiting into the grass.

"I can't," she said, shaking her head as she heaved again. "I can't do that."

Jet sighed again in irritation. He held out his hand for the knife, which she handed to him. "I have to do everything around here," he mumbled bitterly.

Nyx shook her head as she wiped her mouth and walked away. She couldn't even be near him as he cleaned the kill. She walked back toward the fire, sinking to sit beside it. She pulled a canteen toward her, gulping down water to wash the vomit-taste from her mouth. She sat there by herself for a long moment, looking up at the trees overhead.

They were massive, with huge, reaching branches. The sound of exotic birds and animal calls was like music to her as she watched the forest become a bit lighter with the rays of the sun. She turned her head quickly when she heard Jet's footsteps.

"It's done," he said, still irritated.

Nyx winced as he held out the bloody, gutted carcass. "Gross," she whispered.

Jet rolled his eyes as he knelt to the ground. He'd already picked up sticks to use for a spit, and he set it up, not bothering to explain how to her. He knew she would never be a hunter.

After he'd set their breakfast to cooking, he turned toward a bag he'd brought, digging around in it.

"What's that?" Nyx asked, watching him.

He glanced at her, suddenly too pleased with himself. "Your armor is done."

Nyx watched as he pulled pieces of metal from his bag. She picked up a shoulder piece, admiring the smooth metal and the engraving carved into it. It was beautiful, but it looked complicated.

"Come on," Jet said, standing and motioning for her to do the same.

Nyx rose to her feet, watching as he dropped the breastplate in front of her, pulling straps around her middle.

"It'll protect your front," he said as he fastened the straps over her stuba-leather jacket. "You'll have to watch your back."

Nyx looked down at it, rubbing her hands across it. "It's so light," she said absently.

"Can't get better pieces than this," Jet said as he reached for the shoulder pieces. He lifted her arm and buckled the piece around her shoulders and the top of her arm. After he'd done both sides, he handed her the last two pieces.

"Where do these go?" Nyx asked, feeling stiff as she tried to lift her arms.

"Forearms," Jet said, turning to check their kill.

"Oh," Nyx said softly, buckling them on. Once she was done, she turned to face him. "How do I look?"

Jet looked up from where he was kneeling, watching her lift her bow. She looked like a warrior, and it made his heart jump in his chest, forcing him to look away quickly. "You look like you might know what you're doing," he said.

Nyx started to smile, but then he continued.

"It's too bad you don't."

Nyx pursed her lips at him, mentally cursing. "Why can't you ever just compliment me and leave it at that?" she asked. She eased to sit, the metal on her chest making it difficult for her to slouch.

Jet smirked at her. "Why would I want to do that?"

Nyx leaned forward, picking up a stick nearby. She twisted it in her fingers as she looked at the rabbit-thing roasting on the fire. Now that her armor was ready, she knew it meant they would leave soon. "How much longer do we have here?" she asked softly, looking up at him.

Jet looked up at her, knowing what she meant. "We shouldn't stay much longer," he said, turning the spit to cook the other side of the rabbit-creature. "Maybe a day or two. This has already taken a lot more time than I anticipated." He looked back to her, seeing that she was trying to keep the emotion from her face.

"Do you think that we'd be found if we stayed?" she asked then.

Jet frowned at her. "You know we can't," he said sternly. "And every moment we spend here puts us and Melinda and her father in danger. You know this."

Nyx nodded, feeling tears pressing at her eyes. "It's just..." She shook her head. "I feel normal when I'm with them."

Jet sat back on the ground, sighing deeply. He felt the urge to apologize, but he swallowed it. "You'll be fine once we reach Liana."

Nyx wiped her eyes, nodding her head. She knew he was right, but it didn't ease the pain in her heart. She looked away, turning her eyes back toward the tree-tops. She was trying to clear her mind, when suddenly a shadow flashed over the trees. Nyx felt her heart skip a beat.

"Jet," she whispered, moving slowly to her feet.

Jet looked up, seeing her staring at the canopy. Confused, he followed her gaze. "What?" he asked, surveying what sky he could see beyond the branches. He looked back at Nyx, seeing her holding her bow and arrows. "What is it?"

"I thought I saw something," Nyx murmured, still staring at the sky.

Jet frowned, looking back down at the meat. "It's probably nothing."

Nyx nodded, kneeling slowly. "I guess you're right." She looked at him, still feeling the hairs on her neck standing on end. Even if he didn't think so, she knew she'd seen something. Something big. She told herself that it was just an unfamiliar bird as she set her bow down.

It didn't take much longer for the meat to be ready, and Jet offered her a piece.

"Thanks," she said as she took the chunk. She lifted it to her nose, taking a whiff. "Ugh." She held it away from her face. "This is disgusting."

Jet leaned back as he bit into a piece, smirking. "It's what you killed, so eat it."

Nyx scowled, picking a piece off and tucking it into her mouth. She grimaced at the taste, forcing herself to chew and swallow. "Oh, god," she gasped. She wished she had a toothbrush. "That's horrible."

Jet's smirk widened. "Lesson number two," he said, holding up the meat in his hand. "Don't kill the males."

Nyx threw the chunk into the fire. "That's nasty," she said, rubbing the back of her hand across her tongue. She leaned forward to grab her flask, when a wave of cold washed over her. Her heart skipped a beat, and she looked up at Jet, seeing his smirk slowly slipping into a frown.

Trusting her gut, Nyx grabbed her bow and an arrow,

spinning on her knees. Jet was beside her quickly, both their eyes finding the figure lingering in the branches of the trees.

"Well," a woman's voice called. "Isn't this sweet."

Nyx felt her jaw tighten, recognizing the voice and understanding her Sarotian words. "It's her," she breathed.

"You two shouldn't be out here all alone," Savra taunted, dropping down from the branch. She landed lightly on the ground, flexing her clawed hand. A sword was in her opposite hand.

Nyx lifted her bow then, seeing Jet summon blades from the corner of her eye.

"What's this?" Savra asked, tilting her head. She turned her eyes on Jet. "What have you been teaching her?"

Nyx aimed her bow at Savra. "He taught me how to kill you," she snapped, loosing her arrow. Her eyes widened when Savra lifted her taloned hand, a blast of hot magic meeting the arrow, incinerating it.

"Oh," Savra said, a reprimand on her face. "He should have taught you better than that." She gasped when Jet suddenly materialized in front of her, swinging his blades.

"I did," he growled as she barely managed to dodge his attack.

"What have you got there?" Branimir asked, watching his daughter pack food into a satchel.

Melinda smiled at him. "I thought they could use a break," she said. "They've been out there all morning."

Branimir pulled his glasses from his nose. "Are you sure you know where to find them?"

Melinda nodded as she pulled the satchel around her shoulders. "I sent them to the game trails," she said easily. "I'm sure I won't have any problems."

Branimir nodded, slipping his glasses back on his face.

"Just be careful," he said, turning the page on his book.

Melinda leaned down to kiss his cheek. "I will, Papa," she said. She pulled on her cloak. "I'll be back in an hour."

Branimir nodded, glancing up at her as she closed the door behind her. He laughed to himself. Melinda cared too much sometimes, but he loved that about her. She definitely got that from her mother.

Melinda walked quickly toward the barn, pulling a stall door open. She led her tall rapere into the aisle, tethering him before throwing a saddle across her his back. She smoothed his bright blue feathers, listening to him chirrup as she tightened the belt. "Sorry, Eder," she said, patting his shoulder. She smiled when he turned to nip lightly at her elbow. "It'll be a short ride."

The rapere flapped its wings a bit, shifting its weight from one foot to the other. Melinda knew he was fussy about the saddle, but he loved a good run. Once she was done, she grabbed the reins and hoisted herself onto his back. With an excited squawk he trotted out of the barn and toward the spiraling wooden pathway that led to the forest floor.

Jet surprised Savra as he swung his blade, forcing her to leap back. She dodged his second attack, using her clawed hand to charge a powerful blast of magic. Jet threw up his own hand to stop her, forming a silver shield. He pulled the hunting knife from his belt, flinging it in her direction. He watched as it sank into her flesh over her heart.

Savra staggered back a step, a scowl pulling at her lips. "I don't understand," she said, grasping the handle of the knife. She winced as she pulled it from her flesh, flinging it into the ground. "I don't understand why you're doing this."

Jet paused, noticing how serious her face was. Rage and hurt were in her eyes. "I don't have to explain anything to you," he said shortly. He was prepared for whatever she might throw at him next. Or at least, he thought he was.

Savra drew a slow breath. "How can you have forgotten?" she asked, lowering her sword.

Jet gritted his teeth. "I've forgotten nothing, Savra," he snapped.

"Don't you think it hurt me, too?" she demanded suddenly. Her brow was furrowed in distress, but Jet didn't buy it for an instant. "All those years, knowing where you were and being unable to come for you?"

Jet shook his head. "You made your choice." He lifted his blades. "I've made mine."

A tear suddenly slid down her face. "I loved you," she said softly. "Does that mean nothing?"

"Not anymore," he said stonily.

Savra lifted her chin as her eyes shifted over him. "Do you remember that day, on the plains of Vespertili?" she asked slowly. "I remember it like it was yesterday."

Jet drew a slow breath, uncertain of what her ploy was. He didn't answer her, listening to the sounds around them. Were there more with her?

She laughed lightly. "The smell of blood in the air," she continued, "the way the Vespertilians fell by our hands." Her deep blue eyes were distant for a moment. "It was beautiful." She fixed her gaze on him. "You were beautiful."

Jet could feel a grimace pulling at his face. He didn't want to remember that day. He didn't want to remember any of the days after it, save for the first day of the rest of his life; the day Liana set him free.

"I never understood how Liana captured you," Savra said. Her eyes were suddenly angry. "If I had been there, I would have cleaved her head from her shoulders."

Jet smirked then. "The past is gone," he said. "And if

you must know, they used an illusion." He glanced down at his hand, remembering the weight of the gold ring they had used to bind him.

"Hessa nearly died without you," she said suddenly, lifting her clawed hand. "It was only by the power of the *drac'duni* that she was saved."

Jet scowled. "You had no right to trap her like that," he said, his voice biting.

Savra returned his scowl. "I did it to keep her alive," she snapped. "I did it for you." She let her arm fall to her side. "I thought you would come home."

Jet shook his head then. "Shut up about home," he snarled.

Savra lifted her sword again. "I thought there might still be a chance," she said bitterly. "I thought your father might have been wrong about you." Fury filled her eyes. "I can see now that he wasn't."

Jet snarled, suddenly lunging for her. He didn't want to hear what his father thought about him. He would kill Paraximus when the time came.

He traded blows with her, narrowly avoiding her whistling blade. He caught her unaware, causing her to stumble back a step. Unable to counter his attack, she braced as he drove a blade into her stomach. Despite the pain, she laughed, her own sword having pierced his side. Jet didn't seem to notice or care as he pushed her away from him, watching her stagger backwards.

"I see you still feel no pain," she said, gasping softly as she pressed her hand to her wound.

Jet titled his head. "There is nothing you can do to stop me this time," he said quietly.

Savra lifted her hand, blood dripping from her fingers. "Maybe not," she said slowly. "But I don't need to stop you."

Her eyes shifted over his shoulder suddenly. "There are others who will do that for me."

Jet snarled at her, fighting the urge to turn around. He moved toward her, intending to grab her, but she swung her sword in an easy maneuver, dancing out of his reach. She leapt past him, and he spun around to see what she'd seen. A figure was moving through the brush, just beyond the trees.

Jet felt his heart drop into his feet. "Nyx!"

Nyx spun quickly, hearing Jet's voice echoing through the trees. She'd run when he engaged Savra, trying to put some distance between them. Fear caught at her at the tone to his voice. Something was wrong. She turned and ran back the way she'd come, notching an arrow in her bow. She steeled herself for what she might find as she climbed the steep side of the riverbed and jogged down the game trail.

Melinda froze, confused at the sound of Nyx's name being called. She felt her heart skip a beat. Were her friends hurt?

She'd left Eder near the beginning of the trail, tethered to a tree. She could hear his squawks fading into the distance as she jogged down the trail, looking for the clearing she'd told Jet about this morning. She figured they would be there, and she prayed to the goddess that everything was okay.

She gasped in surprise when a woman suddenly dropped in front of her. Fear made her blood run cold as she watched the woman twirl a sword slowly. Blood dripped from her middle, and Melinda could see clawed fingers on her free hand.

"A—are you hurt?" she asked, feeling an intense need to run. "My father is a doctor. He can help you."

The woman shook her head, smirking darkly. "Oh,

child," she said tauntingly. "It will be quite a loss to him, won't it?"

Melinda stepped back, clutching the strap of her satchel. "Wh—what do you mean?" she asked, her voice trembling.

"I hate that I have to do this," the woman continued. "You were just in the wrong place at the wrong time."

Melinda knew then that she intended to hurt her. She stumbled back a step and turned to flee. She didn't make it very far before the woman was on her, pressing her sword to her throat.

"Savra, enough!"

Melinda gasped, wincing painfully as the woman turned her, Jet standing in the pathway behind them. His eyes were focused on her assailant. Hope flashed through her.

"Your fight is with me," he continued.

Melinda felt the woman press her blade harder into her flesh, feeling it biting into her skin.

"Oh no, love," Savra said then, her voice deadly. "I will leave a trail of bodies in your wake." She seemed humored. "There will be no one that will take you and your princess in. Nowhere for you to hide from me."

Melinda's eyes widened. Was she talking about Nyx?

Savra's grip suddenly tightened on her as the sound of running met their ears. "Speak of the devil."

"Melinda!" Nyx screamed as she caught sight of her friend. She readied her bow, aiming for Savra's face. "Let her go now!"

Jet caught her arm, forcing her to put the bow down. Tears were crowding Nyx's eyes.

"Have you come to care for this one?" Savra asked mockingly. She looked at the auburn-haired girl. "Is she important to you?"

"Yes," Nyx managed, tears slipping down her cheeks.

"Please don't hurt her."

Savra's eyes were dancing with malicious delight. "And what would you do to save her?" she asked darkly.

Nyx looked up at Jet, desperation in her gaze. She watched his jaw clench.

"Take me in her place," he said finally.

Melinda's eyes widened. "No," she whispered, wincing around Savra's grip.

Savra laughed then. "You would give your life for a peasant?" she asked in surprise. "You certainly are not the same person I knew." Her humor faded as she brushed Melinda's hair away from her face. "But I'm afraid it's too late." Hate filled her blue eyes. "This is what I will bring wherever you go."

"No!" Nyx screamed. She felt like her world was falling apart as Savra dug her sword into Melinda's neck, blood suddenly pouring down the front of her cloak. Nyx felt like she was moving in slow motion as she ran to Melinda, catching her as she crumpled to the ground.

She pressed her hands tightly against Melinda's wound, feeling her blood running across her fingers. Melinda choked, trying to draw a breath, gurgling and drowning in her own blood. She lifted a bloodied hand, gripping Nyx's coat. She looked afraid, and it made Nyx's heart ache painfully.

"No, please, no," Nyx said, trying to stem the bleeding with Melinda's cloak. Her tears were falling quickly, landing on Melinda's face. She held her friend's gaze, trying to make herself believe her own words. "You'll be okay. Just hang on." She looked up, seeing Jet standing just beyond them.

He'd run past them, as if to pursue Savra, but she was gone now.

"Jet, help me!" she yelled, watching as he walked slowly

toward them. Her heart shattered at the way he was watching Melinda, a guarded look on his face. "Help me get her to her father! He can help her!"

"Nyx, stop," Jet said, kneeling beside her and catching her hands.

Nyx looked down at Melinda, seeing that she'd gone still, the light fading from her brown eyes. "No," she whispered, still pressing Melinda's cloak against her neck. "No, we can save her."

Jet pried her fingers from around the fabric. "Stop," he said softly. "You can stop now." He pulled her against his chest, holding her tightly as she crumbled, giant sobs racking her. "She's gone," he whispered. "It's done."

Nyx grabbed the front of his shirt in her hands, painful sobs wrenching from her lips. She felt like she wanted to explode, and she screamed against his chest, her grief consuming.

Jet held her tighter, not surprised when she clenched her fists, trying to punch his chest pitifully. "I'm sorry," he whispered, pressing his hand against the back of her head to still her. "I'm sorry, Nyx."

✴

Branimir was sitting on the steps to their house, smoking a pipe when Nyx and Jet came up the wooden walkway. He stood, seeing the bright orange crest of Melinda's rapere behind them. His welcoming smile faded as he saw the blood covering Nyx and Jet in the fading light. He choked as he pressed his hand to his mouth, seeing a body draped over the rapere's back. His knees buckled as they came closer, and Nyx ran to him.

She wrapped her arms around him as he sobbed uncontrollably. "I'm so sorry," she managed, weeping with him. "I'm so sorry."

The village of Festra, Abjure Forest, Ymber.
The twenty-third day of winter, the 851st
year of the reign of Queen Liana Estrella.
Thursday, January 12, 2012.

BRANIMIR WAS SITTING SILENTLY AT the kitchen table. His eyes were glassy as he stared at the fire in the grate of the stove. Nyx sat silently across from him, her eyes red and puffy from her tears. Jet had taken the mount back to the barn after bringing Melinda's body into the house and laying her on her bed.

"I can't protect you," Branimir said finally, looking over to Nyx. "The Ka and the elders will find out."

Nyx looked up at him, feeling the lump still in her throat. It was just past midnight and neither of them had moved from the table. "I don't understand," she said, sniffling against the grief she still felt.

Branimir looked down at the floor. "Melinda was murdered," he said softly, his eyes filling with tears once more. He looked to Nyx, pain on his face. "I can't stop them from blaming you two." He pressed his hand against his face.

"They will be out for vengeance. They will put you and Jet to death."

Alarm filled Nyx as she sat up straighter in her chair. "It wasn't us," she said quickly. She glanced at the bedroom, seeing the bloody sheet covering Melinda's body. "Melinda is—" Pain filled her as she caught her words, "was a sister to me." More tears filled her eyes. It was her fault that Melinda had died.

"I know, Nyx," Branimir said, catching her hand. "I believe you." He squeezed it tightly. "But the elders won't. They will only want retribution."

Nyx couldn't believe this was happening. "Will you be okay?" she whispered, looking into his eyes.

Branimir's tears were falling into his beard, and a sad peace was in his eyes. "Yes, my child," he said gently. "I will be fine."

Nyx wiped her face as the door suddenly opened. She turned to see Jet close it quickly behind him, his eyes distracted.

"We have a problem," he said shortly, crossing the room to grab his bag. He looked to Nyx, seeing that she was still wearing her armor from earlier. "Someone must have seen us."

Branimir rose to his feet quickly, crossing to a window and pulling the edge of a curtain away. "It's the elders," he said softly. He turned to them, grabbing Nyx's bow and arrows from beside the door. "Quickly, to the back."

Nyx jumped to her feet, looking at Jet as she followed Branimir. She couldn't look at Melinda's body as they went into the bedroom, her stomach turning painfully.

Branimir quickly pulled back a rug, revealing a trap door in the floor. He yanked it open, hearing someone banging on his door. "Go," he said. "Be quiet. Once they leave, I will come for you."

Jet ushered Nyx into what appeared to be a secret basement, helping Branimir pull the door closed. He motioned for her to move away from the door quietly.

Nyx realized she was holding her breath as she glanced around. The basement was filled with paints and clothing, and Nyx felt her heart twist. It was where they stored Melinda's mother's things. She pressed her hand tightly over her mouth, feeling more ragged sobs trying to force their way out. Branimir had suffered enough. She shouldn't have caused him to lose his daughter, too.

Jet stepped toward her then, pulling her into the far back corner, pressing his hand over hers. He kneeled, pulling her down beside him. "You're going to be okay," he whispered softly, his hand strong against hers. "We just have to get out of here."

Nyx nodded, pressing her other hand against his. Somehow, it was comforting. After a long moment, she pulled his hand away, drawing a ragged breath. She felt like her heart was beating too loud as footsteps and voices filled the cabin overhead. She leaned into Jet, burying her face in his shoulder, feeling terrified.

Eventually, the voices faded and the footsteps left the room.

Nyx still didn't feel like she should breathe as she sat there with Jet, waiting for Branimir's signal. It seemed like an eternity passed as they waited, but then the sound of footsteps came thundering back into the room.

"Don't try to hide them, Branimir!" a voice boomed. "My men will tear this house apart to find them."

A sudden chorus of voices filled the room, Branimir's among them. "Please, lord Ka," he begged. "They aren't here any longer. And even if they were, it wasn't them!"

"Don't lie to me, Branimir," the Ka thundered. "My men saw no one leaving your house." Silence filled the room for a moment. "Let us do our jobs." Footsteps shuffling across the floor filled the air. "I know you are being threatened and they are forcing you against your will. We will find them."

Branimir made to protest more, but Nyx shrank back against Jet as the rug was yanked away, allowing light to pierce through the slatted floor.

"Please, Ka—" Bright light suddenly filled the basement, making Nyx close her eyes.

"We've found them!" a man yelled.

Nyx pressed her back harder against the wall as Jet moved to his feet, swinging at the first guard. He managed to knock the man down, but more were on him quickly, swarming him in the tight space.

"The chains!" a man barked.

Nyx watched as Jet tried to fight his way through them, but one managed to catch his wrist, clicking a thick metal cuff around him. It took three more men to force Jet to his knees so that they could secure the other cuff around his free hand.

"To the cells," the Ka ordered.

Nyx didn't fight the man who walked toward her, yanking her to her feet and taking her bow and arrows. She went without protest, unable to look at Branimir. She could hear him weeping as they were escorted from the house and into the cold night air. They were marched through town, past the smithy and the bathhouse, to a small building that was attached to the temple.

It had a thick iron door, which the guard opened so that they could be pushed inside. Once they were secured, the guard locked the door, shaking his head, his eyes scornful.

Nyx crossed to Jet, catching her arm around his as he pressed his back against the far wall. She knelt beside him as he slid to the floor. "What do we do now?" she whispered, feeling the cold pressing inside between the metal bars.

Jet surprised her when he maneuvered so that he could swing his hands from behind his back, putting his feet through them. He lifted his wrists triumphantly in front of him. "First,

I need a way to get out of these," he said, looking around the small cell.

It was bare, the floor dirty stone.

"You can't break them?" Nyx asked.

Jet shook his head. "They're chalargentum," he said, sighing shortly. "Even I can't break out of these." He looked at her, his eyes still searching for something to pick the lock. He surprised her when he suddenly reached up as if to caress her face.

Nyx felt her face flush. "What are you doing?" she asked, unable to tear her eyes from his.

Jet smirked when he suddenly plucked a hairpin from her braid. "Borrowing this."

Nyx realized her hands were clenched tightly as she watched him try to fiddle with the pin in the lock. Melinda had tucked it into her hair this morning to keep stray strands in place. She'd forgotten it was even there.

"Let me," she said. She drew a shaking breath as she reached to take it from his fumbling fingers. She licked her lips as she bent the pin a bit before shoving it into the lock and jiggling it.

It took a long moment for her to find the right angle, but soon the cuff popped open. Jet tilted his head as he watched her work on the second one. "How did you learn to do that?" he asked, drawing her gaze.

Nyx offered a small smile. "The locks in our house were like these," she said. "I got bored a lot as a kid."

"Hm," Jet said as he watched the second one pop open. He rubbed his wrists absently, clearly stewing up a plan. He turned to look at her. "How well can you act?"

"That won't be necessary."

Nyx jumped, trying to hide behind Jet's arm. She looked up at the big man standing in front of their cell, realizing it was the Ka. He cut an intimidating figure with the moonlight casting a shadow over his face.

Jet didn't seem overly impressed. He didn't say anything as he watched the Ka silently.

"I must say, you did an impressive job of hiding amongst my people," the Ka continued. He looked to Nyx. "I really did believe that you were related to the Laxman family." Disappointment eased across his face. "This is your one opportunity to tell me why you killed Melinda."

Nyx felt tears press against her eyes. "We didn't—"

Jet surprised her when he held up his hand to silence her.

"Didn't what?" the Ka pressed. "Didn't kill her? Didn't mean to?"

Nyx looked at Jet, seeing him glaring at the Ka. Why wouldn't he defend them?

"It doesn't really matter," the Ka said then. "Whether it was you or someone you brought here, we can't allow you to live."

Nyx swallowed thickly. That answered that question.

"You'll both be hanged at dawn," the Ka continued. He sighed then, lifting his hand much in the way a priest would to administer last rites. "Caeles be with you both, and bring down her swift hand of judgement."

Jet was practically growling at the man as he finally disappeared. "Pompous jackass," he said finally. He looked around the room for a long time before a scowl settled on his face.

Nyx knew that wasn't good. "How are we getting out of here?" she asked.

Jet rubbed his face, sighing shortly in frustration. "It looks like we're not."

24

The village of Festra, Abjure Forest, Ymber.
The twenty-third day of winter, the 851st
year of the reign of Queen Liana Estrella.
Thursday, January 12, 2012.

RIAN REINED IN RAIMI, LEANING forward as her
talons caught a thick tree branch. Around him, the
rest of the Pangere nestled in a massive tree, overlooking
the dimming lights of the town in front of them. It was un-
like anything he was used to seeing, built high into the bows
of the trees.

"Is this it?" he asked, looking over his shoulder to Ellie.

Ellie leaned around him, nodding. "I think so," she said
softly. "It looks like what I saw."

Rian motioned to his Pangere to take to the sky and
scout the area. "How will we find this girl?" he asked Ellie,
his eyes surveying the town.

Ellie shook her head, feeling her gut twist. "I don't
know," she whispered. "But I don't think we have much
time." She watched as Rian looked over his shoulder to her.
"I saw her on the gallows in my vision."

Rian frowned, leaning forward. "You're right then," he said, unhappy. "We don't have much time." He looked up to see Zaida's black dragon circling overhead. "But maybe we can use this to our advantage."

⁕

Nyx had barely managed to fall into a fitful sleep when a guard suddenly appeared at the cell door. He banged against the bars, laughing and jeering. He ordered Jet to put the cuffs back around his wrists before opening the lock with a thick key.

"You can sleep when you're hanging from that rope!" he barked, opening the door. "On your feet!"

Nyx looked to Jet, her heart in her throat. She watched as he complied with the guard's orders, and she did the same, hoping beyond hope that he had a plan. She gasped in fear when the guard suddenly clipped cuffs around her wrists and yanked a hood over her eyes.

The guard was rough as he walked her from the cell, handing her off to another guard who loaded her into what she was pretty sure was a wagon. She felt Jet forced to sit next to her, his hands finding hers, his fingers entwining hers tightly. The thought that he was afraid too was enough to make more tears slide down her cheeks.

The wagon ride was bumpy as it carried them toward the gallows. Nyx didn't have any idea where that was, and she flinched as the guards announced to the just-waking townspeople their crimes. She tried to block out the yelling of the people as they were told that she and Jet were murderers. She wished that she could go back and rewind time.

Finally, the wagon and the crowd of people they had gathered arrived at the gallows. Nyx knew that's where they were when the guard yanked her from the wagon and led her up a set of hollow, wooden steps. She felt the floor creak beneath her feet and a thick rope was put around her neck.

Ellie hunkered down beside Rian in a patch of tall grass, watching as he passed a spyglass to her. "That's her!" Ellie gasped as she watched what was going on down below. "And that man…I saw him, too."

Rian turned to Zaida. "We need to move in closer."

Zaida nodded, moving gracefully to her feet and talking to Amaya.

"What should I do?" Ellie asked.

Rian caught her hand and pulled her up, away from the hilltop where they were spying on the gallows. "You're coming with us," he said.

Ellie nodded, watching as Zaida and Amaya returned with bows and arrows.

"This is so exciting," Amaya said, grinning to her cousin. "An old-fashioned shoot out."

Zaida rolled her eyes. "We're just going to shoot the ropes," she said shortly. "Nothing else."

Amaya rolled her eyes and grinned to Ellie. "Party pooper."

Ellie returned her smile as Rian shushed them and led them down the hill, closer to the gallows. Once they were within range, Rian signaled for Zaida and Amaya to find high ground while he and Ellie hunkered down in the brush.

Zaida easily scaled the branches of a tree, and Amaya did the same. Both notched arrows and drew back, ready for Rian's signal.

"Do you think this will work?" Ellie whispered.

Rian smirked as he glanced at her. "Let's hope so."

Jet drew a slow breath, taking in the scent of the burlap sack over his head. He could hear the murmur of the men standing around him, speaking softly to each other.

"Horrible what they did to the doctor's girl."

"They deserve more than hanging for that."

Disdain and disgust was clear in their voices.

It was annoying.

The creaking of wood underfoot caught his ears. He closed his eyes, drawing an involuntary breath as the sack was yanked from his head. It took a moment for his eyes to adjust in the faint morning light. The crowd that had gathered at the edge of the platform went silent as he turned his head, looking to his right.

His stomach dropped as another sack was pulled from Nyx's head. He'd known this would be their fate, but seeing it was different than imagining it.

She gasped softly, her brow furrowed, blinking quickly. Tears were rolling slowly down her face, fear in her eyes.

"Any last words?" the Ka asked, drawing their attention from the front of the crowd.

There was a smugness on his face that Jet didn't like. He didn't say anything as he drew a slow breath, straightening his shoulders, ignoring the pompous man. If the Ka expected him to beg, he was going to be disappointed.

The Ka didn't seem fazed as he turned to address the people. He spewed some general nonsense about sins and punishments and that this was the wrath of Caeles. Jet stopped listening as the Ka's booming voice both scared and stirred the crowd. Finally, he turned and nodded to the executioner.

Jet strained at the chains that bound his wrists, feeling the chalargentum groan. He knew he should feel desperate, but in that moment, all he felt was fury. It was shit that they were going to die like this, in some no-name village, accused of a crime they didn't commit. When Liana found out, she would have his head.

The executioner crossed the wooden platform to a handle, which Jet knew led to the trap door under their feet. He looked to Nyx as the man began to say the traditional death prayer for those sentenced to die for their crimes.

"I'm sorry."

Nyx turned her head, surprise on her face. Tears were still rolling slowly down her cheeks, fear in her eyes. The look on her face was more than any words she could have said. It made Jet's heart twist painfully.

"I wish things could have been different," he continued.

Nyx turned away then, drawing a steeling breath as a man stepped forward and tightened the noose around her neck. "I'm not afraid to die," she whispered, her voice trembling.

Jet drew a shallow breath at her words, mildly surprised. He knew she was telling the truth. "It won't take long," he said. He knew that their weight would be enough to guarantee a swift death at the height the platform had been built.

"Will it hurt?"

Jet shook his head. "I don't think so."

The sound of the latch clicking as the executioner threw the lever was deafening. Panic gripped Jet suddenly.

All the times he'd stood in battle, bathed in his enemies' blood, he'd never been afraid of death. But he'd always known he would win. Had there ever been a time when he was even at risk of dying? The monster had always come through. But that wouldn't happen now. Things would happen too fast for it to even have a chance to save him.

His eyes were clenched shut, the wind suddenly knocked from his chest as he landed on hard ground. He blinked in confusion, looking up at the hole where he'd fallen from, seeing fading morning stars overhead. Sudden gasping caught his attention, as well as a single arrow stuck into the beam where the rope had been tied.

"Jet…"

He rolled to his feet then, seeing Nyx laying on the ground beside him. She was confused and disoriented, pulling at the rope around her neck.

"What happened?" she asked.

Jet shook his head, pulling the noose from around his own neck and pulling her to her feet. "I don't know, but we should run now and ask questions later!"

Nyx nodded, hearing the roaring of the crowd and the Ka barking orders to his guards.

Zaida lowered her bow, looking over her shoulder. "They will flee into the wilderness," she called from her perch.

Rian nodded. "We will catch up to them." Beside him, Amaya had dropped to the ground and was grinning, and Ellie looked impressed.

"That was a great shot, eh Zaida?" Amaya asked, slinging her bow over her shoulders.

Zaida sighed. "Now is not the time, Amaya."

Amaya sighed deeply, feigning irritation. "You never let me have any fun." She followed her cousin, Rian, and Ellie quickly back up the hill to where their mounts were waiting.

"What took you guys?" Liam demanded. He was clearly put out, having to wrangle all the dragons while they were gone.

"Baby," Zaida said, catching Zayde's reins. She patted his thick-scaled shoulder, swinging quickly onto his back

"We must catch up with them," Rian said, drawing their attention. He pulled himself onto Raimi's back, along with Ellie. "Fly low to avoid being seen. We'll stop them at the river."

Liam scowled as he boosted Amaya onto Declan's sky-blue shoulders. He hated flying low.

25

The Abjure Forest, Ymber.
The twenty-third day of winter, the 851st
year of the reign of Queen Liana Estrella.
Thursday, January 12, 2012.

NYX WAS OUT OF BREATH as she stopped running. She let her hands rest against her legs, her back aching with the awkwardness of running with her hands bound. Her mind was still racing as she looked up, seeing Jet beside her.

"Do you think we lost them?" she whispered. Fear was still coursing through her, even though the sounds of any pursuers had died out.

Jet nodded mutely as he pulled at the cuffs that bound his wrists. Aggravation and confusion were distracting him. Who had saved them?

Nyx straightened, remembering the pin in her hair. She pulled it from behind her ear. "Here."

Jet paused as she reached for his hands, using the pin to pick the lock. He frowned at her as the cuffs fell away. "We can't stay here for very long," he said, looking around to get his bearings.

He watched as she twisted her fingers to use the pin to unlock her own cuffs. Once they fell to the ground, she rubbed her wrists. "Now what?" she breathed, her brow knitting.

"We should try to make it to the river," Jet said, drawing a slow breath. If they kept pressing to the north they might be able to find the Caelin. The thought didn't sit well with him, but the Caelin would be more likely to protect them from Savra and help them get to Regius Carmen.

Nyx followed him silently as he began to push his way through the trees. Her thoughts were jumbled and afraid. She'd finally started to feel a sense of normalcy with Melinda and her father, but things had gone to shit so quickly. But that wasn't what was plaguing her now. She couldn't shake the look on Jet's face as he'd turned to her and apologized.

It could have been her imagination, but she was certain there was more to his words than just the fact that they were about to be executed. She snuck a glance at him as she bit her lip.

"I accept your apology."

Jet paused then, looking over to her, confusion on his face. "What?"

Nyx brushed her hair from her face. "What you said back there," she said slowly. "I accept your apology."

Jet frowned at her for a long moment, crossing his arms. "Well. Good."

Nyx rolled her eyes as he turned away and continued through the brush. She knew that was the best she'd ever get out of him.

The sun had reached its highest point. Infinity flowers were blooming around them, imbued by Nyx's magic. They had begun to release their pollen, fuzzy seeds floating through the air. Jet glanced over his shoulder, seeing Nyx waving her hand, the glowing fuzz swirling around her. The soft glow of the flowers was illuminating her face in an innocent way, her eyes wide as she watched the seeds dance through the air. Jet drew a slow breath as she looked up at him.

"They like me," she said softly. They reminded her of Melinda, and it made her heart ache.

Jet rolled his eyes, feeling his heart jump into his throat. "Stop playing around," he said shortly. "We're almost to the river."

Nyx frowned at his back, but she pushed after him, the scent of water on the air suddenly.

Soon they were standing on the steep bank of a rapidly running river. The water was fierce, tipped with white caps. Rocks jutted at odd angles through the current. The bank was nothing but a sheer wall that was marked with where the water had previously been. It looked like this part of Ymber hadn't had as much rain as usual.

"Now what?" she asked, looking to Jet. She felt like she asked that question a lot lately.

Jet was frowning. "We need to find a place to cross." He inclined his head up-stream. "Let's try this way."

Nyx followed him, glancing over the water every so often. She'd never seen anything like it before, and it was captivating to watch. She could feel the spray rolling off the water as the wind picked up, stirring up a fine mist. She was lost in thought as the mist tickled her face. Surprise made her heart jump when the edge of the embankment crumbled under her feet, causing her to stumble. She thought she'd end up on the ground or in the water, but she was surprised when she realized Jet had caught her.

He was frowning down at her as he pulled her back to

her feet.

Nyx felt her heart catch at the way he was looking at her. His eyes were pensive, as if there was something he wanted to say to her. It made her brain screech to a halt as she looked at him, not sure what to expect. She watched as his brow furrowed slightly as he glanced down. He looked guilty, but Nyx didn't know why. It made her chest clench, her breath sticking in her lungs.

Was he trying to apologize for not saving Melinda? Or maybe for their nearly being hanged?

The lingering silence was becoming uncomfortable as he looked down at his hand, which was holding onto hers. Nyx didn't know how much more of it she could take, when a shadow suddenly blotted out the sun. She looked up, feeling her heart plummet to her feet.

"Savra," she breathed, cold fear filling her. She realized that she didn't have a weapon to protect her this time.

Jet's eyes were following her gaze, a scowl on his face. "Go," he said, pushing her ahead of him. "Let me handle this."

Hessa landed heavily on the ground, Savra sliding from her back. She drew her sword, her eyes blazing.

"I think I finally understand," she said angrily, twirling her blade. She used the *drac'duni* to form the claw on her arm, Hessa dissolving to form her limb.

Jet waved his hands, forming his Geminaci blades. "What do you think you understand?"

Savra's eyes blazed darker, hatred coming into them. "You love her."

Jet snorted. "Are you kidding me?" he demanded. "Why do you have to act like such a crazy bitch?"

Savra's blow was much stronger than Jet anticipated, a familiar fury in her eyes. She disengaged her sword from his blades, swinging it quickly. She surprised Jet when she flicked her wrist, another sword forming. It had a curved blade, and she swung it at his chest. He barely dodged her swing, rolling from his knees to his feet. The *fax* twisted in his chest suddenly, making him wince. This was the Savra that the beast recognized; the Savra that was just as hungry for blood as it was.

"I can see the way you look at her," Savra said angrily. "Did you think I wouldn't be keeping an eye on you?"

Jet's breaths were shallow, his chest tight with anticipation. "You mean with my eyes?" he asked sarcastically. "Like everyone else?"

Savra smirked darkly. "I'm going to gut you," she growled. She leapt at him, swinging her swords ferociously. It was all Jet could do to stop her attacks, listening to her rage like a banshee.

He felt out-of-sorts for a long moment before his brain pushed away the feeling in his chest. To keep Nyx safe, Savra had to die. That was a fact. He watched as her swords arched through the air, recognizing a pattern to her blows. With ease, he outmaneuvered her, ducking under her swing and driving a blade between her ribs, carving it deeply into her side.

Savra gasped, taking a step back. Her blood littered the ground, but it made her scowl deepen. "I'm going to kill her slowly," she said darkly. "I want you to hear her screams."

Jet clenched his jaw tightly. He didn't know where this side of her had been hiding, but he was ready to be rid of her for good. His eyes widened when she suddenly winced, digging her dragon-fingers into the gash in her side. A cruel smile pulled at her lips, despite the pain on her face.

"I've been learning new tricks while you've been gone," she said, withdrawing her fingers. Her blood was thick as it dripped in fat drops to the ground, running down her wrist. In a swift move, she swung her hand, using the dragon's magic to form razor-sharp waves of blood.

Jet lifted his hand at the last moment, releasing one of the Geminaci to summon his silver shield and block the razor waves. His feet slid across the dusty ground beneath him, forcing him off-balance. He tried to block Savra's swing as she appeared in front of him, bringing her sword down in an arch, but instead he only managed to stagger backwards, losing his footing. Savra's malicious grin was victorious as she pressed harder into him.

"I hope you kissed her goodbye," she said, her face close to his.

Jet scowled darkly at her, realizing he was one misstep from being forced over the ledge and into the roiling river. His heart dropped to his feet as Savra suddenly disengaged her sword, swinging her fist. Her punch didn't really hurt, but the way his heart leapt into his throat did as he lost his balance, the sandy soil beneath his feet crumbling away and sending him over the edge.

The water was cold as he was submerged momentarily. He felt his feet touch bottom and he pushed off toward the surface, drawing a quick breath as he broke through. The water was unforgiving as it washed over his head, pushing him farther downstream from Nyx and Savra. He barely managed to keep his head above the capped waves, struggling toward a fallen log that had wedged itself against the sandy wall. Screaming was filling the air as he paddled desperately toward it.

"Jet!" Terror was in Nyx's voice as she called for him.

Jet dug his claws into the saturated wood of the log, knowing he would be unable to get to her in time. The water was too deep and his feet were sinking into the mud as he tried to pull himself out. "Run, Nyx!" he called, hoping she could hear him.

Despite the sound of the rushing water, he could hear scuffling above, as well as Nyx's cries as she struggled against Savra. He hoped that she would remember her training as he managed to climb onto the log and find handholds to climb the steep, sandy wall before him. A string of curses was filling his mind as the toes of his boots slipped when the sand crumbled away. The desperate desire to help Nyx seemed to be the only thing that kept him from tumbling back into the angry waves.

Finally, he was close, one more reach away from the top, when the sound of Nyx whimpering reached him. Fury fueled him as he grabbed onto the top of the ledge and heaved himself over. His eyes were searching the scene quickly, the anger worse when he saw Savra kneeling over Nyx, her hands pressed against Nyx's throat. Nyx was quickly losing consciousness, her hands sliding from around Savra's wrists. Both of them were covered in dust, and Jet saw blood dripping down Savra's chin from where Nyx had managed to get in a blow or two before Savra overpowered her.

A wave of emotions washed over Jet as he pushed down the burning weariness in his limbs, rolling to his feet. Nyx suddenly gasped and choked as Savra released her, yanking her with her to stand. Jet snarled as Savra pressed a short blade to Nyx's neck.

"Don't come any closer," Savra said evenly, her eyes blazing hatefully. "You know I'll cut her up the way I did that little peasant girl."

Jet's eyes shifted from Savra to Nyx, seeing that she was barely standing. Her face was pale and she seemed disoriented as Savra pressed the knife harder against her skin. Time seemed to stand still as Savra glared at him.

"This is a side of you I've never seen before," she said suddenly, drawing Jet's eyes back to her.

He scowled at her. "Don't get used to it," he said angrily. "You're going to die."

Savra laughed then. "If you so much as flinch, I'll slice her open," she said. Her voice was sweet and patronizing. "And we wouldn't want that, would we?" She looked down at Nyx then, using the tip of the knife to lift a strand of her golden hair from her face.

Nyx turned her face away then, regaining some semblance of mind. Disgust was on her face.

"Our king would be delighted to meet you, Princess," Savra cooed then.

Nyx scowled. "The feeling isn't mutual," she said, her voice hoarse. Her eyes shifted to Jet then. She was surprised by the way he was watching them, worry beginning to furrow his brow. It was slight, but Nyx knew what he was thinking. He didn't think this would end well.

"That little Inerse taught you some manners, didn't she?" Savra asked, the edge returning to her voice. Nyx winced when Savra pressed the knife harder against her skin. "You should use them."

Nyx dug her nails into the leather covering Savra's arm. "You should just kill me," she said darkly. She looked up to Jet. "But do it so I bleed out slowly." She smirked bitterly, rage sweeping her. "I want to see you die for what you did to Melinda."

Savra growled softly then. "Quite a mouth on you," she commented, looking to Jet. "You've obviously been spending too much time with Jet." She offered a sardonic grin to him. "But I can see why you like her."

Jet realized his nails were digging into the palms of his hands. He had no words as he watched them. The fear that was filling his chest was heavy. If Savra intended to take Nyx back to Celo Cavus, that would be the end of everything. Nyx would never survive a meeting with his father. Hell, by the time Paraximus was done, Nyx would be begging for death. The thought made his blood run cold. He started to move toward them, but an arrow suddenly sailed through the air past him.

Jet watched as it struck Savra in the shoulder, sending her reeling back. Nyx collapsed to her knees, coughing as she struggled to her feet and away from Savra. Jet took the distraction to jump toward them, swinging his fist at Savra. He wasn't surprised when she managed to block his blow, rolling to her feet.

She raised her blade, snarling angrily as she ripped the arrow from her shoulder. "It seems your rescuers have finally found you."

Nyx watched as a massive red dragon landed in the dust in front of them. A young man slid from the dragon's back, his armor glinting in the sunlight. His cloak was a dark red and it swished around his knees as he brandished a sword. Only his eyes and mouth were visible underneath the helmet he wore. A massive dragon was carved into his breastplate, with scaled shoulder pads accentuating his stance. Along his forearms were thick, pointed spikes. He looked like he was ready to do battle with a wild dragon instead of a more-human opponent.

"Are you hurt, Milady?" he asked, his Sarotian more accented than she was used to.

Nyx shook her head as he helped her to her feet. A black dragon landed next to the red one, its rider aiming a silver bow. She wore similar armor to the first, a purple plume fluttering from the top of her helmet, her cloak the same color to match. She looked fierce in her silver armor, a dragon etching curling across her chest. She didn't have the wide shoulder scales that her companion did, but the same spikes covered her forearms. A thick braid of black hair fell down her back with her movements.

The rider's dark eyes were cold, focused only on Savra. She said something in a language Nyx didn't understand, to which the man raised his hand to still her.

"Who are you?" he called to Savra. A scowl formed on his face. "Why do you possess the power of the *drac'duni*?"

Nyx watched as Jet backed toward them, carefully putting himself between her and Savra. "What's going on?" she whispered, catching the back of his jacket.

Jet shook his head, taking in the scene.

Savra laughed then. "You must be the Pangere," she said then. "We have heard much of your work."

The man lowered his hand, as if to ready his archer. "Paraximus has brought all of this and more upon himself."

Nyx glanced at him, seeing that he was angry.

Savra shook her head, turning her eyes on Jet. "It seems we will have to pick this up later, love," she taunted.

Jet scowled at her, watching as she released the dragon, allowing Hessa to form from her arm.

"Monster!" the man barked suddenly.

Nyx gasped when the woman released her arrow, thinking it would strike Savra again. She was surprised when Hessa roared, using her thick wings to knock the arrow away.

The man beside her mumbled words that sounded like curses as Savra pulled herself onto Hessa's back. She didn't say anything as Hessa took flight, spiraling high into the sky. The man turned quickly, barking orders to the dark-haired woman, who swiftly turned her black dragon after Hessa.

"You're wasting your time," Jet said, turning to the man.

He turned to meet Jet's gaze. "An enslaved dragon is not

a waste of time," he said shortly.

Jet frowned. "This one is," he said. "You won't find Savra."

The man didn't seem to care as he turned back to his red dragon, pulling off his helmet. "Zaida will find her."

Nyx had let go of Jet, watching the young man. She was surprised to notice an unarmored girl sitting on the dragon's back. "Are you the ones who saved us?" she asked.

The man paused, looking over at her. "Yes," he said, holding out his hand to the girl. "I am Rian, and this is Ellie." He offered a smile. "You should be thanking her. She's the one who sent us to save you."

Nyx was confused as she looked at the girl. She looked to be about Nyx's age, maybe a bit younger, with platinum-blonde hair. Her eyes were a startling blue. "How…?" Nyx shook her head, not understanding.

Ellie stepped toward her, her eyes wide and surprised. "You're just like in my vision," she said, pausing within arms' reach of Nyx.

Nyx frowned. "Your vision?" She looked to Jet to be sure she was translating that correctly.

"You're a Seer?" Jet asked, crossing his arms.

Ellie nodded. Her eyes were guarded as she looked at him. "But I can't control my powers yet," she said. "It was just by accident that I saw you." She looked back to Nyx, lowering her voice to a whisper. "I know who you are."

Nyx felt her heart skip a beat. "You do?" she asked, afraid.

"We are going to Regius Carmen," Ellie said. "I know we are meant to help you get there, too."

26

The Abjure Forest, Ymber.
The twenty-third day of winter, the 851st
year of the reign of Queen Liana Estrella.
Thursday, January 12, 2012.

NYX WAS SITTING CLOSE TO Jet, her knees pulled to her chest. She watched the dragon riders build a camp around them, Ellie crossing beside the large fire to sit beside her.

"I know this is unusual," she said, offering a friendly smile. "It's a bit odd for me, too."

Nyx nodded, watching Ellie's straight hair fall over her shoulder. She still couldn't get over how bright the girl's eyes were. She looked like some sort of porcelain doll, with her pale skin and large eyes.

"Are you hungry?" Ellie asked, offering a piece of fruit. "It's not much, but it's what we've been getting by on."

Nyx reached out slowly to take the fruit from her. "Thanks," she said, glancing over her shoulder to Jet. She noticed that he was watching Ellie carefully, his face guarded.

"Where have you come from?" he asked suddenly, drawing Ellie's gaze.

"Sorona," Ellie said, looking down at the dirt.

Nyx sensed that there was much more to that story. "Why did you join up with these guys?" she asked, nodding to the Pangere.

Ellie looked up at them as they put together the camp. They were being more cautious than usual, tying strings with noise-makers around the perimeter to alert them to intruders. Their dragons were nestled along the edges of the camp, but they were constantly looking, as if they knew someone was hunting them.

"They saved me," Ellie said finally. "I was kidnapped." She kept her eyes turned away, a hitch in her voice.

"You should go home," Jet said. "Whatever these dragon-people are into is nothing you want to be a part of."

Ellie shook her head. "I can't," she said sternly. She looked over at them. "Paraximus sent men to destroy my home and kidnap me and my sister." She shook her head again. "I can't stop until I get her back."

Nyx felt her heart twist and she looked up at Jet.

His brow was furrowed in confusion. Her words didn't make sense to him; Paries' Wall should have kept Paraximus out, and what did he want two little girls for? Was her Sight really that important to him? Neither of them pushed the girl anymore as Rian and Zaida approached them.

"We should be safe for tonight," Rian said, looking to Zaida.

"I could find no sign of that woman," Zaida said, her voice cold and stern. "But I doubt she will attempt to come back tonight."

Jet made an irritated noise and moved to his feet. "That's cute," he said mockingly.

Rian tilted his head. "Sorry?"

Jet motioned around to the camp. "This," he said. "Whatever you think you're doing." He smirked darkly. "It's cute. But it won't stop Savra if she wants to come back."

Nyx looked up at him, surprised at his tone.

"Do not confuse us for fools," Zaida suddenly snapped. "We are perfectly capable of defending ourselves and *her*." She tilted her head, motioning to Nyx.

Nyx felt her heart leap into her throat. "Whoa, hold on," she said, standing as well. "I don't need protection." She looked to Rian. "Jet and I can handle ourselves."

Zaida mirrored Jet's smirk. "That's not how it looked this morning."

Jet scowled at her. "We had everything under control," he snapped.

Zaida rolled her eyes. "Of course you did," she said. "You're lucky we knew where to find you."

Rian suddenly stepped between them, holding up his hands. "Enough," he ordered, looking to Zaida. "I think we need to introduce ourselves properly." He looked at Jet. "So that you can know why we came here."

Jet crossed his arms tightly. "Be my guest." Since the moment that these dragon riders picked them up, they'd been treating him and Nyx like they were all friends and like they were expected. It didn't make much sense to him, but, ever so slowly, the pieces were starting to come together.

"I am Rian," the sandy-haired leader said. He motioned to his side. "This is Zaida." He pointed over his shoulder. "Liam and Amaya." He put his hands on his hips, his face brightening a bit with pride. "We are from Fornax, and an elite team of riders. We call ourselves the Pangere; the Fang of the Dragon."

Nyx glanced up at Jet, watching his scowl never waver.

"And you're the ones who cut us down from the gallows?" Jet asked slowly, his voice guarded. "Why?"

"Ellie had a vision of Eomryr Lani," Rian said, nodding toward the pale-haired girl.

"Who?" Nyx breathed, glancing at Jet again.

"Our god, the Sky Dragon," Rian clarified. "He told Ellie that we needed to save you and where to find you." He looked to Ellie. "We were near Angulus and Ellie had the vision and told us to turn around and go to Festra."

Nyx felt her breath stick in her throat. She didn't expect that at all. She looked back to Jet, unable to read his face. Was he just as surprised as she was?

Jet looked at Ellie, his eyes narrowing. "What else did you see?" he demanded.

Ellie looked afraid as she twisted her fingers together, stepping closer to Liam and Amaya. "Just the Sky Dragon," she said softly, her eyes turning to Nyx. "And you two."

Jet scowled darkly then. "Do you know what you're getting yourself into?" he demanded, looking to Rian. This kid was asking for trouble in more ways than one, trusting a novice Seer to come and get him and Nyx.

"It is our mission from the Sky Dragon," Rian said steadily. "We must obey his commands." His eyes were bright with his faith in his deity. "Obviously Eomryr Lani thinks you have a part to play in helping us."

Jet rolled his eyes, looking at Nyx. That wasn't really an answer, but he didn't want to ask if they knew who he and Nyx were. In the off-chance they didn't, he didn't want to out them. "Fine," he said darkly. "We'll stay with you until we can catch a boat to Regius Carmen."

Rian frowned. "Our dragons would take you there," he said simply.

Jet shook his head. "You've helped us, just like your god

commanded you to do," he said. "Once we get to Angulus, we're on our own."

Rian didn't seem happy, but he nodded curtly.

Jet didn't feel appeased by how easily he relented, but he knew it was a start.

27

A Ceremonial Caelin Site, Abjure Forest, Ymber.
The twenty-third day of winter, the 851st year of the reign of Queen Liana Estrella. Thursday, January 12, 2012.

SAVRA LOOKED UP AT THE giant moons overhead. She knew that it was almost midnight. She looked back at the stone slab in front of her, seeing the dried blood and cut marks. She knew that on this day the moons would align, and for a short time, all magic would be at a peak. She looked down at her clawed hand, feeling a twinge of guilt.

In order for her plan to work, she would have to slay the dragon.

She dropped her pack onto the stone altar, pulling a carved-handled knife from it. It was white bone, with a cha-largentum blade, sheathed in a piece of thick leather. She thought back to when it had been given to her.

"Only this knife can undo what has been done, should you wish to release the drac'duni."

Savra drew a slow breath, preparing her slaughter table. She didn't have much time.

Nyx realized her mouth was open when a small bug flew into it. She sputtered, trying to do it quietly, so as not to wake the others. She'd been watching the bright moons as they crossed behind each other, the farthest hiding behind its bigger sibling. It was fascinating to see; Nyx had never seen anything like it and she'd lain awake for the last few hours watching their dance beyond the clouds. They were finally beginning to move out of alignment when the bug had been so rude and interrupted her watching.

She sat up slowly. It had been a nice distraction from the weirdness around her and the pain in her chest from losing Melinda. Unfortunately, it was all rushing back to her now as she looked around.

The fire was smoldering softly, barely pushing away the cold. Bedrolls were laid out all around the clearing, the dragons circling it protectively. The Pangere members were all asleep, most of them curled into the protective embrace of their dragons. Ellie was lying near the fire, her hair fanning around her head as she slept peacefully. The only one missing was Jet.

Nyx pushed the blanket that she had pulled up to her chin away. The night was still, and she couldn't sleep. It was odd, just like Ellie had said to her earlier. She couldn't believe that she was here, in Gexalatia, with a pack of dragon riders and a girl who could see the future.

She stood slowly, looking around. No one stirred, not even the dragons. Nyx thought that was weird, but she didn't mind it as she left the fading light of the fire. She was careful to step around her pile of armor, not wanting to make a ruckus. She figured if Jet was around somewhere, he wouldn't be hard to find.

The forest was dark as she walked slowly through the

brush. She stepped carefully over the lines with the noise-makers, not wanting to wake anyone. She crossed her arms as she walked, realizing that the night had gone quiet. Rian had taken them to the other side of the river, where they would at least be safe from the Festrans.

Snow had started falling again, littering whatever ground it could find between the branches. Nyx was glad that it wasn't windy as she walked slowly. She didn't go far, pausing in the darkness to listen.

"Jet?" she called quietly.

The only thing that answered was the silence of the forest.

Nyx frowned as she turned to walk the perimeter of the camp. She kept her eyes peeled for any sign of him. It took a while, but finally, she ended back up where she started. She could feel a frown on her face, worry making her chest feel tight.

"Jet," she called again. "This isn't funny."

A loud call filled the night, making her jump. She spun around toward the sound, seeing a light flickering in the distance. Her heart caught in her chest. Was that Savra? Did she have Jet? Thoughtlessly, she broke into a jog toward the light, forgetting the others at the camp.

Nyx lifted her arms, using her *stuba* coat to force her way through the brush. The light was piercing through the trees in a weird way as she ran toward it. Her heart was racing, her mind conjuring images of what she might find when she reached it. As she came closer, she stopped short, seeing that the light was creating a bubble of sorts. Her hands were shaking as she reached to touch it, wondering what the heck it was.

A yell suddenly pierced the night, making her jump. She tried to look past the light, fear trickling down her spine.

"Jet?" she called softly.

When she didn't receive an answer, she drew a quick breath and decided that she had to press on. She pressed her hands against the bubble, feeling them pass through with little resistance. The barrier was cold as she moved through it, coming out onto the other side in one piece. She shook the cold away, turning toward where the light seemed to be originating.

Her footsteps slowed, her throat feeling tight as she looked around.

A stone slab sat in the middle of the clearing, surrounded by torches. The light was intensely bright here, but it dimmed as she came closer, revealing the bloody body of Savra's black dragon.

Nyx pressed her hand to her mouth, feeling her stomach flip. Was that the calling she'd heard? Hessa's death cries?

Hessa's head had been cut off, her eyes staring blankly as her tongue lolled from a fanged mouth. Nyx didn't know what to think as she stared at the dead dragon. She blinked as she stared at the slab, realizing it was some sort of altar, symbols carved into the stone base. The light finally began to fade, revealing a tall figure standing over Hessa's body.

Nyx took a step back, realizing how stupid she was as she reached for a weapon that she didn't have. She couldn't move as she stared up at Savra, watching her lift her hands, her missing hand having somehow reappeared. She turned her eyes on Nyx, a devilish grin pulling at her lips.

"I knew you would come," she said, stepping over Hessa's body to the edge of the altar. She crossed her arms, long, talon-like fingernails digging into the leather of her jacket. She looked up at the barrier that surrounded them. "I wasn't sure that Hessa's blood would be enough."

Nyx took another step back, looking around. "Where's

Jet?" she demanded.

Savra tilted her head. "It's just you and me, Princess," she said, suddenly stepping off the edge of the stone slab. She landed easily on her feet. She lifted her hand, the one that had once been a dragon claw, curling her perfectly re-formed fingers. "I thought we could...talk."

Nyx didn't like the sound of that. "I don't think that's a good idea," she said, knowing she needed to run.

"I wouldn't," Savra said, as if reading her mind. "You can't leave my trap." She motioned to the barrier around them. "And no one can find you." She walked toward Nyx, her blue eyes filled with murderous intent.

Nyx drew a quick breath when Savra grabbed the front of her jacket. She gritted her teeth, pulling against Savra's grip.

"Now, we can do this two ways," Savra said slowly.

Nyx surprised her when she suddenly swung her fist. She'd be damned if she let this bitch get away after everything she'd done. She caught Savra across the face, but it seemed to have little effect as Savra lifted her off the ground.

"Guess it's the hard way," Savra growled, slamming Nyx onto the altar.

Nyx gasped as pain rushed down her back, the wind knocked from her lungs. She tried to turn over and roll off the altar, but Savra caught her arm.

"I think I'm going to enjoy this," Savra said, leaning over her as she wrapped a rope around Nyx's wrist.

Nyx was stunned, realizing too late that Savra was tying her down. She tried to fight against her, but Savra was too strong as she wrapped another rope around her opposite wrist, securing her to the table. "Why are you doing this?" Nyx managed, letting her head rest against the cold stone. Her thoughts were on Melinda. "Why?"

Savra paused then, looking down at her. Her eyes were pensive and angry. "I waited for him," she said finally. "For a century." She turned away, lifting the ceremonial knife that she'd used to cut off Hessa's head. "Do you know what that's like?"

Nyx swallowed thickly as she looked at the knife in her hands. It was coated in dried blood, the white handle stained with red. She didn't know if Savra was expecting an answer as she looked up at her. "You two—" She drew a shaking breath. "You had something, didn't you?"

Savra tilted her head as she looked down at her. "Something?" She laughed bitterly. "It was more than *something*." She braced her hands against the edge of the stone, looking toward the sky. "He was going to take me as his bride."

Nyx was surprised when something like genuine pain crossed her face.

"He was supposed to be with *me*," Savra growled, looking down at her. She lifted the knife. "But now he wants to be with you."

Nyx flinched as she leveled the knife at her face. "You've got it really wrong," she said quickly. "Me and Jet—we're not a thing."

Savra smirked darkly. "Please, I see the way he looks at you," she said shortly. "It's not a mystery to anyone."

Nyx shook her head. "Ask him yourself," she said, feeling desperate.

"It doesn't matter," Savra said then. "Even if it doesn't hurt him, I still have to kill you."

"Why?" Nyx breathed, feeling tears in her eyes. "What purpose does that serve? What does all of this death get you?"

Savra smiled cruelly. "You really don't know anything, do you?"

Nyx drew a ragged breath as Savra lowered her hand, pointing to the sky.

"It's the night that Deimos and Pistis cross in the sky," Savra said. She looked down to Nyx, seeing the confusion on her face. "It's the one night in their cycle that the magic is at its strongest." She lifted her blade again, watching the moonlight reflect in the bloody surface. "The peak has already passed." She turned eyes to the dead dragon beside Nyx. "But I've already taken Hessa's strength. It's all I need to take yours, too." She smirked darkly. "Then I'll use your magic to kill Jet."

Nyx struggled against her restraints as Savra held the blade near her throat. "Wait!" she gasped. She tried to calm her racing heart when Savra paused. "I need to know."

Savra scowled at her. "You're just trying to put off the inevitable."

Nyx shook her head. "No," she managed. "You're going to kill me anyway." She was desperate, knowing she was using time she didn't have.

Savra's eyes were narrowed suspiciously.

"Before you do it," Nyx's eyes shifted to the knife, "tell me what Jet was like when you knew him."

Confusion pulled at Savra's face. "Why?" she asked.

Nyx twisted her hand against the rope, feeling her wrist slipping a miniscule amount. "Everyone acts like he was some sort of hero," she said, continuing to try to subtly wiggle free. "Or a monster."

Savra drew a slow breath then, her eyes turning away. "He was both," she said, reverence in her voice.

Nyx pulled at the rope, feeling it cutting into her hand. She tried not to grimace at the pain, knowing if she could keep Savra talking, she could pull free.

"Jet was the most powerful warrior to have ever walked

Gexalatia," Savra continued. "And with the beast inside, he was unstoppable."

Nyx frowned then, stilling. "The beast?" she whispered.

Savra looked down at her, surprise and delight on her face. "You've never seen the monster?" she asked, laughing shortly.

Nyx shook her head. "What are you talking about?"

Savra laughed again, as if she'd just uncovered a most delicious secret. "Jet's body is a vessel for a demon," she said, leaning forward. "A monster that is only sealed away by blood." She shook her head. "You've never noticed anything peculiar about him?"

Nyx's breaths were short as they ghosted over her lips, her thoughts racing. There were a lot of *peculiar* things about Jet.

Savra leaned closer, lowering her voice. "He needs blood to feed the monster. If he doesn't keep it fed, it will kill until it is satiated." Her eyes were pensive suddenly, a new idea forming behind them. "But, with your strength, Jet can defeat the monster."

Nyx wasn't sure what she was hearing as she looked up at Savra. "What?" she breathed.

Savra smirked, as if she'd just had the most brilliant idea in the whole world. "You didn't think I'd just let him go, did you?" she asked quietly. She leaned back then, the smirk still on her face. "He's much different than I remember, but he won't turn away from a chance to become what he once was, and more."

Nyx could feel the surprise and fear on her face. "Jet would never do that," she whispered. "Jet won't kill me."

Savra shook her head. "You're so naïve," she said slowly, a maniacal gleam in her eyes. "Jet lusts for power. He may think he's changed, but, deep down, what he really wants is the strength to destroy both Liana and Paraximus." She brushed a strand of Nyx's hair from her face. "And with the blood that flows through your veins, I can give that to him." Her smile was demented. "He'll come back to me."

Nyx knew that she didn't have much time. She pulled hard at the rope, feeling it burning against her skin as her hand slipped free. Savra barked something that Nyx didn't catch as she threw her legs over the dragon's body. She didn't know what she expected, but she gasped, the other rope tightening around her wrist as she hit the end of it.

"Nice try, girl," Savra snarled, advancing on her. "You didn't think that one through, did you?"

Nyx pulled harder. She would have pulled her arm off at that point to escape. She gasped in pain when Savra caught her around the neck, her nails digging into Nyx's skin.

"Don't worry," Savra said, pulling Nyx toward her. "I'm not going to kill you." She smirked. "Jet will."

28

The Pangere Camp, Abjure Forest, Ymber.
The twenty-fourth day of winter, the 851st
year of the reign of Queen Liana Estrella.
Friday, January 13, 2012.

JET WAS QUIET AS HE walked toward the fire. He could see, even at his distance, that the Pangere members were asleep. He'd volunteered to be on first watch, but things had been quiet all night. He looked up at the moons, knowing that dawn wasn't very far off. He'd decided at some point that it wasn't worth waking the next watch.

He slowly stepped across their perimeter line, walking into the faint light of the fire. He frowned at how deeply the dragon riders seemed to be sleeping. None of them had stirred, even still lying in the same positions they'd been in when he'd left. He turned his head to where Nyx had been lying.

Jet clenched his jaw, his heart skipping a beat as he saw that her bed roll was empty. He turned and moved back into the woods, hoping that she'd just stepped away for a moment. Once he was out of the light of the fire, he looked around, listening carefully.

"Nyx?" he called.

Silence greeted him. In fact, everything was *too* quiet. No birds, no insects, not even the rustling of grass or leaves in the wind.

Jet spun around, running back toward the campsite. He stood just beyond the trip lines, realizing that even the Pangere were silent. He couldn't hear the rumbling snores of the dragons, or even the soft popping of the dying fire. He turned his back to them slowly, feeling his blood run cold.

"Jet!"

He jumped suddenly, spinning around. "Nyx?"

The sound of her voice calling him had echoed all around him, but there was no one there. On edge, Jet scanned the darkness. It seemed impossibly thick between the trees, despite the bright moonlight that should have been filtering down to the forest floor.

"Jet, help me!" Fear and panic were in her ragged cry.

He turned his head quickly, his heart racing in his chest. A crawling feeling came over him as he realized that, this time, the voice had a direction. He turned, his whole body tense as he broke into a sprint. He drew up short after a moment, barely able to hear anything over his quick breaths.

A scream tore through the night, making him spin around.

A dim light flickered in the distance, and he ran toward it. He didn't have any idea what he was running into, but he had a feeling Savra would be at the center of it.

Before long, he'd broken through the foliage, into a clearing. He stopped as he looked around the clearing. It was dark and empty, save for a tall stone table. Torches were unlit around the table. He knew it was some sort of ceremonial site, but he didn't know how it got here or why he hadn't seen it before on his patrol. His breath caught in his chest when a soft noise drew his attention, a familiar aura pressing against him.

Jet gritted his teeth as he turned toward where he felt her, summoning his blades. "I know you're there," he called quietly. He wasn't surprised when Savra materialized out of the shadows.

She offered a small smile. "I didn't come here to fight you," she said. "I'm glad you came."

Jet felt his heart lurch in his chest at her words. "It's not like I had a lot of choice," he snapped. "Where is Nyx? If you hurt her, I swear—"

"Why do you care so much about her?" Savra demanded. "How can you care so much about a weakling like her?"

Jet scowled at her. "It's my job," he ground out. His heart was racing at the thought of her being in Savra's clutches. He glanced around the clearing, seeing no sign of her.

Savra's navy hair fell over her shoulder, the wind catching strands of it and pulling it around her face. Her eyes were soft and bright as she watched him. "It doesn't have to be," she said gently. She took a step closer, keeping her reformed hand hidden, waving it slowly to draw on Hessa's stolen magic. "You don't have to do this."

Jet relaxed his shoulders a bit, still scowling, a calm sensation creeping over him. It was so slight, he barely noticed it. "What do you know?" he demanded. "Last time I checked, you didn't know a damn thing about me."

He knew she was trying to distract him, but for some reason he couldn't seem to muster the energy to be mad at her. In fact, all his emotions and senses felt dull suddenly. He shook his head slightly, trying to shake off the fog that seemed to be slowly coming over him.

Savra took another step toward him, pleased that he

hadn't sensed her trap. "I know you're angry," she said.

Jet smirked darkly, leveling his blade at her neck, her words sparking a fire in his chest. She was close enough that he could have killed her right there. "That's an understatement." He should have killed her. He didn't know what was stilling his hand.

Savra's blue eyes flicked to his blade before back to his face. "You're angry at the wrong person," she said softly. "I wanted to come for you." She looked down at the sharp edge at her throat. "Your father wouldn't let me."

Jet still didn't lower his weapon. "Is that supposed to make me feel better?" he asked. Once again, the slow, creeping numbness was easing through him, making his limbs feel heavy.

Savra drew a slow breath as she held his gaze. "I thought about you every day," she whispered, her eyes suddenly filling with tears. "I never stopped loving you."

Jet's brain felt muddled at her words. He lowered his blade slowly, watching hope flash across her face. He looked down at her hand when she held it out to him.

Savra knew that her spell was working. "Things can be like they were before with us."

Jet felt his heart twist at her words. *Like they were before.*

What did that even mean?

He looked back up into her face, remembering lazy afternoons in the palace courtyard with her. He remembered standing beside her in battle and celebrating victories with her in his father's ballroom. He remembered a time when there was nothing else except her and whatever future she promised. He remembered never wanting that to end, and how dark and alone he felt when it did.

Jet shifted his eyes back to her open hand, feeling the

need to reach out to her. Could things be like they were before? Why did her words make him feel so confused?

"Please," she pressed at his hesitance. "I know what you want, and I want to make that happen for you."

Jet looked back into her face, his eyes narrowing, despite the fog that was clouding his mind. "What are you talking about?"

Savra took another step closer, searching his gaze. "You're angry at your father," she said softly. "For what he did to you." She was close enough now that she pressed her hand against his arm. "And angry at Liana for stealing your life from you."

Jet's eyes shifted down to her hand, warmth spreading through him from her touch, pushing away the fog in his mind and replacing it with desire. His heart was racing as he stared at her, listening to her words. How was it that after all this time she still managed to enthrall him? His eyes were traveling over her face, his mind knowing every inch of her still.

"I can help you become strong enough to kill them both," Savra said, her hand sliding down his arm and her fingers finding his. Her words were low and coated with rage. "I will help you take your revenge."

Jet scowled at her suddenly, but didn't resist her touch. "How?" he demanded. "You had to steal Hessa's strength to even face me. How could you possibly have a power to defeat them?"

Savra lifted her opposite hand then, pressing her soft palm against his cheek. She smiled when his eyes widened. Rage flitted across his face, but it dimmed just as quickly as it came with her touch.

"What did you do to Hessa?" Jet demanded, trying to ignore the feelings that were twisting in his chest. He wanted to be furious with her, but he couldn't seem to muster the energy. A tightness was filling his chest, pushing out anything else he might have felt.

Savra turned then, holding his hand still and leading him toward the stone table. "Tonight is *travecto*," she said.

Jet's eyes shifted toward the sky, where the moons were already moving past one another.

"I have consumed Hessa's magic," Savra said, drawing his gaze. "And I intend to use it to make you unstoppable."

Jet didn't move as he watched her let go of his hand and step away. Somewhere in the back of his mind, he knew that Hessa's magic was strong enough to hide Nyx, but his thoughts were jumbled as he stared at her. The thought slipped away like a puff of smoke on a windy day.

Did he want what she was offering? He wanted to kill those who had wronged him more than he'd ever wanted anything else in his life.

"Why?" he asked, the edge easing from his voice. "Why would you do any of this?"

Savra grinned, stepping close to him. "Because I love you," she said softly. "And I want to see them suffer just as much as you do." She leaned forward on her toes, pressing her lips against his.

Jet leaned into her kiss, his mind blanking. The warmth that she had brought made him feel empty. His thoughts and reason fled as he blinked, watching her lean away. This seemed too good to be true. But what if she was serious, and so were her feelings?

He held her gaze, feeling as if he'd been taken back in time, to a place where nothing mattered except being with her. He stepped toward her, grabbing her and roughly pressing his lips to hers.

"Jet!" Nyx screamed, yanking at the ropes that held her against the table. Tears were running down her face as she watched him with Savra. She yanked harder against her bonds, feeling the rope cutting into her skin. "Snap out of it!"

She'd been yelling at him since he'd stepped into the clearing, but she knew he couldn't hear her. Frustration and despair made her heart ache in her chest, and she let her head fall back against the table, her eyes never leaving his face.

"She's using you," she breathed.

Nyx couldn't stand the way her heart felt like it was being ripped in half. She could see the way he looked at Savra, as if nothing else in the world mattered, and it made her feel like she wanted to puke. She couldn't hear what Savra was saying, but Jet was eating up every twisted word Savra was uttering.

"She's lying to you!" Nyx screamed again, her voice ragged with fear and rage. "She doesn't give a shit about you!" Her breaths were ragged as she looked up at the sky. "She just wants you to do her dirty work."

She turned her head back to them as they came closer, feeling disgusted as Jet pulled Savra tightly into his arms. Her tears fell faster as she watched him kiss her like his life depended on it. She knew that he was done. He'd bought whatever lie Savra was selling, and Nyx knew that nothing she could say would matter. Savra had been right, and it made Nyx feel broken. Jet would always choose power over anything else. Not to mention the fact that his feelings were clouding his mind. If he didn't still care about her, he wouldn't have ever listened to her.

Nyx was silent as she laid on the table, listening to Savra's faint words. Whatever spell she had cast to hide Nyx made her voice sound like it was traveling through water.

"I'm glad you see things my way," Savra said, pulling Jet closer to the table. Her voice was heavy with fake sincerity. "I will always stand beside you."

Nyx hated the way Jet stared at her. If the forest had been burning down around him, he wouldn't have noticed. It made Nyx's stomach turn as realization hit her.

"Do you trust me?" Savra asked.

Nyx shook her head, her tears hot on her face as Jet nodded slowly. "She's controlling you," she whispered. "You have to break free."

"Tell me what I have to do," he said.

Savra was grinning then. She pulled him around the table, her blue eyes sadistically happy. She pulled out her white-handled knife, holding the handle out to him.

Jet didn't react as he took the blade.

"Our time is short," Savra said, her eyes shifting to the moons. "You must do this now." She reached out to press her hands against the table.

Nyx felt her heart lurch. The submerged feeling was ebbing away, and she drew a sharp breath, ready to scream, when a swift, heavy feeling came over her. She realized she was paralyzed, unable to make any sounds as they stood over her.

"Kill her and take her power," Savra said, a command in her voice.

Nyx turned her eyes to Jet's face, feeling her heart drop into her stomach. There was no spark of recognition on his face as he stood over her.

"Do it," Savra snarled. "Kill her."

Nyx blinked against the tears in her eyes, trying to will him to wake up. She tried to pull against the ropes, but her arms didn't want to cooperate. She closed her eyes tightly, trying to force her body to move. If there was ever a time that she needed to use her magic, it was now.

"Do it!" Savra barked.

Jet stepped closer, lifting the knife. Savra was grinning victoriously beside him, waiting for him to plunge the blade into Nyx's heart.

Nyx closed her eyes once more, drawing a breath. She knew that this was the last moment she had. Just when she thought that she would die, the hot warmth of her magic spiked into her finger tips. It flooded her body with power, and she drew a strangled, gasping breath as if she'd surfaced from water.

"Jet, don't!" she yelled hoarsely.

Jet froze, his eyes confused as he looked at her.

"Shut up!" Savra screamed, lunging for Nyx to hold her still. She looked to Jet, lifting her hand, the pull of cold magic strong as she tightened her spell over him. "Kill her now!"

Nyx felt anger filling her as Savra's hands gripped her tighter. It was white-hot and consuming, and suddenly the image of a sword flooded her mind. She hadn't been able to summon it before, probably because she didn't really need it, but she needed it now. No, she *wanted* it now. Jet's teachings rushed back to her, and she held out her hand, feeling a warmth pressing against her skin.

"No!" Savra growled, realizing she was drawing on her magic. She tried to restrain Nyx, but the fiery anger inside her had taken control. Savra looked up at Jet. "Do it now!"

Nyx turned her eyes on him, watching as Savra's spell took hold of him, and he swung his hands down in a death stroke. The magic took control of her body, a blast of heat throwing Savra away from her and disintegrating the ropes around her wrists as the golden sword formed solidly in her hand. It was bright as she swung it, barely managing to stop the knife in Jet's hands.

Nyx was panting as she held him at bay, leaning into him. "Jet, listen to me," she said quietly. "You don't want to do this."

Jet's dark eyes were blank as he continued to bear down on her.

"Please," Nyx whispered. "Wake up!" She suddenly yanked her sword back, using her free hand to strike him with a blast of magic that flung him backwards. She spun around quickly on the table, her knees shaking as she slid off it. She was panting heavily as she stood there, wondering how in the hell she'd just done that.

"You should have just died," Savra growled at her. She'd picked herself up off the ground, and fury was in her eyes.

Nyx lifted her golden sword, feeling fury fill her as she stared at Savra. "I should be saying that to you." She leapt forward at Savra, swinging the golden blade with as much force as she could. "I'm going to kill you for what you did to Melinda!"

Savra's hands were quick as she summoned two blades, stopping Nyx's blow. Nyx's arms were shaking as Savra pushed her back, but she knew she couldn't quit now. She had to kill Savra.

She ducked as Savra swung her blades at her chest, staggering backwards to stay out of her reach. She barely managed to parry Savra's blows, the swinging of her sword clumsy. She felt like she was barely staying out of reach of Savra's blades as her initial fury wore off, and Savra caught her off-guard, dealing a kick to her chest.

The breath was knocked from her lungs as Nyx fell backwards onto the ground, the golden sword slipping from her fingers. She struggled for a breath as she watched Savra advance. She rolled to her knees, scrambling to grab the sword, but Savra was quicker, dealing a hard kick to her side. Nyx yelled out as she felt her ribs give under the force, pain flooding her and making her head swim. The golden sword dissolved in a flurry of sparkles as the pain pushed away the confidence and anger she'd felt before.

"You're so weak," Savra taunted, rage in her eyes. "You can't avenge your friend, and you won't save Jet."

Nyx pulled herself backwards across the leaf-litter, feeling fear shooting through her. Every breath she drew was painful, and the sound of her breathing was gurgled. She knew that wasn't good.

"Even if he doesn't turn tonight, Paraximus has ways of forcing him to come back."

Nyx reached a tree, pulling herself into its tangled and jutting roots. It felt like a coffin as she watched Savra tower over her. She knew that she had to do something quick, or this was where she was going to die. She lifted her hand as if to summon a blast, but Savra slapped it away, leveling a sword at her throat.

"Any last words?" she sneered.

Nyx narrowed her eyes, unable to speak as a cough shook her. She wanted to tell Savra to go to hell, but the blood that was filling her lungs and dripping from her lips kept her silent. She couldn't do anything as she leaned against the tree, staring angrily down the edge of Savra's blade. If she was going to die, she wouldn't give Savra the satisfaction of seeing her fear.

Savra made a pleased sound and lifted her hand, preparing to strike, when a sudden burst of silver shot through her middle. Her blue eyes were wide as she staggered forward a step, a silver blade protruding from her gut.

Nyx let her head fall back against the tree as she watched Savra sink to her knees, Jet standing over her. His dark eyes were clear and filled with rage.

"Jet," Savra breathed, her eyes wide as she looked up at him. She looked confused, as if she'd expected her spell to hold. "What—what are you doing?"

"You chose the wrong person to toy with," he growled. He watched as helplessness crossed her face. "It's over."

Nyx didn't flinch as she watched Jet swing his blade in an easy motion, Savra's head falling from her shoulders. Her body fell limply to the ground, and for a moment, everything was still before the forest around them began to ripple, light bursting through the trees. The altar and Hessa's body began to fade away, the first light of the morning sun filling the empty clearing. Whatever illusion Savra had conjured was gone.

Jet was breathing hard as he turned away from Savra's body, his hand pressed against his chest where Nyx's magic had struck him. He moved toward her, watching her wipe blood from her lips. He collapsed to the ground beside her, looking just as ragged as she felt. "What happened?" he asked.

Nyx drew a slow, wheezing breath. "Your dumb ass almost got us killed," she managed. She pressed her hand to her side as she coughed again. The relief that had filled her when she saw him standing over Savra made her want to cry, but the betrayal of seeing him kiss Savra still made her want to vomit. Her feelings were jumbled as she sat there.

Jet was frowning as he looked at her. "You have a punctured lung," he said.

Nyx nodded, feeling her ribs protest when she tried to take a deep breath. She leaned back against the tree trunk, closing her eyes for a moment. "I'll be okay," she said, her voice ragged. She could feel what little strength she had left working to repair her body, a warm tingle spreading around her injured side. "I just need a minute."

Jet leaned against the tree beside her. He watched the pain wash across her face, pride sparking through him. He didn't know how she had done it, but she'd managed to somewhat hold her own against Savra. The feeling didn't last long as she turned her eyes on him.

"How did this happen?" she asked, unable to muster an angry tone, even though her emerald eyes were furious. "You were going to kill me."

Jet scowled at her. "But I didn't," he snapped.

"Only because I knocked your ass out," Nyx returned.

Jet sighed in disgust. "You know it wasn't me."

"That's what I'm worried about," Nyx snapped. The pain was diminishing and she leaned forward. "How did she even get her claws in you?"

Jet shook his head, looking across the clearing. "She stole Hessa's magic," he said softly, as if he couldn't quite wrap his head around it. "She used some sort of charm."

Nyx looked at him, feeling her stomach turn. "She knew exactly what to say to you," she whispered. She watched as Jet bowed his head, smoothing his hair from his face. "It was like you needed her." It was like he still wanted to be with her.

Jet forced a scowl to hide the way his brow furrowed. "That's how her charm made me feel."

Nyx's eyes widened, trepidation filling her. "And how do you feel now?"

Jet glared at her. "Don't do that," he snapped, his voice less biting than she would have expected. "I was coming to find you."

"No," Nyx growled. "It's time for you to be honest with me." She glanced at Savra's body. "I didn't forget what you said to me during the festival." Her stomach twisted into a tight knot, making her feel like she wanted to cry. "You said you still cared about her." She looked back at him. "Whose side are you really on?"

Jet looked away, anger on his face. "Yours, obviously," he ground out, moving to his feet. He did not want to talk about this.

Nyx struggled to stand, taking a shaking step toward him. "That's not obvious!" she yelled. "All it took was a little bit of magic for her to manipulate you." She had a hard time believing that it was all Savra's magic. "How you felt just made it that much easier for her."

Jet turned to look at her, his jaw clenched tightly. "Well what do you want me to do about it, little princess?" he demanded. "Do I have to swear my loyalty to you?" He took a step toward her, his voice heavy with sarcasm. "You want me to get down on my knees and pledge my life to you?"

Nyx felt her heart twist in her chest. "I just want some transparency from you," she said, her voice low and angry. "You're the only person I can rely on, and I thought you were my friend."

Jet scoffed then, making Nyx feel small. "I don't do *friends*," he said bitterly. "Once you're safely in Liana's hands, that's where this relationship ends."

The pain that filled Nyx's chest made the lingering pain of her cracked ribs feel like nothing. She tried to mask it, forcing down her angry tears. "At least don't lie to me anymore," she said, her voice lacking any bite. "I've been lied to enough."

Jet was aggravated as he looked at her. "She's dead now," he snapped. "Isn't that good enough for you? I'm not going to tell you every little thing about my life."

"And are there others?" Nyx demanded. "Anyone else who might try to turn you?"

Jet's dark eyes were distant suddenly. "No," he said evenly. "I'm going to kill the rest of them."

"Nyx! Jet!"

Both turned their heads, surprised to see Rian and Zaida pushing through the trees. Rian's eyes were worried as he broke through the trees. Zaida's eyes were shifting around, searching for danger, her bow and arrow ready.

"What the hell happened?" he asked breathlessly. He seemed alarmed as he looked down at Savra's headless corpse. "Are you two okay?"

Nyx glanced up at Jet before back to Rian. "We're fine," she said slowly.

Jet was scowling. "Took you long enough," he snapped.

Nyx wanted to roll her eyes, but instead she winced, the adrenaline and anger ebbing away, leaving her feeling weak. She pressed her hand against her side again as the pain resurfaced.

"We've been searching for you for hours," Rian said, the worry still on his face. He stepped toward Nyx when she leaned forward. "Are you hurt?"

Nyx caught his arm when he moved toward her, wincing around a breath. "I'll be okay," she said.

"We need to get out of here," Zaida said.

Rian nodded as he led the way back to camp, Zaida trailing protectively after them.

29

Celo Cavus, the capitol city of Siccita.
The twenty-fourth day of winter, the 906th
year of the reign of King Paraximus Lamia.
Friday, January 13, 2012.

It was dark and cold. Fear was coursing through her, making her heart flutter. She lifted her head, seeing faint light falling across a stone floor. Beyond a thick door, screaming filled the halls, echoing off the stone. The smell of blood was heavy in the air. She pulled her legs to her chest, tears sliding slowly down her face. She jumped when the heavy wooden door swung open, torchlight filling up the cell.

"He will see you now," a soldier said gruffly, standing in the doorway.

Bailey moved unsteadily to her feet, her body trembling. She stepped slowly toward the soldier, feeling terror streak through her as he caught her arm. Darwren had been easy to deal with compared to the man escorting her. He pulled her after him, not caring when she stumbled up the stairs from the dungeons. He only released her when they stepped into the main hall of the castle.

Bailey was surprised as she looked around, seeing how decadent the castle was. It was full of things that had clearly been taken from other countries. It was extravagant and it made Bailey feel cold. She knew Paraximus always took what he wanted. Her breath caught in her throat when she saw a girl, probably not much older than she was, dressed in rags and cleaning a polished floor. She looked up for a moment when they walked by, her face swollen on one side.

"No one told you to stop scrubbing!" another servant suddenly barked.

Bailey flinched at the sound of a slap, almost grateful the soldier pulled her down another corridor. Her fear was heavy and her heart was pounding hard in her ears. She tried to calm herself when a page opened a tall, gold-coated door.

Paraximus's throne room was filled with people. Entertainers were dancing and playing music, while his guests talked and drank from jeweled goblets. The party didn't stop as the soldier brought Bailey into the room, around the crowd and toward the dais.

Bailey could feel the stares of Paraximus's courtiers as she was forced to kneel on the steps, the soldier standing over her. She couldn't move, keeping her head down as the evil king lifted his hand to silence the room.

"You're not what I expected," he said slowly.

Bailey lifted her eyes slowly, feeling her heart twist. He was leaned back in his throne, his hands on the armrests. His feet were both on the floor, tall black boots shining in the light. His traditional garb was stark white, with gold accents, but a red cloak was around his shoulders. Long tendrils of black hair fell over his shoulder, tethered back from his face, and a gold crown sat on his head. His eyes were dark and there was an angry, hard set to his jaw. He seemed unimpressed as he gazed at her.

"You're just a little girl," he said, the same edge to his voice.

Bailey wasn't sure what he expected her to say. She flinched when he moved to stand. She tried to still her trembling as he stepped down the stairs of the dais toward her.

"Look at me, Seer," he commanded.

Bailey turned her eyes up slowly, trying to choke back her fear. She gasped softly when he caught her chin, tilting her head back.

"You do have the Atturon eyes," he commented absently. His fingers were hard and cold as he looked down at her. "Can you tell me what I want to know?"

Bailey blinked then, feeling a tear slide down her face. "I—we weren't trained to touch the Visus," she whispered. She winced as his hand tightened on her face before he roughly let go of her.

Paraximus scowled down at her, his dark eyes dangerous. "And what has become of your sister?" he demanded.

Bailey shook her head, feeling braver when she thought about Ellie. She looked up at him, anger spiking through her. "She's gone to Liana," she said, trying to keep her voice steady. "Your lackey let her get away. You won't find her."

Paraximus smirked darkly then, his eyebrow quirking slightly. "Is that what you think, girl?" he asked. He waved his hand then, motioning for someone to come forward.

Bailey looked over her shoulder, surprised to see soldiers escorting Darwren. Blood was dripping from his nose and his mouth, and he looked like he'd been put through hell. His hair was disheveled. He fell to his knees, fear on his face.

"Please, My King," he begged, "I will bring you the other girl."

Paraximus didn't seem fazed as he stared at Darwren.

"You only had one job," he said dryly. He motioned to Bailey. "How did a little girl, an Inerse of all things, get away from you?"

Bailey flinched at the way he said Inerse, as if they were the lowest of the low in his mind.

"It won't happen again," Darwren whimpered. "Allow me to bring her to you."

Paraximus grinned darkly then. "You've had enough chances." He motioned to his guards. "Take him away." Sinister delight was on his face. "I'll deal with him later." He turned his eyes on Bailey then. "You're going to help me find your sister."

Bailey gasped when he suddenly grabbed her by her hair, pulling her to her feet. She couldn't struggle against his grip as he marched her through the throne room and into the main hallway.

"I almost feel sorry for you," Paraximus said as he dragged her through the foyer and into a courtyard. He was grinning in a twisted way that made Bailey's fear worse. "Anything I could do to you would be pleasant compared to facing Daya."

Bailey looked up when a temple suddenly loomed over them. She wanted to struggle against him, but he was too strong. She felt darkness pressing against her as a soldier opened the temple door and allowed them in.

The atmosphere inside the temple was oppressive, making Bailey want to claw her way free and run. She tried to twist against Paraximus's grasp, but he only tightened his grip before shoving her away from him. Bailey realized she was standing at the foot of an altar, a white statue towering over her. She turned to look for an exit, but the soldier had shut the door, and Paraximus's tall form was blocking her.

"What have you brought for Our Lady?"

Bailey spun around, her breaths quick and sharp in her chest. Her eyes widened as she watched a woman step toward them from the darkness of the altar. She wore a hood over her head, but Bailey could feel the way the air felt impossibly cold and thin around her.

"As per our agreement, Mara," Paraximus said then. "One of the Atturon girls for Daya."

Bailey couldn't move as the woman stepped toward her. She felt frozen, the woman's eyes flashing with murderous intent, a fanged smile behind her lips. Her touch was as cold as ice as she lifted a finger to brush Bailey's pale hair from her face.

"She will be pleased," Mara said, turning her dark, dead eyes on Paraximus. "You have done well."

Paraximus seemed unhappy at her words. "She hasn't upheld her end of our agreement." He nodded to Bailey. "I only have one."

Mara smiled, baring her rows of shark teeth. "Daya always keeps her promises," she said, turning back to Bailey.

Bailey stepped away from her, feeling the cruel intent in her aura. The woman's hand snaked out, and Bailey attempted to dodge her. "Don't touch me!"

She didn't seem bothered as she caught Bailey's arm, pressing the heel of her opposite hand against Bailey's forehead. "Show me where your sister is," she growled.

Bailey drew a sharp breath, her eyes suddenly turning a bright blue. Her face went slack, her eyes staring at nothing as Mara forced the Visus to surface.

A myriad of colored lights flashed before her eyes. She felt like she was moving impossibly fast, her mind covering vast distances in seconds. Just when she thought she couldn't take anymore, the light exploded, becoming clear.

Trees surrounded a small clearing, a party of dragon

riders sitting around a fire. To one side, a yellow-haired girl lay sleeping on the ground, a man sitting beside her. She instantly recognized the girl as the one that they'd been instructed to help.

The scene went dark.

Bailey staggered back from Mara's cold hands, drawing breaths as if she'd been submerged in water. She pressed her hands against her chest, trying to regain some semblance of mind. Her body was trembling, taxed from the effort of the vision.

"She is in Ymber," Mara said, her voice sounding faint to Bailey's ears. "She is with the princess." A laugh suddenly rumbled from Mara's chest. "And your son."

Bailey's mind swam then and she collapsed to the cold stone floor, Mara and Paraximus's voices lost as her mind faded into darkness.

30

*The Pangere Camp, Abjure Forest, Ymber.
The twenty-fourth day of winter, the 851st
year of the reign of Queen Liana Estrella.
Friday, January 13, 2012.*

No, Bailey, stop!" Ellie screamed, suddenly
throwing her hands over her eyes. She didn't remove
them for a long moment, feeling tears flooding her eyes and
a hand on her arm. Amaya was beside her, her hand on Ellie's
shoulder.

"You're safe," she said quickly, comforting Ellie. "What
did you see?"

Jet turned his head to look at the Atturon girl, moving to
stand. "What's going on?"

Liam looked over at him, Rian and Zaida coming closer.
"She saw something," he said, looking down at her. "Ellie,
what did you see?"

Ellie shook her head, unable to speak for a long moment.
"Bailey," she managed finally. "He has Bailey. He forced her
to find us."

"Who is Bailey?" Rian asked, standing by Liam. "And

who has her?"

"My sister," Ellie whispered, her knees buckling suddenly. Amaya caught her, easing her to the ground. She held her stomach tightly, feeling sick at what she'd just seen. "Paraximus has my sister."

Rian's eyes instantly shifted to Zaida.

Jet pressed his hand against his forehead. "Well fuck," he said, drawing their gazes. "If you see what she sees, then it works the other way, too, doesn't it?"

Ellie nodded. "He forced the vision," she said, trying to catch her breath. "I could feel magic…" She shook her head as if she didn't understand. "He was forcing her to see me, using my eyes to see what was around me."

Rian cursed softly in his native tongue, turning away slowly.

Jet was scowling as he looked at the Pangere leader.

"This isn't good," Rian said, his brow furrowed.

"You think?" Jet demanded. "If Paraximus can see where we are then we're all dead."

Rian's eyes narrowed as he looked at Jet. "What does Paraximus want with you two?" he asked slowly. "He sent that woman and her dragon to try to kill you. Why is he trying so hard to find you and Nyx?"

Jet's scowl deepened. "That doesn't matter," he said quickly, crossing his arms. "You need to take that girl and get away from here."

Rian shook his head. "We won't leave you and Nyx," he said. "Eomryr Lani said—"

"I'm not giving you a choice," Jet snapped. "You need to go now. Savra wasn't the first and she won't be the last to come after us." He pointed angrily to Ellie. "And *she* is like a walking beacon that will lead him straight to us."

"Hold on," Rian barked. "If it wasn't for Ellie, you two

would be dead, and not by Paraximus's hands." He looked at Ellie, who was watching them, her brow furrowed. "It's time for some answers."

Jet stepped away from Rian, putting himself between him and Nyx, who was lying on the ground, sleeping to recover from her injuries. "We didn't ask to be saved," he said shortly. "And we don't need you."

Zaida was watching him carefully, her dark eyes narrowed. "Who are you?" she asked, her voice guarded.

"It's none of your business," Jet said defensively.

"Jet…"

All eyes turned then, seeing Nyx trying to sit up from where she'd been laying. Once they'd returned from their ordeal, she'd been exhausted from the amount of magic she'd used. Jet crossed to her quickly.

"Tell them," Nyx said, holding his gaze. She winced slightly as she struggled to sit up, her side still sore. "Tell them or I will."

Jet shook his head, frowning at her. "We can't—"

Nyx caught his hand, pulling herself up to sit. "We need them," she said softly, so that only he could hear her. "We would be dead or worse if they hadn't come when they did."

The beginning of a scowl was pulling at his face as he turned away. Nyx knew that was his way of relenting, and she turned to look at the Pangere members. She wasn't surprised to see that their eyes were on her, varying levels of distrust on their faces. She winced as she pushed the blanket over her legs, moving to stand.

"Well?" Zaida asked tersely. "Are you going to tell us what's going on?"

Nyx nodded as she stepped slowly toward Ellie and Amaya. "My name is Nyx Estrella," she said slowly. "Liana is my grandmother."

"What?" Amaya asked, jumping to her feet. "How can that be?" She frowned. "All of Liana's family were slain…"

Nyx nodded. "My father and my mother, yes," she said softly. "But I was taken and hidden." She glanced at Jet. "Until the time was right for me to return."

Amaya's eyes were wide suddenly, brimming with a million questions that Nyx could tell she was dying to ask. Rian interrupted her as he addressed Nyx. "So you're the lost princess?" he asked, a hint of disbelief to his voice.

"Ellie knew, but kept it a secret," Nyx said slowly. "She wanted to protect all of you."

Rian's eyes were wide now, too. "It makes sense now," he said. "It makes sense why Eomryr Lani would tell us to rescue you."

"And what about you?" Zaida said coldly, looking over at Jet. She seemed annoyed and unimpressed with this new information. "Where did you come from?"

Nyx turned to look at him, feeling her heart skip a beat.

Jet was scowling darkly, his arms crossed. He looked like a caged animal, ready to escape at any moment. He clenched his jaw for a moment before looking away. "Liana sent me to bring Nyx back."

Tense silence filled the camp, only broken when Liam spoke. "Why you?" he asked, confusion in his voice. He looked at Ellie and Nyx. "What makes you so special?"

"Jet used to be part of Paraximus's military, okay?" Nyx snapped, becoming annoyed with all of their questions. If Paraximus was coming, they were running out of time. "What difference does it make? Liana still sent him for me. And we need to get away from here."

Zaida was still scowling. She held up a hand to silence Liam's retort as they looked to Rian.

"Is this true?" Rian asked quietly, turning his eyes on

Ellie. His expression was unreadable.

Ellie nodded, unable to meet his gaze.

Rian turned away from the group, stepping toward Raimi. His thoughts were chaotic. What the hell was he supposed to do now? He couldn't just abandon them. Nyx was too important.

"What do you want to do?" Zaida asked as she looked at him.

Raimi turned to look at Rian as he put his hand against her shoulder. She looked over at the group, baring her teeth, sensing his distress. Rian pressed his free hand against her face to silence her. He wasn't sure what to do, but one thing was clear.

"We need to move," he said finally, looking at them. "If Paraximus has seen us here, he will come, if what you say is true." He looked at Ellie. "He'll take whoever he can." He turned his eyes to Amaya and Liam. "Take Ellie and go toward Angulus."

Amaya frowned at him, worry in her eyes. "What about you and Zaida?" she asked.

Rian held up his hand. "Just do it," he ordered. "We will catch up with you."

Amaya looked at Liam, clearly unhappy, but she didn't argue. She began to pull her armor over her head, fastening her chest piece in place. Liam followed her lead, and soon they were both ready, their helmets tucked under their arms.

"Are you sure this is the right thing?" Amaya asked again, pausing before she climbed onto Declan. "We're stronger together."

Rian nodded, boosting Ellie onto Emma behind Liam. "We won't be far behind." He looked to Liam. "Now go."

Once they were in the air, spiraling into the clouds, Rian turned to look to Zaida, Nyx, and Jet. Nyx was surprised at the way Rian's face morphed into an angry glare.

"You aren't some nobody like you'd have us all believe," he growled, looking at Jet.

Jet didn't seem fazed as he watched Rian.

Zaida reached for Rian's arm. "Rian—"

Rian turned and glowered at her, yanking his arm away. "Don't tell me to calm down," he snapped, looking back to Jet. "It doesn't matter what you're hiding, you're still Siccitan scum."

Jet crossed his arms slowly, his eyes narrowing dangerously.

"My brother and my uncle died because of people like you," Rian continued, fury on his face. "Give me one good reason why I shouldn't let Paraximus have you. I'm sure defectors don't last long."

Nyx suddenly stepped between them, fierce anger on her face. "If anything happens to Jet, I will make sure Liana doesn't help you," she growled. She could feel Jet's surprised stare on the back of her head. Despite what happened, she still needed Jet. "He's saved my life countless times. He stays."

Rian seemed surprised by her words, but his surprise melted away into frustration. "You have no idea what kind of monster he is," he hissed. "Siccitans are all the same. He'd throw you to the wolves in an instant." He missed the way Nyx flinched, his words ringing too true as he turned his eyes on Jet. "I doubt you were really even sent to get Nyx. Does Liana really know that you have her granddaughter?"

Jet caught Nyx's arm when she moved as if to say more to Rian. He looked at Zaida, who hadn't moved to intervene. She seemed annoyed and worried about her leader, but knew it wasn't her place to stop him. "Look, you go on with your people," he said, pulling Nyx toward him. "We'll be fine." He really wanted this to be the end of their partnership with the Pangere. Rian was asking too many questions.

The dragons suddenly shifted, turning their heads and snarling. Both Rian and Zaida spun around as the dragons moved to their feet and bared their teeth. They curled around their riders protectively. A bright light began to fill the air, swirling magic creating a sucking wind. The light began to spin and spiral together, creating a twisting, bright portal.

"What the hell?" Rian murmured, confused.

Jet scowled as the stench of dirty, decaying, wet dogs hit his nose. "Atrox," he breathed.

Rian turned to frown at him, but Zaida caught his arm, pulling him toward the dragons. "Look out!" she suddenly yelled.

Nyx felt Jet grab her as the sound of yipping and snarling filling the campsite, and a massive, hairy beast flung itself through the portal at Rian and Zaida. She didn't have time to react as Jet pushed her into the trees.

"Run!" he shouted.

Nyx took off in front of him, pushing her way through the brush. It sounded like a pack of very large wolves was chasing them as they crashed through the trees.

"Get to the river!" Jet called from behind her.

Nyx could hear the river in the distance and she ran toward it. She tried to ignore the way howls and barking filled the trees around them, making it sound like they were surrounded. Finally, she broke free of the trees, sliding to a stop in front of a steep drop.

"Now what?" she demanded, turning to look at Jet. She felt her chest clench when he summoned his blades.

"We fight or we jump," he said, his eyes shifting around. The trees were alive with the sounds of the atrox.

"Oh god," Nyx breathed, looking over the cliff. The water had to be fifty feet below them, and it was spinning and churning. Boulders jutted up at odd angles out of it. "What are our chances if we fight?"

Jet looked at her and then to the water. "Not great." His eyes shifted to the drop. "We have to jump."

Nyx shook her head, her breaths harsh and ragged, her heart in her throat as fear filled her. She couldn't make it if they jumped. The water was too fierce, and she wasn't that great of a swimmer. She looked up at him.

"We have a chance if we jump," Jet said, dissolving his blades and turning to catch her hand. "If the atrox catch us, we're definitely dead. There's too many." He knew the odds just as well as she did, but the thought of drowning or possibly living was much better than the thought of being ripped to shreds by teeth.

Nyx held onto his hand tightly. "On three?" she asked, looking at him.

Jet seemed annoyed for a moment, but then one of the atrox burst through the trees. It was snarling as it charged them, standing on two feet, claws bared. "Three!" Jet yelled.

Nyx felt a scream stick in her throat as Jet pushed her, but it was soon swallowed by the raging water as it spilled into her mouth and nose, suffocating her. Her body felt out of control as she spiraled through the water. She managed to break the surface of the water and draw a painful breath before crashing heavily into the side of a boulder. Sharp, blinding pain shot through her skull as her head connected, sending her into the current.

Surprise made her gasp, water filling her lungs again. The current was strong and ripped her feet from under her, sending her spinning through the depths. She fought desperately to the surface, her vision blurred with pain and water as she coughed and sputtered.

Her strength was useless as the river pulled her along, despite how she struggled to paddle to the shore. She thought she could make out Jet's form swimming after her, but the water soon pulled her under again, slamming her into another boulder. She clawed at it desperately, trying to get a hold, but it was too slick, covered in algae.

Nyx gasped and choked when she broke through the water again. She could barely see as the water whipped them down the stream. It curled and spun, like an angry snake, pushing her under again. When she managed to gain the surface once more, she gasped hard for air, feeling Jet's arms around her middle.

His words were lost on her as the water swept her under again. She didn't know which way was up suddenly, and she felt out of control as the water pushed her down. Her arms and legs felt heavy suddenly, and she released her grip on him, feeling the pain from the blow to her head trying to drag her under.

Jet shook his head, drawing a sharp breath as he broke through the water. It was fierce and cold as it yanked him along, and he swam with the current. Hope filled him when he caught sight of Nyx. He'd lost her during the fall from the cliff, and he swam toward her now, catching her wrist and pulling her to him.

"I've got you," he breathed. He paddled the best he could against the current as she groaned softly. He could see blood running down the side of her head. "Stay with me."

Her arms were wrapped loosely around his neck. He could feel her shallow breaths, and he knew she was losing consciousness.

He held his breath as a wave caught them, dragging

them under the surface again. He couldn't see any way out of the water, and suddenly a sharp sound caught his attention. He wrapped his arms around her as he realized they were being pulled ever faster toward a massive waterfall. In the dark it was nothing but a sucking void, and he felt his heart catch.

He swore colorfully as he struggled to reach the shallower water. His boots were scraping across the bottom as they came closer, but he knew it wasn't enough. His heart skipped a beat as he tried to prepare for what was coming.

"Hold on, Nyx," he breathed, pressing her tightly to him.

Her hands clenched at his back as she seemed to realize what was happening.

The sudden sensation of falling erased all thoughts from Jet's mind. It seemed like an eternity passed, and his arms tightened around her waist. The feeling of hitting the water at the bottom was like being slammed into a wall. The pain was blinding initially, but then the cold of the water shocked him back to alertness.

He gasped for air as he surfaced, realizing that Nyx had been ripped from his grasp. Mist distorted the air as he looked around frantically for her, finally catching sight of her paddling weakly near the shore. He winced as he paddled toward her, dragging himself and her out of the water.

"Nyx?"

He was on his hands and knees beside her, his onyx gaze searching her face. She was coughing softly, her breathing harsh. She fell back, laying in the muddy grass.

"We made it," he said breathlessly. His eyes shifted over her, seeing blood oozing from the wound to her head.

Nyx couldn't think straight, fierce pain making her thoughts scatter.

"Just be still for a minute," Jet said.

Nyx felt dizziness and nausea accost her. She pressed her hand tenderly against the cut on her forehead, wincing. "Let's not do that again," she managed. She could feel his eyes on her as he leaned on his elbows beside her.

"I told you we had a chance," he said, his voice humored.

Nyx pinned him with a weak glare. "I could have done without the boulders and the waterfall," she said through a sigh.

Jet drew a slow breath. He could have done without those, too. He looked around, seeing that the short stretch of open grass faded back into thick trees. "We shouldn't stay here too long," he said, pushing himself to his feet. "They'll be looking for us."

Nyx caught his hand and pulled herself up, feeling mildly dizzy. She wiped at her forehead again, the pain having lessened as the wound healed. "Do you think Rian and Zaida got away?" she asked, following him as he started toward the trees.

Jet frowned to himself. "If they know what's good for them, they got the hell out of here and won't come back."

Zaida held her arm as Zayde and Raimi curled around her and Rian. They had fought off a few of the atrox, but once they realized that their prey wasn't here anymore, they'd run off into the trees. Unfortunately, Zaida had taken a clawed swipe to the forearm. It stung like a bitch, blood running down her arm. She turned to look at Rian as he dug through his bag.

"Here," he said, pulling out bandages and a bottle of *drac'vene*. He turned to her, pulling the stopper out of the bottle with his teeth. He knew Zayde's magic would help her heal, too.

Zaida braced herself as he poured the liquid over her arm, feeling the biting sting as it cleansed her wound. It was an antiseptic, and it helped her flesh to regenerate a bit quicker, along with Zayde's magic, but it still didn't keep her arm from twinging painfully. She bit her lip tightly as Rian wrapped her cuts.

"Are you okay?" Rian asked, looking up at her face. He knew Zaida could take pain. She would never complain, and she'd have to be practically dying to ask for help.

Zaida nodded, looking into the trees. "Do you think they got away?" she asked.

Rian followed her gaze, feeling his ire ease a bit. "I hope so," he said quietly. "Eaten by atrox is not the way to go."

Zaida turned to look at him. "We need to help them."

A surprised scowl pulled at Rian's face. "Why?" he demanded. "Jet is a murderer."

Zaida sighed shortly. "Don't you think that Liana considers his crimes paid for?" she asked. "She had to have sent him to find Nyx. Why else would he be with her?"

Rian shook his head, clearly unhappy. "I don't know, Zaida," he said in irritation. He sighed deeply. "You know how I feel about this."

"That's not for us to decide," Zaida said sharply. "And for someone who believes so whole-heartedly in Eomryr Lani, you are quick to cast off his words. He told us to help them."

Rian scowled at her then. "Don't use my own convictions against me," he snapped.

"It only bothers you because it's true," Zaida said. "He still has a role to play in whatever the Sky Dragon's ultimate plan is, and so do we."

Rian rolled his eyes, pressing his lips together tightly. "I hate it when you're right," he said finally.

Zaida offered a dry smile. "Let's find them." She pulled herself onto Zayde's back, watching Rian do the same.

31

The Abjure Forest, Ymber.
The twenty-fifth day of winter, the 851st year
of the reign of Queen Liana Estrella.
Saturday, January 14, 2012.

NYX WAS PANTING AS SHE followed Jet over the crest of a hill. She looked behind her, seeing that they had finally escaped the massive, towering trees of the forest. In front of them, open grassland stretched as far as she could see. She let her hands rest against her knees as she looked up at Jet.

"Where are we?" she managed.

Jet's eyes were looking out over the empty expanse, his face set in a frown. "The locals call it the Calamo Mare." He looked over at her, offering a thin smirk. "The Grass Sea."

Nyx straightened. "Great," she said quietly. "Where are we going?"

Jet nodded into the distance. "We should head toward Angulus, like the Pangere," he said. "We can catch a boat to take us up the coast toward Regius Carmen."

Nyx sighed deeply. The Grass Sea was massive, stretching infinitely into the distance. "Are we walking?" she asked.

Jet looked at her. "I'm not carrying you," he said shortly.

Nyx rolled her eyes, making her way down the hill. This was going to suck.

The grass was thick and a rich, deep blue in the light from the low-hanging midday sun. As they made their way through it, Nyx noticed that the ground sloped slightly downward before leveling out.

"Does it snow here?" she asked, looking over at Jet.

He shrugged. "Sometimes, I guess," he said. "The winds from the bay push most of the weather toward the mountains and the forest."

Nyx nodded, digesting his words. The ground looked wet, the moisture clinging to her boots and pants as they walked. The wind that picked up was cold, but not nearly as cold as it had been in Festra.

Nyx felt a stabbing pain in her heart when she thought about Festra. She tried not to think about Melinda, but she could feel her throat constricting anyway. She would miss her friend, and she wondered if Branimir was okay. She looked up at Jet as she tried to swallow the tears she felt.

"Do you think Branimir is okay?" she asked quietly.

Jet glanced at her, barely hiding the guilt that furrowed his brow. "I'm sure he's fine," he said dismissively.

Nyx pressed her lips together. She wasn't so sure, but it did no good to think about it now. There was no going back. At least Melinda's murderer was dead.

She tried to let her mind wander as she waded through the thick grass. She noticed that small insects would leap from the blades every so often, a spark of light accompanying them as they shot away from them. The sound of their calls was like the crickets Nyx was used to, and it helped to put her at ease as she followed Jet.

They walked in silence for a long time before Nyx looked over her shoulder. The forest was fading, but it seemed ominous as it stood over them. She felt as if eyes were watching them from its black, shadowy depths.

"Do you think the atrox will find us?" she asked finally, looking at Jet.

He scowled at the thought. "I don't know," he said after a moment. He looked around the Calamo Mare, feeling his gut twist. There was nowhere to hide and there was no way for them to outrun atrox. He turned to Nyx. "If they do, you have to fight, like you did with Savra."

Nyx's footsteps slowed, her eyes afraid as she looked up at him. "I don't know if I can fight those things," she said, her voice small. With Savra, she'd been angry. Right now all she felt was fear.

"You are a weapon," Jet said, turning to face her. "You can do anything you can imagine."

Nyx drew a shaking breath. "I'll try."

Jet nodded. "I've taught you everything you need to know, you just have to do it."

Nyx looked down at her hands, realizing her heart was racing. "I should have been able to stop Savra," she said quietly.

Jet felt immense guilt tugging at him. He could handle watching Melinda die, but everything inside him had nearly come undone when he saw Savra standing over her. He tried to push the thought away as he looked up at the sky. He couldn't imagine what he would have done if she had died, or the weight of having her death on his hands.

"You did stop Savra," he said finally, turning his eyes back to her. He surprised her when he stepped toward her, catching her hand. "But you shouldn't have been in that situation to begin with."

Nyx's brow furrowed as she looked up at him. "Is this your way of apologizing?" she asked quietly, her voice sticking in her throat. Her mind had been constantly replaying his words, but she knew what he said wasn't true.

Jet let go of her hand as resolve crossed his face. "I won't let it happen again," he said. "I'll make sure you get to Liana in one piece."

Nyx felt her heart sink at his words. She could only nod as he turned away, motioning for her to follow.

Chatter and growls surrounded a Sagier as he led his pack from the depths of the forest and into the sunlight. He paused at the edge of the forest, looking down across the grassy plains. Like his comrades, he was panting heavily, his tongue lolling from his wolfish lips. His ears turned forward to catch any sound as he placed a hand against a tree. When his eyes landed on two small figures in the distance, he threw his head back, a howl echoing across the expanse.

The atrox on either side of him charged forward into the grass, their thick legs carrying them quickly toward their prey. Their claws were ready as they snarled excitedly. The Sagier joined them, his own yipping sending his pack into a frenzy.

The sound carried across the plain, making Nyx pause to look over her shoulder. Her heart leapt into her throat as she saw the massive beasts charging after them. "Jet … "

"Ah shit," Jet said, catching Nyx's elbow and pulling her after him. The sound of the atrox pursuing them became loud as the monsters closed in on them, excited in their bloodlust.

Nyx struggled through the grass behind him, feeling as if she was slogging through water. Her fear was intense, making her legs feel like rubber. "We can't out run them!"

she called to Jet.

He slowed, turning to look at her before his eyes shifted over her shoulder. The atrox were swift, their eyes glowing brightly as they spread around him and Nyx. He summoned his blades, knowing they had to fight. He looked at Nyx.

"You can do this," he said slowly, holding her gaze.

Her eyes were scared, but she nodded shortly. She lifted her hands as she watched the hairy monsters surround them. Up close they were hideous; their hair was mangy and dirty, their eyes glowing brightly like wolf-eyes. They stood upright, their hands clawed and their back legs like dog's legs. Their chests were thick and muscular, and their arms hung well past their knees. They were hunched over, but that didn't seem to slow them as they surrounded her and Jet. They looked like werewolves. Their stench filled the air, some mixture of wet animal hair and death.

Nyx felt her back press against Jet's as the atrox surrounded them in a circle. She was surprised when one, much bigger than the rest, moved into the circle. His eyes seemed more intelligent than the others, and a piece of armor covered his chest. Nyx noted that it was smeared with what looked like blood. Tangled dreads hung from the back of his head, threaded with what looked like his victims' teeth.

He slowly stalked forward, something like surprise on his face. "Master," he growled, tilting his head. His eyes were fixed on Jet. "Atrox told you dead."

Nyx glanced over her shoulder at Jet. Master? Did commanders have control of these beasts?

Jet lifted his blades defensively. "You were told wrong, Sagier," he said darkly.

The Sagier grinned in a sick, twisted way, baring all his teeth. "No matter," he snarled, murderous delight on his face. "Will make you dead."

Nyx gasped when he suddenly sprang forward. She ducked as Jet used his blades to impale the beast, throwing him away from them. She watched as the Sagier growled angrily, struggling to stand, his blood staining his hair. He snarled a command, which sent the other atrox into a frenzy. They lunged at Nyx and Jet, and she lifted her hands, feeling her heart in her throat.

A yell filled the air, and it took a moment for Nyx to realize it was hers. Her hands were raised in front of her, and for a moment, time seemed to stop. Hot, blistering magic filled her palms as she stared at the teeth of the nearest beast. Just as it was nearly upon her, she released the magic, watching as it strung from her hand like lightning, slamming into the atrox's chest.

Surprise filled her as she watched the beast fall dead on the ground, but she didn't have long to contemplate it. She felt like she was on auto-pilot as she turned, summoning more lightning blasts. She managed to drop two more of the beasts before realizing that Jet had sprung away.

He moved with ease and skill, carving into the atrox's bodies. He looked like a dancer as he twisted under their claws, leaving a trail of fallen beasts in his wake. As he sliced through the last one, he turned to look at her.

Nyx was breathless as she stared at him, her heart catching when his eyes widened. She turned to look over her shoulder, but realized it was too late as the Sagier barreled down on her. The breath was knocked from her lungs as it pinned her to the ground. She dug her fingers into its disgusting coat, trying to keep its razor teeth from digging into her flesh. She didn't struggle long though, as Jet appeared, flinging the beast away from her.

"Are you all right?" he asked as she rolled to her feet.

Nyx nodded, her breaths ragged as she watched the

Sagier stagger to his feet. A sudden anger, much like the one she'd felt before with Savra, filled her. "I've got this," she said slowly, surprising Jet. She held out her hand, the golden sword suddenly materializing. It felt familiar in her hand.

Jet was stunned as he watched her walk forward, lifting the blade as if she'd done it a million times before. Her hands were steady as the Sagier lunged at her. She swung the sword and dodged to the side, cleaving the monster's head from his body without even a scratch. She straightened as the Sagier collapsed, turning to look at Jet.

They were silent as they stared at each other for a long moment. Jet felt on edge as he watched her, remembering the last time she'd come at him with a sword. "You good?" he asked carefully.

Nyx nodded, seeming surprised herself as she looked down at the golden blade in her hand. "I don't know how…" She looked up at him, her eyes confused. "It just seemed like the right thing to do. Like with Savra."

Jet let a small breath leave his lips. All he remembered about the fight with Savra was killing her. He couldn't remember Nyx having a sword. "That's good," he said cautiously. He watched as she let go of the sword, causing it to dissolve into gold sparks. "That might be your weapon of choice."

Nyx looked up at him. "You think so?" she asked.

Jet nodded. "It'll become easier with practice," he said, letting his hands rest on his hips. "I guess our training is finally paying off." He watched as she stepped slowly over the atrox on the ground, uncertain as she walked toward him.

She looked up at him as she came closer. "Are you afraid of me?" she asked.

Jet forced a smirk. "Well, the last time you had a sword you tried to kill me, so," he shrugged.

Nyx felt the tension and confusion leave her. "You know that wasn't me," she said, frowning at him.

Jet's brow quirked. There was irony in her words somewhere. "I feel like we say those words a lot," he said wryly. "At least I don't try to make you feel bad about it."

Nyx sighed in exasperation. "That's not fair," she said quickly. "I didn't know what I was doing."

"Really?" he quipped, crossing his arms. "Because I could say the same."

"It's not even remotely the same, and you know it," Nyx snapped.

Jet scowled at her. "How do you figure?" he demanded. "You were going to kill me, too, if I hadn't stopped you."

Nyx knew she was on the losing end of the fight. "The difference is that I wasn't in love with the person trying to control me."

Jet's scowl deepened and he turned away quickly. "Come on," he commanded sharply. "We need to move."

Nyx followed him as he pressed on, deeper into the Calamo Mare, knowing that had been a low blow. But this whole situation wasn't fair. It wasn't fair that she couldn't trust him, and it wasn't fair that he wouldn't just be straight with her.

"Jet?" she asked, looking up at his back.

He paused, turning to look at her, the sour expression still on his face.

"Why can't you just be honest with me?" she asked.

Jet's eyes narrowed. "Honest about what?" he asked, more vitriol in his voice than he intended.

Nyx drew a slow breath, holding his gaze. "Savra," she said softly. "Your old life." She glanced away for a moment. "I know you have a past, and I'd like for you to trust me with it."

Jet's eyes shifted over her head before back to her face.

"No," he said stonily. "I already told you how our partnership would be." He turned away. "The less you know, the better."

Nyx felt crushed as they walked along in silence. She just couldn't understand him. She was surprised when he came to a sudden stop, and she was instantly on guard. "Why'd you stop?" she asked, her eyes shifting around. She turned her eyes skyward when a shadow suddenly fell over them.

Overhead, the dragons were circling, and Rian was calling down to them. Relief filled Nyx as Raimi and Zayde touched the ground. Rian was grinning as they approached, remaining astride Raimi.

"Need a lift?" he asked.

Nyx returned his grin as she caught his hand, allowing him to pull her up behind him. "I can't tell you how glad I am to see you."

32

Itera-Patet Road, Calamo Mare, Ymber.
The twenty-fifth day of winter, the 851st year
of the reign of Queen Liana Estrella.
Saturday, January 14, 2012.

ELLIE HELD HER HANDS OUT to the fire, warming her fingers. She looked up when Amaya settled beside her, pulling her armor from her arms. She sighed, as if it was confining. Ellie craned her head as Amaya unfastened the buckles of her breastplate, trying to see the design etched into it.

Amaya's lips quirked on one side. "You wanna see it?" she asked as it slid off her chest.

Ellie looked up at her, offering an embarrassed smile. "I've never seen such fine metalwork," she said.

Amaya held out the piece of metal to her. "Rian had our pieces made by his father's smith," she said in explanation. "He does the best work in the Fornax."

Ellie took the piece, surprised at how heavy it was in her hands. Amaya made it seem rather light. Of course, it didn't hurt that all the Pangere members were tall and well-built. She set it across her knees, running her fingers over the etched design. It was a dragon, curling as if made of smoke. Tendrils bloomed from the middle of the piece and swirled around the edges. She started to hand it back to Amaya.

"Are they all custom?" she asked.

Amaya nodded as she took it. "It's neat, huh?" she asked, grinning.

Ellie nodded. "I don't know how you stand to wear it all the time," she said. "It's heavier than I thought."

Amaya shrugged. "I guess I'm used to it," she said. She turned to set it to the side, her thick braid of pink hair falling across her shoulder. She pulled her satchel toward her. She took out a piece of fruit, giving Ellie a sidelong glance. "I'm so sick of fruit."

Ellie sighed, trying not to sound ungrateful. "I don't want to complain about food," she said, taking a piece from Amaya. "But I am too."

"Well, lucky for you girls, I found us some dinner!" Liam called as he walked through the tall grass. He lifted the fowl he'd hunted and cleaned as if it was some amazing trophy.

"Oh, thank the gods," Amaya said, setting her uneaten fruit to the side. She was smiling broadly as Liam came into the light of the fire.

Ellie felt her stomach rumble as she watched Liam lay the bird across the flames. She looked up at him as he settled beside Amaya. He'd shed his armor when they'd first landed. His eyes shifted from the fire to the tall grass around them.

"I spotted a road about a half-mile from here," he said.

Ellie nodded. "The Itera-Patet road," she said. "It goes from the royal city to Paries' Wall."

Liam looked back to their dinner. "Is there anything we need to watch out for?" he asked, glancing up at Ellie.

Ellie shrugged as she watched him. "Maybe highway bandits or something," she said. "I never left Sorona, so I don't know about the people who travel the roads."

Liam frowned lightly as he looked at Amaya. He said something to her in their native tongue, and Amaya frowned, too.

"What?" Ellie asked, watching as they looked at one another.

Amaya shook her head a bit, looking down at her hands in her lap. "It's nothing," she said, forcing a small smile as she looked at Ellie. "Liam was just mentioning things that happened back home."

Ellie tilted her head curiously. "You guys never talk about your home," she said then. "Not very much, anyway." She waited for them to offer her more, but they both were silent. "What's it like in Fornax?"

Amaya seemed mildly surprised as she looked to Liam. "I love it there," she said slowly. "Wonderful, warm weather, with beautiful open fields and beaches…"

Liam agreed, nodding his head. He looked to Ellie. "I think it's something you have to see to truly understand," he said teasingly.

Ellie returned his grin. "I have to be honest," she said. "I'm surprised you guys would come here." She looked between them. "Don't you miss your families?"

Amaya's eyes shifted down to her hands again, her face smoothing. Liam looked to her, as if he was alarmed for a moment. Ellie noticed the change in the atmosphere immediately, and she felt her face flush.

"I'm sorry if that's too personal," she said quickly.

Amaya shook her head then. "No," she said, looking up at Ellie and offering a small smile. She looked at Liam. "I don't have any family to go back to."

Liam looked unhappy. "That's not true," he started.

Amaya shook her head. "Don't Liam," she said darkly.

She looked back to Ellie, seeing the confusion on her face. "Liam and I came from the same small village near the beaches of the Cymacalix. We were sold as children into slavery."

Ellie felt horror streak through her. "How—why would your families do that?"

Liam was frowning at Amaya. "Our village was very poor," he said. "They did it to keep us alive." He looked back to Ellie. "When you can't put food on the table, you have to do things that are extreme or don't make sense to outsiders."

Ellie looked at Amaya, seeing that she didn't feel the same way.

"It doesn't matter the reason," Amaya said. "We were sent away to Forn, the royal city. We would have been like the countless other children sold on the slave market, had it not been for Rian's mother."

"She bought you?" Ellie asked, the words feeling weird and dirty as she spoke them.

Amaya nodded. "She brought us to live in the palace," she said. "Me, Liam, and Zaida."

Surprise filled Ellie. "Zaida?" she asked quickly. "She was a slave child too?"

Amaya nodded again, a grin pulling at her lips. "Queen Genevieve was injured in a terrible accident with a dragon," she continued. "She was unable to have more children and her dream had always been to have many. So she adopted us into her family. Raised us alongside her own children, Rian and his sister, Kaira. She taught us to protect each other and keep each other safe. She wanted Rian to have loyal followers and protectors, and she had us trained to be just that." She looked at Liam. "Of course, we love Rian and his family like they were our own, so loyalty isn't an issue."

Liam nodded at her words, looking down at the roasting

fowl. They would do whatever it took to keep one another safe.

Ellie felt like a light had come on in her mind. "And that's why you follow Rian so faithfully," she murmured.

Liam laughed softly. "Well, when you put it like that, it makes us sound like Rian's lapdogs," he said.

Ellie felt her face turn red again. "Sorry," she said quickly. "I just didn't really understand until now."

"Well, so to Liam's point, the Pangere are my family," Amaya said. "I will never go back to our village or to the man and woman who sold me into slavery."

Liam was once again frowning at her. "I would go back if I had the chance."

Amaya looked at him, her brown eyes deeply hurt before she covered it with a scowl. "That's your choice, then," she said, standing suddenly.

"Amaya, don't—"

"I just need a moment alone," she said quickly, cutting him off. She turned and walked toward Declan, catching his reins and leading him into the grass.

Ellie looked at Liam. "I should apologize to her," she said quickly. She was surprised when Liam reached across the small fire, catching her hand.

"Just let her be," he said, his eyes earnest. "She's mad at me."

Ellie sank back to the ground. "I shouldn't have asked."

Liam shrugged, checking their food again. "It doesn't make it any less the truth," he said, glancing back to her. He turned his head to stare after Amaya, sighing deeply before looking back to the roasting fowl. "I think it's ready."

Amaya felt sick as she leaned against Declan's shoulder. His scales were bright and beautiful in the early-evening moonlight as he turned his head to blow a hot breath across her face.

"I shouldn't be mad at him," Amaya said, brushing her knuckles across his nose. "But I just can't understand why he'd want to return to those people."

Declan purred deep in his chest, his bright red eyes focused on her. He bumped her with his head, wanting more pets.

Amaya caught his head in her arms, hugging him tightly. "You're the only one who really gets it," she said softly. She thought back to the night when they'd broken Declan free from the ship that was taking him to his death.

He'd been little more than a slave then, being shipped to a place where he would surely be killed. Rian, Zaida, and Liam had broken him free from the Siccitan ship where he was being held prisoner. They hadn't known if he would stay or return to the Fornaxian mountains to live among his own kind, but he chose to follow them. He followed them back to Forn, as if he knew that she would be waiting there for him. From the first moment Amaya had seen him, they'd been inseparable.

She was the youngest of the Pangere members, and the last to get a dragon. She'd thought she would have to settle; it was possible to own a dragon and be unbonded to it. But her bond with Declan had been instant and easy. She was glad she'd waited for him to find her. Even now, she could feel the heaviness in her chest easing away with his soft rumbling.

Being bonded with a dragon was something reserved for the royal family. It meant the riders and the dragons shared feelings, and the dragons granted their riders their healing power, and sometimes small other strengths. In rare instances, like with King Fell and his dragon Jasper, a rider could harness the full power of a dragon's magic. Amaya hoped that she and Declan would live long enough to be as ancient and close as King Fell and Jasper.

She drew a slow breath as she looked up at the sky, feeling the tightness in her chest gone. She turned to Declan, tilting her head. "Come on," she said gently. "I'm hungry."

Declan trumpeted his agreement then, making Amaya laugh.

33

Itera-Patet Road, Calamo Mare, Ymber.
The twenty-sixth day of winter, the 851st
year of the reign of Queen Liana Estrella.
Sunday, January 15, 2012.

A TALL MAN STOOD AT the edge of the road, looking out into the distance. Behind him, a team of weather-worn, thick-skinned, horned beasts were resting, hobbled as they pulled sleepily at the grass. Large male raperes laid around the edges of the camp as well, their bright blue feathers ruffled against the cold of the night. A large cart was on the side of the dirt road. Between the beasts and the cart, a handful of men sat silently around a fire.

"What is it, Callis?" one called.

Callis nodded mutely into the distance, the rising sun beginning to obscure what he'd seen. "People," he said shortly. His hands were tucked into the pockets of his pants as he stood there.

"So what?" the same one continued. "We need to get back to Perfide."

Callis turned to look at him then, a scowl on his face.

"Donovan won't be happy with the little bit we're bringing back to him." He nodded toward the fading firelight he'd seen. "Bringing a few more to work the mines might help."

The man turned to look at the others, who were listening silently to the exchange. "Russ, Bakar, go."

Two burly, identical-looking men moved to their feet. One carried a sword at his side and the other a mace. They still wore the armor and colors of their clan, but the house flag had been scratched from the metal. They didn't say anything as they disappeared into the tall grass, in the direction Callis indicated.

The men were silent as they waited for their comrades to return. The sun was half-risen when the brothers came back, just as silently as they had left.

"Well?" Callis asked.

Russ stepped forward, his ugly and scarred face twisted in a grin. "Donovan will be *very* happy with us," he said. His hand was on the spiked end of his mace. "It's people all right, two females and a male, but that's not the best part."

Callis scowled at the man. "Spit it out then."

"Dragons," Bakar suddenly said. His lips were curled in a twisted smile like his brother's, but his face was far less hideous.

Callis grinned to himself, turning to look over his shoulder at the three men. "Looks like we've got a job, boys," he said. He motioned for them to pack up and harness the horses. Dragons would bring a mighty price in Perfide.

34

Near the Itera-Patet Road, Calamo Mare, Ymber.
The twenty-sixth day of winter, the 851st year of
the reign of Queen Liana Estrella.
Sunday, January 15, 2012.

JET WAS STILL AS HE sat beside dying embers. He was watching Nyx on the opposite side of the fire as she slept soundly. He knew she was exhausted from all the fighting. Her sleep was deep, and she hadn't moved since she'd laid down.

He wasn't sure how she and the dragon riders could be so relaxed. Even though they were far from the forest and the carnage they'd left in their wake, Jet still couldn't help but feel like eyes were everywhere. He wondered if it was a side-effect from Savra's charm.

Guilt made him clench his jaw as he thought about Savra. He'd never meant to put Nyx in that position. Of course, he also thought that he was impervious to any type of charm. Obviously, he was wrong, and he didn't like that. He glanced down at the ground, wondering why the monster hadn't tried to free him. He felt worse at the thought that maybe the monster liked it.

Maybe the beast wanted to be with Savra. Or, maybe the beast wanted to take Nyx's power.

Jet shook his head quickly to clear the thought away. He knew he had to be extra careful now. He turned his head as the first rays of the sun filled the morning sky.

It wouldn't be long before Rian and Zaida were awake and ready to find the rest of their party. It was surprising how far the others had traveled, but Jet knew that dragons could cover a lot of ground. He also knew they were getting closer to the royal road, and he didn't want them to linger for too long.

It wasn't uncommon for robbers, or worse, to patrol the road, looking for easy targets.

Jet turned his eyes back to Nyx when she moved, reaching her arms into the air to stretch. She sat up slowly, wincing slightly. When she caught his gaze, she stood and made her way toward him.

"I don't think I'll ever get used to sleeping on the ground," she said, still wincing as she kneeled beside him.

Jet rolled his eyes, standing as well. He motioned for her to be quiet, leading the way into the tall grass. Nyx followed him silently, taking in the landscape below as they crested a hill.

"What's that?" she asked, pointing into the distance. She could see a winding, thick path that cut straight through the countryside.

"The Itera-Patet road," Jet said. "It goes straight to Regius Carmen."

"Is that where we're going?" Nyx asked.

Jet shook his head. "Too dangerous," he said, looking at her. "If we keep heading east, we'll reach Angulus, and we'll take a boat from there."

Nyx frowned at him. "Why a boat?" she asked. "Why not just take the road all the way there?"

Jet sighed. "I just said it's too dangerous," he quipped.

"Well I know, but why?" Nyx asked, put out with him.

Jet crossed his arms. "Thieves, murderers, kidnappers, just to name a few," he said shortly.

Nyx's eyes widened. "Oh," she said. She looked up into his face, seeing that his eyes were lingering on her blood-stained coat.

"We need new clothes," he said absently.

Nyx tried to grin. "Why?" she joked. "This isn't in style?"

Jet pinned her with a look as he turned toward the rising sun. By the time they returned to camp, Rian and Zaida were awake and preparing to leave.

Near the Itera-Patet Road, Calamo Mare, Ymber.
The twenty-sixth day of winter, the 851st year of
the reign of Queen Liana Estrella.
Sunday, January 15, 2012.

C ALLIS MOTIONED SILENTLY TO HIS companions to flank the camp. His heart was racing with excitement as he readied his spear and ropes. It had been quite a while since they'd had such good fortune. With two dragons, Donovan had no reason not to pay them extra this time.

Callis watched as Bakar and Russ moved into position behind the sleeping beasts. Being the largest of the group, they would be able to handle the dragons while Senin, Galex, and Maxin took care of the riders.

On his signal, Russ and Bakar leapt onto the dragons, wrapping thick ropes around their mouths. Startled snarls filled the air, as well as yells of the people. Callis didn't pay them any heed as he leapt forward to help Russ and Bakar.

He leapt to the side when the bright blue dragon whipped its tail, barely dodging a crushing hit. He rolled under a swinging paw, thrusting his spear into the beast's wing and wrapping the rope in his hands tightly around it. The dragon roared in pain and whipped viciously, managing to tear from Bakar's grasp.

Bakar yelled out as the beast swung another clawed foot, catching him across the chest. Fortunately, his armor protected him, but it did little to stop the enraged creature as it knocked him to the ground, baring its teeth.

"Whoa there!" Callis yelled, jumping onto the beast. He yanked at the spear in the dragon's wing, listening to it screech in pain as it fell back from his man. He threw his arms around the dragon's neck, looking desperately to Bakar. "The ropes, Bakar!"

The large man moved to his feet and threw them around the dragon's head, tying up its mouth expertly. With its mouth secured and a wing pinned to its side, Callis wrapped up its legs, bringing it crashing to the ground. Beside them, Russ seemed to have no issue over-powering the green dragon.

"Declan!" one of the females yelled.

Callis turned in time to see her elbow Maxin in the face. She broke free of Maxin's grip, pulling a knife as she ran at him, fury on her face. Callis didn't expect the fierceness she fought with as she swung the knife, trying to gut him. He managed to catch her wrist, twisting it forcefully and causing her to drop the blade.

"That's enough now," he commanded. "I would hate to bloody that pretty face."

She surprised him again when she used her off-hand to try to hit him. Unfortunately for her, Callis was stronger. He caught her wrist, hitting her across the face. With a grunt, she fell to the ground, momentarily stunned.

Rage and tears were in her eyes as she looked up at him, wiping blood from her busted lip. "What is it you want?" she demanded. "We don't have any money."

Callis laughed cruelly, looking over at the two others. The blonde-haired girl was trembling next to the man. Senin had a blade pressed against his throat, probably the only thing keeping him from trying to kill all of them.

"Your dragons are payment enough," Callis said. He looked over at the twins, watching as Bakar helped Russ bind the smaller, green dragon and begin to drag her away.

"You'll pay for this," the man suddenly ground out.

Callis turned to look at him. "Don't worry, you'll get to be with them a while longer," he said. "You're all coming with us." He nodded his chin, a sickening grin on his face. "You'll fetch a nice price in Perfide."

Senin yanked the man to his feet, while Galex and Maxin took care of the women. They forced them through the grass toward where their cart was waiting.

Callis took a moment to look around the campsite, noticing that the only things that seemed to be of value were pieces of armor. He thought he might make some money off it, but decided against taking it as Bakar and Russ returned.

"Let's get this one loaded," Callis ordered, helping the brothers drag the tied-up dragon away. Once they reached Perfide, their reward would be great.

Liam pulled against his bonds for the thousandth time, feeling his heart fluttering in his chest. Emma's head lay near his feet, her mouth bound tightly with ropes. Her eyes were confused and dim as she lay there, barely moving. She glanced at him often, as if trying to understand why this was happening to her.

"You won't be able to hold us for long!" Liam yelled suddenly, gritting his teeth at a burly, armor-clad man. "Our leader will find you and slaughter you like the worthless curs you are."

The man scowled, reaching into the saddlebag of his rapere. He pulled out a stained and dirty rag and slid down from the beast's back. "Quiet you!" he commanded, shoving the dirty rag into Liam's mouth.

Liam shook his head, trying to fling curses at the man behind the rag, but it was useless.

"Liam, don't make it any worse," Amaya suddenly said softly beside him. Her busted lip was swollen, but she looked just as ready to kick someone's ass as he felt.

Liam turned his head, seeing Ellie's fearful eyes as she looked at him. Declan was tied next to Emma, his head near Amaya's feet. They all had been loaded onto a large, flat cart, which was being drawn down the road by a team of asperpellis, horse-like creatures with horns and thick, almost scaly, skin.

All around them, their captors were riding big raperes with ragged blue feathers. They looked just as haggard as the asperpellis and their mounts, with dirty faces and clothing. The strange thing about them was their armor. It appeared to have had a crest carved into the pieces at one time, but it had been rubbed away purposefully.

Liam had a sinking feeling. These men were house deserters, most likely mercenaries.

They were all big, burly, and strong, save for the thin man that appeared to be the leader. It was possible that most of them were related, brothers or cousins, but it didn't matter who they were to Liam. He would kill them all the same for what they were doing to Emma and Declan.

The dragons hadn't gone down easily, but these men seemed to know what they were doing. They'd been able to take down both dragons before dosing them some sort of potion that sucked the life and fight right out of them. With their legs, wings, and mouths tied, the dragons were helpless. They'd all been loaded onto the cart and now they were being taken who knew where.

"How are we going to get out of this?" Ellie whispered, her voice trembling.

Amaya looked to her, feeling pity for the girl. "We'll be okay," she said gently. "Rian and Zaida will come for us." She wished she had better things to say to put Ellie at ease, but that was all she could hold onto for hope. "They'll rescue us." She looked around at their captors. "And they'll slaughter these dirty bastards."

Ellie moved closer to Amaya. "I hope you're right."

36

Near the Itera-Patet Road, Calamo Mare, Ymber.
The twenty-sixth day of winter, the 851st year of
the reign of Queen Liana Estrella.
Sunday, January 15, 2012.

ZAIDA LEANED INTO ZAYDE'S NECK as he twisted quickly into the air. She could feel Jet's hands tighten on her waist, and it made her smirk. She didn't trust him as far as she could throw him, but she knew that they were stuck with him. She looked up as Raimi flew overhead, her massive shadow falling over them.

They'd been traveling for a short time, but Zaida was thankful for the time in the air. The cold wind on her face helped to clear her thoughts. She felt at peace when she was flying with Zayde. At least, she would have, if she hadn't been lugging around a passenger.

She was lost in her thoughts, surprised when Raimi suddenly ducked past her, swooping toward the ground. She felt her teeth clench as she urged Zayde after Raimi, wondering what Rian was doing. Her heart dropped into her stomach as they came closer to the ground, and she caught sight of what Rian had.

Zayde landed easily in the tall grass, and Zaida threw her leg over his head, hitting the ground running. "Amaya!" she yelled, her heart racing in her chest. "Liam!" She didn't hear Rian's words as she ran through the thick grass.

A campsite sat before them, ransacked. Signs of a struggle were all about, the most telling being deep gouges from dragon claws and dark blood stains. Zaida ran toward a satchel that she knew instantly to be her cousin's, seeing her armor strewn about.

Tears were pricking at her eyes as she picked up Amaya's breastplate. "Amaya," she breathed, fear heavy in her chest. She turned to look over her shoulder, seeing Rian, Nyx, and Jet approaching slowly. "Someone has taken them!"

Rian's eyes were wide and surprised as he looked around the campsite. He pulled his helmet from his head slowly, walking toward where the claw marks marred the ground.

Nyx looked up at Jet, feeling worry constrict her chest. "Who did this?" she asked softly.

Jet shook his head, watching Rian study the ground. He was stunned that someone had even managed to go toe-to-toe with two dragons, let alone come out victorious. He watched as Rian knelt slowly, touching the dark stains in the soil.

"Dragon blood," Rian said, his voice heavy. He looked over to Zaida, his eyes worried.

"We have to find them," Zaida said, desperation in her voice. She knelt, her movements panicked as she picked up Amaya's things.

Nyx felt her heart twist. She didn't think anything could upset Zaida. She glanced up at Jet before walking toward her. She picked up a notebook and handed it to Zaida, noticing the tears that were escaping her eyes.

"We have to go after them," Rian said as he approached them.

"Whoa, no way," Jet said then.

Nyx's head snapped up as she helped Zaida pick up Liam's things and put them in his bag. Her heart caught in her chest as she stared at him.

"We can't go with you," Jet continued. "I can't put Nyx in danger like that."

Rian was frowning deeply. He seemed to weigh Jet's words before nodding. "Yes, I agree," he said softly. He turned to look at her and Zaida. "It would be too dangerous."

"No," Nyx said, feeling anger filling her. "We're going to help you find them." She stood, looking at Jet. "They saved us. We owe them."

Jet crossed his arms tightly.

"No, Milady," Rian said. "You don't owe us anything." He looked back to Zaida. "Liam and Amaya are our family." He looked back to Nyx. "I wish we could see you safely to Regius Carmen, but we can't leave them behind."

Nyx shook her head, angry tears pricking at her eyes. "We're not going to do that," she said, her voice steady, despite the way her knees were shaking. She looked at Jet. "I won't let this be like Melinda."

Jet looked away, drawing a short breath. "Nyx, be reasonable," he said slowly. Guilt flooded him at the mention of Melinda's name.

"No!" Nyx yelled, shaking her head. "They're in the mess because of us!" She looked at Rian. "We're going with you."

Rian was surprised, and he looked at Jet, seeing that he was scowling at Nyx, but otherwise silent. He nodded slowly, looking over her shoulder toward Zaida. "We need to go then," he said.

Zaida seemed to have composed herself as she walked toward them, a bag in each hand. She seemed surprised when Nyx took one, throwing it over her back. She was further surprised when Jet did the same, the same scowl still on his face.

Rian caught Raimi's head in his hands, pressing his forehead against hers. She closed her eyes, and Jet and Nyx both felt the pull of magic around them.

"What is he doing?" Nyx breathed.

"He's telling Raimi to find our kin," Zaida said softly beside her. "Raimi is an excellent tracker. She can track a mole in the ground for miles." She brushed at her face. "Raimi will find Amaya and Liam."

Rian slowly opened his eyes, and Raimi drew a deep breath, scenting the air. She turned her head, a soft growl escaping her lips. Her eyes were sharp and focused, reminding Nyx of a pointer dog.

"She's got the scent," Rian said, pulling himself onto her back. "Let's go."

37

The Anemoi Camp, Plains of Pacier, Ymber.
The twenty-sixth day of winter, the 851st year of
the reign of Queen Liana Estrella.
Sunday, January 15, 2012.

RAPHAEL SAT ALONE OUTSIDE OF the tent where he'd been housed. He looked up as shadows fell over him, seeing Bartuk and Ellena swooping across the skies. Men and women were emerging from the nearby tents, eyeing the dragons with distaste.

"Your pets are still new to them," Kadira called, walking up the pathway toward him. "Even after all this time."

Raphael used a crutch to push himself to his feet. His chest felt tight, newly-formed scars twisting across it. He still had trouble standing, infection from his wounds having weakened his body. He only vaguely remembered the first week he'd spent in the Anemoi's care.

"You look nice today," he said, looking Kadira over. She wore white animal-skin pants, with a matching coat. Her hair was pulled up from her face, and a crown of meadow flowers decorated her hair. She seemed light on her feet today.

"It's my wedding day," she said, a smile creeping across her lips.

Raphael had noticed that Kadira wasn't one for idle pleasantries, and he found the little smile on her face endearing. "Then what are you doing here?" he asked. "You should be getting ready."

Kadira clasped her hands in front of her. "I've actually come with a request from the Khanh," she said.

Raphael felt his lips pull in a frown.

"Don't look so nervous," Kadira said, her smile widening. "He asks you to join us for our celebration and night of feasting."

Raphael's eyes widened. These people had treated him like the outsider he was since day one. The healers never spoke directly to him or made eye contact with him. The Khanh had only come to see him a few times, and never asked anything more than how he was feeling and when did he think he would go. He'd been excluded from any celebrations the tribe held, and treated like a pariah. Not that he expected any different, it was just her request surprised him.

"Uh, I don't know if I should," he said finally. He looked overhead to the dragons, who were playing in the clouds. "I really need to be on my way."

Kadira frowned at him, crossing her arms. "You won't get far," she said, motioning to his crutch. "You can barely stand on your own."

Raphael scowled. "I need to find my sisters," he said, for what felt the millionth time. "I'm well enough to go, and your Khanh is ready to see me gone."

"And what do you think you'll do?" Kadira asked. Her eyes were unhappy. "Your campsite is too old to track them."

Raphael sank slowly to sit on the stool behind him. "I know," he said, sighing through his teeth. He'd thought about where Ellie and Bailey might be every day. He truly didn't know how he would find them, just that he had to.

"Listen," Kadira said, stepping toward him. "If you think this is what you need to do, then you should go."

Raphael looked up at her. "It's not what I *think* I have to do," he said vehemently. "I have to rescue them."

"I might know how to help you," Kadira said slowly, ignoring his tone. She looked down, shuffling the toe of her shoe across the dirt. "There's a woman that travels with us, but never comes into the circle." She motioned at the small village of tents. "She goes by Ti. She's a medicine woman, but she practices the dark magic." Kadira's nose wrinkled, as if she was disgusted by the thought of the woman. "She will tell you what you should do."

Raphael looked confused. "Why does she stay beyond the tents?" he asked.

Kadira crossed her arms tighter. "She is *inferi*," she said slowly. Her eyes shifted around as if she was worried someone might hear her. "She gained her powers by taking an oath to the gods of the *nocens magieri*."

"The what?" Raphael pressed.

Kadira sighed in exasperation. "She's a witch," she snapped. "It's bad luck to talk about her, especially on my wedding day." She glanced around again and swallowed thickly, stepping closer to him and dropping her voice. "She can see things. She can tell you where to find your sisters."

Raphael's eyes widened. "Are you sure?"

Kadira nodded and stepped back. "I will let Rais know that you're planning to leave," she said, her tone business-like. "He will make sure you have food and supplies to help you on your travels." Her tone and her eyes softened. "I'm sorry you can't stay for tonight's festivities."

Raphael offered her a smile and moved to stand. He

winced slightly, dull aches spreading through him with his effort. He took a step toward her, and wrapped his arms around her. "Thank you for everything," he said.

Kadira was stiff in his embrace for a moment before she returned his hug. "Be safe, friend," she whispered. When he let go, she put her hand on his arm. "Call on us again, should you ever need assistance."

Raphael nodded. He knew that once Kadira was married to the Khanh, she would have a position of power among her people. He hoped that he never had to take her up on her offer. He didn't say anything else as she turned and walked away. He sank slowly onto the stool, knowing that she was probably right; it was too soon for him to try to go, but he knew he had to. He wasn't sure where his sisters were, but he knew that they needed his help.

38

*The outskirts of the Anemoi Camp, Plains of
Pacier, Ymber.
The twenty-sixth day of winter, the 851st year
of the reign of Queen Liana Estrella.
Sunday, January 15, 2012.*

ARKNESS HAD FALLEN OVER THE plains by the
time Raphael was ready to leave. As promised, Khanh
Rais had gifted Raphael supplies. Raphael just hadn't expected the man to be the one to deliver them. He'd been very
kind and wished Raphael well-travels, but Raphael knew it
was just because he was glad to see him go.

That was fine with him, though. He didn't want to be a
burden, and there was no reason to linger.

Raphael had just finished tying the last of the bags onto
Ellena's back as the sun had fully slipped away. In the distance, light was pouring into the center of the tent-city, and
music was filling the night. The wedding festivities were in
full swing, and it brought a small smile to Raphael's face. He
wished only the best for Kadira and her clan.

Once he was ready, he looked up at Bartuk, who stood
tall over him. "I need some help, old friend," he said.

The dragon rumbled, lowering his silver-scaled body toward the ground. He laid flat, allowing Raphael easier access to the saddle.

Raphael winced, fighting through the pain and weakness as he managed to pull himself onto Bartuk's back. He hated feeling so small and helpless, but he knew it would just take more time for his body to heal. He also knew he was lucky to be alive. His injuries should have killed him, not to mention the havoc the infection had wreaked on his body.

After a moment of regaining his balance and the feel of the saddle, he urged Bartuk on. The silver dragon launched into the air, causing Raphael to grasp tightly to the saddle, but he evened out quickly in the night sky. The cold air was refreshing as it blew across Raphael's face. Behind them, Ellena followed her mate.

Raphael circled the camp, looking into the distance for any sigh of Ti. His eyes finally landed on a small, faint shape in the distance, and he turned Bartuk toward it. It didn't take long for the massive dragon to bring them close, so that Raphael could see a tent like the others set up in a grove of small trees.

"That must be her," Raphael said, leaning forward into Bartuk's neck. He held on tightly as Bartuk began to descend, landing a short distance from the tent. He slid slowly from the dragon's back, wincing at the effort and the stiffness that shot through him.

Ti's home was not what Raphael imagined as he stood beside Bartuk. It was a tent, much like the others, but it was built into the grove, ropes holding the tent up crudely. It leaned haphazardly to one side. Thick grass was grown up around the tent, covering the entrance.

Raphael pulled the cane he used from Bartuk's saddle, hobbling slowly toward the tent. He ignored the way Bartuk whined softly, as if unhappy with his decision. As he came closer, he could see that the tent was dirty and ripped in some places, while patched together with assorted materials in others. There was no smoke coming from the top of the tent, which surprising Raphael.

"Hello?" he called as he neared. He paused to watch for any sign of movement. "Hello? I'm looking for Ti."

The front of the tent suddenly rustled a bit, pulling back as if someone was peeking out from inside. It was dark, however, and Raphael couldn't make out a shape.

"I was told you could help me," he continued. He gasped in surprise when the flap suddenly opened wider. A haggard old woman appeared in the moonlight.

"Magic is what you seek, yes?" the woman croaked, her voice hard like dry clay. She began to move closer to him, so that Raphael could see her face. Her eyes were whitened with cataracts and she seemed like an unassuming old lady, but a feeling of unease began to fill him as she came closer.

"I'm looking for someone," he said. "I was told you could help me find them."

Ti paused a short distance away from him, her face pulled in a scowl. She turned her unseeing eyes to the dragons, something like a hiss leaving her lips. "Send your beasts away," she barked.

Raphael glanced over his shoulder, seeing Bartuk watching the woman carefully. He didn't make a sound or move, but Raphael could see the tension in his neck. Bartuk was ready to attack. It made the anxious feeling worse, but he turned to the dragon. "Go on," he said, waving his hand. "I'll call when I'm done."

Bartuk bared his teeth, clearly unhappy, but turned and wandered away as Raphael instructed.

"That's better," Ti snapped, her scowl turning up in

a grin. "Come inside." She turned away. "I have what you want."

Raphael followed her slowly, the soreness in his limbs increasing. He wondered if he was pushing himself too hard and too quickly like Kadira had said. Once he reached Ti's tent, he pushed the flap aside to follow her. He was surprised when a clap filled the darkness, and a fire sprang to life.

The tent was just as disheveled inside as outside. A bed-roll was to one side, while a small table and a host of vials were to the other. Small parts of animals were hung from her ceiling to dry, and Raphael thought he saw jars full of soft tissue parts among her vials. The unease worsened as he looked to her.

"I know who you seek," Ti said, shuffling toward her table. She pulled a wide-rimmed bowl toward her. "I will help you find them, but it will cost you."

Raphael felt his heart jump. "I don't have any money," he said quickly. "I can give you food or supplies."

Ti looked up at him then, a crooked smile pulling at her face. She was missing a few teeth, and there was an edge to her grin that was dangerous. "I don't need your material things, boy," she said. "You must pay with blood."

Raphael frowned. "Blood?" he asked quietly.

Ti began to empty different vials into the bowl. Raphael wondered how she knew what was what as she went about it without stopping to even smell the ingredients she was adding. Once she was done, she lifted a pestle and began to grind the contents. Once she was satisfied, she lifted a jug of water and poured it into the concoction. She stirred it once with her finger before beginning to chant soft words that Raphael didn't understand.

Surprise filled him as a cold wind suddenly filled the tent. It seemed to have a mind of its own as it snaked around them, tously his hair and moving toward Ti. Her eyes began to glow, as did her bowl of water. Her voice began to change the longer she chanted, and Raphael felt his fists clench. Underneath the hum of her own voice, he could hear the squeals of spirits; the ones she summoned to do her bidding. He clenched his jaw hard when she turned to him.

"Your offering," she commanded, holding out her hand. The cold wind was stilling curling throughout the tent.

Raphael stepped toward her, unsure of what she wanted until she caught his hand in her gnarled fingers. Almost out of nowhere, she produced a knife. Raphael wanted to protest, but she was so quick, she'd pricked his finger before he could do anything to stop her. He couldn't move as she held his finger over the bowl, a single drop of his blood falling into the water.

Light suddenly exploded from the bowl, blowing Ti's hair back and pushing Raphael away. He threw his hand up to shield his eyes from the light, watching as Ti began to be lifted from the ground. Her hands were outstretched and her head thrown back, her eyes wide as her chanting reached a fevered crescendo. She was nearly screaming now, the brightness of the magic she was conjuring filling the tent.

Just when Raphael didn't think he could take much more, everything suddenly went still. The light from the bowl was still bright, but the wind and the chanting ceased. Ti was still hovering over the ground, and she turned to face him, a deep, demonic voice resonating from her chest.

"See what you are searching for," she commanded.

Raphael realized he was shaking as he moved toward the bowl. He leaned over the table slowly, blinking against the bright light. He drew a startled gasp when images began to form.

The first was a black room. A light filtered through a

doorway. The room was built of thick stones, and a straw bed lined one wall, while the other was covered in filth. The door suddenly opened, and a tall guard appeared against the light. There was no sound, but he flung a tray of food onto the floor before slamming the door shut.

Raphael felt his heart in his throat as he watched the scene ripple, shifting to a wide dirt road. A cart was loaded with dragons, and two unfamiliar people sat on either side. An expanse of blue grass stretched around the road, and mountains were far off in the distance. A group of dirty mercenaries surrounded the cart.

The images faded as quickly as they came, leaving Raphael stunned. He backed away from the bowl and the table, his whole body still quivering. He looked up at Ti when she began to laugh, the same deep voice echoing inside her.

"Are you not satisfied?" she demanded.

Raphael wasn't sure what he'd seen in the second image, but he knew what the first was. "One of them is in Celo Cavus," he breathed, feeling sick.

Ti's laughter filled the tent. "You cannot hope to rescue her, boy," it snapped. Ti lowered to the ground. "Not a weakling like you."

Raphael took a step back as she floated toward him, her face suddenly contorting. Rows of razor teeth formed behind her lips, and her eyes turned black.

"A mortal like you could never face the Dark One," she snarled.

Raphael held up his cane, backing toward the door slowly. Despite his fear, anger was filling him. "You know nothing about me, demon," he snapped. He swung his cane at her, watching as she ducked away from it.

Without second thought, he turned and bolted through the tent and into the night. He ignored the way his body was screaming with pain. "Bartuk!" he yelled. He didn't bother to look back to see if she was pursuing.

The silver dragon appeared in a flash, a warning growl emanating from his chest as he curled protectively around Raphael, allowing him to clamber onto his back. Raphael turned his eyes toward Ti's tent as Bartuk flapped his wings, seeing that it was dark inside, no sign of the magic that she'd summoned. He held tightly to Bartuk, his mind and heart racing. He didn't know how he was going to help his sisters.

I hope you enjoyed this book. Would you do me a favor?

Like all authors, I rely on online reviews to encourage future sales. Your opinion is invaluable. Would you take a few moments now to share your assessment of my book on Amazon or any other book review website you prefer? Your opinion will help the book marketplace become more transparent and useful to all.

Thank you!

About the Author

E. Paige Burks is a graduate from Texas A&M University with a degree in Agricultural Communication and Journalism.

Her book, Return to Royalty, won the 2016 Author U Draft to Dream Award in the Young Adult category, the 2017 Dan Poynter Global Ebook Awards in the fantasy category, and is a finalist in the 2017 Best Book Awards.

When she is not writing fantasy and love stories, she enjoys Mexican food, singing out loud, cuddling with her cats, and taking long naps.

E. Paige Burks lives in Houston, Texas with her husband, four dogs, four cats, one horse, and a single bird named Ricki.

Check out her other titles:

The Heart of the Guardian

Return to Royalty, A Gexalatian Tale Series Book One

Jewels for Gemma

A special preview of

ЯETURN TO ШAR

Book Three

of

A Gexalatian Tale Series

PROLOGUE

20 years ago in Regius Carmen

ILENCE HAD FALLEN OVER THE kingdom. It was deafening, and it made the ache in Liana's chest worse. How could this have happened?

Tears crowded her eyes as she brushed dark hair from her son's face. He was still, his bloodied tunic having been replaced by clean clothing for his final trip. Beside him, on the funeral pyre, lay his golden-haired wife. Her only consolation was that their blonde-haired, green-eyed child didn't lie with them.

Finally, she stepped away from the pyre, nodding to the men around her, who held torches. The crowd gathered to witness the funeral was silent as a clergyman said words about Liana's family. One by one, the men lit the pyre.

Liana's tears spilled over as the people around her began to whisper the traditional farewell blessing. Over and over again, her heart was breaking. She should have seen this coming. She should have been able to protect her family.

She turned her violet eyes skyward, watching plumes of dark smoke rise into the morning sky, carrying away the spirits of her loved ones. An all-consuming emptiness filled her. Once again, she was alone. And somewhere out there, her granddaughter was running for her life. The thought made her stomach turn, and she clenched her teeth, bowing her head.

Jet would pay for this.

He had done many heart-wrenching, deplorable things. But this was not something she could overlook.

Liana lifted her head, feeling fury filling her. She looked toward her Captain of the Guard, Antony, who stood at her side. His dark brown eyes were wide with tears, and he blinked in surprise when she placed her hand on his arm.

"I need to see him," she whispered.

Antony's eyes widened further. "I'm not sure that is wise, Your Grace," he said, brushing at his face. "You know he will only twist your misery for the sake of his own pleasure."

Liana nodded. "That is why I need to see him now," she whispered, feeling doubt edge into her heart. "Before I lose my nerve."

Antony drew a slow breath, nodding. He motioned to his guards, escorting her silently from the ceremonial grounds.

Once they reached the safety of the castle, Liana pulled the dark veil from her hair. She wouldn't let Jet think he had won anything. If anything, he had started something that she knew he would have no desire to finish. She would have his blood on her hands this day.

The walk to the dungeons was long and every step sent a pulse of hatred deeper and deeper into Liana's heart. If she had thought that keeping Jet prisoner would drive Paraximus mad, then killing Jet would be the driving blow to her former lover. He would know that she was not what he thought she was, and that she would be coming for his head as well.

Antony and his followers paused as they reached the door where the abomination waited for them. He offered

Liana a beseeching look once more. At her curt nod, he opened the door.

Liana gritted her teeth as the door swung in, light filling the cell. She drew a slow breath as she stepped inside, feeling a guard at her elbow. Satisfaction filled her as her eyes fell across Jet. He was restrained, shackled to the wall. The chains that bound him crackled with electric magic, keeping him from moving.

Despite the fury writhing inside her, Liana still felt her stomach turn when Jet lifted his face, his onyx eyes shifting over her. A sadistic grin slid across his face, which was still splattered with blood. Everything inside her suddenly ached to break his neck, but she held her ground.

"Do I have your attention now?" Jet asked, his voice dark.

"If my attention was all you sought, then there would have been easier ways," Liana quipped. She pressed her hands together, realizing she was trembling.

Jet grunted in annoyance. "Too easy," he said indifferently. "I prefer the pain I have brought you."

Liana fought for control, feeling her fury escalate. She knew Jet could feel it pulsing through her aura, but he ignored it. It suddenly occurred to her that he was too calm for what he had just done.

"You must think that you have every move I will make calculated," she said.

Jet's glittering eyes shifted to her, narrowed dangerously.

Liana felt a small smile slide across her face. His look said volumes, and she suddenly understood his intentions. "Do you tire of my dungeons already?" she asked, hearing the condescending tone in her voice.

Jet scowled darkly. "Is a hundred years not enough for you?" he suddenly snapped, frustration lacing his voice. "Just kill me like you came here to do."

Liana drew a slow breath, feeling the tension suddenly ease away. That was his game, wasn't it? He knew she would never let him go, so he tried to force her hand. Unfortunately, he didn't know who he was dealing with. "I have no intention of killing you," she said easily.

The fury that suddenly creased his face once again spoke volumes. He said nothing as he turned his face away. It took a long moment for him to school himself into indifference again. Liana braced herself when he finally drew a slow breath.

"Then perhaps it will please you know that I enjoyed killing them," he said quietly, keeping his eyes trained away from her. "I enjoyed the way they begged and pleaded for me to stop." A soft smile pulled at his lips. "Especially the woman." Regret crossed his face. "It's a shame that the child escaped. I would have—"

"Enough!" Liana clenched her fists, feeling her jaw clench tightly. The pain was still fresh, and she took a quick step toward him.

A devilish grin was on his face as his eyes shifted to her before away again. His words had hit where he had intended.

"I will not bend to you!" Liana suddenly yelled at him. She felt tears fill her eyes. She knew she needed to get herself together. She was only playing right into his hands and doing what he wanted. She took a moment to control herself, her voice soft when she finally spoke. "You will spend the rest of your days here." She nodded at the stone around them. "These walls will be the last thing your eyes will ever see. You will not have the satisfaction of a murderer's death."

With that, she turned, walking quickly from the cell. Once Antony had shut the door behind her, she waved her hand. Golden magic wove around and into the wood of the door, sealing it.

"He may only be released by my hand," she said, looking among her guards. "No one may see him without my knowledge and permission."

~ Some Time Later ~

The night was dark. Liana could feel her heart racing in her chest. Carefully, she blew the candle beside her out, sitting for a moment in the darkness. Jet was out of time. Doubt was starting to ease into her heart about if he would make the right choice.

Her violet eyes shifted to the door when a gentle knock sounded.

"Your Grace?"

Liana moved to her feet, crossing to open the door. She wasn't surprised to see Antony standing before her.

He bowed quickly. "He is asking for you."

Liana nodded quickly, keeping her face void of emotion. Inside, her heart was racing. This was what she wanted. It was crucial that Jet chose to come to her of his own free will, otherwise her plan could never work.

Without a word, she stepped into the hall, following her Captain of the Guard to the dungeons. It was mostly silent, save for the soft sounds of water leaking between the rocks. Her eyes were steady as she paused in front of the door she knew well. She had spent many sleepless nights standing before it, wondering what she could do and what she could say to the wayward hellion inside.

She realized once more that her heart was racing, and she drew a calming breath. She caught Antony's dark brown eyes, nodding once. The key grated in the lock and Antony stepped back. Liana swallowed thickly as she stepped to the door, reaching for the handle. The sealing enchantment that she had placed on the door evaporated with her touch, allowing the heavy door to swing on its hinges.

It took a flash of a moment for Liana's eyes to adjust to the consuming darkness inside. She felt the pull of the void that Jet created around himself. She ignored it as she stepped inside. She hated the way his dark eyes narrowed, catching the faint light. It was all she could see of the monster before her.

Words were hard-pressed to leave her lips as she gazed at him. "You asked for me?"

Soft scuffing let her know that he had heard her. He stepped toward her, the light from Antony's torch falling over him. Even in torn, dirty clothing, he still set a frightening figure in the darkness.

"I've been considering your offer," he said slowly. His onyx eyes were narrowed in a way that Liana didn't like.

"And?" she asked. She tried to school her voice into calm. She couldn't let Jet think he had any control over her, even though everything hinged on this moment. Her plans were nothing without him.

Jet crossed his arms, lifting his chin in a defiant manner. "What makes you so certain that I'll do as you command?"

Liana grinned then, feeling all her doubts ebb away. She had him. "Because you have no other choice," she said easily. "Once you commit to me, whether it be in word or in truth, you can never go back."

Jet's cocky manner slid into a scowl.

"You must be sure," Liana continued. "I will require all of you, and there will be no escaping for you." She knew once word reached the City of Fear of Jet's allegiance, Paraximus would stop at nothing to destroy him.

And Jet knew it, too. His glittering onyx gaze shifted

away, his thoughts racing behind his eyes. "And what's in it for me?" he asked, his voice softened.

"Freedom," Liana said simply. "There will be no commands from me. You will do as I ask of your own free will."

Jet's eyes narrowed as he looked back to her. He'd never been asked to do anything of his own free will. Every move he made had been carefully planned and controlled by Paraximus. How could Liana stand here and trust him? Twenty years passed like minutes for creatures such as them. She couldn't have forgotten.

"Why are you so confident in me?" he asked finally, feeling baited by the poise in her aura. She knew what she was doing, and she was happy about it.

Liana drew a slow breath, gathering her thoughts. "I'm more than happy to let you rot here in this cell," she said. "But offering you this opportunity will give you more satisfaction than it will give me."

"How so?" he demanded. How could he ever be happy about serving his sworn enemy?

"You will spill the blood of the ones you so loathe," Liana said simply. "What more could you ask for?" Her violet eyes sparkled dangerously in the darkness. "Do not think that I don't know your true nature, Jet Lamia."

Jet looked away, his brow furrowing at the thought. For years he had dreamed about having the chance to destroy her. But thinking about destroying his once-comrades brought a different sort of thrill to him. Killing them would be much more satisfying, by far. And knowing the anger it would bring his father would maybe begin to ease the rage he felt at his father's abandonment and betrayal.

He looked back to her, meeting her gaze. "Fine," he said shortly. "I'll play your game."

Liana smiled benignly. "Good."